The *Dirty* Girls Book Club

SAVANNA FOX

HEAT | NEW YORK

THE BERKLEY PUBLISHING GROUP
Published by the Penguin Group
Penguin Group (USA) Inc.
375 Hudson Street, New York, New York 10014, USA
Penguin Group (Canada), 90 Eglinton Avenue East, Suite 700, Toronto, Ontario M4P 2Y3, Canada
(a division of Pearson Penguin Canada Inc.) • Penguin Books Ltd., 80 Strand, London WC2R 0RL,
England • Penguin Group Ireland, 25 St. Stephen's Green, Dublin 2, Ireland (a division of Penguin
Books Ltd.) • Penguin Group (Australia), 250 Camberwell Road, Camberwell, Victoria 3124, Australia
(a division of Pearson Australia Group Pty. Ltd.) • Penguin Books India Pvt. Ltd., 11 Community
Centre, Panchsheel Park, New Delhi—110 017, India • Penguin Group (NZ), 67 Apollo Drive,
Rosedale, Auckland 0632, New Zealand (a division of Pearson New Zealand Ltd.) • Penguin Books
(South Africa) (Pty.) Ltd., 24 Sturdee Avenue, Rosebank, Johannesburg 2196, South Africa

Penguin Books Ltd., Registered Offices: 80 Strand, London WC2R 0RL, England

This book is an original publication of The Berkley Publishing Group.

PUBLISHING HISTORY
Heat trade paperback edition / September 2012

Library of Congress Cataloging-in-Publication Data

Fox, Savanna.
The dirty girls book club / Savanna Fox. — Heat trade paperback ed.
p. cm.
ISBN 978-0-425-25315-1 (pbk.)
I. Title.
PS3606.O95653D57 2012
813'.6—dc23
2012007749

PRINTED IN THE UNITED STATES OF AMERICA

10 9 8 7 6 5 4 3 2 1

AUTHOR'S NOTE

The idea of the Dirty Girls Book Club has been in the back of my mind for years, and I'm delighted to have finally brought the girls to life on paper.

Thanks to my editors at Berkley, Katherine Pelz and Wendy McCurdy, for giving me this opportunity. Thanks also to my agent, Emily Sylvan Kim of Prospect Agency, for her enthusiasm and unwavering support.

Special thanks to my friends and critique partners, Michelle Hancock, Elizabeth Allan, and Nazima Ali, who help me make every book the best it can be.

I'd also like to recognize my own book club: Kate Austin, Kate Denby, and Alaura Ross. Ladies, thanks for your friendship and the wonderful discussions over the years. And yes, in case readers are wondering, my club has been known to read dirty books!

If you enjoy *The Dirty Girls Book Club*, I hope you'll check out my other titles at www.savannafox.com, where you'll find excerpts, behind-the-scenes notes, recipes, a monthly contest, my newsletter, and other goodies.

I love hearing from readers. You can contact me through my website at www.savannafox.com.

One

"I t took me a while to get into it; then I was hooked." Georgia Malone touched the cover of the trade paperback lying in the middle of the book club's table at Rogue, a trendy restaurant/bar near Vancouver's downtown harbor.

It was just after four thirty on a warm May afternoon. The four club members had settled at an outside table and ordered drinks and appies.

"The characters came to feel like friends," Georgia added. "I like books that take me on an emotional journey."

Lily, who had selected this month's book, said, "I enjoyed it too. Such beautiful writing."

Marielle gave a snort of disgust and shook back a curtain of wavy dark brown hair. "You mean pretentious. Masturbatory writing, where the writer's only stroking his own ego and doesn't give a damn about the reader."

"Aw, come on, tell us what you really think." Kim's near-black eyes danced.

"It won the Man Booker." Lily defended her choice, and Georgia nodded in support.

In the three months the club had been meeting, it had quickly become clear that the four of them were quite different. That made for stimulating discussions, which was what Georgia had hoped for when she responded to the "Want to create a book club?" notice posted by Marielle at a downtown coffee shop. Though Georgia loved her job in marketing, the fast pace and hype meant that these chats over appies and drinks were a welcome break. The four busy women had decided that rather than commit to a whole evening each month, they'd meet Mondays for a quick get-together between the end of the workday and whatever they had planned for the evening.

"I don't know what the Man Booker is," Kim said, "but it sounds pretentious too." An art student from China, her spiky black hair streaked with tangerine highlights, she looked anything but pretentious.

Lily frowned and tucked a breeze-blown wisp of short, stylishly cut blond hair behind her ear. "You didn't like the book either?"

Kim shrugged. "I couldn't get into it. It was dense, too literary, and depressing. I'm so not in the mood for being depressed." Although mostly the women talked about the book they'd chosen for the month, personal information occasionally slipped out, and Georgia had the impression things weren't going well with Kim and her boyfriend.

A ponytailed waitress in jeans arrived with calamari and yam fries to share, and drinks for each of them: a martini for Lily, a fruity cocktail for Marielle, a fancy lager for Kim, and a cup of coffee for Georgia. "Sure you only want coffee?" the waitress asked.

Georgia nodded. "I have to work tonight."

"Bummer, George," Marielle said. Two or three years younger than Georgia, she worked as a temp and her social life was her top priority.

"No, it's good. A new assignment, and I'm excited." Her boss at Dynamic Marketing had just appointed her, not her competition, Harry, as account manager on a major new campaign. She'd worked her butt off to win this opportunity.

The initial meeting with the client was tomorrow afternoon, and she had meetings all Tuesday morning, so that left only this evening to prepare. The client, VitalSport, was an American company that manufactured sports and leisure wear and equipment and was about to expand into the Canadian market. Her boss, Billy Daniels, had recommended a figurehead campaign. The figurehead—a Canadian hockey star—had just been signed. Billy had given her a video of an interview with the man and said, rather ominously, that he hoped she was up for a challenge.

Of course she was, and she was happy to put in a long night of preparation. At least she could work at home, where she could peel off her tailored office clothes, free her hair from its businesslike knot, and curl up with her cat.

Marielle took a healthy sip of her cocktail, said, "Yum," then, "I agree. The book was depressing."

"Is there a rule that says a book club can't ever read anything fun?" Kim asked.

"Exactly," Marielle agreed. Then, her attractive coffee-colored face lighting with mischief, she said, "Or sexy. What's wrong with sexy? I just started a cool book." She reached into her large purse, extracted her iPad, and clicked it on.

A moment later, she turned it around. "Here."

The other three of them peered at the image. "You're not serious," Georgia said. The cover had all the romantic clichés. A blond woman with flowing locks, clad in a lacy, old-fashioned undergarment, was being untied down the front by a black-haired man, naked to the waist, his rippling muscles on full display.

"*The Sexual Education of Lady Emma Whitehead*," Kim read the title. "Now, that looks like fun."

"It's historical erotica," Marielle said. "Lady Emma's a twenty-year-old widow. Her husband was an old guy who sucked in bed. Her father arranged the marriage. Emma didn't love the dude, but at least she had some kind of life. Now she's supposed to be in mourning, she's running out of money, and no handsome, sexy young guy's likely to marry her when he could get a lovely young virgin with a dowry."

"Groan," Lily, the only married member of the club, said.

Georgia could relate to Emma, at least a bit. She was a young widow too, though in her case her husband had been her soul mate. She'd married at age twenty-one and lost Anthony in a horrible car accident—one she'd survived almost injury-free—before she turned twenty-five. In the three years since, she'd learned to be happy living alone. From what she'd seen, few marriages were as wonderful as hers had been. A man like Anthony—and a connection so deep and special—was a rare thing. Maybe one day, if she was lucky, she'd find another soul mate, but she couldn't imagine it happening soon. For now, she'd focus her energy on her career. And, like Lady Emma, she'd be celibate. Sex without an emotional connection didn't attract her in the least.

Marielle continued. "A married girlfriend invites Emma to spend a month at her husband's family's country home, and she's thrilled to escape her boring rut. The first evening she's there, the family entertains friends and neighbors for a musical gathering. Emma discovers that there's another houseguest." She clicked her iPad.

"Don't stop there," Kim said.

"No way. But it's better if I read it."

Emma was late arriving downstairs due to the maid's insistence on ridding her demure gray widow's weeds of their travel creases. She entered the noisy, crowded music room nervously, unused to being alone at a social gathering, and gazed about for her friend and hostess. Margaret, Lady Edgerton, sat talking with two middle-aged women, and Emma hurried to join them.

Marielle's normal speaking voice had a slight Caribbean lilt and it was fun to hear her attempt an English accent.

Once seated, she surveyed the room. A group of pretty young girls gathered in a corner, and with their fluting voices, silvery laughter, and colorful dresses, they reminded her of a flock of tropical birds. What had captured their interest?

The crowd parted and a black-haired man walked from among them. Emma's breath caught in her throat as the man strolled over to speak to Lord Edgerton, Margaret's husband, with the flock of chattering girls trailing him.

Emma could understand their fascination. This was no conventional English gentleman. There was a . . . je ne sais quoi . . . about him, from his stylishly cut Continental clothing, almost indecent in staid old England, to the cocky tilt of his head and his persuasive smile as he spoke to his host.

Lord Edgerton nodded, and moved away purposefully.

Sipping her coffee, Georgia thought that Woody Hanrahan, the hockey player she'd be dealing with, likely had little in common with the je-ne-sais-quoi man in the book. Hockey was big in Vancouver, but the appeal totally escaped her. She didn't know one hockey player from another, so she'd studied the biography Billy had given her.

Woody—Woodrow—Hanrahan was born in a small town in Manitoba twenty-eight years ago. He'd played hockey from a young age and been mentored by a friend's father, who became his agent. Woody had been drafted into the NHL at age seventeen by the Atlanta Thrashers. Vancouver had traded for him seven years ago and, along with a couple of other players, he was credited for turning a second-rate team into one that had won the Stanley Cup four years ago and lost out by a single goal last year. This was his third season as team captain. He'd also played on the gold-medal-winning Team Canada in the 2010 Olympics.

It all sounded relatively impressive—if athletes impressed you—but Billy had warned her that she'd need to transform a sow's ear into a silk purse. Obviously there was more—or less—to Mr. Hanrahan than appeared in his bio.

Realizing she'd become distracted by thoughts of work, Georgia focused again on what Marielle was reading.

The cosmopolitan man gazed about the room, a sparkle in his dark eyes as he glanced past the pretty girls, on to a group of men rather loudly discussing politics in the corner, and then to Margaret, the two middle-aged ladies, and Emma.

For a moment, his eyes met hers. She felt something extraordinarily disconcerting: a quick flush of heat, not just in her cheeks but all through her body; tingly prickles across her skin as if someone had stroked her with a feather; a pulse that throbbed in her throat, at her wrists, and—oh my!—at that secret feminine place between her legs.

The man's gaze moved on, leaving her hot, prickly, and throbbing. Oh dear, was she coming down with an illness? And yet, she didn't feel ill, exactly. More . . . unsettled.

"Oh, good God," Lily broke in, rolling her eyes. "Enough."

"No, it's just getting good," Kim said. "Go on, Marielle. You can't leave us hanging here."

Marielle grinned. "I told you her husband sucked in bed, right? The poor woman's never had an orgasm, and she doesn't even recognize arousal."

Georgia focused on the yam fry she'd lifted to her mouth, not daring to look at the others. Though she'd loved Anthony with all her heart, and intercourse with him had been emotional and wonderful, the truth was she'd never had an orgasm either. Nor was she all that familiar with arousal, or at least not the purely physical kind Marielle was talking about. For Georgia, sex was about an intimate sharing of heart, mind, body, and soul with a man she'd committed her life to and who had committed his to her.

Though she'd dated a couple of men since Anthony died, she'd quickly realized there was no real connection and had broken things off.

She was glad she wasn't a very sexual being. Celibacy was easy. Marielle began to read again.

Margaret leaned over and whispered to Emma, "That, my dear, is Comte Alexandre de Vergennes from France. He will be staying here too. He arrived this afternoon, while you were resting after your journey."

"I didn't know there was to be another guest."

"Nor did I," Margaret said tartly. "I am not best pleased, but in this I will bow to my husband's wishes. They are old friends, although I cannot imagine why. The Comte is, to use the most polite word available, a rake."

Emma's mouth opened in a silent "O."

Margaret's lips kinked up and her eyes sparkled. "I must tell you the most delicious secret. The Comte was caught in the bedchamber of a married woman. Her outraged husband challenged him to a duel, and instead of doing the manly thing and fighting, the Comte fled the country. He sought refuge with my husband."

"Oh my!"

Across the room, bottles of champagne had arrived and were being opened. The Comte, usurping the role of host, handed glasses to the colorful young ladies. "He is making free with your husband's hospitality," Emma commented.

"Actually, he brought the champagne with him. Cases of it."

Margaret tsked as bright laughter rang out. "I see it will be my task to ensure that none of our innocent maids—or," she added as two young married women headed over to join the fun, "married ladies—fall for the Comte's charms and jeopardize their reputations."

"Surely no one would be so foolish." Charm was such a superficial thing.

Besides, there wasn't the slightest chance the Comte would wield that charm on her, a drab widow.

Marielle stopped reading. "You know they'll end up in bed. Won't it be fun seeing how they get there, and what happens when they do?"

"I vote for this book," Kim said promptly.

"I vote against," Lily said. A doctor, she could put on a brisk "I have spoken" tone.

It didn't daunt Marielle. "We went along with your last choice. I say it's time to get dirty, girls."

"Oh, for heaven's sake," Lily said. "George, back me up."

"Let's read it." The words just popped out.

"Hurray! Three votes win," Marielle said. "Thanks, George."

"Now," Lily said sternly, "can we please get back to discussing *this* month's book, before we run out of time?"

As the blonde rattled off what sounded like a review from a literary journal, Georgia wondered at her own quick agreement with Marielle's choice. Historical erotica? She'd never felt the slightest desire to read erotica. Yet the short passage had intrigued her. It might be fun to read something that was such a complete departure from her personal experience.

Two

Off balance—literally, since the one-inch heel of her sensible pumps had snapped off in a sewer grate five blocks away—Georgia opened the door to one of Dynamic Marketing's conference rooms early Tuesday afternoon. She stepped inside to see a good six and a half feet of naked male back.

Back, and backside. Naked backside. Naked, extraordinarily well-muscled back. And a tight, taut, amazing butt.

Well, all right, not entirely naked. She noted a thin "T" of black fabric. *What self-respecting heterosexual man wears a thong?*

No, wait. Shouldn't the question be, *Why am I gaping at a near-naked man when I've obviously entered the wrong room?* She should be retreating quietly and sliding the door shut before anyone noticed her.

She was about to do exactly that when the naked giant said, "No straight dude's gonna wear a fucking thong. I didn't fucking sign on for this."

"Woody," a much calmer male voice started, in a placating tone, "now, just—"

"Woody?" Georgia exclaimed. *This* was Woodrow—Woody—Hanrahan?

"George?" That was her boss, Billy Daniels's, voice. She hadn't even noticed he was in the room.

"George?" the naked man said.

She was dimly aware of the calm-voiced man, someone she didn't know, joking, "Is there an echo in here?" But only dimly aware, because the giant had swung to face her.

Her eyes widened. He was leaner than she'd thought a hockey player would be, but oh, my, did he have muscles. Shoulders, arms, torso, legs. Abs.

Her gaze traveled south and fixed on the front pouch of that skimpy black thong. She had never, not in ads or movies much less real life, seen a man who filled out his underwear so impressively.

The giant crossed powerful-looking arms across his broad chest. "Who's George?"

"I'm George." Her voice came out breathy because, let's face it, the sight of him had stolen her breath. She forced air into her lungs and went on. "It's a nickname. I'm Georgia Malone."

Holding her hand out to offer a firm handshake, she stepped forward, forgetting that her right heel was no longer there. Her ankle wobbled, her knee buckled, her briefcase slipped, and she tumbled ignominiously toward the floor—only to be caught by one large, firm hand grasping her elbow.

"You're a woman," he said disbelievingly.

Woody Hanrahan no doubt intended to steady her. Instead, her heart jerked and her pulse raced like she'd been zapped by an electrified fence. Or a Taser.

Except, the heat that rushed through her, the tingles that darted across her skin, the pulse that throbbed at every pulse point, felt incredibly good, in a way she'd never experienced before, yet somehow recognized. Why did she— Oh, there'd been a similar description in the passage Marielle had read yesterday.

"George, are you all right?" Her boss's voice was sharp.

"Yes, of course." She answered automatically, belatedly realizing she was mere inches from that six and a half feet of muscled nakedness. From that black pouch, its skimpy fabric doing its best to contain all the masculinity inside.

His package. That was one of the less crude terms people used for male genitals. A package, wrapped in black—was that silk?—and just begging to be unwrapped.

No, wait—what was she thinking? Georgia Malone, the girl who had, without a moment's hesitation, sworn chastity vows as a teen, did not think about unwrapping men's private parts. Not unless there was a wedding night involved, which wasn't likely to happen anytime soon—and less likely with this guy than with any other she'd ever met.

"Should get that shoe fixed," Woody said.

"Right." Striving to find her balance—in all meanings of that word—she stepped away from him. "And I apologize for being late. I left my last meeting a few blocks away, and that's when my heel snapped off." She hated to look unprofessional. This marketing campaign, her first as account manager, was a critical step on the path to her ultimate career goal: to have enough clout to choose the campaigns she worked on, or to set up her own agency. While she loved putting all her expertise and energy behind products she believed in, a few campaigns had made her feel like a snake oil saleswoman.

She set down her briefcase. "Let's try this again. My name is Georgia Malone, and as Mr. Hanrahan so astutely observed, I'm a woman." She limp-walked, trying for as steady a gait as possible, toward the third man in the room. "You'd be Marco Sanducci of VitalSport?"

"Indeed. A pleasure to meet you, Ms. Malone."

They shook hands. While her boss, Billy, was mid-thirties and metrosexual, this man was perhaps a decade older and more casual in appearance. He looked fit, vigorous, and attractive with silver-streaked black hair, tanned skin, and the right kind of wrinkles around his eyes and mouth. He wore nicely tailored pants, a sports jacket, and a blue shirt open at the neck, no doubt VitalSport designs. As a visual symbol for his company, he made a great impression. Pity he wasn't the person the campaign would center around.

She forced herself to turn back to Woody, and finally studied his face. Yes, she saw a resemblance to the video clip Billy'd given her of an interview between the periods of a hockey game. Except, in it, Woody's hair was stringy with sweat, his face flushed and angry, and his eyes slitted as he spat out obscenities that challenged the censor's bleeper. As the crowning touch, a slash high on one cheek dripped blood down his face.

Now his mahogany hair was clean and glossy, his face sculpted, and his eyes the deep blue of a lake in summer. The slightly crooked nose and a scar cutting one cheekbone—from that same slash?— saved him from being a pretty boy. His hair needed styling and the overgrown beard had to go, but he could be made to look good in an ad. That was a relief.

Billy's market research indicated that Woody was not only Canada's favorite hockey star, but one of the country's most recognizable athletes. Recognizable even though, unlike many players, he'd stayed out of the media limelight and he hadn't done product endorsements. Snagging him for the VitalSport campaign was a coup.

Briefly, she wondered why Woody had signed. Hockey players made an obscene amount of money. Did he really want more? Had staying out of the limelight been a ploy to win him even bigger bucks when he finally agreed to an endorsement? She shook her head. Motivation didn't matter. He'd signed and he was locked in.

And she was the account manager and this was supposed to be her meeting. A *meeting*, so what was the hockey star doing in his Skivvies?

"Gentlemen," she said crisply, "I understood this was to be an initial discussion of the marketing campaign for VitalSport's Canadian launch." She raised her brows in Woody's direction. "I assume there's an explanation for your state of undress."

"Not a fucking good one," he grumbled.

Trying not to look below his neck again—the view was too distracting, and the fact that it was distracting annoyed her—she said, "Perhaps you'd like to get dressed; then we can discuss the explanation, or lack thereof."

"First good idea I've heard." He hooked his hands in the sides of the thong as if . . .

Oh my God, he was going to take it off! "Stop!" She raised both hands, almost losing her balance again.

He grinned. It was a thoroughly wicked, extremely sexy grin. "Got a problem with nudity? You wouldn't survive in the locker room."

She frowned. "No, I do not have a problem with nudity, in appropriate circumstances." Like between two people who were in love. "And why on earth would I want to be in the locker room?"

He snorted. "Right. A lesbian. *George*. Figures."

It wasn't the first time her nickname and tailored style had led to that assumption. Her sexual orientation, like her gender, was irrelevant in the workplace, so she didn't bother to correct him.

Also ignoring Woody's comment, Marco Sanducci explained, "Journalists visit the locker room. Sports reporters. Women as well as men."

"Oh." Women mingled with a whole team full of men like Woody, in various states of undress? The thought struck her that her mother'd be in seventh heaven. But Georgia was nothing like Bernadette. In fact, they had a standing joke—one neither of them found very funny—that she must have been swapped at birth.

"I'll turn around while you get dressed, Mr. Hanrahan. Let me know when you're decent."

She was about to turn when laughter, in three different male tones, stopped her. Fine, that hadn't been the smartest thing to say. Her brief research had told her that "decent" wasn't a word typically used to describe Woody. On the ice, he was a forward, captain of his team, and known not only for high scoring and being a good team player, but for collecting penalties and never backing off from a fight. Off the ice, he had the reputation of being "forward" too—in other words, he was a *player* in a whole other sense of the word.

Woody picked up a ratty hockey jersey with the logo of his Vancouver team, but, rather than pull it over his head, he stood there, holding it. Like he was thinking about something—and thinking was a painful process.

It dawned on her that she'd seen a lot of those chocolate-and-caramel jerseys on the streets of Vancouver recently, but she'd never paid particular attention. Now she studied the stylized logo: a little brown creature up on its back legs, with a big tail, bright eyes, and two huge front teeth.

For her first solo campaign, she had to transform a man named Woody, who was captain of a team called the Beavers.

Life just wasn't cutting her a break.

Three

Nudity didn't give Woody one bit of trouble, but the idea of strutting around in his underwear in front of a camera did. There was such a thing as dignity.

And he wanted to get this fuckup settled right now.

He tossed his jersey back on a chair and turned to George.

For a moment, he forgot what he was going to say. When Billy Daniels had talked about George, he'd never imagined the account manager was a woman. But she sure as hell was.

She dressed like she was trying to hide the fact, all buttoned up in a starchy white shirt and a tailored charcoal pantsuit, with her red hair slicked back in some weird knot. But he saw her curves, the creaminess of her skin, and big eyes the color of his favorite Granville Island amber ale. He'd felt a sexy charge when he'd gripped her elbow, and that charge hadn't faded.

He was turned on by a lesbian, one of the few women he'd ever met who didn't get excited about the thought of visiting the locker room. Man, he must really be stressed over this stupid campaign, not to mention his mom's illness and his agent's betrayal, which were the only reasons he was here, needing money so badly he was letting himself be turned into a model.

But not a gonch model.

And George was not a puck bunny. This was about business, and he had to get his head—and body—into that game.

He narrowed his eyes and leveled George with a "no one's fucking with me" glare. "You're handling this campaign, so that makes you the head coach. Tell them I'm not modeling gonch."

Her brow creased in puzzlement. "'Gonch' means underwear?"

He rolled his eyes. What red-blooded Canadian woman didn't know that? Oh, wait. A lesbian. One who, from the way she'd gaped at him when she'd first seem him in that god-awful thong, might never before have seen a semi-naked guy in the flesh.

For some stupid reason, he wondered if he impressed her.

George turned to the other two men and said briskly, "He has a point. My understanding was that Mr. Hanrahan would model sports and leisure wear. No one mentioned underwear."

Woody nodded firmly. "Damn right."

The dude Sanducci from VitalSport said, "Underwear is clothing, just as much as T-shirts and jerseys."

"It hardly falls under the term 'leisure clothing,'" George said.

"Sure as hell doesn't," Woody pitched in, taking her assist and shooting for the goal.

Sanducci blocked the shot with, "You don't wear underwear when you undertake leisure activities?"

It was a great save. Despite his state of pissed-offedness, Woody had to grin. "Depends on the activity." And damned if now he wasn't thinking about one specific leisure activity: getting George out of that tailored suit and shirt and checking out what lay beneath. Curves tempting enough that his body throbbed with awareness.

Of a lesbian. Yeah, he was losing it.

"We have a team of designers," Sanducci said. "When one of the women heard we'd signed you for the Canadian campaign, she said, '*The Cowboy Way.*'"

Woody groaned. All his life, he'd heard the Woody jokes. Little kids had made that Woody Woodpecker *ha-ha-ha-ha-ha* laugh sound, and adolescent teasing had centered on "woody" being slang for a boner. As an adult he'd been compared to Woody Harrelson in every role the actor had ever played—not just the various athletes, but the dim-witted bartender in *Cheers*, the psychopath in *Natural Born Killers*, and, yeah, the gonch model in *The Cowboy Way*. He wished his mom's granddad's name had been anything but Woodrow.

George said, "What are you talking about? Mr. Hanrahan's a hockey player, not a cowboy."

"It's a movie," Sanducci said, "with Woody Harrelson."

"Oh."

"There's a huge billboard with Harrelson in a cowboy hat and boots and Calvin Klein underwear," Sanducci said. "Woody Harrelson, Woody Hanrahan. Athletic guys in tight underwear. Grown-up guys with real male bodies." He grimaced. "Sorry; I'm quoting the designer. A lot of male underwear ads have models who look like they're barely legal. Anyhow, the designer said we should start an underwear line, and whipped up some samples. It'll be something special for the Canadian launch. We figure it'll appeal to men because they respect and identify with Woody, and it'll appeal to women because, well"—he shrugged—"the designer says that one's obvious."

Woody scowled. He had the feeling he was screwed. In the short time since his agent had betrayed him and lost all his money—millions of fucking dollars, including the money that should have paid last year's income tax—he'd been flying solo. He'd trusted his own judgment when he'd read the VitalSport contract, which now seemed like a dumb move.

He honored responsibilities, but what had he gotten into? He wasn't comfortable with the media, not like the phenoms like Crosby who'd grown up with it—and who didn't have shitty family secrets to hide. Woody had avoided interviews and product endorsements until now, when he had no choice. Sanducci and Daniels liked how he hadn't been "overexposed," to use their word.

Well, now it seemed he'd be about as exposed as a guy could be.

"George," Daniels said, "I want your team to meet with Woody tomorrow. Brainstorm; start on a strategic plan. The Beavers are in the Western Conference finals, so you'll have to work around Woody's game schedule. And speaking of games"—he turned to Woody—"don't forget to wear a face shield."

"What? What the hell?" The only time he wore a face shield was to protect a broken nose or similar injury. He was an old-style player and didn't like having something in his field of vision.

"Did you read the contract?" Daniels asked.

"Sure." And it hadn't said anything about a face shield. Of course, it hadn't said anything about gonch either.

"Then you'll have seen the clause about protecting your face. Cuts and bruises, not to mention broken bones, aren't photogenic." The man's voice held a note of warning.

Photogenic. He groaned. He was a hockey player, not a goddamn model. All he'd ever wanted to do was play hockey. And look after his mom. Which, right now, meant not only covering the mortgage and expenses for her luxury home in Florida, but paying for full-time care, medical bills, and now the special cancer treatments in Switzerland. The very expensive alternative treatments that were the last hope of saving her life. Damn it, she wasn't even fifty, and she'd had such a crappy life. She deserved a future.

He pulled his attention back to Daniels, who was rising and saying, "Marco and I will go to my office and sign some papers. George, I suggest you make sure Woody is clear on the details of the contract."

She nodded. "Good idea." Despite her words, she sounded less than enthusiastic.

Sanducci joined Daniels at the door, where the Dynamic Marketing dude turned back. "I forgot to mention—let's target the Boys and Girls Club fund-raiser next month."

"The what?" she asked warily.

"What d'you mean?" Woody asked. It was a charity he supported—one that the VitalSport deal would let him keep supporting—and they'd asked him to be guest of honor at their event. By that time, if things went the way Woody intended them to, the Beavers would've won the Stanley Cup.

He'd agreed to attend, on the promise that he didn't have to give more than a five-minute speech. He was no public speaker and he sure as hell wasn't going to give one of those sob-story motivational talks. The world knew all it was going to know about his personal history: he'd had a tough childhood, and it was his best friend's dad who'd helped him get into hockey.

What guy wanted to reveal that his dad had beat up on him and that, even worse, he'd had to lie in bed and listen to his dad beat up on his mom? When, at the age of five, Woody had tried to help his mom, she'd slapped him—it was the only time she'd ever hit him—and told him to go back to his room and mind his own business.

Hockey'd been his escape. Getting out on the frozen lake in winter with his best friend, Sam. They'd been tough, scrappy kids, and they bashed each other around a lot, but it was equal and it was sport, so it was okay. Man, he'd loved the purity and power of skating, shooting, blocking, tussling with his friend. It was all so clean and simple.

Hockey'd been his ticket out of small-town Manitoba, thanks to his innate talent for the sport, and to Sam's dad, Martin.

Martin Simpson. The man who'd been Woody's agent since he was fourteen. The man he'd trusted to run his career and manage his money. The man who had confessed in tears that he had a gambling problem and had lost all Woody's money—the money Woody needed now, *right now*, to save his mom's life.

Martin belonged in jail. But Woody couldn't turn him in. He owed his career to that man, and it'd shatter Sam if he found out what his father'd done. Woody'd told Martin that if he joined Gamblers Anonymous and stuck with the program, his secret would be safe.

Martin had left a message on Woody's voice mail a couple days ago, saying he'd followed through and was going to meetings. He'd asked Woody to give him a call. That wasn't happening—at least not yet. Woody was still too pissed off.

Tuning back into the conversation, he realized Daniels had been explaining about Woody's involvement with the Boys & Girls Club. "A couple of days ahead, we'll do the formal campaign launch. There'll be lots of interest, and eyes'll be on Woody. George, you should aim for having a few ads ready by then: one that yells 'sports,' another that's more leisure, and one of the underwear ones." With that parting shot, Daniels and Sanducci left the room and the door closed firmly behind them.

"I thought it was my campaign," a soft voice said.

He turned to George, who was frowning at the closed door. Absently, she rubbed the back of her neck where the stiff collars of her shirt and suit jacket met up with a few curly red hairs that were too short to be captured in that tight knot.

"Got the GM breathing down your neck?" he asked with some sympathy.

"What? Who?" Her hand dropped away from her neck and she turned to him, a dazed expression in those amber-ale eyes. Big eyes, fringed with darker lashes. Really pretty eyes. A man could get lost in there.

She didn't look away for a long moment, then finally blinked and did. "What's a GM?"

He blinked too. "General manager." That had been weird. If she wasn't lesbian, he'd have thought she wanted to kiss him. He'd have wanted to kiss her. In fact, under that scrap of thong, his cock was stirring.

"I wish you'd get dressed," she said irritably. She seemed to be making a deliberate effort to not look below his neck.

For some reason, he wanted to rattle her buttoned-up cage. "You really do have a problem with nudity."

"It has its place," she snapped, "and this isn't it."

"Man and a woman alone together," he teased, moving closer to her, so close that he realized she smelled like vanilla. He preferred that scent to sultry perfume. "Seems to me that's a pretty good place to get bare-assed naked." Then he snapped his fingers. "Oh yeah, you bat for the other team."

Her brow pinched. "Are you homophobic?"

He stepped back. "Hell, no."

"You made that comment about only a gay man wearing a thong, and now you're down on lesbians. I have no patience with homophobes, and it won't play well in a marketing campaign."

"Jesus, I'm not homophobic. Don't you have a sense of humor? I was just having a little fun with you."

"Your idea of fun isn't the same as mine," she said, all starchy to match up with her clothes.

"Believe me, I get that." Then, because he wasn't a total jerk, "I'm sorry. Guess sexual orientation isn't something I should joke about."

She nodded stiffly. "Apology accepted, and no, you shouldn't." She took a breath, let it out. "I apologize too. I haven't been entirely honest. I let you think . . . Well, the truth is, I'm not a lesbian."

"Aha!"

"What does that mean?"

"That my body's not all confused." In fact, his cock surged as if he'd given it permission to really get turned on.

She shook her head. "I don't know what you're talking about."

"I've wanted you since I first saw you."

"Wanted me?" Fine brows arched. "Give me a break. Does any woman fall for that line?"

Women threw themselves at him without him even opening his mouth. "It's not a line."

"Just because you're in your underwear, that's no reason—" On the word "underwear" she'd lowered her gaze, and now she stalled completely.

The thong had given up the battle and his swollen cock bulged out the top. Weird how he could be naked in the locker room with female sports reporters and have no physical reaction, yet this woman with her man-tailored suit and skinned-back hair really got to him.

How long was that flaming red hair, and what did it look like when it was down?

Her gaze was still fixed on his package. Maybe there was something to be said for the stupid black gonch, after all.

Her body quivered, but other than that she didn't move. "You really are aroused." Her voice was barely a whisper.

"Man, yeah."

She wasn't moving away. Wasn't looking away. Wasn't slapping his face or acting insulted. She was quivering. With arousal. He knew it.

He moved past her and locked the door to the conference room. "George"—no, that wasn't right—"Georgia," he corrected himself. She was no guy, even if she downplayed her femininity.

"Wh-what?" Her eyes were huge as they stared into his.

"There's something I need to know."

"To know?"

He went to stand behind her. When she started to turn, he caught her shoulders and held her still. "Hang on."

"What? What do you need to know?"

Her hair was secured by a clip. "How long your hair is."

"What are you doing?"

He eased out the clip. "This." Shiny locks tumbled past her

shoulders, halfway down her back. Fiery locks, and he knew there'd be fire in her blood. He wanted to know the woman inside the starchy exterior.

No, he wanted to be inside that woman.

She froze as he ran his fingers through her glossy hair. It slipped and slid like silk as he delved beneath the flames to touch her neck, circling it loosely. He stroked down her throat and found her pulse points. Their wild rhythm made him smile.

At least one thing was finally going right today.

Four

Georgia couldn't believe the hockey player was stroking her. Couldn't believe she was letting him, and that each caress from the rough pads of his fingers made her body throb with an intensity she'd never experienced.

She couldn't believe he was standing, all but naked, behind her, fully aroused. Aroused by her.

She wasn't that kind of woman. Not the kind who got aroused, and not the kind to engage in suggestive, much less downright erotic, behavior.

Woody moved closer so that the front of his body pressed into her back, and through the light wool of her pants his hard shaft thrust against her. She should be shocked. Appalled. And yet it took every ounce of self-control to not wriggle her backside against that firm pressure. What was she doing? She had to pull away, had to stop him.

His hands eased deftly under the front of her jacket to cup her breasts through her white cotton shirt, and she sucked in a breath. Oh my gosh, that felt good.

She'd never found celibacy to be a burden, not as a teen and not since Anthony died. She'd never related to girls who moaned about how hard it was to resist temptation and stay pure.

Temptation . . . Ooh, there was temptation in the tongue that traced her earlobe, the soft whisper of his breath against her damp flesh, even the tickle of his unkempt beard. Temptation in the fingers that slipped open a few shirt buttons, found their way under the fabric of her bra, and gently squeezed her nipple.

She moaned, then clapped a hand over her mouth.

"Don't do that," he murmured. "Let me hear you. Tell me what you want."

"I w-want you to stop." She forced herself to speak the words, but they didn't convince even her.

"No, you don't."

"I . . ."

"You don't." Now his hands were on her shoulders, turning her to face him. Firm, but not harsh. If she'd felt the least bit forced, she'd have yanked away. Instead, she felt as if he was guiding her body in the direction it wanted to go.

She wasn't short, but he was so much taller, so much bigger, and somehow she'd put her hands on his arms to steady herself. Just to steady herself.

But the last thing she felt was steady, and it had nothing to do with her broken-heeled shoe and everything to do with the man whose deep blue eyes gleamed with some fierce, intense expression she didn't recognize.

The man whose naked torso pressed against her, whose muscled back was hot and hard under her hands, whose erection thrust insistently against her lower body.

The man whose lips . . . Oh my God. Whose lips were on hers.

His mouth must be the only part of him that was soft. Firm, yes, but soft and tempting rather than hard and demanding. Seductive. Teasing her into responding in a slow, subtle dance. Overcoming her common sense one lick, one nibble, one gentle suck at a time. One tongue-flick between her lips.

He held her head firmly between both hands, tilting it where he wanted it, the curls of his mustache and beard a softly abrasive caress against her sensitive skin.

She had to tell him to stop. This was wrong. This wasn't like her; this couldn't be her. She had to pull herself together and stop him.

No, this wasn't her. This wasn't the girl whose mom's boyfriend had groped her, the teen who'd embraced celibacy, or the wife who'd enjoyed gentle intimacy with her husband.

This was a woman who was sensual and turned on, and who couldn't bear to have it end.

When she parted her lips, it wasn't to say, "Stop," but to sigh with need.

A moment later his tongue was in her mouth.

Heat licked through her, heavy and pulsing. Arousal. She'd been aroused before, but never so quickly, so intensely. Before, it had been a mellow buzz that never built to orgasm.

But now, as his tongue delved into her mouth and his fingers wove their way under the waistband of her pants to stroke the upper curve of her buttocks, as his erection thrust insistently against her belly, the sweet, sensual, downright sexy sensations *were* building. Between her thighs, a spiraling ache of need craved more, more, more of this man.

She couldn't stop herself from wriggling her pelvis against his shaft.

He groaned, pushed away; then he shoved her jacket down her shoulders and yanked it off. "Shit, Georgia, I want you."

Some part of her brain registered that he, unlike everyone else, called her Georgia. That he was undoing the remaining buttons of her shirt. But most of her attention was focused on his body. Specifically, on his swollen penis. At some point, without her noticing, he'd stripped off the thong and now he was totally, gloriously naked.

The dense, dark curls of his pubic hair matched those of his beard, and the shaft that sprang confidently forward was long and thick.

Had any man ever had such an amazing, seductively gorgeous body?

She'd always believed she didn't care about physical appearance, but now the mere sight of him made that hungry ache strengthen. "Woody," she protested halfheartedly, "we shouldn't—"

"Oh yeah, we should." He flipped open the fastener at the waist of her pants, yanked down the zipper, and the fabric slid down her legs.

About to protest again, she could only gasp, "Oh!" when his long fingers slipped between her legs.

He stroked back and forth along the crotch of her panties and she realized she was wet. Soaking wet. How could this stranger's touch make her respond as she'd never done before?

She leaned her head against his naked chest and closed her eyes, unable to do anything but lose herself in what he was doing.

His finger found one particular spot and focused, circled.

She gasped as sensation rocketed through her. It dawned on her that she might actually have an orgasm.

Who cared about celibacy when she might finally find out what it was like to climax? Shamelessly, she pressed herself against his fingers, silently demanding more.

He gave it to her, one hand under her butt, anchoring her, the other toying with her sex through the thin barrier of her panties. And then—oh God—he pulled the crotch of her panties aside, probed gently with a long, broad finger, and then that finger was entering her.

She dragged in air on a gasp, realizing she'd been holding her breath. Her eyes were squeezed shut too, and she slowly opened them, to focus on his engorged penis.

Just the sight made her private parts pulse and moisten. Unable to resist, she reached out to cautiously wrap her hand around his shaft. He was so big, she couldn't fully circle him, so hot, he branded her palm.

His moaned, "Oh yeah, that's good," encouraged her to stroke up and down, feeling the slide of his skin, the firm strength underneath.

Touching him turned her on. These sensations were so unexpected and glorious.

His finger thrust into her, gently but insistently, in a rhythm that coiled the achy need even tighter. She'd never come so close to orgasm, and oh, she didn't want to lose it now.

As he thrust in and out, his thumb pressed her clitoris, taut with aroused nerves.

She twisted with arousal, with desperate need. "Please," she panted.

His thumb pressed a little harder at the same time as, deep inside her, he touched a spot that made her cry out with pleasure. He did it again, again, and— "Oh God!" she sang out as the coil of tension broke in waves of blissful, shattering release.

So this was orgasm. Unbelievable.

Unbelievably good. No wonder people made such a big deal of it.

She shuddered as delicious ripples of sensation continued to pulse through her. If Woody hadn't been holding her up, she'd have collapsed in a quivering mass on the floor.

As she gradually came to her senses, she realized she was gripping his penis like she had no intention of ever letting go.

Woody caught her hand in his and tugged it away. "Gotta put on a condom."

He didn't know she'd just had the first climax of her life, and an earthshaking one at that. He thought she was a normal, sexy woman.

Wow. How about that?

Fleeting thoughts of her intent to remain celibate, of her career—this wasn't exactly professional—flickered through her head.

She shoved them away. She'd had an orgasm and she was with an outrageously virile naked man who quite possibly could give her another.

W oody struggled to force a condom over one of the biggest hard-ons of his life. Oh yeah, he'd been right about Georgia Malone. She had the responsiveness and passion that went along with that red hair. A woman who'd go at it in the conference room at her office was his kind of woman.

A hand on each of her hips, he maneuvered her backward.

Eyes wide with surprise, she stumbled in her broken-heeled shoe with her pants pooled around her ankles. Impatiently, he waited until she kicked out of her shoes and stepped free of her pants; then he sent her panties skimming down as well.

He kept maneuvering her until her ass met the edge of the table.

Even though his cock demanded action, Woody paused a moment to enjoy the view. Red hair tumbled every which way and rosy patches flushed her cheeks. Her tailored white blouse was unbuttoned and hung free over a plain white bra, and below that she was naked: creamy skin, fiery curls, the pouty, swollen lips of her sex gleaming with her arousal.

What a turn-on.

He shouldn't just give in to his own need. He'd bury his face between her legs and eat her until she came again, and then it'd be his turn.

He hoisted her up on the table, gripped her knees, and parted her legs.

The sight of her, spread, glistening, ready for him, sent pure lust surging through him. He had to have her now. Couldn't mess around with more foreplay. "Fuck." He yanked her closer to the edge of the table.

"Oh, Woody." Her fingers, surprisingly strong, wove into his hair and locked onto his skull.

"Oh yeah." He nudged her opening with the head of his cock. Man, she was tight. Wet, but tight. He eased in slowly, struggling for self-control, fighting to ignore the urge to drive, and drive hard.

Bit by bit she softened, opened, gripping him with wet, silky heat as he slid in.

Torture. The best torture in the world. Sweet enough it made him groan.

She let go of his head and reached behind her, bracing her hands on the table, arching her body backward so she was even more open to him.

So much for self-control. With his big hands holding her hips steady, he had to take her now. To give her everything he had. To pound and drive like he was racing toward the goal net and no one could stop him. Adrenaline blazed through him, firing him up, and his whole being focused on one thing: the need to climax inside Georgia Malone.

He pumped in and out, his blood pulsing so thick, so hot, his body couldn't survive it. He was going to explode.

Tension rolled through him, centering in his cock, the base of his spine, everything gathering and building until there was no holding back. He jerked hard, deep inside her, felt his come jetting out in long, full pulses, and groaned with satisfaction.

Hell, yeah, that felt great.

As he thrust one final time, caught up in his own lust and pleasure, he was dimly aware of a female cry. Realizing he'd squeezed his eyes shut, he forced them open. Saw his cock buried to the hilt in swollen pink folds, saw those sexy red curls of pubic hair. Shit, he'd been carried away by his own need and had forgotten about his partner's pleasure.

He wasn't that kind of guy. He was a good lover.

"Georgia?" he said tentatively, raising his gaze past her smooth, creamy belly and ribs, past the plain cups of her white bra clinging to sweet curves, up a delicate chest and neck, to her face. Her cheeks were rosy and her amber eyes looked stunned.

"Sorry," he muttered. "That was . . . I mean, uh . . ." He had to know how bad he'd been. "Did you come?" Even as he said it, he wanted to whack himself upside the head. What kind of lover didn't know if his partner'd climaxed?

She blinked. "What?"

He forced himself to ask again. "Did you come that time?"

Her cheeks flooded with even deeper color. "Y-yes," she stammered, not meeting his gaze.

Was it the truth or was she lying to salvage his pride? Shit, he was damned sure no woman had ever done that before. And nor had he ever had to apologize for his skill in the sack before. Knowing his own face was ruddy with embarrassment, he muttered, "I didn't mean to do that." To lose control and nail her like a cock-driven adolescent. "I'm sorry."

He eased out of her, let go of her waist. His grip had been so tight he'd left red marks on her pale skin. Sure hoped she didn't bruise. He had no qualms about body-checking an opponent into the boards, but he would never intentionally hurt a woman.

Now her gaze fixed on his face. "You're sorry," she repeated. "Sorry . . ." Her eyes widened and suddenly she thrust him away and jumped down from the table, stumbling over discarded clothing. When he reached out to steady her, she jerked away. "For God's sake, put your clothes on!" she demanded as she scrabbled to find her pants.

She was acting like a virgin who'd let herself be seduced by a football player behind the bleachers, and now wished she hadn't. Guess that made sense, if the football player'd been as clumsy and self-centered as Woody.

"Yeah, sure," he muttered. He found the pile of clothing he'd discarded when Sanducci and Daniels had persuaded him to try on the VitalSport gonch. After pulling on his own boxer briefs, old jeans, and jersey, he crumpled the discarded thong into a ball and tossed it toward the wastepaper basket.

He missed.

He'd always been good at physical stuff. Like basketball. And sex. Now he was sure off his game. He'd need to get back in the zone by tonight, when the Beavers were playing the Anaheim Ducks in the Western Conference final.

When he turned, Georgia was briskly pulling her jacket over her buttoned white shirt. She didn't glance his way. She pulled her hair back into its tight knot. Then she gazed over to where he stood, a few feet away.

"I'm sorry too," she said. Her voice was firm but she didn't meet his eyes.

He'd just bet she was. Damn it, he had a *reputation* as a good lover, and he'd blown it.

"What we did was bad," she said, her cheeks bright pink.

"Yeah, it was kind of crappy," he admitted, "but—" He was about to swear it'd be better next time.

She stopped him by holding up both hands. "No! Stop talking about it. I don't want to dissect just how bad . . . Oh, never mind. The point is, it can never happen again. We have to work together, and we need to put this behind us."

Now he was sure she hadn't climaxed the second time, and the last thing he wanted was to fucking *dissect* how bad he'd been. What his pride demanded—along with his cock, which for some perverse reason found her protests a turn-on—was that he seduce her again, and this time show her a fantastic time. Not on a hard wooden conference table. He had those high-thread-count Egyptian cotton sheets women loved, and champagne in the fridge. He'd buy her flowers, maybe an orchid plant. Women were into orchids.

"Are you listening, Woody?" Her amber eyes spat sparks, and they didn't look like sparks of desire. "No one can know about this. At the meeting tomorrow, we'll start fresh, like this never happened." She crossed her arms over her chest, all stiff and starchy again.

She wasn't his kind of woman, this Georgia who went by the nickname George. He liked them warm and easy, laughing and fun, sexy and provocative. Hell, maybe that was why his sexual performance had been less than stellar.

And she was right about business. Yeah, he had this stupid Vital-Sport contract he needed to honor, but his real business was hockey. He never let sex interfere with his work ethic, especially this close to the playoffs. Best to forget about the sheets, champagne, and flowers. "Okay, it never happened. And neither of us are gonna tell anyone. Right?" He didn't need her spreading the word that Woody Hanrahan had lost his sexual edge.

"Agreed," she said fervently.

Five

Struggling to be professional, Georgia said, "I need to set up a meeting. How's your schedule?" Professional? She'd never been so unprofessional in her life. What the hell had just happened? That had to be the single most out-of-character thing she'd done in her life.

She'd dated two men in the past year and never even wanted to kiss them, yet with Woody . . . She drew her attention back to what he was saying.

"Game tonight. An early practice tomorrow, same on Thursday; then we fly to Anaheim in the afternoon for an away game Friday."

"So tomorrow, Wednesday, would work, after your practice?"

"I guess." He said it begrudgingly, as if the last thing he wanted was to get together again.

Not that she wanted it either. The man had made her lose her mind. Her body still hummed with the aftereffects of that craziness.

She'd had not just her first orgasm, but a second one for dessert.

How? How had that happened?

Woody really didn't look the least bit appealing in that tattered jersey with the ridiculous beaver on it, though the way the faded cloth hugged his body, more than hinting at muscles that she'd seen up close and personal . . .

Again she dragged her thoughts back to business. "Please bring a copy of your schedule tomorrow."

He gave her a "you have to be kidding" look. "It's on the website."

If she'd had more time to do her homework, she'd have known that. "Along with the practice schedule and your travel times?"

"Nah," he admitted. "Just the games. Okay, I'll bring it."

A point to her side. Except she and Woody were on the same team. Why was she seeing this as a battle?

She'd been off balance since the moment she saw his all-but-naked butt. And now she'd actually had sex with him. Oh God, she'd climaxed with a boorish hockey player, a man she'd barely met, with whom she had absolutely no intellectual or emotional connection. In four years of marriage to Anthony, she'd never experienced more than a pleasurable buzz.

Although, of course, the lovemaking had been so much better with her husband. So intimate and loving.

With Woody, it had been . . . stunning. As in, it had stunned her utterly.

He'd called it crappy. He was sorry they'd done it. And so was she. Really.

Now that she'd experienced orgasm, she knew it was just a physical thing. An incredibly pleasurable physical thing, but all the same—

"So, you wanna set a time for this meeting?" he asked impatiently.

She struggled to focus on business. "When's the earliest you can be here after your practice?"

They firmed up the details and exchanged contact information. Now that she was coming to her senses, she remembered something else. "Billy asked me to review the contract with you." She didn't want to spend one more moment in his company.

He scowled. "You think I can't read?"

"Of course not. And I assume your agent went over everything with you."

His mouth tightened. "I got a handle on it."

Billy *had* asked her to go over the contract, but her pulse still raced and her sex tingled. She'd had two orgasms, for God's sake. She had to get away from Woody and recover her composure, aided by one of the chocolate bars stashed in the bottom drawer of her desk. "Good. You'll remember to wear a face shield tonight?" She couldn't imagine why a player wouldn't wear one in every game, but Woody must not, or he wouldn't have the broken nose and scar.

"Hate those fucking shields."

In her line of work, she'd heard the F-word enough times that it didn't make her wince, but they'd have to clean up Woody's vocabulary before he made any public appearances on behalf of VitalSport. "It's a term of the contract, and you signed the contract."

He muttered something under his breath that sounded like, "Fucking contract."

Impatiently, she asked, "If you weren't happy with the contract, why did you sign? I can't imagine you need the income."

His jaw tightened and his face looked hard, almost bitter. For a long moment he didn't respond. "I'll wear the shield." He stalked out of the conference room.

When the door closed behind him, Georgia let out a long breath. Her legs were wobbly, so she sank into a chair. "My first meeting on my first campaign as account manager."

A bubble of hysteria rippled through her. "Now, didn't that go swimmingly?" A giggle escaped her; then her gaze snagged on the crumpled ball of thong underwear, and she giggled again.

No, there wasn't one single funny thing about this. But every once in a while, even the most sensible woman was entitled to a bout of hysteria, wasn't she?

* * *

Later that afternoon, Georgia met in a conference room—a different one; she couldn't imagine sitting at that particular conference table again—with Viv Andrews and Terry Banerjee, her team on the VitalSport campaign.

Terry was an obvious pick, for his love of sports as well as his creativity and enthusiasm. She was less sure about Viv—their styles were very different—but Billy said the other woman was a genius when it came to image. It was clear that, if Woody'd ever worked with a publicist, that person had done an appalling job.

"Let's do some groundwork for the meeting with Woody tomorrow," Georgia said.

She'd have to face the man who'd given her mind-blowing orgasms. She had to forget—no; no woman could forget her first orgasms, especially if they were that incredible. She had to put all of that behind her and focus on business.

"Terry, did you find some videos?"

He nodded enthusiastically, his carefully styled black hair not moving. In his early twenties, he reminded her of a young Bollywood star. "Sure did, George. Interviews, YouTube candids shot by fans, clips from sports news on TV."

"Good. Let's take a look."

"Afternoon movies," Viv said. "Where's the popcorn?"

Georgia was almost sure she was joking, but she didn't know Viv well. The woman, a few years older than Georgia, was vibrant and feminine. Her blond hair was wavy and gleaming, and her lips always matched her fingernails. Today's dress and jacket were an abstract design of rich plum and sour lemon that screamed "look at me," and the silky fabric clung to her curves.

Her appearance reminded Georgia of her mother. Bernadette

was always on the lookout for the next guy to give her life meaning and make her feel valued as a woman. She dressed to lure them, and shaped her personality to please them. She'd encouraged Georgia to be a "girly" girl and to be charming with men.

That had never sat right with Georgia—especially not when that jerk boyfriend of her mom's had fondled her. After a lot of stress and trauma, teenaged Georgia had decided that a woman should have her own identity, be strong and independent, and not be seductive or slutty. She'd joined the chastity club, and sworn to never use feminine wiles in either her professional life or her personal one.

Still, she shouldn't judge Viv by appearance. Billy had recommended her for a reason, and it was Georgia's responsibility to pull this team together and utilize everyone's strengths.

"I'd rather be watching almost anything other than hockey," Viv groused.

"You're not a fan either?" Georgia asked.

Viv shook her head. "A violent sport. Ugly uniforms."

"Have either of you ever actually watched a game?" Terry asked.

"My ex used to," Viv said. "Another reason to hate it."

Georgia and her husband, Anthony, had agreed on the subject of sports. The amount of time and money devoted to teams chasing balls was ridiculous.

"All set," Terry said, projecting the image from his computer onto the wall screen.

"Okay," Viv said. "Let's size up our raw material."

"Size up" and "raw." The words make Georgia remember Woody in that outrageous thong. And out of that outrageous thong. When she'd seen him erect, felt him nudge between her legs, she'd wondered if she could open wide enough to take him in. A warm pulse throbbed against the crotch of her panties. Oh yes, she'd opened, and he'd felt glorious. Even if he—used to more experienced women— had categorized the sex as "kind of crappy." The bastard.

Grabbing her notepad and pen, she forced herself to focus on the clip Terry was playing. She had to view the man on-screen objectively, not as a well-endowed bastard she'd had sex with.

After half an hour or so, Terry said, "That's the last clip." His tone awestruck, he added, "Isn't he amazing?"

Amazing. Yes, Woody was, in some ways—and not just sexual prowess. He was very male and powerful and he definitely had presence, even if that presence sometimes verged on Neanderthal. She turned to Viv. "What do you think of him?"

"He's crude, one-dimensional"—she gave a mischievous grin— "and he's a hottie."

Georgia tapped pen on notepad. "Expand."

"Which of those words didn't you understand?" Viv asked impishly.

"Tell me how you see them fitting Woody."

"Okay. Starting with crude. He's rough around the edges and isn't great at channeling his testosterone. With the media, he parrots meaningless platitudes, then occasionally forgets the script and verges on being offensive. VitalSport is an upscale line, and a large segment of the market wouldn't connect with him."

Georgia turned to Terry. "I agree. What about you, if you can put aside the fanboy thing?"

Terry made a face. "I'm a fan for a reason, and it's the reason VitalSport wants him for this campaign. He's the biggest Canadian star playing for a Canadian team in Canada's favorite sport. At the age of twenty-eight, he's on his way to being a legend. And he's all guy, which is something men and women both relate to."

He took a breath. "But, yeah, I hear what you're saying. Players are coached on things to say and coached not to swear, but Woody could use more work. He's from the backwoods, his career built slowly, and he hasn't acquired the same polish as some players."

Georgia nodded. "Billy said we'd have to make a silk purse out of a sow's ear."

"Silk purse?" Terry snorted. "Give me a break."

"It's the wrong analogy," Viv said. "We don't want to lose his masculine edge, that sense of power and something a little raw, a little wild, just below the surface."

A shiver rippled through Georgia and that pulse between her legs throbbed again. "Good point. Now, Viv, what do you mean by 'one-dimensional'?"

"All he seems to be interested in, or be able to talk about coherently, is sports. Not just hockey; other sports too. But on those subjects, he can be articulate, informed, and entertaining. Good jokes, good use of nonverbals. He makes you see a person, hear him."

Georgia glanced up from her notes. "Are you saying he's intelligent? I've been wondering if there's a brain at work." Okay, that was insulting, but when she'd still been in a mellow post-orgasmic glow, he'd said sex with her was crappy. She was entitled to snipe.

"I wouldn't swear to intelligence, but he's a good observer and mimic, at least when it comes to sports."

"You're a good observer too. Thanks, Viv. That's something we can work with."

"You're underestimating him," Terry said.

"Excuse me?" Georgia asked.

"The words 'dumb' and 'jock' don't necessarily go together. Hockey's not an easy sport. It takes smarts, skill, instinct, discipline. And Woody's one of the best."

"Didn't he quit high school after grade eleven?" Georgia remembered that fact from his bio.

"For a career that earns him more in one year than any of us are likely to make in a lifetime," Terry said. "Doesn't sound like such a dumb decision to me."

"Hmm. That's good information too. Thanks, Terry." Yes, this team was shaping up well. She turned to Viv. "Now tell me about the, uh, hottie bit."

Terry groaned, but Georgia persisted. "You really think he's attractive?" Viv was a sophisticated woman who dressed in designer clothes and dated successful, handsome men.

The blonde flicked a curl back from her face and laughed. "He's not the kind of man I normally go for, yet at a primitive level I feel his appeal. We have some good raw material there." She winked. "I look forward to dressing Mr. Woody Hanrahan."

Georgia tried very hard not to remember seeing him naked. "Thanks, both of you. This is a good start."

Yes, this was going to work out. It simply had to work out, and a little thing like a muscle-bound jock who'd seduced her into doing something totally out of character wasn't going to stand in her way. She would make a glorious success of the VitalSport campaign.

Georgia enjoyed the challenges of her career, but she had high principles and sometimes had to grit her teeth. Her goal was to get enough experience and credibility within Dynamic Marketing that she could specialize in the kind of campaigns she enjoyed handling—not the snake oil ones—or else set up her own firm.

"Tomorrow," Georgia said, "we'll brainstorm and see if Woody has any ideas to offer. Including him in the planning is the most likely way to win his cooperation." That was one of the principles she believed in, though it would have been easier to not have to see him again.

"I can't wait to meet him," Viv said. "By the way, rumor has it VitalSport's introducing an undies line for this campaign?"

Trying to keep her face expressionless, Georgia nodded.

"Every job has its perks," Viv said with a cat-that-ate-the-cream smile.

"Jesus, Viv," Terry said.

Georgia glanced at the other woman, so pretty and feminine. Tomorrow, Woody wouldn't even notice Georgia, not with Viv in the room.

No, she'd make sure he paid attention, Georgia vowed silently, because she was in charge. As for noticing her as a woman—that was the last thing she wanted. Honestly.

"I can't wait either," Terry enthused. "And you should both watch the game tonight." He pumped a fist in some kind of cheer. "Bash 'em, Beavers!"

Georgia and Viv exchanged eye rolls.

Six

Georgia spent the evening on the couch with her laptop on her knees and her tortoiseshell cat, Kit-Kat, curled up beside her. Mostly, she typed campaign notes. Still, in the name of research, she had turned on her TV—rarely used, because she was more of a reader—and tuned in to the hockey game. As she worked, she glanced at it occasionally.

The Vancouver Beavers were playing a team from Anaheim called the Ducks. Despite the silly bird name, at least their jerseys featured only the team name, not an animal caricature.

Within each team, the players were virtually indistinguishable in their padded clothing and helmets, and oddly, they almost all had scruffy beards. Hanrahan was number 77 for the Beavers, and she was glad to see he wore a face shield when he was on the ice.

Not that he was there for very long at a stretch. He was on the bench or in the penalty box as much as he skated. She shuddered as number 77 sent yet another body crashing into what she'd learned were called the boards, though only the bottom part was board; the top was Plexiglas.

It was surreal watching, and knowing that number 77 had been inside her. The same man who had a stadium full of fans on their feet cheering when he took an opposing player into the boards and freed up the puck for a teammate, or groaning in sympathy when the Ducks' goaltender blocked one of his shots. The thought that he'd given her two orgasms was ever-present in her mind, and in the warm, not unpleasant, ache between her thighs.

Woody had probably already forgotten. He was sorry they'd had sex. That was what he'd said, when she was still in a rosy glow of sexual satisfaction.

And who cared? She had to stop dwelling on it and put the whole thing behind her.

Georgia focused again on the game. The Beavers were losing. To her untutored eye, it would be better to spend more time shooting the puck and defending their goal, rather than smashing into members of the opposing team and getting penalties. Hockey seemed so useless and violent. Why were players paid millions per year? What was the appeal for all those fans?

She tried to grasp what was going on. Players got credit for assists as well as goals, and the referees handed out penalties for behaviors like hooking and high-sticking. Icing—which had nothing to do with cake—resulted in stopping play, and a face-off. There was something called a power play, which seemed to be a good thing. The Ducks got more of them than the Beavers, and scored on them twice.

In the intermission between the second and third periods, an interviewer shoved a microphone into Woody's face. "It's not a good night for the Beavers," the man said.

"The Ducks are doing a good job out there." Woody's face was grim and it sounded like the admission pained him.

The interviewer said, "You're wearing a face shield. Did that high stick you took in the last game break your nose or cheekbone?"

Woody snorted. "I'm healthy."

"No player ever confesses to an injury during the finals."

"Then why'd you ask the"—he paused, like he was swallowing a curse—"question?"

Georgia huffed out a sigh. She'd actually had sex with that Neanderthal? It must have been temporary insanity. There was no other logical explanation.

Temporary insanity that led to two orgasms . . .

Notes finished, she clicked off the TV. Yes, she hoped the Beavers won because it would be good for the VitalSport campaign, but she had no desire to watch the rest of the game.

Half an hour later, she'd purchased an electronic copy of *The Sexual Education of Lady Emma Whitehead* and was snuggled in bed with her e-reader.

The first chapter expanded on the background Marielle had summarized. Lady Emma had been widowed a year earlier. Her life was circumscribed and her finances dwindling. Her father proposed arranging another marriage, and she knew it would be to another much older man. Her brother was pressuring her to live with him. He said he'd look after her, but she knew he wanted a glorified servant to care for his children and his wife's ailing mother.

Georgia shuddered, relieved to have been born in more enlightened times.

Emma, faced with a no-win situation, was happy to avoid it temporarily by accepting her friend Margaret's invitation to visit her and her husband's country home.

Increasingly caught up in the story, Georgia came to the scene Marielle had read last night, then moved on to the next chapter. Lady Emma, too, was reading. It was afternoon and she was alone in the library.

Books were a great pleasure to Emma, a temporary escape from worries about her future. When the library door opened, she glanced up to see the Comte de Vergennes, a man she'd barely exchanged two words with.

Her pulse raced, no doubt because of his scandalous reputation.

She stood quickly. "Good afternoon, Monsieur le Comte. I will leave the library to you."

"No, please." He waved a hand in a charming Continental gesture that would have looked foolish from an Englishman, just as no Englishman could have worn those stylish clothes with such flair. "Please do not go on my account, my lady. I would be distraught to think I drove you away."

She felt most uncomfortable around this man, and particularly discomfited at the notion of being alone with him; still, she did not wish to be rude to another houseguest. Slowly, she sank down again.

Unfortunately, rather than search out a book to read, the Comte seated himself across from her.

In such close proximity, Emma couldn't help but notice that he really was most attractive, with wavy black hair and chiseled features. He flashed a smile, and how could she not admire his even white teeth, dimple, and coffee-brown eyes that sparkled with . . . Well, she had no idea to what one might attribute that sparkle, but it really was most attractive. No wonder women clustered around him.

She felt the same disconcerting reaction as last night: an odd, tingly, pulsing heat that reached even the most private parts of her body.

"You enjoy reading, my lady, and music also. Do you play an instrument?"

How drab and boring she must seem, compared to the women he'd charmed last night. Why did he feel compelled to make conversation? Her pulse raced, making it difficult to draw breath. Striving to ignore her unusual reaction to him, and to be polite, she responded, "The violin, but only passably well."

"You have an affinity for music."

"I do?" How could he know that?

"Last night, your body swayed to the music as if you wished to be playing yourself. Or dancing, perhaps?" He cocked an eyebrow.

Her cheeks heated and the bodice of her dress felt hot and confining. How improper to mention her body, to have noticed her body. Of course, it should come as no surprise that this man did not abide by the conventions of polite society. Stiffly, she said, "I do not dance. Perhaps you do not know, but I am a widow."

"Ah yes, the absurd convention that when a man dies, his widow must for all practical purposes give up her own life too."

Her eyes widened. Yes, she chafed against the restraints placed on her, but while she might confess as much to her dear friend Margaret, this was not a fit topic of conversation with a gentleman, much less a rake. Again, she rose. "I really must go."

He rose too, with a rueful and most charming smile. "I have offended you. My sincere apologies, Lady Whitehead." He gestured toward her chair. "Please. I promise to be more circumspect. Shall we discuss composers, perhaps? Who is your favorite?"

She had no experience with a situation such as this. Still, he was a houseguest and she was a widow, and surely chatting about music in the library was the most harmless of activities. The truth—and she always tried to be honest with herself—was that she wanted to stay. There was something intriguing about the man, perhaps because he was so different from the Englishmen she'd known.

Her reason for staying was not—it most certainly was not—that his presence sent those pleasurable tingles and throbs racing throughout her body.

Ah now, was she still being honest with herself?

"Don't give in to those tingles and throbs," Georgia advised. And yet, of course Emma would, because this novel was erotica.

As Georgia read on, she couldn't help but compare Emma's first meeting with the Comte to her own with Woody. The Comte, handsome and suave, also proved to be well educated, knowledgeable about music, and interesting company. He charmed and flattered in a sophisticated way that appealed to a femininity, a sensuality, that inexperienced Emma had never before felt in herself.

As Emma's attraction to the man grew, Georgia could almost feel it herself. A man like that would be hard to resist.

Woody Hanrahan—the Neanderthal—was a completely different matter. Forcing him from her mind, she turned back to the story.

"We must play together," the Comte said, flashing that dimple again.

"Play?" Emma asked, breath catching in her throat. What on earth did he mean, and why did it sound so wicked?

"I play the pianoforte. We would make beautiful music together."

He spoke of musical instruments, and yet his suggestive tone and the gleam in his dark eyes hinted at something far more personal. If she did not know better, she might believe he was attracted to her, but why would he choose a drab widow when there were younger, prettier women who would welcome his company? It must be second nature for him to flirt with every member of the gentle sex.

"Come with me to the music room," he said, holding out his hand. "Lord and Lady Edgerton are visiting an ailing neighbor, so there will be no one to hear and judge. We may play whatever our hearts most desire."

She clasped her hands tightly together, resisting an absurd impulse to put one of them in his. Bad enough she was alone with him in the library, but somehow the idea of playing music—beautiful music, the kind of music that stirred her body and soul—seemed far less appropriate. After all, the man had a reputation as a seducer. "I don't believe it would be proper," she stammered awkwardly.

"Proper?" He withdrew his hand and his lips curled. "And is being proper so very important to you?"

Knowing her cheeks were rosy, she said, "Of course. I am not the kind of woman you are used to."

"Which makes you even more a delight." He studied her, head

tilted to one side. "But I must ask, Lady Emma, what kind of woman do you believe I am used to?"

Surely her entire body had flushed as pink as Margaret's prize roses. Regretting that she'd left her fan in her bedchamber, she said, "Sir, this conversation is most improper. Let me just say that I have heard of, er, your troubles in Paris."

"Ah, the gossipmongers have been at work. You have heard that a woman's husband caught us in flagrante delicto."

Despite her shocked gasp, he carried on. "Yes, it is true, and he issued a challenge to a duel. I am excellent with a pistol, and could not bring myself to kill him, as would inevitably happen. The most circumspect course of action was to depart France."

"I cannot listen to this." She would have risen and swept out, but her legs had taken to trembling.

His eyes danced, as if he understood her plight. "There is more to the story than the gossipmongers know."

"More?" Despite better reason, she was intrigued.

"I will tell you the truth, my lady, because you have been married and will understand such delicate matters."

Oh my! What on earth did he refer to? Curiosity came close to overwhelming her better judgment, but she forced herself to say, "No, I should not listen to such—"

He held up a hand, silencing her. "I have been misjudged, and I wish one person—you, my dear Lady Emma—to know the truth."

In the space of an hour she had gone from Lady Whitehead to Lady Emma, and now my dear Lady Emma. She should protest, but sat mute.

"I did not take advantage of the lady in question. She was married to a man who could not—how would you English say this?—perform his marital obligations."

His marital obligations? Did the Comte mean that the man could not support his wife financially?

"In the bedchamber," he murmured.

"Oh!" Could he actually be talking about . . . ? Her heart raced so fast she could barely draw breath. She could not, should not, listen, but already he was going on.

"She begged me to give her the pleasure she craved, and I did not refuse that plea."

Emma's eyes opened wide with astonishment. The French-woman found pleasure in conjugal relations? For Emma, those acts had been painful and embarrassing—a part of marriage she never, for one moment, missed. Surely no decent woman could enjoy something so base.

When the Comte reached for her hand, she was so shocked she didn't resist. He stroked the back of it, sending shivers coursing through her entire body. "I see from your reaction that I was wrong about you, my dear. I sense your husband did not teach you the joy a man and woman can create together. The beautiful music their bodies can play. My lady, there is no duet to compare."

Her lips quivered as she tried to form words to tell him she could hear no more of this. Her legs trembled too; else she'd have sprung to her feet and dashed from the room.

He leaned closer and her breath stopped entirely. And then—how shocking, but oh, how sweet—his lips touched hers.

Kit-Kat tried to crawl onto Georgia's chest, blocking her view of the e-reader. "Oh no, you don't," Georgia muttered. "I'm not stopping now."

She nudged the cat aside and read on, enthralled, as the Comte skillfully seduced Emma, playing her body as if it were a beautiful instrument and he the most talented and appreciative of musicians. He overcame her embarrassment, her inhibitions, and taught her that sex could be an act of supreme pleasure.

Lying on the sofa in the library, surrendering to the caresses of his deft fingers and tongue, Emma climaxed for the first time in her life.

And then, when he entered her slowly and tenderly, patiently teaching her the rhythm of intimacy, the dance of two bodies moving in perfect harmony, she climaxed again.

Lying in bed, Georgia's body tingled with the memory of her own orgasms. She flicked off the e-reader. Two orgasms. What a strange coincidence.

Of course, her own circumstances were very different from Emma's. Emma's husband had been a cold, inconsiderate man, whereas Georgia's Anthony had been warm and loving. And then Emma had been coaxed toward climax under the attention of a charming man, a subtle seducer, a skilled and patient lover who devoted himself to his partner's pleasure. Georgia could, perhaps, understand how Emma had let herself be persuaded.

Her own actions with Woody made far less sense. She wasn't even attracted to him. Not really. Only to a splendid body. He certainly wasn't suave or charming, and his idea of seduction was to rub his erection against her. Admittedly, he'd been generous in giving her that first orgasm, but then the only thing he'd devoted himself to was getting his own rocks off. The Comte had ensured Emma's second climax before finding his own release. Woody hadn't even known if Georgia had come.

And yet she had. A second time. The memory of it, combined with reading about Lady Emma's seduction, had her body all atingle.

She clicked off the light. The bottom line was, she'd been unprofessional. A part of her didn't regret it, because the experience had been incredible, yet she knew it couldn't happen again.

Orgasms weren't like chocolate. She could enjoy those first two wonderful ones, and not become addicted.

Seven

Woody drifted into consciousness gradually and painfully. He lay absolutely still, inventorying the damage. Oh yeah, this hurt a lot, and it wasn't just the shoulder he'd dislocated a couple of weeks ago, which hadn't had time to heal and which had taken another hard hit against the boards last night. He opened an eye, winced, and then groaned as the movement shot splinters of pain piercing into his brain and gut. The last time he'd had such a massive hangover was almost a year ago, when the Beavers lost the Stanley Cup in double overtime in the seventh game of the finals.

He sure as hell couldn't show up for practice like this. Gritting his teeth against nausea, he hauled his ass out of bed and into his jogging shorts. He added a ratty T-shirt and gingerly bent to put on socks and running shoes.

Each step was more agonizing than the one before. Out the door, down the hall, into the elevator where the sickening swoop downward from the penthouse floor almost made him toss his cookies. Into the street. Fresh air, thank God. His condo was in Vancouver's Yaletown, and he always ran along the seawall. His trembling legs took him across the grass of David Lam Park toward the water.

It was a beautiful morning, which added insult to his injury. Sunshine stabbed his eyes like shards of glass, penetrating and lodging deep in his brain. He closed his eyes, but that made the nausea worse.

For the first mile, he figured he would puke or die. Probably both. Sweat ran in rivulets off his body.

He spent mile two trying to remember why he'd tied one on. After handily winning the first game in the Western Conference finals on the weekend, they'd lost the second last night. A home game, with all those fans rooting for them and being disappointed.

Woody hadn't played his best. The shield drove him crazy, and it reminded him of the fucking contract, and the fact that his near-naked body would soon be on billboards. Not to mention the fact that he'd nailed Georgia Malone with the finesse of a rookie at training camp. His performance in that boardroom had been . . .

As bad as his performance on the ice last night.

But none of it was an excuse for getting hammered, especially during the finals. He thought back. A bunch of the guys had gone for a beer after the game. He'd ordered a Granville Island amber ale. Usually, he drank out of the bottle, but before he'd noticed, the waitress had poured the beer into a glass. The amber bubbles had reminded him of Georgia's eyes. And somehow one beer had turned into—

No, he didn't want to remember. He was into his third mile and his stomach was almost steady.

Woody's head came up and he started to appreciate the blue sky and puffy white clouds. In the fourth mile, as he turned for home, the bark of a frolicking terrier, the shriek of wheeling gulls, and the glint of sunlight off the ocean barely made him wince.

Mile six. His legs pumped fast and strong, his shoulders had loosened up, and his head was clear. He'd call his mom in Switzerland and see how she was doing, then have breakfast in the players' lounge and get in a good practice.

*   *   *

After practice, Woody drove to Dynamic Marketing.

At the reception desk, the same pretty Asian girl who'd been there yesterday gave him a stunning smile. "Good morning, Mr. Hanrahan!"

"Hey, sunshine. Call me Woody."

She smiled even brighter. "I'm Sandra, and a huge fan." She pumped her delicate hand in the air. "Bash 'em, Beavers!"

He returned the trademark salute.

"Go on in, Woody. It's conference room B, beside the one you were in yesterday."

As he headed down the hall, his stride faltered. He'd shoved Georgia out of his mind, but now she was back. Yesterday, she'd gone from snippy to businesslike to passionate—man, had she been passionate—to pissed off. And no wonder, after he'd plowed into her like a rookie.

Not knowing what to expect, he stepped into the conference room.

No Georgia. Just, sitting across from each other, a knock-your-socks-off blonde wearing a jacket in shades of pink and green that made him think of plastic flamingos on a new spring lawn, and a young man in a trendy shirt and tie who might or might not be the actor from *Slumdog Millionaire*.

"Sorry," Woody said. "Got the wrong room."

The young guy leaped up and hurried forward. "No, you're in the right place." He stuck his hand out. "Man, is it great to meet you, Mr. Hanrahan."

"Woody." He shook.

"Bad luck about the game last night."

"Tell me about it."

"You'll bash 'em in Anaheim on Friday."

They'd sure as hell better.

A female cough made him turn toward the woman. "Terry," she said, "introductions?"

"Sorry. Woody, I'm Terry Banerjee, and this is Viv Andrews. It's going to be so great to work with you."

Woody turned to the woman, who didn't rise but held out her hand. "Nice to meet you," he said.

"You too." She gave him a warm smile and studied him intently, like she was analyzing him in detail.

Georgia must've been so mad at him, she'd bailed on the campaign, transferring him to these two. Maybe that was for the best. Working together would've been tough. "So," he said, "Georgia . . . ?" What had she given them as an excuse? What had she said about him?

Viv's arched brows rose, maybe because he hadn't used the nickname George. "I'm sure she'll be here any moment."

So she hadn't dumped the campaign.

"Have something to eat?" Viv offered. "A cup of coffee?"

"Don't drink coffee, thanks." He went to look at the selection on a sideboard. High-fat muffins, which he ignored. He poured a glass of orange juice, then sat at the foot of the table.

When Terry started to talk about last night's game, Viv steered the conversation toward world events. Watercooler chat. Woody'd never been good at that stuff. The women he went out with were usually happy talking about sports, or about themselves.

He gave Viv short answers, finished his juice, went for a refill. He hated the whole idea of the VitalSport contract, but he'd signed it. So could they just get on with things? Restless tension sent him over to the twentieth-floor window.

Vancouver Harbor was busy this morning. A red-striped float

plane bounced down onto the water. Sky was blue; sun was climbing; he could be out doing something. Georgia was fifteen minutes late. If that was some kind of pointed message directed at him, he wasn't grasping that point.

The door crashed open and she rushed in, gasping for breath the way he'd done on the first mile of his morning run. She wore a suit that looked like the navy twin of yesterday's charcoal one, except today the bottom half was a straight skirt that covered her knees. Her cheeks were pink, and loose tendrils of hair escaped the knot to straggle around her face. As she wheezed, today's white shirt rose and fell in a manner that made him remember the pretty curves underneath. He'd been inside this woman. And been a crappy lover. They'd promised they'd put all that behind them, but it wasn't going to be easy.

She choked out a few words between gasps. "Car broke down. So sorry."

Broke down, he wondered, or just ran out of gas?

Viv went over to her, face anxious, and touched her shoulder. "Are you all right?"

"Yes, except I speed-walked from Robson and Burrard." The gasping was easing.

"What did you do about the car?" Woody asked.

Defensively, she said, "No, I didn't leave it sitting in the middle of the road. I pulled off—" She shook her head. "Forget the car. I'm sorry to delay the meeting."

She sat at the head of the table, yanked her hair back into its neat knot, then pulled a laptop out of her briefcase.

Figuring she could use a glass of water, Woody poured one.

When he put it down in front of her, she froze, staring at his hand. It made him remember stroking her pussy, thrusting a finger inside her steamy depths, teasing her clit.

Realizing he was getting hard, he let go of the glass and took a seat. Thank God for the loose Beavers jersey that hung down over his swelling fly.

"Thanks," she muttered, then took the glass and downed half the contents. "Terry, can you hook up my laptop to project?"

"Sure."

While he did, Georgia went over to the side cabinet and returned with coffee and a chocolate chip muffin. "We'll start with a little brainstorming." She turned to Woody, her gaze sliding past his without meeting it. "Brainstorming, Mr., uh, Woody, is a creative process where we toss out ideas without worrying whether they make sense." There was an edge to her voice that said, "You should be good at that."

Yeah, he got the message yesterday: she didn't think much of his brain. It was true he'd never done well in school, preferring to be outside and active. True, too, that he'd always been more interested in the sport of hockey than the business side, so he'd left contracts and finances to his agent. He used to think that playing well was all that mattered. Now he was learning differently.

Damn it, he wanted to impress this woman, and if he'd failed in the sex department, he didn't stand a hope in hell when it came to smarts.

Why did she get to him? Why were those amber eyes more intoxicating than beer?

"I'll type up our ideas as we go along," Georgia said briskly. She clicked through menus until a document appeared on the wall screen, blank but for the title "VitalSport Canadian Campaign—Brainstorming Notes" and today's date. "We want to be creative and open to discussing ideas, not critical."

Woody chose to stay quiet and listen. The best strategy was to size up the opposition, and even if this marketing campaign wasn't exactly opposition, it was a challenge.

He learned that Terry was a sports junkie and knew as much

about the Beavers and hockey as Woody did. The women weren't into sports. They were smart, though, and creative.

Would Georgia be creative in bed? No, he wasn't supposed to be thinking about sex with her, but how could a guy concentrate on business when his throbbing cock kept telling him it wanted to get back inside that woman? Not that she'd allow it, after his miserable performance.

Viv caught his attention when she said, "Woody, let's look at what you're wearing now. Old jeans—not designer ones, am I right?—and a rather worn Beavers jersey."

"Nah, not designer." The concept of *designer* jeans was stupid.

"He wore the same clothes yesterday," Georgia put in as she got up to refill her coffee. She'd demolished the muffin. Fat, sugar, caffeine. She'd never survive on the ice.

"Different jersey," he said, offended. Did she think he didn't do laundry?

"On the video clips," Viv said, "you and the other players wore suits when you went in and out of the stadiums."

"They have to," Terry said. "They're going to work, they're paid a lot to do that work, and they're supposed to look professional. Right, Woody?"

Woody nodded. "Yeah, and it sucks." He hated those uncomfortable suits. He also hated having the press shove microphones in his face. Why couldn't a guy just play hockey?

"Okay, then," Georgia said. "Let's talk about the concept of uniforms." She typed the word and it appeared on the wall screen.

"Uniforms?" he asked.

She glanced at him, then away again. No, even if she wanted to forget yesterday, he could see she wasn't succeeding. "You wear one on the ice, for the game," she said, "and I assume it's mostly about safety, right?"

He nodded.

"You wear another—a suit—going to and from games. That's about professional image."

"Yeah, I guess." He'd never thought of those suits as a uniform, but she was right.

"You'll have to wear VitalSport clothes, not just for the photo shoots but when you're out in public."

"My jeans and jerseys are comfortable." Did he sound like he was whining? He really wished they hadn't had sex. Especially bad sex. It made things way too awkward.

Viv jumped in. "Woody, here's my take on it. You're wealthy and could dress however you want, yes?"

Not these days. It had been true before his agent lost all Woody's money and got him in debt with the tax people—but even then Woody'd never been into acquiring stuff. Yeah, he'd bought himself an apartment, a sports car, and a big TV, but what else did a guy need? Pretty much the only money he spent—and yeah, it was a small fortune—was on his mom. "I guess," he hedged.

"But you don't care about clothes," Viv said. "You dress for comfort, you don't like shopping, and you'll wear clothes until they're falling apart rather than buy new ones."

Hey, this woman knew him.

"You buy off the rack, making choices as quickly as possible."

"Yeah."

"I saw that in the video clips. Your suit jackets don't fit right."

"They don't?"

"Don't you find they pull across the shoulders?"

"Yeah." He'd figured that was what suits did, and that all ties felt like nooses.

"Woody," Georgia broke in, "you're going to have to dress differently."

He grimaced. He had no issue with taking direction from a woman, but he'd have been way happier about it if he'd given her great sex rather than humiliating himself. He'd have been way happier if just the sight of her didn't make him want to do it again, slow and thorough and hot and sweet this time.

Viv crossed one leg over the other. "Clothing should drape and hug and caress. Like a balmy breeze, a tropical ocean against bare skin, the touch of a lover's hand."

Girly words, but the way her very adult voice lingered over them made his flesh tingle. This was not the way to get his mind off sex.

Georgia ran a hand inside the paired collars of her shirt and jacket. Were they too tight, or was she imagining the touch of a lover's hand? His hand? When he'd stroked her pussy and made her come, he'd done it right. It was only later that he'd lost control and been a selfish bastard.

Viv went on. "Woody, you'll see that being stylish doesn't have to mean being uncomfortable. I promise." She gave him a dazzling smile.

That, plus her reassurance, made him smile back and say, "Thanks, sunshine. I'm counting on you." He didn't get any sense she was flirting with him, just that she was all woman and didn't mind showing it in the workplace. The blonde's approach was sure different from Georgia's, passionate though the redhead was once she let her hair down.

Viv's foot, in a bright green shoe with a mile-high heel, swung in circles. With a glint in her eyes, she said, "Of course you'll wear VitalSport underwear, too."

Jesus. "No one's seeing my gonch," he protested.

"Ah, so you're not dating anyone these days?" the blonde asked.

Since when was his dating life their business?

Eight

Georgia, typing notes at the head of the table, froze at Viv's words. Why had that question never occurred to her? She'd had *sex* with the man and he might be involved with someone. Well, no, Billy's background research made it clear Woody didn't get "involved"—he was anti-commitment—but he might be dating someone. And Georgia was *not* the kind of woman who'd sleep with a guy who was seeing someone else.

Of course, until yesterday, she'd never figured herself as a woman who'd have random sex with a near stranger whom she didn't even like, much less respect. Never figured she'd have the first orgasm in her life, much less two, at the hands of said near stranger.

Ever since she'd broken her shoe heel, her life had tipped upside down.

Looking annoyed, Woody ran a hand over his bushy beard, and the diamond on a big ring he wore flashed. "I don't date much during playoff season. It's too distracting."

Right. And having sex with her wasn't distracting in the least. It was just a little tension release. Something he felt *sorry* about the minute it was over.

"Bet that pisses off the puck bunnies," Terry said.

"The what?" she asked.

"You know, George," Terry said, "like buckle bunnies who follow rodeo riders. Hockey players have puck bunnies who—well, you get the picture."

"Right." Grimly, she stared at Woody. Did he think she was a puck bunny, getting her kicks from screwing a hockey star?

"It's good you feel that way, Woody," Viv said.

Startled, Georgia glanced at the other woman. No, Viv couldn't have read her thoughts.

The blonde was going on. "A man's judged by the company he keeps, and puck bunnies aren't the right image for VitalSport. I know this sounds offensive, but—George, do you agree?—I'm thinking that if you want to go out with someone, you should run it by us first."

"You want to approve my dates?" Woody asked disbelievingly.

"It's all about image and brand," Viv said.

"I do agree," Georgia said coolly.

Woody shook his head. "No way. Stay out of my private life."

"The contract—" Georgia started.

"Doesn't say anything about who I date."

"It contains a morals clause," she pointed out. "If you're involved in a scandal, VitalSport can terminate the contract."

"Morals clause?" he echoed. "Jesus."

"It's there for good reason," she said stiffly. "Billy Daniels and VitalSport did their background research. I understand there was a, uh, situation last year. With a woman who said you'd promised to marry her, made her fall in love with you, then dumped her."

"Crap. It was all lies. I was up front all along. Told Angela I'm not into serious relationships." He snorted. "I'm not even into serial monogamy. No way was she in love. She was a wannabe actress who liked dating someone famous. When I broke up with her"—he shrugged—"I guess she figured going to the tabloids would get her some PR and hook her a movie or TV role."

Terry chimed in. "It never went anywhere. She and her story

weren't that interesting. Everyone knew Woody's rep and no one believed he'd led her on, much less proposed to her."

Georgia nodded. "So I read in Billy's notes. He and VitalSport didn't figure it was a significant detriment to having Woody as the campaign figurehead. Still, we don't want anything like that blowing up now."

Woody slitted his eyes. "You're not seriously going to tell me who I can sleep with."

Was there a threat in those words? A threat that, if she pushed too hard, he might reveal what the two of them had done? Warily, she said, "We're asking that you use good judgment." Heat rose to her cheeks, and deepened when he raised his eyebrows. No, what they'd done was most definitely not good judgment.

Georgia squeezed her eyes shut briefly. "Let's move on."

"Okay," Terry said. "What's up with the underwear line?"

Ignoring another groan from Woody, Georgia turned to Terry. "One of the VitalSport designers is female. She remembered a movie called—what was it now?—*The Cowboy Way*."

"Oh, yes!" Viv said, but Terry shrugged, clearly not recognizing the reference.

Viv filled him in, then Georgia said, "The designer thought an underwear line could be a special feature of the Canadian launch."

"I'm guessing our Woody will look even better than Woody Harrelson did in a pair of tighty-whities," Viv teased.

Woody gave a third groan.

It was interesting, but despite Viv's attractiveness, Woody wasn't flirting with her the way Georgia'd expected. He treated Viv and Terry equally, nodding in agreement or groaning or making a face when he hated an idea. As for Georgia herself, she'd catch him watching her; then he'd look away. He probably wondered what crazy impulse had made him come on to her, just as she was wondering why she'd been insane enough to go along.

Well, there had been those two orgasms. . . .

No, this was a business meeting, and they'd been discussing . . . Right. Underwear.

Ignoring Woody, Georgia addressed Viv and Terry. "The question is"—she held out both hands, palms up—"would underwear ads be effective, or tasteless?" She jiggled her hands up and down, weighing alternatives on an imaginary set of scales.

Viv ran the tip of her tongue around lips painted hot pink. "Hardly tasteless, I'd say. And just what are you juggling there? Could it possibly be balls?"

Terry snorted, and the double entendre hit Georgia. She dropped her hands immediately. "It was scales! I was weighing . . . Oh, never mind." She took a breath, then said, knowing she sounded stiff and self-conscious, "Obviously, Viv thinks underwear ads would be effective, at least with female buyers." It was hard to argue with that.

"And gay men," the other woman added. "Terry, how about straight guys?"

"So long as the ad's masculine and not too arty. Arty works for metrosexuals and gays, but not guys who think of themselves as 'real men.' Maybe have him in his gonch doing stuff like sharpening his skate blades."

Georgia typed the idea, trying very hard not to imagine that picture. "Would that work for metrosexuals and gays? And women?" It sure worked for her, if the throb of need between her thighs was any indication.

"Yes," Terry and Viv said simultaneously.

"Shit," Woody said.

She ignored him, drumming her fingertips reflectively along the bottom of her keyboard. "Good. That's an idea to develop."

"No thongs." Woody's voice grated and his gaze met Georgia's, pleading. "Please, Coach, no thongs. They're not, you know, dignified."

Dignified? This, coming from a man in a ratty jersey with a cartoon beaver on it? Still, she could sympathize. "It might turn straight men off," she mused.

"Kids watch the games," Terry said. "Thongs don't project a family image."

"You can say that again," Viv agreed.

"Fine. No thongs." Georgia typed it as Woody said a heartfelt, "Thank God."

She turned to Viv. "Moving on. Viv, you can handle physical appearance. We'll want to play on his, uh . . ."

"Sex appeal?" Viv provided.

"Yes." Georgia eyed Woody dubiously. He was handsome, physical, and masculine, but his lack of polish and questionable clothing choices diminished his appeal.

He caught her gaze, raised an eyebrow, then ran a hand over the conference table in slow, caressing circles. Reminding her that her bare butt had been plunked down on the matching table in the room next door, as she let him spread her wide—in fact virtually begged him to enter her.

Ooh, he wasn't playing fair. He'd agreed they would put the sex behind them.

But yes, he had effectively made the point that, despite his flaws, he did have sex appeal.

Deliberately, she typed "sex appeal" so the words sat up there on the screen, and said in an all-business voice, "We can't alienate the male half of the market. Woody has to be a man they identify with."

"He's all man," Terry said, "and he has a talent for telling sports stories and making them come to life."

As Georgia typed that, Viv leaned forward. "All man is good. A masculine edge is great. But crudeness isn't. Nor swearing."

Georgia nodded firmly.

"I don't swear in interviews. They teach us not to."

"I saw an interview where you did," Georgia said. "Repeatedly. You had blood dripping down your face and the censor's bleeper could barely keep up with you."

He winced. "Yeah, I know the one. Got reamed out for it."

"The game with the Flames?" Terry asked.

Woody nodded. "It was the last few seconds and I could've tied the score. Asshole defenseman slashes me across the face and hip-checks me into the boards. Buzzer goes off; we lose. Skating off the ice, someone sticks a mike in my face. Yeah, I was steamed; didn't watch what I said."

"Beaver fans were steamed too," Terry said. "They were swearing too."

"Which doesn't excuse it," Georgia said.

Woody shook his head. "Nah."

"We can help you with communication," Viv said. "So you can talk articulately and not offend anyone."

"Yeah, yeah, I know all the stuff we're supposed to say. Mostly, I do it."

"True," Viv said. "Terry can help you make it sound more fresh and genuine."

"Really don't like talking to the media," Woody grumbled.

"I'm afraid you'll have to," Georgia said. "And we'll set up public appearances with sports and recreation groups." She glanced at Terry. "I guess they'll want him to talk about hockey, his career, sportsmanship, things like that?"

"And the Olympics and Stanley Cup," he added. "We'll figure out the kinds of questions people are likely to ask, then work out good answers and rehearse them."

"Rehearse?" Woody asked grimly.

They certainly didn't want to rely on him to say the right thing.

While Georgia struggled for a polite way to phrase that, Terry spoke up. "Think of it as training camp."

She shot him a grateful look.

"He should be able to talk about more than sports," Viv said. "Politics, world affairs, culture."

"Oh, is that all?" Woody asked sarcastically.

"You're a jock," Terry said. "No one's going to expect you to talk like a rocket scientist or a foreign diplomat or a Pulitzer Prize–winning author."

Georgia muttered, "Thank God," under her breath. She did a quick mental review of what they'd covered so far, and reached a conclusion that appealed to her about as much as putting on one of those huge, ugly hockey uniforms and skating onto the ice. Still, this was her campaign, her responsibility. Billy had given it to her over Harry, her competition, and she was determined to prove herself. "Viv's handling appearance and Terry's handling the sports end, so I'll take the other communication aspects."

"Can't think of anything I'd rather do than communicate with you," Woody said in a tone that was half taunt, half protest.

"And deportment," she added.

"Deportment? Jesus, it sounds like a girls' finishing school."

She ignored him. "Moving on. We've talked about scheduling sports interviews and appearances. Let's think more broadly."

For a few minutes, she and Terry and Viv batted around ideas like TV interviews, talk radio, podcasts, YouTube, Twitter, and so on.

Woody listened, looking unhappy. "If I gotta do this kind of stuff, how 'bout *The Ellen Show*?"

"Ellen?" Georgia asked.

"You know, DeGeneres."

What was the man thinking? "That won't work. It's American,

and we'd never get you on." He really did have an inflated idea of his own importance.

"Oh, okay." Woody frowned. "Guess I misunderstood. Thought you said brainstorming meant discussing, not ruling things out."

Georgia glared at him.

A chuckle escaped Viv before she cut it off.

He was right, and Georgia hated it. "I stand corrected," she said grimly. "Fine, let's discuss *The Ellen DeGeneres Show*."

Viv said quickly, "Lots of Canadian women, even a number of men, watch it. I think it's a good idea, Woody, but I'm afraid Georgia's right and it might be difficult to get you on it."

That was what Georgia should have said. Woody did *not* bring out the best in her. Probably because her body was so aware of him, tingling like there was an electrical charge in the air.

Woody smiled at Viv. "I met Ellen at a charity event. She's nice. We talked about her doing a show on how women view sports like hockey and football."

He had to be blowing hot air. The urge to call his bluff was irresistible. "I think that's an excellent idea. Are you willing to give Ms. DeGeneres a call, Woody?"

"Sure," he said offhandedly.

"Do let us know how that goes." The thought of his ego being taken down a notch made her smile with genuine pleasure.

To her surprise, he returned the smile. "You got it, sunshine."

She frowned. Earlier, he'd called Viv "sunshine." Was it some generic thing he used for all females? Probably he called the puck bunnies sunshine too. It might work on them, but Georgia didn't find it the least bit flattering.

Viv said, "Let's talk about the schedule. I'll arrange a wardrobe fitting with VitalSport, and custom tailoring for suits so Woody will be comfortable, and for hair—"

"Yeah, yeah, I'll get a haircut," he said.

Viv's blue eyes told Georgia, "Leave this to me." The other woman smiled sweetly. "There's a wonderful man I'd like you to see, Woody. Many of my clients go to Christopher Slate, and I do myself. He's very talented. I don't think you'll be disappointed."

Georgia pressed her lips together to hold back a chuckle. She caught Terry's gaze, also full of suppressed amusement. *The poor sucker hasn't a clue what he's in for,* their eyes telegraphed.

Viv gave Woody her most charming smile. "Will you do this for me?"

"Uh, sure, I guess." He shifted in his chair, then flashed her a grin. "Anything for you, sunshine."

Georgia's amusement vanished. "Woody, did you bring your schedule of games and travel?"

His guilty expression told her he hadn't.

Terry took over the laptop, pulling up the game schedule on the Beavers' website, then typing it into a spreadsheet along with the practice and travel times Woody provided from memory.

Georgia frowned at the screen. "So, Woody is heading out of town tomorrow, Thursday, and won't be back until Monday." She turned to him. "It's going to make things difficult, you traveling so much."

"And once the Beavers win the Western Conference," Terry said, "they'll be into the finals for the Stanley Cup, against whoever wins the Eastern Conference."

"Thanks for the vote of confidence," Woody said, shifting restlessly.

"And that means another travel schedule to work around," Georgia said. "On the other hand, it will certainly work better for the campaign if the Beavers win the Stanley Cup."

Woody shot her a nasty look. "I'll be sure to tell the coaches and my teammates. It'll really help motivate them."

"I'm just saying—" She stopped herself. She was in charge, and didn't have to justify herself to this man. "Terry, for the next couple of days, can you work on a tentative schedule for interviews and appearances, and some interview questions and suggested answers? Let's you, Viv, and I get together on Friday to discuss them."

Staring at the dates projected on the screen, she accepted the inevitable. "Woody, we need to start working on communication and *deportment*. The only possible time before next week is today. Are you available?"

Something sparked in his eye. Something very masculine, that made something very feminine inside her respond. "Available?" he drawled. "Guess I could be available. For you."

That spark, that drawl, and all she could think of was sex on the table. But no, that would never happen again. She only hoped she and Woody could be civil, and work productively together. "Great," she said, trying to sound enthusiastic.

The four of them left the conference room together, and Terry and Viv branched off toward their offices.

Woody said, "So, Georgia, your car's okay, right?"

"My car?" She stopped dead. "Oh, damn, I forgot about it."

Nine

Women. Abandon a broken-down car, then just forget?

Georgia closed her eyes briefly, then opened them. "I'll get it later, see if it starts, call for a tow or whatever. Our priority is the campaign."

Yeah, she'd made that clear in the meeting. Interviews, rehearsals, *deportment* lessons, haircuts, clothes fittings. They wanted to twist him all out of shape and force him to talk to the media. And model gonch.

Nervous energy coiled in his body and the idea of sitting and talking for another hour about his own inadequacies drove him nuts. He needed to move, to do something.

Georgia might be the head coach, but sometimes a guy had to take charge. "We're supposed to be working on communication. We can communicate while we deal with your car."

A rare smile flashed. "Are you saying you can do two things at once?"

That smile transformed her. The stiffness left her face as her lips curved and her eyes danced. Man, she was pretty.

Starting to feel better, he said, "Been known to happen." A fact she'd have known if she had the slightest understanding of hockey.

He reached toward her, intending to cup his hand around her upper arm and head her in the direction of the elevator.

She leaped away before he could touch her, saying in a falsely hearty voice, "You win—the car it is."

This morning, there'd been tension between them. Sometimes, like yesterday, tension meant sex. Now the way she reacted to his touch told him that wasn't going to happen again. He'd had his chance with her, and he'd blown it when he blew his cork like an adolescent.

So yeah, he'd try to put that humiliating experience behind him.

He exchanged a few words with Sandra, the receptionist; then he and Georgia took the elevator down to street level. They walked in silence to the lot where he'd parked his Porsche Carrera—a car he'd have had to sell but for the VitalSport deal. He opened the passenger door, but, rather than get in, she stood studying his car.

"What's wrong now?" he asked defensively. All morning, she'd criticized him. Was she going to pick on his car too?

"Nothing." She sounded surprised. "It's classy rather than flashy. Black was a good choice. Yes, I'd say it's distinctive but not pretentious."

Relieved, he winked at her. "Drives fast too."

Her eyes flared in what looked like fear. What was that about?

The thought vanished as she maneuvered herself into the car, and he enjoyed the way her navy skirt rode up to reveal delicate knees clad in sheer hose.

He slid behind the steering wheel, very aware of how close she was. The last time he'd been this close to Georgia, he'd been screwing her. His cock pulsed to life, and again he was glad of the loose jersey that covered his fly.

"It's awfully small, isn't it?" she said, a little breathlessly.

"Excuse me?" Now she was insulting his cock?

She gestured, and he realized she meant the inside of the car.

"Kinda like the cockpit of a plane," he said. If he'd been on his own, he'd have put the top down, but he figured she'd complain about the wind messing up her hair. "Where'd you say you left your car?"

"I was coming down Burrard and it was in the intersection of Robson, so I pulled into the nearest loading zone around the corner. Let's see, uh . . ."

"You don't know the name of the street where you left it?"

She shot him a nasty look. "I know exactly where it is. Drive and I'll direct you."

He threaded the Porsche through traffic-clogged downtown streets until, after a few misses, they arrived at the right place. Except there was no car. He'd expected that. "Towed."

"Oh no."

Woody slipped the Porsche into the loading zone, clicked off the ignition, and turned to her. "You left it in a commercial loading zone. Didn't you figure it'd get towed?"

"I didn't have a choice," she flared. "I had to get to the meeting. Well, damn. Where would they have taken it?"

"How should I know? I'd never let anyone get their hands on this baby." He stroked the leather dash. "Terry might know. Give him a call."

"Good idea." She reached down for her briefcase, then groaned. "My cell's in my purse."

"Where's your purse?"

She sighed and rubbed the back of her neck. "In my car."

He stared at her, and another thought struck him. "Did you take your keys?" Maybe her car hadn't been towed, but stolen.

"Of course I did," she snapped. "And yes, I locked the car."

He reached into his jeans pocket, pulled out his cell, and said, "Crap. Mine's dead." Coming home hammered last night, he'd been lucky to make it into bed, much less charge his phone. But he did have a battery charger in the glove compartment. He reached over to open the compartment and his hand grazed Georgia's leg.

She jerked. "What are you doing?"

He yanked his hand back. "Jesus, woman, don't be so jumpy. You do it, then. Open the glove compartment and dig out my cell charger."

"Sorry," she muttered. She fumbled with the release button and the compartment sprang open, the contents cascading out in a mad, noisy tumble.

With quick reflexes, Woody grabbed the cell charger while the rest of the items landed on Georgia's lap and the floor at her feet.

"Sorry," she said again, beginning to collect them and put them back. A package of tissues, miniature flashlight. Corkscrew. Swiss Army knife. She bent and scrabbled around at her feet, coming up with a bunch of condoms.

She dropped the cellophane packages like she'd picked up a handful of worms, and they cascaded back to the floor.

Woody wasn't going to try leaning across her again, and she made no move to retrieve them. In fact, she'd pretty much frozen into a block of ice.

He plugged in the charger, and in a few seconds the phone was functional again.

She gave him her office number, he got through to Terry, and then he pulled away from the curb. "The lot's near the Main Street SkyTrain Station."

She rubbed her neck again, something she'd done a number of times yesterday and today. "We really don't have time for this."

"You okay?"

"Just a bit of a headache."

"You get 'em a lot, huh?"

She stretched and he heard the crinkle of condom wrappers under her feet. He hoped her shoes weren't trashing them. He relied on condoms. Had since he'd first had sex at age fourteen. In fact, he had condoms stashed—

"Do they occur frequently?" she asked.

"Huh? What? Condoms?"

"What?" She sounded shocked, outraged. Then, suddenly and unexpectedly, a laugh spluttered. "I meant headaches," she managed to say, giggling. "I was trying to"—giggle—"work on communication skills."

Now he got it, and laughed too. When he glanced over, his eyes met her dancing ones. "You mean like this?" He put on his best imitation of a snotty upper-crust English accent. "It occurred to me to wonder whether your headaches occur frequently, Ms. Malone?" By the time he finished, his voice had disintegrated into laughter again, and she was chuckling.

This was good, the two of them laughing together rather than her picking on him or ordering him around. Man, she was pretty when she laughed.

She shifted position, and wrappers crackled under her feet.

Pretty Georgia, animated and laughing.

Condoms.

And his growing hard-on. "We'd better get a move on," he said gruffly. He accelerated to catch the tail end of a yellow light, and heard a soft gasp beside him. When they'd cleared the intersection, he glanced at his passenger. Her hands gripped the seat belt, knuckles white.

"I'm a good driver. Never had an accident."

"I believe you." She gritted the words out between clenched teeth. "But I'd appreciate it if you'd slow down."

He sighed and obeyed. "Yeah, okay, but it takes all the fun out of it."

He slid the driver-side window down and rested his arm on it, driving with just his right hand as he took the Georgia Street Viaduct toward Main.

"Do you have to drive with one hand?"

Ticked, Woody lifted both hands from the wheel. "Guess not. She's a good little car; she can manage on autopilot for a while."

He repented when he saw Georgia's face. Her normal skin color was pale, but now she'd gone as white as his Egyptian cotton sheets.

"Sorry." He put his hands at ten and two, eased off on the gas, and puttered along like a little old lady out for a Sunday afternoon drive.

He found the lot, stopped the Porsche, and climbed out.

Georgia clambered out awkwardly, clearly not a woman who had experience with sports cars. "I wonder if these people only tow away parking violators," she mused, "or if they do other towing? I'll need to get the car to my repair shop."

"Hold your horses. First we'll find out if your car's here, and what's wrong with it."

"How would we know what's wrong with it?"

Woody rolled his eyes and stomped over to the claim window, with her scurrying to catch up. When she gave her license number, the pimply kid in the booth said, "Yeah, it's here. Over in that corner." He pointed.

"So what happened?" Woody asked Georgia as they headed in that direction. "Run out of gas?"

"I did not. No, I think the engine caught on fire."

"What?" He stopped abruptly and grabbed her arm. "Fire?"

This time, she didn't jerk away, just gazed up at him. "Traffic was crawling, the intersections were gridlocked, then I saw smoke pouring from under the hood." She shuddered, eyes wide. "It terrified me."

"I bet."

"I pulled into the first loading zone I saw and . . ." She wrinkled her nose. "I've been pretty stupid, haven't I?"

"Leaving your car to burn up?" He shook his head in wonder. Women never failed to surprise him. An idea occurred. "You're sure it was smoke?"

She frowned. "It looked like smoke."

"Did it smell like smoke?"

"I don't remember."

"Scorched metal, burning oil?"

She shook her head. "If it wasn't smoke, what do you think happened?" She gazed up at him like she actually thought he might have the answer.

This was a first, and Woody got off on it. He hoped he wouldn't bomb out. "Any funny noises when you were driving?"

"Not today. Yesterday it sounded odd; then it was okay again."

"Odd?"

"Kind of a clacking, whirling sound?" Her face scrunched up as she tried to remember.

"Where was the noise coming from?"

"How do you mean?"

He could do a lot of eye-rolling around this woman. But then, she probably felt the same way about him. "Under the hood?"

"I guess."

"Any funny lights on the dash?"

"I didn't look. I mean, I don't know what lights there are supposed to be. All I look at is the fuel gauge. And yes, it does work."

"Let's check her out." His best guess was a broken fan belt.

Georgia led him over to an older model Toyota sedan the same navy as her suit.

No signs of fire. He grinned to himself. Honestly. Couldn't she tell steam from smoke? He hoped she did better in the kitchen. Speaking of which, he was starving.

He took the keys she handed him, unlocked the driver's door, and popped the hood. One glance was enough, but he reached a couple of fingers in and jiggled things around, checked out the radiator. Piece of cake. He eased the hood down, wiped his fingers on his jeans, and turned to her.

"Well?" she asked.

"I'm hungry."

"What?" she almost yelled.

"Aren't you?"

"Yes," she admitted, "but what about my car?"

"Need to pick up a fan belt for this baby."

"Fan belt?"

"Yeah, it's the belt that . . ." Nah, what was the point? "Damn, Georgia, I'm hungry. I can fix your car, but I need some fuel in my tummy first."

"You can fix it? Honestly?" Her amber eyes were wide and dazzly in the sunshine.

Yeah, intoxicating was the right word. He smiled at her. "Yeah, sunshine. Would I lie to a pretty lady?"

Her eyes narrowed and her mouth went all tight and prissy.

What the hell was wrong with her? It wasn't like he'd mentioned sex.

Georgia rubbed the back of her neck. Her headache had been coming and going, and Woody's insincere flattery didn't help. No, he was definitely not the charming Comte de Vergennes.

He was right about food, though. It was well past noon, and her headaches got worse when she didn't eat. "I suppose your idea of a lunch spot is McDonald's?"

He gave an exaggerated shudder. "I got more respect for my body. There's an Italian place nearby, Campagnolo, that makes good pasta and pizza."

She hoped his taste in restaurants had more in common with his taste in cars than in clothing.

They returned to his Porsche. "Please don't drive too fast." He had terrified her earlier. Since the accident and Anthony's death, she never felt truly comfortable in a car.

Campagnolo was in an area of town she wouldn't have ventured into alone at night, but it was almost full and the patrons were fairly upscale, mostly in their twenties and thirties. Some wore business suits; others looked more like artists, of the successful rather than starving variety; a few might have been students. Woody was among the most casually dressed.

Georgia settled herself in a minimalist chair that looked like it had come from a hospital waiting room, and found it surprisingly comfortable. Eyeing the décor, she said, "Industrial chic. It reminds me of the Chan Centre."

"Huh?"

"The Chan Centre for the Performing Arts at UBC. It doesn't have ice on the floor, so you've probably never been there."

He chuckled, and that made her smile a little. "It has the same concrete walls and light wood," she told him. "It's supposed to be great architecture, but it reminds me of a parking garage."

"Probably not what they were going for."

She was beginning to relax. "I know stark décor is trendy, but I like something softer."

"Wouldn't have guessed that."

"No? Why not?"

He gestured toward her. "Dark tailored suits, white shirts, hair all yanked back. You dress kind of like this place."

It was a surprisingly perceptive comment. She did choose an image that was on the stark side, rejecting her mom's notion that a woman should dress to attract men.

Woody's eyes gleamed. "Of course, underneath it all, you're curvy, warm, passionate."

Ooh! How dare he use a line like that on her when yesterday

he'd said the sex was crappy? "Don't say that," she said stiffly, cheeks burning. "We agreed yesterday was a mistake and we'd put it behind us."

The gleam died. "Yeah. Sorry." He turned away and flashed a smile at a waitress, who hurried over.

"Like a drink?" she asked brightly. "And are you ready to order?"

"I'm starving," he said. "D'you still have that pizza with salmon and spinach?"

"Sure do."

Georgia opened her menu. Small, but enticing. She'd have lingered over it, but the complex aroma of garlic, herbs, and everything else that was cooking made her stomach growl. Besides, it was annoying listening to Woody banter with the waitress.

"I'll have the risotto with calamari and fennel," Georgia said when she could get a word in edgewise.

Woody chose the pizza and a salad.

"And to drink?" the waitress asked. "A bottle of wine? Beer?"

"Diet Coke for me," Georgia said firmly.

"Just water." Woody gave the waitress another smile.

Somehow, the girl managed to tear herself away and head for the kitchen.

"I would have taken you for a beer man," Georgia said.

Was that a shudder? "Yeah, that's what I drink when I'm drinking, but I don't usually have alcohol during the day. It's not a good habit to get into, even during the off-season."

"I agree. But at some point we'll have to educate you about wine."

"How come?"

This was going to be an uphill battle. "Woody, it's better to say 'why' rather than 'how come.'"

"Oh. Uh, why?"

"Well, beer is—"

He interrupted. "No, I mean why is it better to say 'why'?"

"It sounds more polished."

"Polished. Shit."

She wasn't sure whether to grin or groan. "You're supposed to be avoiding expletives."

"Huh?"

"Swearwords," she said, before noticing the twinkle in his eye that said he was having her on. "Let's try to enrich your vocabulary with more descriptive words."

The twinkle grew. "Seems to me words like 'shit' and 'fuck' are pretty descriptive."

Ten

How could Woody be so annoying, so amusing, and so—okay, she admitted it—charming? His charm wasn't the sophisticated style of the Comte's, but it did exist. "Are you determined to make this difficult?"

"Seems to me that's what you folks at Dynamic Marketing are doing. But okay, go on. Why do I need to learn about wine?"

"I know you're a sports figure, and beer is big with men who are into sports—"

"Lots of women too," he interrupted.

No doubt he'd gone drinking with dozens, maybe hundreds, of—what had Terry called them? Puck bunnies? "With the sports crowd, beer will often be an appropriate drink. However, there will be occasions—black-tie functions like the Boys and Girls Club event—where beer won't convey the right image."

"You mean it's lower class," he said grimly.

"Not so much anymore, with all the microbreweries and designer beer. It's more about matching beverage selection to circumstance."

"So you figure they'll be drinking wine at these black-tie deals?"

"Try using 'functions' or 'affairs' rather than 'deals.'"

"Affairs? Seriously? I thought that meant—"

"I know what you thought." She was getting to know that twinkle, almost enjoying the sparring, and her headache had eased. But they had work to do. "And yes, at events like that, wine will often be served. Or champagne."

"I like champagne."

"Oh. I hadn't realized. . . ."

His eyes narrowed. "That a boor like me would drink champagne?"

That was exactly what Georgia had been thinking. "Of course not. I just gathered that you only drank beer."

"Beer and champagne." His deep blue eyes were steely. "I like champagne best when I'm drinking it out of the Stanley Cup."

"The Stanley Cup?" The hockey trophy. "Are you saying that if you win it, you drink champagne out of it?" She had an image of a locker room and a bunch of half-naked, sweaty hooligans capering around, dousing one another with champagne and drinking out of some giant silver loving cup.

"Yeah," he said softly. "It's just as bad as you're imagining."

She stared at him guiltily. "Sorry."

"It's a drunken brawl, except what we're drunk on is success more than booze." His eyes, his tone, were intent. They held her mesmerized. "We're exhausted, injured. We've pushed ourselves way past our limits. We've fought with everything we've got; we've fought against another team that's as skilled as us, that's probably got as much heart. And we're the ones who, in the end, triumphed. So, yeah, Georgia, we celebrate. We just about go out of our minds celebrating. Sorry if you find that so offensive."

He finished with a sarcastic edge, but she'd heard the truth: how important his sport was to him, and how much he hated to have it ridiculed.

Grown men chasing a black disk around the ice and getting paid a fortune to do it. Yes, but clearly there was more to it. She didn't understand hockey, but he'd taken her a step closer. She did understand sincerity, and the passion to do something well. Not to mention, he looked incredibly sexy when he spoke with that passion.

"I'm sorry. I had no idea. I never thought about it that way, and I should have. Woody, there are things you need to teach me too." Without thinking, she reached across the table and rested her hand on his forearm, bare and muscular below the pulled-up sleeve of his jersey. His flesh was firm and warm under her hand and she could sense the energy just below the surface. Her palm tingled and a current ran up her arm and zinged through her body, straight to her sex.

This man had been inside her.

It had been a bad idea. They both knew that. She forced herself to remove her hand.

But she couldn't look away from those indigo eyes.

Woody opened his mouth, but their waitress arrived with their lunches.

He must have been grateful for the interruption, because he began demolishing his food. Georgia turned her attention to her risotto, which was delicious.

Woody's left arm was on the table, curved protectively around his meal. He leaned forward over the pizza plate and ate methodically, without a break.

She sighed. "No one's going to take your food away before you're finished."

Bent forward as he was, his face was close to hers when he looked up, startled. "What?"

"A deportment lesson. You eat as if it's a race to get through the meal before someone takes it away from you."

Something flashed in his eyes. Something dark; a hint of pain, perhaps. It reminded her that his bio didn't say much about his childhood, but suggested it had been rough.

Softly, she went on. "Meals—especially meals with friends or colleagues—are supposed to be relaxed and social. People eat a bit, chat, eat some more. They take it slowly."

He frowned as if he didn't understand.

"Look around," she suggested. "See how that man is sitting, listening, while the woman across from him talks? Then he takes a forkful of salad, sits back, says something to her. There's a pace and balance."

"Oh yeah? I never think about it when I'm out with the guys. We're hungry; we eat."

"What about when you're on a date?"

His gaze flicked downward. "Guess I eat my meal, and talk before and after. No one's ever said anything," he added, a little belligerently.

"When you're finished with your meal, what's the woman doing? Is she finished too?"

"I guess not. Women are such slow eaters. You pick at food like you feel guilty about every calorie."

Georgia chuckled. "I'm not suggesting you act that way either." She had an inspiration. "When you tell sports stories, you do great imitations of people. You're a good observer and mimic. Why don't you use that man as a model, and try imitating him?"

Woody was still staring down at his plate. She'd embarrassed him and, while his table manners were poor, the blame likely lay with his upbringing. "It's like what I said about wine and beer, and knowing what fits the circumstances. If you're out with the guys on the team, and you're all ravenous after a game, then it would probably be natural to, uh . . ."

"Chow down like pigs at a trough?" Now he looked up, a dangerous gleam in his eye.

He really did have a knack for reading her mind, and calling her on it. "Uh, well, maybe not quite like that."

Fortunately, his gleam turned into a twinkle. "Whereas when I'm with a lady I oughta eat like a constipated Englishman?"

She remembered his imitation of a snotty English accent. "What have you got against Englishmen, anyway?" The thought of the novel she was reading flashed into her mind. Lady Emma might agree with Woody about the stodginess of upper-class Englishmen, especially when compared to the Continental charm of the Comte.

If Woody had the Comte's flair, this campaign would be so much easier. And he'd be so much more appealing. Or would he? According to Viv, Woody's raw masculine edge was part of his appeal. Georgia's body—if not her mind—agreed. She was so physically aware of him, it was as though an energy charge, a sexual one, ran constantly through her body.

Forcing her mind back to the topic at hand, she said, "Okay, Woody, let's look around the room and see if we can find a constipated Englishman."

His laugh boomed out, hearty and very male. Heads turned. Most people smiled, then turned back to their meals, but several women, having noticed Woody, now had trouble keeping their eyes off him. One stylish young man in a business suit was also staring. He said something to his companion, another man like him, who turned to stare at Woody. The pair got up and made their way across the room.

Georgia frowned. Surely they weren't going to complain because Woody'd laughed so loudly. He had a wonderful laugh, rich and contagious. They could use that in the campaign.

The first young man, looking eager but painfully embarrassed, reached their table. Ignoring Georgia, he spoke to Woody. "You're Woody Hanrahan."

Woody smiled easily. "So I've been told."

"Wow! Like, in person! Just having lunch here like Tim and me. Hey, can I shake your hand?"

Still smiling, Woody held out his hand.

The other man gaped at it. "Oh shit, that's your Stanley Cup ring." Reverently, he shook Woody's hand.

Georgia glanced at the knuckle-duster, heavy and gold with a sparkling diamond, as the fan rattled on. "My name's Benjamin and this is Tim—I already said that—and we have season tickets. Haven't missed a single home game, and we've seen the rest on TV. You're awesome, man, totally awesome."

"Thanks, Benjamin." Woody shook with the other man as well. "Nice to meet you, Tim."

"You deserved the Conn Smythe last year." Fervent words poured out of Tim. "It was a crime they gave it to LaBecque."

Woody shrugged. "I've had my share, and Pierre LaBecque led his team to the win. Besides, he scored more goals than I did last season."

"Yeah, but you had way more assists," Tim said, "and that's what it's really about. Any idiot can wham the puck into the goal if the other guy sets him up right."

Woody chuckled. "Trust me, it's not quite that easy."

Benjamin flushed. "You know what I'm saying. You're the next Gretzky, for Christ's sake."

"Thanks for your support, guys. Now, if you don't mind, the lady and I would like to get back to our lunch."

The two men glanced at Georgia as if she'd materialized out of thin air. "Yeah, sure." Chattering to each other and glancing over their shoulders at Woody, they headed back to their table.

"Apparently I'm invisible," she said dryly.

"Sorry about that."

She glanced at him curiously. "Does it happen a lot?"

"You mean, 'Does it occur frequently?'"

"Right." She smiled, remembering her lesson in the car.

He made a self-deprecating face. "The price of fame. Sometimes it's cool—gives me a boost if I'm feeling low, like if I've played a bad game." He grimaced. "Like last night. Sometimes it's a pain in the ass, like if I'm out with a woman."

"You handled it well."

His mouth twisted. "You don't have to sound so surprised."

She bit her lip. "Sorry. But you seemed at ease, genuine, polite." Attractive, and too darned appealing. "It's different from how you come across in interviews. And yes, I understand that the interviewers may catch you at a bad time, but you don't want to come across as raw and violent."

He scowled. "I'm not violent. But I'm not gonna come across like a wuss. Hockey players are tough, Georgia. It's part of the sport."

"All that whacking into each other, bashing each other into the boards, it's uncivilized," she protested. "Other sports aren't like that, are they?" She'd caught only glimpses of sports like basketball and baseball as she changed channels, but she'd never seen the kind of violence she'd noted in last night's hockey game.

"Hockey's a Canadian game." He grinned. "We're tough guys up here, north of the forty-ninth parallel."

His grin was infectious, but she resisted. "I can't believe that's the image Canada wants to present to the world."

"Yet hockey's our unofficial national sport."

"Unofficial? What's the official one?"

"Lacrosse."

"Lacrosse?" No image came to mind. Had she ever channel-surfed past a game of lacrosse?

"See, you don't even know what it is. Fans go for hockey. They like seeing guys getting bashed into the boards by a good, fair hit."

"That doesn't say much for the fans."

"I'm sure there's a psychological explanation. Bottom line, better they cheer for me smashing LaBecque into the boards than they go home and beat up on their spouses." His voice was heavy, his blue eyes shadowed.

She wrinkled her nose. "I hate to think those are the only two options."

He gave a solemn nod. "Me too. Alls I'm saying is, there gotta be reasons hockey's so popular."

They were conversing, and he hadn't touched his lunch for a good ten minutes. She'd let his poor grammar slide by. Instead, she took a bite of risotto and chewed slowly.

His fork went down and came up with a much larger portion of salad.

When he'd finished it, she said, "What were those men talking about? Conn Smythe?" She took another forkful of risotto to eat while he responded.

"The Conn Smythe Trophy is the award for the MVP in the NHL Stanley Cup playoffs. Uh, MVP means—"

"Most valuable player. That much I know. And NHL is the National Hockey League. But I'm not sure exactly what that is."

Following her example, he'd eaten some pizza while she was talking. "Can't believe you live in Vancouver and know so little about hockey."

Some people had better things to do than watch grown men chase pucks. But saying so would be rude, and not an effective strategy. "I've never been into sports. Enlighten me."

"Okay. The NHL is a formal organization with thirty clubs—what you'd think of as teams—that are franchises. Mostly American, seven in Canada. The players come from all over the world, and lots of Canadians play for American teams."

"How's it decided what team a player's on?"

He swallowed the bite he'd been eating, and she realized he'd picked up the back-and-forth flow of eating and conversing. "There's a draft, trades, free agents. It's complicated."

"And the season has all these games that build toward the Stanley Cup playoffs?"

"Pretty much. First we play some exhibition games against NHL clubs, European clubs, and so on. Then it's regular season and we play clubs within the league." He lifted his water glass.

Georgia stared at his hand, so large and brown. Surprisingly well shaped, but so very strong looking. That hand had touched her most intimate places with amazing delicacy. And deftness. As if he knew her body better than anyone ever had.

A tingly ache throbbed between her legs, craving more of that touch.

When Woody took a long swallow of water, his throat rippled.

She'd never been so physically aware of a man, but then, she'd never been with a man who made his living with his body. As well as his mind, if Terry was to be believed. She'd also never been with a man who'd brought her to climax.

"Then there's postseason," Woody went on.

Throat dry, she swallowed and tried to remember what they were talking about.

"That's the Stanley Cup playoffs. An elimination system involving the top eight clubs. Two clubs play until one has won four games; then the winner advances to the next round."

"Terry said the Beavers are in the Western Conference finals?"

"Yeah. There's two groups, Eastern and Western Conference. We're in the playoffs against the Ducks for Western Conference title. That club will play the Eastern Conference champs for the Cup."

"You must've played a lot of games to get to this point." Thinking back on what he'd said earlier, she said, "No wonder players are tired and injured."

He nodded. "The further you go, the harder it is. But that's how it's supposed to be." He flashed a grin. "Tough, remember?"

Georgia realized she was enjoying this. Woody could be good company. She was starting to like him. "How about you? Are you injured?"

"If I was, I wouldn't say. We don't talk about that stuff. Don't want our opponents knowing our weaknesses."

It was the same thing he'd said to the interviewer last night. The concept made sense, but she wasn't an opponent or an interviewer, and she felt a little hurt that he wouldn't tell her.

How silly. They weren't friends. This was a business relationship. Except for the sex. The momentary lapse she needed to ignore. "You said the Conn Smythe Trophy goes to the MVP?"

"Yeah, in the Stanley Cup playoffs. There are other awards, like the Hart Memorial for the MVP during the regular season, voted on by the Professional Hockey Writers Association. And others based on statistics, like highest-scoring player."

"You've won some of them." She'd skimmed the details in Billy's research, the names of the various trophies making no sense to her.

A smile flickered. "All of 'em."

And, she recalled, some more than once. Georgia finished the last bite of risotto. She'd assumed Woody had an enormous ego, but that wasn't proving to be the case. It made him even more appealing. That was good for the marketing campaign—which, after all, was the only thing that mattered. "Which one most recently?"

He shrugged. "Hart Memorial this season."

This lunch was enlightening. The man had more depth than she'd given him credit for, he learned quickly, and he had a sense of humor. As well as a rough brand of sex appeal that didn't quit. Even when she tried to concentrate on work, her body hummed with awareness of him. "What was the other thing that man called you? The next Gretzky? That's Wayne Gretzky, right? Even I have heard that name. He was a really successful Canadian hockey player, wasn't he?"

"Yeah. He was my hero, growing up."

Something Terry had said finally sunk in. "Hockey is Canada's favorite sport, and right now you're the biggest Canadian star."

"Jeez, don't put it like that. A guy's only as good as the men he plays with, not to mention the coaches, athletic trainers, medical staff, equipment manager. It's a team."

It was the same kind of thing he'd said in interviews. There, it had come across as a platitude. Now it sounded totally sincere. Terry needed to overcome Woody's awkwardness with the media and bring out this genuineness.

Woody shoved his plate away. "You finished? We should get that fan belt."

Again, she'd forgotten her car.

They were arguing over the bill, with her insisting it was a business expense, when his cell phone rang. As he reached into his jeans pocket, she grabbed the bill, making a mental note to tell him to turn off his cell in restaurants.

"Yo," Woody said into the phone. "Yeah, I'm great. Probably because I ran six miles first thing this morning when you were still in bed. Or hanging on to the toilet."

Georgia's stomach, full of risotto, did a somersault. Delightful. And a needed reminder that, despite his good qualities, Woody still required a lot of work.

"Yeah, that was one hell of a bender," he said. "God knows how I staggered home."

At least he'd had the sense not to drive.

As she listened to Woody's side of the conversation, she glanced around the restaurant, noticing other women covertly watching him. Did they recognize him, or was it just that he was hard not to look at, with his large, rangy frame, tousled mahogany hair and beard, and rolled-up sleeves showing off muscular forearms? Female eyes checked her out too, no doubt thinking she and Woody were an odd couple.

"Nah, I can't this aft," he said. "All booked up."

As Georgia calculated a tip and punched her PIN into the card reader, she listened to Woody say, "Oh, nothing special."

He glanced at her. "No, I can't blow it off."

"Okay, it's this girl I met." He actually had the audacity to wink at her. "Yeah, sure she's hot; why else'd I be spending time with her?"

Ooh! How dared he?

He ended the call and turned his attention to Georgia. She glared at him.

He grimaced. "Sorry. Wasn't really talking about you. Don't take it personally."

Oh good, that helped immensely—of course he didn't really think she was hot, despite having had sex with her on a conference room table.

He gazed wistfully out the window. "Great day for golf. S'pose you don't play?"

"Hitting balls of any kind isn't my idea of fun." Her Diet Coke was finished, but she crunched the remaining ice. "Why did you say those things to your friend? Is it essential to come across as a super-stud?"

He grinned. "Only semi-essential." The grin died. "I should've just said I was hanging out with a friend. Didn't think fast enough, and I didn't want to spill anything about the fuck—stupid— endorsement deal." All parties had agreed that the campaign would launch with a formal announcement, and Woody's involvement would be a secret until then.

"You're clearly not pleased about the contract. What's the issue? You're making a lot of money. Is it just about the underwear thing?"

She couldn't see his leg but could tell he was jiggling it; the table vibrated rapidly. "Money's good, but the figurehead thing is embarrassing. And modeling gonch sucks." He rose. "Let's go."

As they walked to her car, she said, "You were out drinking last night."

"I guess."

"I hope you don't do it often."

"Often?" He stopped and glared down at her. "None of your business. Alls you need to know is that I won't tie one on at one of your fancy champagne *affairs*."

"All," she said coldly. "The word is 'all,' not 'alls.' There is no such word as 'alls.' And thank you for that extraordinarily articulate and convincing assurance."

They climbed into the car in silence.

Eleven

Woody turned the key and the Carrera's engine roared to life.

Should have known it was too good to be true, those few minutes when he and Georgia'd been getting along. Didn't take long for her to climb back on his case. According to her, there wasn't one fucking thing he did right.

Well, he could damn well fix a car.

He headed to a parts and repair shop and picked up the right fan belt. When he drove back to the tow lot and parked, Georgia said rather grudgingly, "It's nice of you to do this."

Yeah, it was. And he was going to make her help, rather than sit all high-and-mighty on her tush. A tush that hadn't been all that high-and-mighty yesterday, when he'd popped it up onto that conference table.

"Could you ask the kid in the booth for a bucket of water? Gotta fill up the rad."

She nodded and walked away.

Woody, using the small toolkit from his car, cleared out the old fan belt, tightened a few screws, and by that time he was whistling. Nothing like productive work to put a guy in good spirits. Besides, he had a plan for taking Ms. Georgia Malone down a notch.

He unscrewed the cap from the radiator as she returned, awkwardly lugging a bucket. A gentleman would take it from her, but she'd made it clear she didn't see him as a gentleman. So he pointed. "Pour it in there."

Her eyes narrowed, but she hoisted the bucket. Woody stepped back. Water gushed every which way, mostly onto Georgia's skirt and legs, but probably enough got into the radiator to do some good.

"Thank you," he said politely.

She put the bucket down. "What now?"

"Take off your panty hose."

Her expression made up for everything she'd put him through.

"What did you say?" she spat, eyes huge and disbelieving.

Trying to sound innocent, he said, "You are wearing panty hose, right? Not stockings with a garter belt?"

Her eyes widened further. "What business is that of yours?"

Woody fought to control his laughter. "Can't install the new fan belt without the right tools, which are at my place."

"You tell me that *now*? I could have had the car towed to my repair shop."

"No need. Easy to fix, just need the right tools. But for now, we need to move the car, which means jerry-rigging a fan belt. Panty hose works." It was true that he needed proper tools, and true that panty hose made a fine short-term fan belt. Not that the car would need one to go a few kilometers.

No reason Georgia had to know that.

Her squinty-eyed look told him she was doing her best to read his mind.

He tried to look innocent.

Finally, she ground out, "Turn around."

"You forgetting I've already seen what you've got?"

"Oh! Well, you're certainly not seeing it again!"

Laughing, he turned around.

But then the joke was on him. When he heard the slither of skirt fabric against hose, his mind jumped to what he'd seen yesterday:

those slim, creamy legs, the fiery pubic hair, the slick, pouty lips of her pussy.

His body stirred, reminding him that a man and woman didn't have to like each other to want sex. Not that she seemed to be inclined that way at the moment.

"Here," she said grimly. A hand reached around him with a bundle of pale silky stuff.

He took the panty hose, which was damp from the water she'd spilled, still warm from her body. Was she naked under that skirt, or wearing panties?

"Well?" she demanded. "Do you need something else?"

Trying to focus on the unnecessary task he'd created, he said, "My pocketknife. Mind getting it? In the glove compartment, right?"

The same place he stored condoms.

If she brought a condom back . . . But of course she wouldn't.

Against the fly of his jeans, his swollen cock throbbed insistently. He stared down at the empty bucket. Where was the cold water when a guy needed it?

Bending under the hood, he fiddled needlessly until she returned and handed him the knife. He improvised a fan belt, then straightened and looked at Georgia. If he expected admiration, he wasn't getting it here. "Where do you live?"

"Why?"

"Trying to decide whether we take your car there or to my place."

"Kits, between Fourth Avenue and Jericho Beach."

Not much farther than his condo. If he took her to his place he'd have the home ice advantage, but she'd prowl around his apartment while he worked on the car. Nope, he'd rather have a chance to scope out her digs. "Here's what we'll do. You drive home slow and easy. I'll follow, make sure you get there safely. Then I'll whip over to my place, get the tools, and come back and fix her up for you."

Brow furrowed, she said, "It's nice of you to want to help, but if I can drive it, why not just take it to my repair shop? It's not far."

That made sense, but his pride was engaged. "Will they have it ready for you to drive to work in the morning? Don't bet on it. Besides, we've already bought the fan belt."

She tossed her hands up in one of those fluttery, female gestures. "All right, have it your way. I admit it would save me a lot of hassle."

But you don't want to be indebted to me. His mind supplied the rest of her thought. *You don't want to be indebted to a dumb jock. Tough. Guys like me are good for something, and it's time you learned it.*

I t was an unaccustomed treat to be home—an apartment in an old character house that had been renovated to make six units—on a workday afternoon. Georgia shed her confining suit jacket and traded her damp skirt and bare legs for beige cotton pants. Normally, she'd also have let down her hair and put on a tee, but she didn't want to get that casual with Woody.

Settling on the couch with Kit-Kat beside her, she turned on her laptop and checked e-mail. After responding to a few work messages, she clicked on a message from Marielle, addressed to the book club members.

So, have you started the book? I'm dying to know what you think.

Kim had responded with,

I got it on my Kindle Monday night and I'm totally loving it. How come I never meet men like le Comte? Wasn't that first sex scene hot? I mean, he started out as a stranger, she didn't even like him, and he seduced her so totally and she loved it. When you think about it, it's pretty unbelievable, right? A terrific

fantasy—and yet I totally bought it. And I want some for
myself!!! LOL.

Was Kim joking or, as Georgia suspected, was all not well with
her and her boyfriend? Although the four women's reason for getting together was to read and discuss books, Georgia liked the way
they were slowly getting to know one another.

Though she had a couple of close girlfriends who went back a
long way, the three of them didn't get together so often these days.
One was a newlywed, the other a new mom, and they were tied up
with their own lives. Though Georgia was busy with her job, and
liked her own company and that of her cat, sometimes she felt lonely.

Turning back to her computer screen, she read Marielle's reply
to Kim.

Hey, no one wants to read about a normal, boring life, right?
Besides, I don't think it's pure fantasy. I could totally see myself
doing it.

Georgia smiled at that. Marielle was gorgeous, vivacious, and
fun. Her motto was to enjoy life. She sampled drinks, jobs, and men
with abandon.

Marielle's e-mail ended with:

Lily, George, what do you think?

Fantasy or reality? A stranger who seduced the prim Lady Emma
and awakened her sexuality. On Monday night, Georgia would have
agreed with Kim that it wasn't believable. Yet she was living proof
that it could happen, even when the man was far less suave than Le
Comte de Vergennes.

Lily had chimed in with a brief message:

Haven't bought the book yet, but I will. That's what the club's about. We have to read everything, even if it's not something we'd choose ourselves.

Marielle responded:

Yeah, you gotta give it a try. Lady Emma tried something different, and hey, she liked it a lot! George, you out there? Have you started the book yet?

Slowly, she typed:

Yes, and I've read the scene you're talking about. It did seem out of character for Lady Emma, but I bought into it. Why do you think she did it, though?

If she better understood Emma's motivation, maybe she'd be clearer on her own.

She didn't expect an immediate response, but an e-mail from Marielle popped in:

For me, good old chemistry would be enough. But for Emma, I think it's more than that. She'd never been treated that way before. Never been appreciated for being a beautiful, sexy, desirable woman. And also, she'd never had an orgasm, never really even been turned on. How could she resist?

How indeed?

A double knock sounded at the door. Kit-Kat, who was shy around strangers, took off in a tortoiseshell blur. Georgia typed quickly:

Have to go. Business meeting.

Before she could rise to answer the door, it opened and Woody invaded her peaceful living room. His jeans and jersey were streaked with dirt, his skin was glossed with sweat, there was a dark smudge across one cheek, and his face wore a satisfied grin. "All done. Purring sweet as any kitten."

"Thank you." She put her laptop on the coffee table, feeling both gratitude and resentment. She had vowed to never be like her mother, to never need a man. But of course she did need a car mechanic, so perhaps it shouldn't be an issue that the man was someone she knew, not an anonymous guy in the back of the repair shop.

Of course, Woody wasn't just someone she knew; he was the man who'd given her orgasms. Who had, in his own un-suave fashion, made her feel sexy and desirable—at least until he'd made it crystal clear he was sorry they'd had sex.

He waved his hands, smeared with black grease, in front of her face. "Need to wash up."

Definitely un-suave. She wrinkled her nose. "Use the kitchen. I suppose you opened the door with one of those?"

A brow went up. "Nah, with my tongue."

She refused, absolutely refused, to think of that tongue tangling with hers. "Don't be any more disgusting than you need to be." She followed him into the kitchen. While he scrubbed busily, she took household cleaner and a roll of paper towels to the front door.

Returning, she handed him paper towels to dry his hands on. "You have a smudge on your cheek."

He reached up and she said, "No, the other cheek."

When he missed it again, she said, "Stop; I'll do it." She wet a paper towel and stretched up.

Stupid move. He was so tall compared to Anthony, and his raw masculinity was unsettling. Especially when it was raw masculinity she'd been up close and personal with, in that moment of temporary insanity. No wonder her heart was thudding like it wanted to burst out of her chest. Marielle had mentioned chemistry. Was this what it felt like?

When she inhaled, his scent was raw and masculine too. There was a tang of something like pine or cedar, and the distinct odor of male sweat. Not bad, just not something she was used to. The most exertion Anthony'd ever engaged in was walking and lovemaking, and she couldn't remember ever seeing him sweat.

Oh yes! She smiled. Right before he had to defend his master's thesis.

"What's so funny?" Woody asked.

Startled, she gazed into those mesmerizing blue eyes, far too close to her own. "Nothing." She stepped back. "We need to get back to our communication lessons." She eyed his grubby clothing dubiously. "I'd suggest the living room because it's more comfortable, but your clothes might stain the upholstery."

He glanced down, apparently surprised to find dirt all over himself. "I've got clean clothes in the car."

"Oh." It was a sensible, considerate suggestion. Why should it make her uneasy? Yes, the last time he'd taken his clothes off, the consequences had been . . . Her brain sought for the right word. Disastrous? Amazing? But neither of them was going to go insane again. They both regretted yesterday. "Thank you, Woody. That's good of you."

"Shower'd feel good anyway." He was out the door again.

She gaped after him. A shower? She hadn't offered a shower.

A few minutes later, he was in the bathroom with the water running, whistling. Badly.

She listened. She couldn't not listen. Any more than she could avoid imagining him naked, with water streaming over him. Soaping up his hands and slicking them over his bulging muscles.

His body was so different from Anthony's. Her husband had been five foot nine, two inches taller than her. She'd loved his body, in all its subtlety and ascetic fineness. Woody was the opposite. Blatant, not subtle.

Not that he was overdeveloped, like the steroid-pumped men who built their muscles to the point of absurdity. Woody's body really was quite appealing. For marketing purposes, she reminded herself. That was what counted.

When Woody had said clean clothes, she'd assumed jeans, but he emerged from the bathroom in baggy gray, mid-thigh-length gym shorts and a loose black T-shirt with the sleeves ripped out. Oh no, he was not fine-boned and ascetic. There was so darned much naked flesh, tanned and toned and utterly masculine.

He caught her staring. "My squash clothes."

"Is there any sport you don't play?"

"Sure. Cricket, lacrosse . . ." Looming above her, he rested his hands on his hips. "Is there any sport you do play?"

"No. I walk, but I don't play sports."

"How come? Oops, I mean, why?"

She bit her lip. "I don't mean to offend you. Honestly. I heard what you said at lunch about hockey. But I never saw the point to ball-chasing, ball-throwing, ball-hitting." Not to mention, she had no skill in any sport. Anthony was the same. They'd had so many things in common and had truly been soul mates. "I'm more into reading."

Woody stood in the middle of her room, gazing around, not bothering to hide his curiosity.

She felt a little vulnerable, having him check out her place. Yet she could work with this. Rather than let herself react to all those tanned muscles, she'd concentrate on her job. "Let's work on powers of observation and analysis. What do you see when you look around, and what does it tell you?"

"It's cozy," he said on a note of surprise. "Homey. I hadn't figured you for the nest-building type. Nice comfy furniture, everything easy on the eye, lots of different, pretty colors." He turned to her. "How come—I mean, why—don't you dress in colors like that?"

He, whose idea of style was a ratty jersey, was critiquing her wardrobe? "Plain, tailored clothes are appropriate for business."

"Viv disagrees."

"She and I have different approaches." And who cared that he obviously preferred Viv's?

He looked around some more. "Nice paintings. They show that you like flowers and the Pacific Northwest. And you can't stand to throw out plants when they get old and sickly."

"What's wrong with that?" she demanded.

He flashed her a grin. "Nothing. I'd say it's good news for your parents, and whatever guy you end up with. You won't toss them when they're old. Got a high loyalty quotient, Georgia."

Her heart had thumped at the mention of parents—her father hadn't been in her life since she was a toddler, and she and her mom argued over every little thing—and of her guy. Yes, she'd been loyal to Anthony, and wished she'd had the opportunity to be loyal well into her eighties or nineties. She cleared her throat. "Loyalty quotient?"

"It's a term the head coach uses. It means—"

"I get it. I'm just surprised to hear you say it, and surprised you picked up on that about me. It's true. I can be exceptionally loyal. To people who earn my loyalty." The thought of her mom put coolness in her voice.

Woody shot her a questioning look, then walked over to the bookcases that took up the walls on either side of the gas fireplace. "See what you mean about liking reading. And you've got real, uh, mixed tastes. There's a word for that."

"Eclectic?"

"Yeah, eclectic. Bestsellers, autobiographies, marketing, business, and sociology." He turned to her, scratching his head. "You really read all this?"

She curled her legs under her. "A lot of it, but most of the sociology books were my husband's." She and Anthony had spent so many nights curled up side by side reading, she couldn't bring herself to get rid of his books.

Woody gaped at her. "You're married?"

He thought she'd cheated on her husband yesterday? "No, of course not," she said hotly. "I was. He died."

Suddenly Woody was in front of her, dropping to his knees. "That's awful. I'm sorry."

The compassion in his eyes led her to go on. "It was a stupid car accident. Anthony wasn't the world's best driver; he got distracted easily. We were discussing a play we'd just seen." She swallowed, still feeling guilty about that. "It was dark, raining. It happened so suddenly. The police said he ran a red light and the other car was going too fast, one of its headlights was burned out, and it T-boned our car." She swallowed again. "On the driver's side." The car had been totaled. She'd never looked at it again, not even at pictures.

"My air bag blew up and I blacked out. When I came to, I was in the hospital. Barely injured." And Anthony was gone. Dead at the scene of the accident. She'd never had a chance to say good-bye.

"Man." Woody reached out to take her hands. "I'm sorry I was such a jerk about my driving. And I'm really sorry about your husband, but I'm sure glad you were okay."

Sincerity warmed his striking blue eyes. The grip of his hands was comforting. More than comforting.

He was too bare-skinned, too masculine, too close. Too different from Anthony, too disconcertingly attractive.

She tugged her hands free and pushed her body into the back of the chair to increase her distance from him, when what she really wanted to do was lean into him and have him put his arms around her.

"It happened three years ago," she said, trying to sound brisk and professional. "Yes, it was tragic, but these things happen." It shouldn't have happened. One brief moment of inattention, and she'd lost her soul mate. "I'm . . ." Despite her best efforts, her voice broke. She gave a choked laugh. "I was going to say I'm over it, but that's not true. I'm doing fine, though, really."

The melting sympathy in his eyes would be her undoing. She felt it dissolving her defenses. A woman could lose herself in those deep indigo pools. She could dive in and never resurface. She'd just go down and down and—

No, what was she thinking? This was a hockey player, a man who didn't even believe in serial monogamy, much less marriage. A man who had condoms in his car, condoms in his pocket. Here, there, everywhere a condom. A fact she hadn't protested about yesterday. Oh God, she was usually so in control in work situations. Why did this man rattle her so badly?

"I appreciate your concern," she said, managing to sound calmer.

He nodded, then rose and returned to the bookcase, where he picked up the small wedding picture that sat on one side. She knew the photo by heart. Anthony, slim and handsome in a tux; Georgia in a lacy white dress, her red hair a mass of curls barely confined by the pearl-studded band of her veil. She and Anthony stood at the top of the church steps, arms around each other's waists, a shaft of sunshine slanting in to pool at their feet. Smiling as if it was the happiest day of their lives. As it had been.

They'd been joining their lives, their hearts, their souls, and anticipating the wedding night when for the first time they'd join their bodies.

Woody gazed at her. "You were a beautiful bride."

Nostalgia crowded her heart. Softly she said, "I felt beautiful. I guess every bride does. And is." She pulled herself together. "Not that beauty is important."

Woody was examining her intently from across the room. Judging her beauty, or lack thereof?

Oh God, she'd had sex with this man. She and Anthony had waited for their wedding night because, for them, lovemaking was such a meaningful, emotional act. Yet, she'd had sex with the hockey player, in an act that was unemotional and meaningless. What was wrong with her?

She popped out of her chair and headed toward the kitchen. "Want a Coke?" she asked from the doorway.

"No, thanks. Got any fruit juice or milk?"

"Sorry. Coffee?"

"I don't do caffeine."

"Pardon?"

He came over, the photograph no longer in his hand. "It's a drug. I mostly don't do drugs." He tapped his chest with his knuckles. "This body's a temple. Gotta take care of it."

She stared at him.

He rolled his eyes. "Joke. But seriously, you gotta respect your body if you want it to come through for you. I ask a lot of my body, so I take care of it."

She cocked her head. "Going on a bender is taking care of your body?"

He shook his head. "Nah. That was dumb."

A man who would admit a mistake. It was another thing to like about him. "Then why did you do it?"

"Didn't play well; we lost the game. I dunno. Looked into the glass of beer and—" He broke off, gazing into her eyes.

Funny shivers—warm ones, not at all unpleasant—rippled through her. "Yes?"

He gave his head a shake and looked away. "And didn't come

out." He turned and headed back to the bookcase, saying over his shoulder, "Water'd be good. With ice."

Oh yes, ice was a very good idea. It was a relief to escape him, a relief to plunge her hands under the cold water tap. How absurd to react this way to Woody Hanrahan, a man who was the opposite of Anthony. She turned off the water and extracted the plastic ice tray from the freezer.

"You dating anybody?" His voice came from the living room.

Under her clumsy hands the tray snapped, spilling cubes all over the counter. He thought she'd had sex with him while she was dating someone else? "No," she called back. "Why?"

"No reason."

Did he always ask questions without the slightest reason? Surely, he couldn't be interested in dating her. He was sorry they'd had sex—crappy sex, for him—so the last thing he'd want would be to go out with her. It was the last thing she wanted, as well. Well, the last thing she *should* want. Oh damn. She'd never had this kind of problem working with a man before.

She dumped ice into his glass and swept the rest of the cubes into the sink.

When she walked into the living room, Woody was crouched down between the chair and the bookcase. Kit-Kat sprawled shamelessly on her back with Woody's fingers buried in her white belly fur, and gave him her most throaty, sexy purr.

Georgia stared, dumbfounded. "She doesn't like strangers. Especially men."

Woody grinned up. "Guess I'm special."

"You just keep thinking that," she said dryly, holding back a grin.

He chuckled. "What's her name? Figure if I'm stroking a girl's belly, I oughta know her name."

"I'm impressed by your high moral code. Her name's Kit-Kat."

She and Anthony, both chocolate lovers, had come up with the name together.

"Kit the cat," Woody was murmuring to the feline flirt. "Kit for short and practical, Kitty for cute, and Kitten when you're acting like one."

"And just plain Kat when she's misbehaving," Georgia finished, surprised that the hottie jock would have picked up on the cat's nicknames.

"Aw, I bet she doesn't misbehave. Do you, Kitty?"

The cat gazed up at him soulfully and Georgia shook her head. Kit-Kat had fallen head over heels: a cat who was easily seduced by Woody's magic fingers. Just as Georgia had been yesterday.

"On the subject of names," she said, "I notice you call me Georgia. Everyone else calls me George."

He gazed up. "George is a guy's name, and you ain't no guy."

That hadn't stopped anyone else. She'd labeled herself George as a teen—when she joined the chastity club and rejected feminine wiles. Everyone had accepted the nickname. Even Anthony.

Not sure what to do with Woody's comment, she decided it was high time they got on with the deportment lesson. "Sit, Woody. Let's get started."

He chose the couch, sprawling easily in the middle of it, starting to lift his bare feet to the oak coffee table, then thinking better of it.

"Thank you," she said, "but they're clean, so it's okay."

She took the chair and consulted her notes. "Here are some preliminary items I'd like to clear up: your use of 'sunshine,' the appropriate time and place for cellular phones, your rather inadequate and often questionable vocabulary, and . . ." Was that a groan? "And your attitude. Why aren't you committed to this campaign?"

He picked up his water glass and slugged down half the contents. "I'm committed," he said grimly. "Go on." A smile tugged at his lips. "Start with 'sunshine.' Can't wait to hear what that's all about."

"I've heard you call Viv 'sunshine,' and the receptionist at the office, the waitress at lunchtime, and me."

"Something wrong with that?"

"We're not interchangeable females. We have names."

"Yeah." He gave a puzzled frown. "Sandra, Viv, Tawny, and—"

"Tawny?"

His eyes gleamed in triumph. "You mean you didn't know the waitress's name?"

"You're making that up."

"Nah, but I have an advantage. When you were in the ladies' room, she gave me her phone number."

"Of course she did." *Tawny* had assumed Woody couldn't possibly be dating Georgia, or else she hadn't given a damn. Georgia was glad she hadn't given her a sizable tip. "You remember what Viv said, that if you want to date someone, you should run it by us?"

"You remember what I said? My private life's private."

He'd also said he didn't date during the playoffs because it was distracting. Sex with her hadn't been, though.

"So what's wrong with calling a woman 'sunshine'?" he asked.

"Why do you do it, when you know their names?"

He reflected. "It's when, you know, they give a big smile, or laugh, or their eyes sparkle. When they're all bright and sunny and they make me smile. No one ever seems insulted."

Her turn to think. Sandra, Viv, the waitress . . . They hadn't seemed insulted. Georgia was the only one. Why did it get to her? Surely, she didn't want to be special to him. And was he saying that he sometimes saw her as bright and sunny?

Damn, her headache had come back. She rubbed the base of her neck. She didn't like taking pills, but it was hard to concentrate when she was in pain. Oddly, her headaches happened only when she was working—and yet, for the most part, she loved her job.

"Still got the headache, huh?"

"Vocabulary lesson. There are better ways of asking questions than making a statement and following it with 'huh.' In fact, 'huh' is not a word. I'd suggest you expunge it from your vocabulary. Uh, I mean, get rid of it."

Suddenly he was there in front of her, on his knees. "How about we start by *expunging* that headache?" A huge but gentle hand landed on her shoulder and urged her out of her chair. "Sit on the footstool. Here, facing this way."

Arguing with him made her head ache, so this time she went along. Or maybe it was because that hand felt so right there. Decisive and reassuring. Masculine and sensual. A shiver of pleasant awareness rippled through her.

She sat where he'd placed her, with her back to him. His hands eased her body upright until her spine was a straight line. Not rigid, but straight.

"Why d'you always wear your hair pulled back so tight?"

"It's professional." Then, "Ouch." Was he pulling her hair?

"You ever think it might be the reason you get headaches?"

She couldn't resist a comeback. "No. I thought it was you."

"Oh, man, you wound me," he joked. "Why not just cut it short?"

"I only pull it back for work. I like long hair. Oh!" She realized he'd tugged out her hair clip. Long strands of hair tumbled over her shoulders and down her back and brushed her cheeks and ears. He shouldn't have done that—and yet the tension was easing from her temples.

"You can't be professional with long hair?" His hands settled at the sides of her neck and began to massage, very gently.

She sucked in air in a little gasp, and tensed. He shouldn't do this. She shouldn't let him.

"Relax, Georgia." One palm cupped her forehead, holding her steady while the fingers of his other hand worked the back of her neck.

This wasn't professional; it was personal. Nowhere near as personal as sex, but still . . .

But still, it felt wonderful. There were calluses on his fingers but the slight abrasiveness was enjoyable, like the rough caress of Kit-Kat's tongue. Georgia went for back massages on occasion, with a female massage therapist. This was therapeutic. No doubt that was the way Woody viewed it.

"Didn't answer my question," he said.

Question? Oh yes, about long hair not being professional. "In my opinion, gender should be irrelevant in the workplace."

"How d'you mean?"

"Work assignments, promotion, success shouldn't relate to gender."

"Sure, but what's that got to do with hair?"

"If women wear short skirts, have their hair long and wavy, and wear lots of makeup, then they're bringing gender into the workplace."

"But . . . gender exists. Thank God. And just 'cause men and women dress differently, it doesn't mean they're not equal."

"I'm glad you believe that. I guess I'm biased," she admitted. "It's not that there's anything intrinsically wrong with a woman dressing in a feminine fashion, but I grew up with a mom who took it too far."

"Too far?" He soothed her temples with his fingertips.

It loosened not only the tension, but also her tongue. "She dresses to attract men, to seduce. Being attractive to men is all she cares about. It's the basis for her sense of identity."

"That's scary."

"Tell me about it. So, maybe I go a little overboard in the other direction. At least I'll know I've never won a promotion due to feminine wiles."

"Huh." He reflected for a minute. "I guess that makes sense."

Did he really get it, or was he being polite? No, this was Woody. Subtle was not his middle name. If he disagreed, she'd hear about it.

His thumbs eased out tension knots in her neck, loosened her locked-up shoulders, stroked down the muscles of her back. He knew instinctively where and how to touch.

"That feels wonderful," she said. Even when his touch hurt, it was a good kind of pain, a pain that promised relief. Like when she went to the massage therapist.

But Woody had much bigger, stronger hands. Masculine hands. Hands that made her feel both strong and fragile, and definitely feminine. That thought shattered her accepting mood, and she came alive with a different awareness. The awareness of Woody as a man she'd had sex with, even if they'd agreed it was a mistake.

A man whose hands now explored her body with the intimacy of growing knowledge. Of increasing sensuality. What had been therapeutic massage was turning into something more erotic. Or was that merely her perception?

His hands were around her neck, strong hands that could strangle her or snap her neck without effort, yet they stroked her as appreciatively as a lover.

She felt an overwhelming impulse to tilt her head and rest a cheek against one of those hands, to press her lips against his skin—

She wouldn't. Of course she wouldn't. The man was being kind, trying to ease her pain. She wasn't so pathetically starved for male touch, starved for sensuality, tingling with the memory of her first orgasms, that she would misinterpret this for something else. Something that, of course, she didn't want. Not with Woody Hanrahan.

Yesterday had been an aberration. When she made love again, it would be with a man she loved. A soul mate, a man like Anthony.

Of course, yesterday hadn't been making love. It had been sex. A physical act, not an emotional one.

For her, an extremely satisfying physical act. One that had made her whole body tingle, vibrate, and throb with pleasure, then peak and shatter in rapture.

Twelve

Georgia had stopped talking, and Woody was glad. He wanted her to concentrate on the physical sensations.

Sitting behind her, his hands lost in the red silk of her hair, her flesh warm and soft under his fingers, he had the hard-on to end all hard-ons. Thank God he was wearing gym shorts rather than jeans or he'd be in serious pain.

Yeah, his reaction was physical, but he'd massaged women before and didn't get this turned on. He'd behaved himself today, tried to put yesterday out of his mind, but damn it, Georgia got to him. Was it her unique blend of prissiness and passion? The sparkle in her amber eyes? The way she guarded herself, yet let him see glimpses of the real woman—the one who wouldn't throw out scraggly old plants, and was bound and determined not to be like her mom?

Yesterday she was sorry she'd had sex with him, but now, maybe, he was getting under her skin. Perhaps winning a second chance to prove he was a good lover?

She liked how he was touching her. He could tell by the way she arched into his hands, pressed against him, stretched her neck. She was just like her cat, letting herself be caressed into a state of bliss.

Which was exactly what he wanted to do. Maybe he shouldn't, but he did. Why not go for it?

Reaching from behind, he ran a finger gently across her forehead, down her nose, along a delicate cheekbone, and then to her lips. He dragged his finger, letting it tug at her bottom lip, and felt her warm breath.

He used both hands to smooth the hair back from her face and behind her ears, then slid his hands down the length of her neck. Up until now, he'd stopped at the collar of her shirt, where only the top button was undone. Now he undid the next one and the next, and slipped his fingers inside, stroking firmly around her collarbone.

She tensed, but only momentarily, before surrendering.

This was how he'd win her, by alternating genuine massage with seductive caresses. He'd keep her off balance, give her a reason to persuade herself he was just looking after her health, but all the time he'd be seducing her into arousal. "Starting to feel better?"

"Mmm. Much."

He wanted to slide his hands lower and cup her breasts, but instead raised them to her shoulders, outside her shirt again. He began working down her arms, squeezing into the muscles and working out tension. "You're all locked up, Georgia. Not getting enough R and R."

"I relax," she protested halfheartedly. "I go for long walks and I spend hours reading."

"Do you ever stretch?" He spoke quietly. "Go for a massage?"

"I get a massage now and then, and I love a long bath."

He had a big whirlpool tub at home, to ease achy muscles. He sure wouldn't mind playing with Georgia in it. "Can't take your body for granted. Especially when it's such a nice one. You gotta respect it, take care of it." He hoped she got the message that he was doing exactly that.

Though he loved the feel of her under his hands, this was costing him, and not just with the ache in his groin. His banged-up shoulder protested the pressure he was exerting. Later, he'd ice his shoulder. And sooner, he hoped, his cock would find its own relief with the woman who sat in front of him, for once not lecturing or arguing, just enjoying his touch.

She stirred, and her cheek brushed his bare arm as it reached over her shoulder. Whether or not it was intentional, it heated his skin. Hell, he knew his way around women almost as well as he knew his way around hockey rinks. Why was he pussyfooting with Georgia? Whatever else she might be, or pretend to be with her tailored suits and slicked-back hair, underneath she was all woman.

His fingers had been reminding her of that for the last ten minutes. Now that he had her full attention, he could up his game.

He fanned his fingers and drifted the tips across her collarbones and the top of her chest, his touch as light as he could make it.

She quivered.

He did the same thing, but lower, so his pinkie fingers stroked the line where the top of her bra cups met the silky skin of her breasts.

He heard a tiny indrawn breath. She knew he'd gone beyond massage, and wasn't stopping him. It seemed he'd convinced her, with his patient, sensual touch, to give him another chance to prove that he not only had the right equipment, but could use it with skill.

At the moment, his equipment begged for release from the boxer briefs that contained it, but he vowed that this time he'd hang on to his control if it killed him.

He ran his palms lightly over the cups of Georgia's bra and felt her nipples, unmistakable hard nubs. He also discovered that today's bra had a front clasp.

Her head came back, neck clearly not hurting now as she arched to thrust her breasts more firmly into his hands.

Accepting the invitation, he slipped the clasp free and cupped her sweet, naked curves. He leaned closer, to nuzzle her ear and run the tip of his tongue along the edge of her lobe.

A scent rose from her skin, nothing as blatant as perfume but something that combined innocence and passion: vanilla and aroused woman.

Woody wasn't a guy for flowery words or thoughts, but right now he could relate to the guys who wrote poems, or lyrics for love songs.

Her long, slender neck, her budded nipples, they were too much to resist. He risked breaking the spell, rising quickly to move around the footrest where she sat.

Her eyes were closed, an expression of concentration on her face, as if she was totally caught up in the physical experience.

He knelt in front of her and leaned in to kiss a trail down her neck, thrum her wildly throbbing pulse with his tongue, and taste the upper curves of her breasts.

She gave a sigh-moan and wove her hands into his hair.

Oh yeah. He undid a few more buttons and peeled back her shirt and unhooked bra. Such beautiful breasts, pale and full, crowned with tightly furled pink buds. He captured one between his lips, licking and sucking it until she gasped. A pulse throbbed in his cock each time he touched her.

Woody wanted to tell her how pretty she was, how sweet she tasted. But if he spoke, he might jolt her out of the sensual spell he was doing his damnedest to weave. Besides, he had better things to do with his mouth.

He moved to her other nipple and suckled it, using her reaction to tell him exactly how she liked to be touched: a little rough, then gentle licks, then another firm assault to ramp her up again. It was exactly the way he'd like her to touch his cock.

Her breast thrust against his mouth; her fingers roamed restlessly through his hair and gripped his scalp; her lower body stretched and twisted. When he nudged her legs apart, she separated to let him kneel between them, then closed her thighs around his hips.

His hard-on rubbed against her. Even through the layers of their clothes, it felt unbelievably good.

Now, finally, he let himself kiss her, his lips taking hers the way they'd done her breasts. A little rough, a little tender.

She gasped, and kissed him back fervently, like she was hungry, needy, for his passion.

Firmly, he gripped her head, tilting her face to the exact right angle, and slanted his lips to match hers as he deepened the kiss. He thrust into her mouth, seducing her tongue, then pulled back to tease her lips with licks and nibbles.

Her tongue got into the act, chasing his, invading his mouth.

He pulled her forward, or maybe she slid, until she'd come off the footrest and was kneeling in front of him, their bodies plastered together as they battled to own each other's mouths.

His hips thrust against her involuntarily and she ground her pelvis against him. He wanted nothing more than to rip off their clothes and be inside her, but he held back. He'd screwed things up once with her, and wouldn't do it again.

Somehow, he managed to tear his mouth and body away from hers and ease her back onto the rug that partially covered her hardwood floor. He spread her shirt and bra wide-open to admire her soft skin and seductive curves.

Then he bent to take up where he'd left off, teasing her taut nipples. From there, he kissed his way to the waistband of her pants, and unfastened the button. Her lower body twisted needily as he slid her zipper down, and her hips lifted without prompting so he could slide her pants off, taking her panties with them.

When he kissed her belly, he felt the tautness of the tension that was building inside her. The sweet musk of her desire drove him so wild he could barely hang on to his sanity.

He cupped her pussy, warm and damp, and had to taste her. Her creamy thighs spread easily under his touch and then he was gazing at her lush, rosy folds.

A sight like that could turn a guy into a poet or a madman. Or a lover.

He hooked his hands under her thighs, lifted her, and bent to lick the sweetest damn pussy he'd ever seen.

"Oh!" she gasped.

"God, Georgia, you're sweet." He licked again.

Suddenly, her thighs clamped together, gripping his head so tight she stopped him. In a panicked voice, she cried, "No! Oh my God, Woody, no! What are we doing?"

Seemed pretty damned obvious to him. Cautiously, he eased her legs apart and extricated himself. "It'll be good. This time it'll be good."

She scooted back, all the way off the rug until her ass thumped down on the hardwood floor. "No! We can't. This is crazy. I don't do things like this."

"Things like have great sex?" She'd lost him, totally.

"No!" Her eyes were wide, panicked. "I mean, this is wrong. It's unprofessional. I don't even know you."

Body aching with need, he growled, "Seems like we were getting to know each other."

"Not that way! Good God, do you think I just . . . leap into bed with every random man who comes along?"

Okay, now he was pissed off. "Fuck, Georgia. I'm not some random man. I'm Woody. You—" He was about to say that she did know him, better than most women he'd dated, but she cut him off.

"Oh yeah, the big hockey star. The next Wayne Gretzky. Listen, mister, I'm no damned puck bunny!"

With that, she scrambled to her feet and ran out of the room, giving him a tantalizing view of her firm, curvy ass jiggling with each step.

A door slammed.

"Oh, fuck." Should he go after her? Try to explain? Hell, he didn't even know what her problem was. Of course she wasn't a puck bunny, any more than he was some random man. What the hell was up with her?

Fuming, he hauled himself and his serious case of blue balls off the floor. She was the moodiest damned woman he'd ever hooked up with.

If he had even one brain cell in his head, he wouldn't try to get personal with her again, no matter how tempted he might be.

S unday night, Georgia realized she hadn't finished her assignment for book club: to read the first third of *The Sexual Education of Lady Emma Whitehead*. She'd been so busy with the VitalSport campaign, she'd had time for little else. Or was she avoiding the book because it made her think of sex?

She'd let Woody do things to her, deeply intimate things. She'd even encouraged him. But it was so wrong, on so many levels. It wasn't professional. It certainly wasn't flattering, because Woody clearly thought of her as an available female body. Though he hadn't really enjoyed sex with her the first time, he'd gladly use her again to get his rocks off. And she was no better! She felt disloyal to Anthony that some jock she barely knew could arouse sensations she'd never experienced with her beloved husband.

And here she was, thinking of Woody again, even when she wasn't reading the book.

Did she want to go to book club and participate? Yes. So that meant she needed to finish the reading assignment. There hadn't been any further e-mails among the club members, not after Lily complained that she hadn't started the book and she didn't want to be influenced by everyone else's chatter.

Curled in her reading chair with half a Ritter Sport dark chocolate peppermint bar, Georgia picked up where she had left off. Emma had run from the Comte after they'd had sex.

Shocked by her wanton behavior, Emma pleaded a headache and remained in her room for the rest of the day. Perhaps she indeed was ill. Her body and her mind felt feverish, yet every time she lay down, a certain restlessness forced her to her feet. She must have paced her spacious chamber several hundred times, yet all that walking had brought her no closer to an understanding of what she had done.

She'd let a man touch her intimately, the way only a husband should do. But when the Comte had touched her, it was so very different from what she'd experienced in the marital bed.

What kind of woman was she, to take such pleasure in the act? Was she no better than a common harlot?

She paced, fanning herself vigorously with her ivory fan, though it failed to cool her heated body.

A knock at the door interrupted her tormented musings. "Yes?"

The door opened and Margaret swept into the room. Her expression, at first concerned, brightened. "Ah, you are feeling better, my dear?"

Caught out of bed, what could Emma say but, "I am somewhat improved, yes; thank you."

"Will you take some soup? Perhaps a cup of tea? Or why not come down and join us for a nightcap? We have a sherry I'm sure you would enjoy."

Go downstairs and face the Comte? No, she couldn't possibly. And yet, tomorrow she would have to.

Yes, but that was tomorrow. Perhaps she would feel stronger then. "Thank you, Margaret, but I think it best to stay in my room. I could perhaps take a bowl of soup and a glass of sherry, if the maid has time to bring them up."

"Of course. I'll see to it immediately."

As her friend turned to go, Emma found herself saying, "Wait. There is something I was wondering."

"Yes? Come, let's sit and talk." Margaret guided her to two

chairs beside a neatly laid fireplace. Emma, feverish as she'd felt, had not lit it, but now her hostess did so, and it crackled to cheery life. "What is it, Emma?"

Emma took the seat beside her. How on earth could she even hint at the question foremost on her mind? "It's about the Comte. . . ."

"He makes you uncomfortable, doesn't he? I noted that at breakfast. I am so sorry."

"It's . . . his reputation. This, er, married lady he, er, was involved with in France . . ."

"Yes?"

"Why, Margaret? Why would a woman do such a thing? A decent married woman should never be tempted by, well, by . . ."

"By a charming man?"

"Charm is a superficial thing. It does not justify breaking one's marriage vows."

"No, of course not. And yet"—a knowing look crossed Margaret's face—"if that charm promises certain delights, pleasures that perhaps the lady does not experience with her husband . . . Well, of course it does not excuse infidelity, but perhaps it makes it more understandable."

Delights and pleasures? "Perhaps so," Emma said tentatively, hoping her friend would elaborate.

"After all," Margaret said, a smug smile curving her lips, "not every woman is blessed to have a husband like my dear Edgerton."

"The Lord is certainly an admirable man," Emma ventured, unsure exactly what Margaret was referring to.

The other woman's smile widened into a mischievous grin. "Indeed he is." She winked. "Admirable in all the ways that most matter to a woman, if you take my meaning. Oh yes, I am a most satisfied wife."

Heat spread through Emma's body. She stood abruptly and paced away from the fire, again wielding her fan. "Dear me, I do believe I have a fever."

Margaret rose promptly. "I will send the maid with soup and sherry, and she'll assist you in getting into your bed gown. I do hope you're not coming down with something."

"I am sure I'll be quite well in the morning."

When her friend had departed, Emma strode even more quickly about her chamber. So it was true, what the Comte had said. It was not wanton for a woman to experience such pleasure.

Of course, it was indeed wanton to experience it with a man other than her husband.

But she hadn't experienced it with that esteemed and unbearably stodgy gentleman, and in all likelihood she would never wed again. Indeed, she would rather be the widowed aunt and glorified servant in her brother's household than to be forced into marriage with another man such as her first husband.

So, this one moment—no, two extended moments—of physical bliss were all she was to ever know?

That was where the chapter ended, and Georgia reluctantly clicked off her e-reader. She'd finished the first third of the book, and the club's pact was that they'd read only a third each week, then discuss it before anyone moved on.

Sitting cozily in her chair with Kit-Kat on her lap, she mused about Emma's story. It was different in many ways from what was going on in her own life, yet the similarities were intriguing. Emma, she was sure, would let herself be seduced again by the Comte. The book couldn't be erotica without sex.

As for herself, she got to write her own story. It wouldn't include sex with Woody. That would be unprofessional, and she wouldn't risk her career. Her pride mattered too. She wasn't another puck bunny. She wasn't pathetically desperate for pleasure, for a man's touch, for that amazing feeling of sexual tension cresting in her body, for— Oh, damn.

She'd last seen—and run away from sex with—Woody on Wednesday afternoon. Four days ago. She wouldn't see him again until Tuesday; tomorrow the Beavers would be traveling back to Vancouver.

She had, strictly in the name of business research, turned on the Friday and Sunday night games in Anaheim, watching bits and pieces while she did work and chores. The things Woody had said over lunch had helped her view the sport differently. She still thought it was ridiculous to get so obsessed over shooting a puck into a goal, but she saw how excited the fans were, and how seriously the teams took it. It wasn't rocket science, they weren't saving the world, but they were pouring their strength and drive—and maybe even their hearts—into what they were doing.

The Beavers lost the Friday night game, and tonight they'd lost again, when the Ducks scored a goal in overtime. This meant, the announcers said, that the Beavers were down one to three and would have to win the next three games to clinch the Western Conference title. Georgia worried about the impact on the VitalSport campaign if the Beavers lost, and particularly if they lost badly.

She worried about Woody too. The game meant a lot to him. His team meant a lot to him. How would he handle it if they lost to the Ducks?

He wasn't playing his best, according to the announcers. She winced every time he smashed another player into the boards—and winced even harder the times he got slammed. Tonight, his left shoulder had hit hard and he'd crashed to the ice. It had taken him only a second or two to rise, but those seconds had gone by in agonizing slowness.

He'd said everyone was playing injured but taking pains to hide that fact. Was he, and was that why he wasn't at his best?

And here she was again, spending not just her work hours but her free time thinking about Woody Hanrahan.

Thirteen

She was getting ready for bed when the phone rang. Call display showed her mother's number, and she groaned. No point in not answering. Her mom would keep trying until Georgia picked up.

"Hi, Bernadette," she said resignedly into the phone. Her mother had never wanted to be called Mom, figuring it made her seem old.

"Hey, baby, how are you?"

Before Georgia could respond, her mother was going on. "I want you to come over for dinner. There's someone you have to meet."

"Let me guess. It's a man." Her mother had broken up with her last boyfriend a month ago, so it was time to find a replacement.

"Well, of course." As if no one other than a man was worth meeting.

"And this one's special." Georgia had heard that story so many times she'd lost count. Bernadette's marriages numbered five now, but there'd been many men besides her husbands.

"He's the best," her mother gushed. "I've never met a man like Fabio."

"His name's Fabio? Seriously?"

"It's a perfectly good Italian name," her mother said huffily. "And who are you to judge? I bet you're not seeing anyone, are you?"

No, I only screwed a man named Woody. I can top you in the silly name game. "Why is that the only thing you ever ask me?"

"Because you're still moping over Anthony. You need to move on."

"I'm not moping. Yes, I miss him, but I'm busy and happy."

"Women weren't designed to live alone."

"Better to live alone than to settle for second best." Why did she bother arguing? She and her mom were black and white when it came to their opinions on pretty much everything, and most definitely on relationships. More out of habit than any hope of changing Bernadette's mind, she found herself saying again, "I don't believe a woman's life is somehow *less* if there's no man in it. We can be strong and independent."

"What's the fun in that?"

"Your generation invented women's lib. How can you be such a throwback?"

Her mother ignored that. "So, what night works for dinner?"

"I'm really busy. I've been put in charge of my first marketing campaign."

"And working all the time's more rewarding than sharing your life with someone special?"

"I knew it was too much to hope for congratulations."

"Oh, baby, I'm sorry. It's great that you're doing well at work. I just hate to think of you being lonely and unloved."

"I'm not!" Occasional loneliness was better than being with the wrong man.

"Okay, okay. So what's the big campaign?"

"This is a secret for now, okay? We don't want word getting out before the official launch." One thing she'd say for her mom: she didn't spill other people's secrets.

"Ooh, exciting! Tell me."

"It's the Canadian launch for an American sports and leisure company. We're doing a figurehead campaign based on a hockey star who plays for the Vancouver Beavers."

"Yeah? Who's the player?"

"Woody Hanrahan."

"Woo-hoo, girl! That man's hot. Now I see why you're so excited."

"It's not about the man!" Georgia drew a breath. She really, really must have been switched at birth. "This is a step forward in my career."

"Why don't you bring him along for dinner?"

"Sure, fine, I'll do that," she said, tongue in cheek. "I'll ask him what night works, and get back to you."

"You don't really mean that."

"You got it."

Monday after work, the book club met at Steamworks, again lucking into fair weather and an outside table. After putting in long hours on the VitalSport campaign, Georgia figured she could take the night off. And so, when the others ordered alcoholic drinks, she joined in with a glass of pinot grigio.

When the drinks arrived, Marielle took a sip of her Hemingway Daiquiri. Her attitude toward drinks was the same as her attitude toward men: if it looks like fun, give it a try. "Ooh, nice." She peeled off her suit jacket—these days she was temping as receptionist at a law firm—and said, "Well, girls, are you loving the book? I sure am."

Lily flicked her short, wheat-colored hair back. "I'm confused. Has anyone figured out exactly when it's set?"

"When?" Kim, her spiky black hair streaked with purple today to match the long, skinny top she wore over black leggings, frowned in puzzlement. "It's historical."

"I mean, is it Regency, Georgian, Victorian, or what?" Lily demanded. "I don't think the author's done her research. I'm sure there are inconsistencies in the descriptions of clothing, décor, and social customs."

"Jeez, Lily," Marielle protested, "it's fiction. The author made up the characters, so who cares if she makes up other stuff?"

Lily frowned over the rim of her martini glass and turned to Georgia. "What do you think?"

Usually, the two of them—the older, more serious women—had similar opinions, while Marielle and Kim thought more alike. This time, Georgia said, "That hasn't bothered me. I'm more interested in the characters. I'm trying to understand Emma's motivation for being so tempted by the Comte."

"The classic allure of the bad boy," Marielle said promptly.

"Who can resist?" Kim put in, her dark eyes sparkling as she sipped a light beer called an Ipanema.

"A woman whose brain is in her head, not her crotch," Lily said sharply.

Marielle hooted. "What's the fun in that?"

Georgia, who had, until last week, always believed her brain was firmly lodged in her head, asked Marielle, "What's the classic allure of the bad boy?"

"That he's kind of dangerous."

"Yeah, he's a real man," Kim said with relish. She gestured around the bar. "I mean, look at these guys. They're either metro-sexual, which, sorry, just isn't very sexy"—her smooth brow furrowed for an instant, then she went on—"or they have beer bellies, or they're immature students like the guys I go to art school with. Do you see a single 'real man'?"

If Woody'd been there, he would have caught Kim's eye—as he caught so many women's eyes. Even if he didn't dress well, he radiated masculinity. Tomorrow, Georgia would see him again, and she was antsy with nervous anticipation.

"By 'real man' you mean a caveman?" Lily asked. "No, thanks."

"But that's the fascination," Marielle said. "You want to be the one woman who can tame him."

"But you don't want to tame him too much," Kim said quickly. "Otherwise he'd lose his charm."

Hmm. This was interesting information for the VitalSport campaign, and in line with what Viv had said, about needing to maintain some of Woody's edge. Not that Georgia could imagine him being converted into a trendy metrosexual.

Marielle nodded vigorously. "So, Kim, that's what your guy's like? Only partially tamed?"

Kim shrugged. "Yeah, well, there's fantasy and then there's reality."

"And the reality is," Marielle said, "that there's all kinds of guys and lots of them have their own charm." She winked. "As for the bad boy, let's face it—the true allure is sex. You absolutely know he's had dozens of lovers and he's fantastic in bed, and you want to get yourself a piece of that smoking hot action."

A ripple of sexual awareness moved through Georgia. Was that why she couldn't stop thinking of Woody?

"Because," Marielle went on, dragging a slice of bread through the artichoke and cheese dip, "after all, it's all about the orgasms."

Georgia felt as if her entire body was flushing at the memory of the ones Woody had given her. "No, it's not," she protested. Her brain was *not* in her crotch. "There's much more to a relationship, and to sex." Feeling defensive about her marriage, she said, "It's about having a true connection: minds and hearts and souls."

"Wow." Kim's eyes widened. "Yeah, that's the dream, isn't it? You had that with your husband?"

She nodded.

"I'm so sorry you lost him."

"Me too. But at least I had him for a while."

Kim nodded. "It's more than a lot of women find, I guess." Her mouth twisted. "Or you think you've found it, but then it just kind of fizzles." She tossed her purple-spiked head and said to

Lily, "You're married. You have all that great connection stuff going on?"

"Of course." Lily said it in such an unemotional tone that Georgia had to wonder if she was telling the truth. The blonde, the oldest in their group at thirty-two, had said little about her husband.

"Hey, girls." Marielle waved red-tipped fingers at them. "There's one thing George left out in that description. Physical connection."

"Yes, of course," Georgia said quickly.

"Which brings us back to orgasms," Marielle said.

Georgia didn't respond. She was okay with the conversation taking a personal turn, but she wasn't about to confess that with her wonderful husband, her soul mate, she'd never climaxed.

"If a woman bases a relationship on orgasms," Lily said, "that's about lust, not love."

Georgia nodded firmly.

"So many factors go into a good relationship," Lily went on. "In my practice"—she was a doctor with a family practice—"I see lots of women who have great sex but unhappy relationships, and lots more who don't or can't achieve sexual satisfaction but have great relationships."

"I've read that," Kim said. "That a lot of women never climax."

Until last week, Georgia had thought she was one of them. She listened with interest as Lily said, "That's right. Sometimes there's an actual physical problem, and treatments that can help. Or it's just personal physiology, so some women can't have orgasms through intercourse, but can through"—she glanced around as if she'd suddenly realized what she was talking about in the middle of a crowded patio, and lowered her voice—"clitoral stimulation."

"Which is always a good idea," Marielle put in.

"Sometimes, inability to climax is due to a horrible experience," Lily went on, "like sexual abuse. Also, there are strict religions that don't believe women should experience sexual pleasure. Then there are women who react to social pressure that makes them believe their bodies are unattractive and inadequate."

Georgia's mind was stuck back on sexual abuse. When she was thirteen and one of her mom's boyfriends groped her, it had traumatized her. She'd gained a lot of weight, started wearing boy's clothes. But she'd gotten over that long ago. Besides, if that experience had been responsible for her inability to climax, surely the man who'd have helped her get over it was the one she loved, not the near stranger.

"Man, this stuff is complicated," Kim said.

Georgia nodded, and Lily said, "Yes, sexuality is incredibly complicated."

"Which is why every girl should masturbate," Marielle said cheerfully, "and learn how her body works and what turns her on."

Georgia had tried that a few times, but couldn't arouse herself. Yet Woody'd done it effortlessly when she'd barely known him an hour.

So far, she'd held back from contributing to a discussion she knew so little about, but now she ventured, "Does it ever have to do with the partner? Some special chemistry or something?"

"Or that bad-boy talent?" Marielle said. "You bet it does. I have much better sex with some guys than others."

Kim said, "Don't some cultures believe that virgins of either sex should be initiated by someone experienced?"

Marielle chuckled. "Good idea. I mean, can you imagine two virgins on their wedding night? Would they ever figure out what they were doing?"

Georgia busied herself spreading dip on bread. She and Anthony had figured out what they were doing. That was part of the wonder of the experience, both making love for the first time. But she'd sound hopelessly old-fashioned if she said that. These women weren't the chastity club type.

"Ladies," Lily said in her brisk doctor voice, "we're straying off track. Let's get back to the book."

"Much as I'm loving the book," Kim said, "talking about sex is more fun. But okay, here's something I find interesting. It's all in Emma's point of view. We never get to know what the Comte is thinking."

"That's pretty obvious," Marielle said with a laugh. "He wants to get into her—what did they wear back then?—knickers or bloomers or whatever, and he's going to seduce her into agreeing."

"But why?" Kim demanded. "He can have all those younger, vivacious girls."

"Because she's a challenge?" Marielle suggested. "The one who doesn't immediately fall for his charms?"

"She's not a puck bunny." Georgia didn't realize she'd said the words aloud until the three other women stared at her.

Marielle laughed. "Yeah, exactly. I see you're really getting into the hockey thing, eh?"

"You have no idea."

Hoping that a good, hard game of squash with a friend would burn off some restless tension and break him out of his bad mood, Woody bounded up the steps to the Chancery Squash Club on Hornby. He greeted the pretty brunette at the desk, and headed for the change room.

His partner wasn't there, but he arrived a minute later, out of breath, his suit jacket already off and his tie loosened. "Sorry; had some orders to sign," he said as he pulled off his clothes.

Tom Westin was a judge on the British Columbia Supreme Court, and a hockey fan. They'd met at a fund-raiser, hit it off, and been playing squash for the past two years.

"I'm gonna slaughter you today," Woody announced.

Tom pulled on a T-shirt and shorts. "That'll be the day. In this sport, I'm king." More than a decade older than Woody, he was a big man too, and in great shape thanks to frequent games of squash plus early morning jogging.

"Prepare to be dethroned."

"Take your best shot, pal," Tom said as they headed for their court.

"Bet on it."

Even so, Woody, pissed at himself for being off his game in the all-important Western Conference final, had trouble finding his rhythm. Didn't help that his injured left shoulder had taken another beating in the last game.

It also didn't help that Georgia'd been on his mind. Last Wednesday she'd been totally into sex; then she'd freaked out. What the hell had happened?

He'd always figured dating during playoffs was a bad idea because it distracted him. Now he was just as distracted by *not* having sex with a woman.

Seeing Tom's ball hurtling toward him, Woody swung his racquet and connected perfectly, sending the ball off the front wall and down the side one.

Tom tried, but failed, to scoop it up. "Good one," he said, wiping sweat from his face. "But your playing's erratic today." That was something Woody liked about Tom. He didn't talk down to Woody, just used his regular vocabulary as if he figured Woody would understand. Mostly, he did. Even the legal jargon Tom sometimes dropped in.

"Today's not the only time," Woody muttered.

"The Beavers will get back on track," Tom assured him. Then he slanted the ball to send Woody racing to the front of the court.

Woody missed and hurtled into the wall, smashing his bad shoulder. "Fuck! Fuck, fuck, fuck." He peeled himself off, rubbing his shoulder.

"You okay?"

"Sure. And yeah, you bet we'll come back." It was his job, as captain, to make sure of it—and to fix his own game. Since he'd been a kid, there was this thing that happened to him on the ice, like he could envision the individual parts of the game and the pattern they formed, even as it changed second by second. He sensed when someone was coming up behind to steal the puck, knew where his teammate would be to field a pass, saw the exact spot the goaltender couldn't cover. For him, that was part of the beauty of the game, along with the crisp slash of skates against ice, the hard smack of a well-shot puck off his stick, and the knowledge that at that moment in time, nothing else in the world mattered.

His head coach used terms like "spatial and situational intelligence." Said Gretzky and Crosby had it too.

Whatever it was, Woody had to get it back. He wasn't playing badly, but his team deserved his best. Each of the men had his own strengths, but they needed him to be on top of his game, not to mention keep them motivated and focused. And he'd damned well do it. "We're always up for a challenge." Besides, it'd be a home game and Vancouver fans were the best.

"We'll be rooting for you Wednesday night." Tom grinned. "Bash 'em, Beavers."

They whacked the ball around some more; then Tom said, "Something else on your mind?"

"Nah. Well, yeah, maybe," Woody confessed. "A woman."

Fourteen

Tom served. "That figures. You ought to get married, my friend. It settles a guy down."

Woody smashed the ball with all his strength. It cracked against the front wall, flew up in the air, and fell neatly into the angle where side wall met back wall. Where it was virtually impossible to hit. Tom left it alone and Woody whooped.

"Don't wanna be settled," he proclaimed, retrieving the ball for his own serve. His parents had soured him on marriage for life. Besides, he couldn't imagine spending the rest of his life with any of the women he'd dated.

He won the second match, put up a good fight in the third, but lost to Tom's superior skill. He slapped the other man on the back. "Not bad for an old guy."

"Better than you can do, superstar."

"One of these days," Woody threatened.

Back in the change room, they headed for the showers. Warm water sluiced the sweat from Woody's body; hot water eased the ache in his shoulder; cold water invigorated him.

"You're tone-deaf," Tom shouted from the stall next door. "What the hell are you trying to whistle?"

Woody hadn't even known he was whistling. He thought back. Damn, it had been "Sweet Georgia Brown." His palm slammed the shower off.

Next door, the shower stopped too, and both men emerged, toweling off.

"Do you have plans for the evening?" Tom asked. "Maybe with the woman?"

"No way. Want to go for a beer?" They sometimes did that.

"How about dinner?"

"You don't have to get home?" Both busy guys, the most they'd done before was play squash and go for an occasional beer. They had little in common, yet they'd always been able to talk. Woody had learned about Tom's family life and his work on the court, and the judge always seemed interested in what was up with Woody.

Tom grinned. "Maureen's out of town, Jason's at a friend's, and I'm in the middle of a trial and am actually caught up with my work. In other words, I have the evening completely free."

Woody, remembering Georgia's lessons, said, "A rare occurrence."

"Indeed. And worthy of celebration. Let's go for a nice meal."

All set to agree, Woody remembered his poor table manners. Would he embarrass himself? Then he thought of Georgia's suggestion that he find a model to imitate. He grinned at Judge Westin. "Sounds good."

"Do you like French food?" Tom asked. "There's a restaurant Maureen and I like. Small, one of the old standbys rather than a trendy newcomer. Not too much chance either of us will be pestered."

When the two of them went for a beer, it was a toss-up whether more people came to kowtow to the judge or to beg autographs from Woody. "Sounds good, but alls—all—I brought to change into is shorts and a tee."

"We're about the same size. I brought jeans, but I guess I could live with climbing back into my work clothes." Tom took neatly folded clothes from his gym bag and handed them over.

Woody pulled the jeans on over his underwear, finding they were a bit tighter than he was used to wearing. He held up Tom's beige shirt, which was classier than anything he owned, enjoying the rough texture. Wondering what it was made of, he read the label. Cotton and linen. He squinted at the name. "Zeg-na?"

"It's pronounced 'Zenya,'" Tom said matter-of-factly. "Italian."

"Nice." Woody put it on and started to do up the buttons. "Nicer than that suit you're stuck wearing. Sorry, man. I'd have brought proper clothes if I'd have known." Proper clothes meaning one of the suits he hated.

"No problem."

As they walked out together, Tom said, "So tell me about the woman."

Woody groaned. "Name's Georgia."

"Pretty. Images of southern lushness come to mind."

Nah, that was more Viv's style. "She's more, uh, confusing. All buttoned up tight for work, but when she lets her hair down, man."

"Confusing. I hear you."

Out on the street, Tom said, "You're on foot?" He knew that was Woody's habit, since the squash club was less than a mile from Woody's condo.

"Yeah."

"My car's in the courthouse lot."

They walked in that direction, and a few minutes later were cruising through the West End in Tom's Mercedes.

"How are things going with Jason?" Woody asked, knowing that the judge's son was a constant source of worry.

"Fifteen is a hellish age," the other man said gloomily. "If it weren't for those season tickets you gave us, I doubt I'd ever see the boy. Thank God at least we've got hockey in common." He glanced toward Woody. "Maureen wanted me to ask if you'd come by for dinner. Jason, though he'd never admit to anything as uncool as hero worship, is dying to meet you. Maureen too. She says you sound more interesting than most of my colleagues."

"Don't know about that."

"She says all that lawyers and judges talk about is law, and it gets boring."

"Well, I sure wouldn't be doing that."

The judge stopped at a light. "You didn't finish high school, right?" There was no judgment in his voice.

"No, just grade eleven."

"You got drafted into the NHL when you were what? Seventeen?"

"Yup." It had been his ticket out—away from small-town Manitoba, his abusive dad, his guilt and anger that he couldn't get his mom to leave his dad. "Never was fond of schoolwork. Hell, if a guy can make millions a year without putting himself through the agony of schooling, I figure he'd be a fool not to go for it."

Tom's expression was serious. "It's not many who can do that, though." He pulled away from the light. "Jason wants to drop out of school and play in a band, but I doubt he and his group have what it takes to be successful. The talent, discipline, drive. Connections. Luck." He pulled the Mercedes into a parking spot on Alberni Street, two or three blocks up from Denman.

Woody nodded. "Takes all of that if you're going to get ahead without an education. It's not something I'd recommend for many folks."

"I'd appreciate it if you'd come for dinner and have a man-to-man with Jason." Tom flashed a grin. "Bring Georgia."

Yeah, right. "Don't think that's gonna happen, but dinner sounds good. When the playoffs are over."

"It's a date."

They climbed out of the car and Woody studied the heritage house that had been converted to a restaurant called Le Gavroche. He'd never been there before.

Tom led the way in the front door, where a distinguished man rushed forward enthusiastically. "Judge, how good to see you. We weren't expecting you tonight."

"A spur-of-the-moment decision. I hope you have room for us?"

Woody got the impression this place would always have room for his friend. He trailed the other two up the stairs to a medium-sized restaurant with windows at the far end. He could see why a husband and wife might favor this spot for an intimate dinner, particularly if they got the window table currently occupied by an attractive couple.

How about that? The woman was Viv Andrews, in bright turquoise and purple tonight, sitting across from a sleek, dark-haired guy in a suit.

Viv glanced up, mouthed, "Woody!" and beckoned him over with a vivid smile and a curled finger.

"And I figured you might be safe from fans here," Tom murmured, following him.

"She's a business acquaintance," Woody said. Then, as they reached the window table, "Hey, there, Viv. This is a surprise."

"Hi, Woody. Woody Hanrahan, this is my friend Jeremy Grant."

"Pleased to meet you." Woody shook his hand. "And this is Tom Westin."

"Tom Westin?" Grant said. "Judge Tom Westin?"

"The same," Tom said easily, also shaking Grant's hand.

"I thought so. Saw you on the news a month or two back, when you were handling that drug conspiracy trial."

"Yes, that was a mess," Tom said. "And everyone knew that whichever way I decided, it would be appealed. Now it's the Court of Appeal's problem."

Viv tugged gently at Woody's sleeve. "Nice shirt."

He was about to tell her it wasn't his, but then a devil made him say, "Zegna," making sure he pronounced it exactly as Tom had.

"Very nice," she repeated, studying him from head to toe in an appraisal that made him wish he was in his own loose jeans and a jersey.

"We'll let you get on with your meal," Woody said, and he and Tom walked over to the table they'd been assigned.

Once seated, Tom said, "Want that beer, or shall we go with a bottle of wine?"

Georgia had said that different drinks were appropriate for different occasions. Taking his cue from Tom, he said, "Let's have wine. Your pick."

While Tom deliberated over the wine list, Woody studied the food menu. Lots of French words, but there were English translations. Still, if he was going to use Tom as his role model, he should probably order the same thing. Unless the judge chose something gross like sweetbreads, which Woody knew damned well did not refer to the dessert tray.

Tom chose an appetizer salad and rack of lamb cooked rare.

Relieved, Woody said, "The same for me, please."

Carefully, he watched as Tom tasted the red wine and approved it. When Woody sipped from his own glass, he said, "That's nice." It didn't have the refreshing, almost-sour edge of beer, but it wasn't sweet either. It was interesting on his tongue, with lots of flavors that came together well. He picked up the bottle and studied the label.

"I chose French because we're eating French food, and hearty to stand up to the lamb," Tom said. "Glad you like it."

"I'm trying to learn more about wine," Woody said. "Tell me some of your favorites, and why you like them."

Tom seemed happy to oblige, and Woody concentrated, looking for mental hooks to remember at least a tiny portion of what Tom said. He did pick up some of the lingo, about bouquet, nose, hints of vanilla, oak, blackberry, smooth finish.

He realized Tom was studying him with amused curiosity. "All right, my friend," Tom said, "who are you trying to impress? Georgia?"

Woody gave a wry chuckle. "Yeah, but not in the way you're thinking." He fiddled with his wineglass. "This is confidential, right?" He had total trust in Tom.

"Of course."

Woody told him about the VitalSport endorsement, omitting only his reasons for doing it. When he finished, Tom gave a low whistle. "You're going to be even more famous."

"Yeah, I'm not keen on that part." Or any part except the money.

"You must have a hell of a good reason for doing it."

Woody heard the curiosity in his voice. He should have anticipated it. Tom was a perceptive man. Not sure how to respond, Woody was glad when the waiter served their salads.

Tom glanced at his plate, thanked the waiter, but didn't pick up his fork. Instead, he returned his gaze to Woody's face, looking interested and concerned.

Woody muttered, "It's embarrassing."

Tom picked up the smaller of the two forks and separated a couple of leaves of lettuce. "Sometimes it helps to talk, but don't feel pressured." He chewed the mouthful slowly.

Woody ate his own first bite of salad, then sighed. "I'm still steaming, and I'm mad at myself for being such a fool." Suddenly, he really did need to talk. He told Tom about how he'd trusted Martin, and how his agent had lost all the money Woody'd made in a career that spanned more than a decade.

When he was finished, Tom said, "Shit."

Woody raised his eyebrows. The judge never swore.

"That's fraud. I hope you reported him to the police."

"If it wasn't for Martin, I'd never have become a hockey player. I owe him for that." He explained how it was his boyhood friend's dad who'd taken the kids to the rink, then to practices and games. He'd even forked out some of his own money for equipment. "He was more of a dad to me than my own was; that's for sure."

"But he betrayed your trust."

Fathers did that. Woody should've known better. "Guess it was dumb of me to trust him."

"It's always wise to keep an eye on people, but this man gave you every reason to trust him." Tom sighed. "Sounds as if he's a gambling addict."

"Yeah. Seems he got into it after his wife died a couple years ago. Anyhow, I told him I wouldn't turn him in if he joined Gamblers Anonymous and sticks with it." One day, maybe he'd return Martin's call and see how things were going. One day. After he'd paid for his mom's treatments, paid the back taxes he owed, and got over being royally pissed.

"You're generous."

Woody shrugged. "Bet you'd do the same thing."

Tom's eyes narrowed as he thought for a long moment. "Maybe. People screw up. They deserve another chance."

He picked up his fork again, and Woody realized neither of them had eaten for at least ten minutes. The same thing had happened when he'd had lunch with Georgia.

Woody chewed on a mouthful of salad, feeling pretty good. He was glad he'd told Tom. Nothing had been solved, but one person in the world knew, and was on his side.

"Have you hired a new agent?" Tom asked.

"Not yet. It's hard to trust someone else."

"Until you do, let me know if I can help with anything."

"Thanks." Too bad he hadn't asked Tom to read the VitalSport contract before he signed it. Woody might not have been stuck modeling gonch.

In companionable silence the two men polished off their salads.

Two racks of lamb appeared as if by magic and again Woody studied Tom for behavior cues.

Tom sliced one of the chops off the rack, cut a bite, and raised it to his mouth.

Woody did the same.

"Tell me more about Georgia," Tom said. "How do you know her?"

"She's in charge of the marketing campaign."

"What's she like? Pretty? Smart?"

"Smart, businesslike. Pretty's not the right word. Striking. Creamy skin, fiery red hair. Eyes like amber ale with little sparkles in them. Long, slender neck." He remembered stroking the length of that neck, down to the delicate collarbones. He'd never realized that a neck could be such a turn-on.

"Nice. But you're not dating her?"

"She's not that impressed by me."

The judge raised his eyebrows. "I had the impression women threw themselves at you."

Woody shrugged. "Some do."

"So Georgia is a challenge."

"Nah, I'm not interested." He had been, but he could recognize a lost cause. Woody sliced into his lamb again.

"That's not what I'm hearing."

"I'm not gonna force myself on a woman who isn't interested."

"Of course not. But you just said you weren't interested anyhow."

"Oh, hell, you're tying me up in knots. Bet you were a damned good lawyer."

"I was. Damned good. Good enough not to let you get away with changing the subject that way." Tom rested his elbows on the table, interlocked his fingers, and leaned his chin on them. "Let's see. You're not interested, and Georgia's not interested. Have I got it right?"

"Yeah."

Tom's eyes twinkled. "Then why are we spending so much time talking about her?"

Woody snorted. "I'm not. That's your doing. You've been married so long that you're desperate for any hint of sex."

"Shows you don't know the first thing about my marriage."

Wrangling cheerfully, they finished their dinners. Woody could see that there was something to be said for Georgia and Tom's slow and easy approach to dining. He really tasted his food, and he and Tom got in some good conversation.

Woody made his first glass of wine last, and let the waiter refill the glass halfway, then stopped him. The judge did the same. When the waiter had gone, Woody said, "Great wine, but I'm taking it easy on the booze these days." That one bender had reminded him of a lesson he'd learned years ago.

Tom nodded. "And I have court tomorrow."

After dinner, they split the bill. Then, feeling more mellow than he had in days, Woody turned down Tom's offer of a ride. He'd walk home, ice his shoulder, and get a good night's sleep. Tomorrow, Georgia and her team had a busy day scheduled for him. Clothes fittings, and God knew what else. He wasn't looking forward to it one bit.

He definitely wasn't looking forward to seeing Georgia. A guy could take only so much rejection.

If there was a tingle of anticipation in his body, it was about something else entirely. He wasn't sure what, but definitely not Georgia.

Fifteen

Woody was scheduled to come in at ten thirty on Tuesday. Georgia's boss, Billy, had asked her, Viv, and Terry to meet before that and brief him on the campaign.

"How's our hockey star shaping up?" Billy asked.

"We're working on him," Georgia said. "The good news is that he learns quickly." The bad news was that he frustrated and aroused her. "Today we're tackling hair, wardrobe, and deportment."

"Interestingly," Viv said, "I saw Woody last night at Le Gavroche and he looked great. And your first deportment lesson has borne fruit. He behaved perfectly."

"He was out for dinner?" And at a rather classy French restaurant. Not that she gave a damn, of course. Not in a personal sense, anyhow. "He obviously doesn't intend to get our approval of his dates." And so much for him saying that he didn't date during the playoffs. It had just been another of his lines.

"Oh, we'd approve this one."

She tried not to grind her teeth. Of course she wasn't jealous. "Really?"

"Judge Westin of the B.C. Supreme Court."

"He's dating a judge?"

Viv's eyes gleamed. "Judge *Tom* Westin. They're friends."

"Really?" How ridiculous to feel relieved that his companion hadn't been a woman. "Woody's table manners were all right?"

"Excellent."

"Hmm." Had he been having her on at lunch, or was he really that quick a learner? She'd suggested he find a role model to mimic, and who better than a distinguished judge? "Well, good for him." She actually felt a little proud.

"He was wearing a Zegna shirt," Viv said.

"A what?"

"Ermenegildo Zegna," she said, while Terry nodded. "Honestly, George, you're as hopeless as Woody."

How was she supposed to know about designer clothing for men? Anthony certainly hadn't been into that kind of thing.

Georgia turned to Billy. "Have you had a chance to read the game plan I e-mailed you?"

He lifted a sheaf of papers. "Yes, but don't we usually call them 'strategic plans'?"

"Terry's been teaching me some of the lingo"—she gave a nod of recognition to the young man—"and I'm trying to use it."

"I like that. And I like your plans for the image makeover, rehearsing for interviews, and the proposed interview and appearance schedule."

"Thank you." Her initial draft had included *The Ellen DeGeneres Show*, but she'd deleted it from the final version. Woody had just been blowing hot air.

Billy glanced down and fiddled with the pages. He wasn't a fidgeter by nature, and Georgia sensed he was hunting for words. "You're going to hand-hold Woody at the first half dozen or so events? To make sure he can deal with whatever comes along?"

She winced. It was an aspect of the plan that didn't thrill her. An introvert, she was fine when she felt confident about her work and was dealing with clients and coworkers, but public appearances weren't her forte. They were second nature for Viv. But this campaign was Georgia's responsibility, and if she wanted to be an account manager and maybe one day run her own firm, she needed to step up. "I will."

"You might, uh . . ." Billy's eyes met hers, then danced away. "When Viv's consulting with you and Woody about his wardrobe, perhaps she could come up with some suggestions for you too, for public appearances."

"You're criticizing the way I dress?" she asked disbelievingly. "I'm totally professional."

"Yes, of course," he said quickly. "Your suits are perfectly, uh, suitable for the office, but I think something a little more, uh, well, different is called for when . . ." He glanced at Viv. "You get what I'm saying? The two of you could go shopping together. Dynamic Marketing will pay for anything you need, within reason."

"Terrific!" Viv's eyes sparkled with excitement.

"Fine. Whatever you want," Georgia said evenly, seething inside. Billy wanted her to dress like Viv. Like her mom, Bernadette.

Terry gestured toward the clock on the wall. "Woody'll be here any minute. I'm meeting with him first, right?"

Georgia nodded, relieved to postpone seeing the man. How could she face him? She had let him bury his face between her legs; then she'd run away. And now she had to reestablish her professionalism and authority.

She still couldn't believe she'd behaved so badly. "Great, Terry," she said with forced enthusiasm. "You work on those interview questions with him. After that, it's the hair and clothing appointments. Viv, I know you'd suggested I come along, but really, you're the expert on those things, as Billy so tactfully pointed out." She avoided glancing at her boss. "You don't need me there."

Viv's blue eyes gleamed. "Oh, but I do. You're the one with the overall concept of this campaign."

"Yes," Billy said, "you should be there, George."

"Fine, fine. I'll be there."

Grudgingly, she realized she was acting immature and cowardly—like Lady Emma, hiding in her room so as to avoid the Comte. As they all left the conference room, she firmed her jaw. "Terry, when Woody arrives, would you ask him to come to my office? I need five minutes with him before you two get going."

She hurried to her office, pulled her hair out of its knot, ran a brush through it, then gathered it up even tighter. Though she usually left the collar button undone on her tailored shirt, now she fastened it.

When Woody walked through the door, she jerked to her feet and pressed her lips together as if that could hold back the flush that heated her cheeks and chest. He looked unbelievably masculine and sexy in jeans and a tee—and his mouth had touched the most private parts of her body.

But she couldn't think about that. Or, at least, she shouldn't.

"Please close the door," she said stiffly.

Expression wary, he obeyed. He didn't sit, and she didn't suggest it.

"I want to apologize," she said.

"Oh, yeah?" His tone was as cautious as his expression.

"I've behaved unprofessionally and it won't happen again." Her tight collar was doing its best to strangle her and she could barely swallow.

He tilted his head and studied her face. "Why?"

At least he'd lost the "how come?" if not his penchant for asking questions. "Why what?"

"Both. Why did you, and why won't you?"

She really didn't want to answer, but he deserved an explanation. "You must think I'm crazy, like I can't make up my mind."

"I don't know what to think, Georgia. You're the most confusing woman I've ever run into. I know you're attracted to me."

How embarrassing. She could almost feel the air between

them vibrate with tension. She closed her eyes briefly. Should she lie to save face? No, she refused to be such a coward. "I guess that's obvious."

"As obvious as the fact that you turn me on something wicked."

"I do?" Despite her better intentions, her lips curled. Wow. She straightened them again. "But there are all sorts of reasons that nothing can—should—happen. We're totally different people and our relationship is a business one. I'm not one of your puck bunnies."

"Jesus, I know that." He kept studying her. "You're saying you'd like to, though?"

"Like to, uh . . . ?"

"Have sex again. If it wasn't for business and how different we are."

He was the most virile, masculine creature she'd ever seen and her whole body tingled with the desire to have him touch her. "Woody, I was with one man for years and years." She wouldn't tell him she'd lost her virginity to that man. "I take relationships seriously."

He nodded slowly. "Okay, I can see that. And you know that the word 'relationship,' with a capital R, gives me hives." He reflected a moment. "But if it wasn't for that stuff, you'd sleep with me?" He didn't seem to be joking, he wasn't flirting, and she didn't know what he was driving at.

Baffled, she planted her hands on her hips. "What are you asking?"

"Did you like it? Would you do it again if it wasn't for all the stuff that's bugging you?"

Oh my God. She gritted her teeth. "Yes, I liked it! Damn it, what are you looking for?"

A slow smile widened on his lips. Such sensual lips, and such a warm, charming smile. "Just wanted to know it was okay for you."

"You're the one who thought it was crappy," she snapped.

"What?" He looked astonished.

"After, you said it was kind of crappy." She fought to keep the hurt out of her voice.

"Shit, no, that's not what I meant. I meant that I was, you know, selfish. I didn't make it good for you. You didn't, uh, come."

Heat flooded her entire body. "I did," she whispered.

"I meant the second time."

Her mouth fell open as it dawned on her that the big tough jock, the guy women flocked around, might suffer from performance anxiety? Immediately, she felt 100 percent better. Her lips curved. "Actually, I did. You just weren't paying attention."

"You can say that again," he muttered ruefully. "But seriously, you did?"

She nodded. "Now are you satisfied?"

He grinned, a sexy flash of white teeth, and his blue eyes sparkled. "Nah, I'm sexually frustrated as hell. How 'bout you?"

She gave a startled laugh. "That pretty much describes it." And for her, the mutual confessions had gone a long way to clearing the air. Did he feel it too? "So, Woody, are we okay? Are we going to be able to work together?"

"If you can keep those pretty hands off me," he drawled, sounding smug.

"Oh, it'll be a struggle, but I'll do my best," she teased back, knowing she spoke the truth.

"Yeah, me too. But you can undo that button. Promise I won't rip your clothes off you." He headed for the door, then tossed a final remark over his shoulder. "Not unless you beg me to."

Laughing, she reached up and unfastened the button that was nearly strangling her. That would be the day. Georgia Malone begging a jock for sex.

Albeit hot sex. Very hot sex.

* * *

An hour later, Georgia walked with Viv and Woody to Christopher Slate's hair salon. The loft-style room had azure walls and half a dozen unusual chandeliers. The décor featured a clutter of funky objets d'art, bright abstracts of nude men and women, state-of-the-art hairdressing equipment, giant plants, couches that belonged on the set of a French drawing-room farce, and even a hot pink chaise longue. Very odd, and it shouldn't have worked, but to Georgia's mind it was both cozy and intriguing.

"Eclectic," Woody said sagely.

Georgia raised her brows. He really did pick things up quickly.

"Yes, it is," Viv said, "and creative. Come meet Christopher."

Christopher Slate, a man of perhaps forty, was willowy and elegant in a black shirt and pants. A mane of glossy black hair cascaded from a silver-clasped ponytail to midway down his back. His features were those of a Spanish grandee, his manner blatantly gay.

His eyes widened theatrically as he took in Woody; then he said to Viv, "My dear, how deliciously raw!"

Georgia choked back a laugh and Woody sent her a thundercloud glare. He squared his shoulders and stuck out his hand. "Pleased to meet you."

"The pleasure is all mine," Christopher returned, clasping Woody's hand enthusiastically between his slender palms. "Now, come with me and we'll get you changed."

"I can get myself changed, thanks all the same," Woody growled.

Georgia bent her head to Viv's. "He's going to kill us for this, you realize."

"Nonsense. I have complete faith in Christopher." The blonde rubbed her hands together and said gleefully, "One transformation coming up."

Woody emerged from a change room, caped in black and purple, looking immensely ill at ease. The stylist seated him in front of a giant mirror and edged gracefully around him, studying his head from all angles, lifting his hair and testing the texture between his fingers. Woody's face was expressionless, as if he'd left his body in the chair and removed his mind to a distant planet.

Christopher finally spoke. "Viv, you suggested a style rather like that of our friend Terry?"

"Terry Banerjee comes here too?" Georgia asked.

"But of course," Christopher said.

"I'd look stupid with hair like Terry's," Woody said grimly, "and I hate putting all that goop in it."

"Product," the stylist corrected. "We could go very short, because your skull has a wonderful shape." He stood back and shook his head. "But no, I like longer hair, especially on a man with such healthy, thick hair."

He glanced at Viv and Georgia. "Woody is an athlete, and long hair is synonymous with virility, isn't it, ladies? Samson, and so on? Isn't every middle-aged man's greatest fear the loss of his hair?" He made a wry face. "Well, his second greatest fear, because after all hair does only *symbolize* virility. The hair is a poor substitute if the real thing is missing. Not that I imagine you'll have to worry about the depletion of either, will you, Woody?"

Woody's lips twitched. "No signs of trouble yet, Christopher."

"I thought not." He patted Woody on the shoulder. "I can always tell these things."

"Longish hair, then," Viv said, "and the beard needs to go."

Georgia nodded.

"No," Woody said flatly, and Christopher glanced at the two women.

"You may hate shaving," Georgia said, "but you're going to have to get used to it."

He shook his head. "It's a playoff beard."

"A what?" she asked, as Viv also stared in puzzlement.

"We don't shave during the playoffs."

"Athletes have superstitions," Christopher said.

"I've noticed that almost all the players for the Beavers and the Ducks have beards," Georgia said. "But we'll be doing ad photos and the scruffy beard just won't work. If you read the contract, you'd know we—"

"Goddamn contract." Woody scowled. "Shaving would jinx our luck. I can't do it."

Pointing out the childishness of the superstition wouldn't be the most effective tactic. "I understand. But, Woody, not to be insulting, at the moment the beards aren't bringing the Beavers much luck."

"We'll turn things around," he said grimly.

"Of course you will," Christopher said. "And I want to help. Here's what I'm thinking. Maybe you need a fresh angle on the beard tradition."

"A fresh angle?" Woody's tone was wary.

"We won't shave it," the stylist said, "but we'll trim it. It won't be rough and sloppy, but neat, focused, and virile. Just like the Beavers' game will be. And"—he turned to Georgia and Viv—"he'll look utterly stunning, I promise you."

Georgia turned to Viv. "It sounds like a good solution to me, but you're the expert."

"I trust Christopher." Viv gave a sunny smile. "And we all want to do everything we can to improve the Beavers' chances."

Woody groaned.

"Shall we leave the boys to play?" Viv steered Georgia over to a corner where one of the delicate French couches sat beside a shiny Italian espresso machine. Clearly a regular, she fixed cappuccinos for both of them.

Georgia took a sip. "Poor Woody. He's going to hate today, isn't he? Hair and wardrobe?" Empathizing, she shuddered. However, her boss had given her a more-than-strong hint, and if Woody could man up to a makeover, she had to do her part. "Billy's right that I could use some new clothes for the events I'll be attending with Woody. Are there stores you'd suggest?" Evening wear had never been part of her wardrobe.

Viv's eyes gleamed. "I'll come with you. We'll have great fun!"

Georgia winced, remembering her mom dragging her shopping as a child, buying her pink frilly dresses, then, as she neared the age of ten, miniskirts and skimpy camisoles. Clothes that made men look at her. Touch her. She shuddered at the memory of her mom's boyfriend fondling her, then forced it away. She wasn't that girl. She was a confident woman.

Dubiously, she studied Viv, today in a magenta and bright yellow pantsuit. Georgia might be confident, but no way would she wear figure-hugging, cleavage-revealing clothes like the blonde's. Would Viv be any help in finding pantsuits in silk or satin, dressy yet tailored and unobtrusive?

Knowing that she'd hate every second of the shopping expedition, Georgia glanced with sympathy toward Woody. Interestingly enough, he didn't look totally wretched. He was getting along well with Christopher Slate.

"Do you have something to wear tonight?" Viv asked.

The schedule called for Georgia and Woody to have dinner at an upscale restaurant and work on his table manners. Even though Viv said he'd acquitted himself well at dinner last night, Georgia couldn't shirk this responsibility. At least they'd be in public, so that even if she did feel that strange sexual attraction to him—the one Woody said was mutual—she wouldn't jump him and beg for more orgasms.

"George?"

"Sorry. I was thinking. Uh, this restaurant you booked—Hawksworth—it's quite formal, right?"

"Yes. You'll enjoy it. Excellent food, lovely ambience, intriguing cocktails, great wine list. And it's in the Hotel Georgia, which seems apropos."

Usually, when Georgia went out with friends, they ate somewhere casual. "I'll wear a business suit." A pantsuit. The one time she'd worn a skirt with Woody, he'd made her peel off her panty hose. Yes, it had been to improvise a fan belt, but she was afraid it'd be all too easy for him to talk her into doing it again, with far less justification.

"A dress with a nice jacket or wrap would be better."

"I don't own any dresses," she confessed.

Viv beamed. "We'll remedy that this afternoon."

Georgia knew she'd be voting for pants instead, a fancier version of her normal business wear.

The other woman tapped a purple-tipped finger thoughtfully against her chin. "As for Woody, whatever suits or blazers we choose today will need alterations, but VitalSport has classy lines of jeans, casual pants, and shirts. Hopefully we'll get a fit on those, and that'll be fine for him tonight." She glanced past Georgia and a smile widened. "Especially now that Christopher has worked his magic."

Georgia looked up to see Woody, uncaped and looking anxious, walking toward them with Christopher almost dancing around him.

Woody's hair was still on the long side, but it had fallen into shiny mahogany waves that complemented the pure masculinity of his strong features. It looked natural, not like he'd spent twenty minutes in front of a mirror. The neat beard and mustache suited his firm jaw and sensual mouth. Christopher had made Woody look more sophisticated and charming without sacrificing an ounce of his formidable masculinity.

Viv murmured, "Oh, my, he really does clean up well," while

Georgia just stared. No, she was *not* going to jump him and beg for sex.

Woody eyed Georgia. "Well?"

"I like it." When she met his gaze, she felt a zing of sexual electricity. Quickly, she turned to the stylist. "Christopher, you're as much a genius as Viv promised."

"I'm glad you think so," Viv purred, touching Georgia's shoulder and guiding her away from Woody. "Because it's your turn. Come and be caped."

"What?" Georgia demanded, freezing in her tracks and trying to hug the floor with her feet. "No way!"

Woody laughed. "Go for it, Georgia. How can you refuse a genius? Not to mention Viv?"

"I don't want a haircut."

"Neither did I," said Woody.

"It's part of the contract you signed."

"Aw, come on." Mischief glinted in his eyes. "We're a team, right?"

She was about to argue when she remembered Billy's criticism of her wardrobe. Had he asked Viv to find a diplomatic way of changing Georgia's hairstyle too? She nibbled on her bottom lip.

Viv took advantage of her indecision and in a matter of seconds had her draped in a dramatic purple-and-black cape and settled in front of the mirror. "What do you suggest, Christopher?"

"No!" Georgia screeched. Then, more quietly, "I'll submit to a haircut but not with the two of you watching. Go away!"

"She wants us to get lost," Woody said to Viv, in a voice of exaggerated hurt.

"You were much more cooperative," Viv said, patting his arm.

"I'm just a cooperative guy. Right, Georgia?"

"Would you just go?" she wailed, knowing her cheeks were on fire.

"Oh, fine." Viv gave a phony huff. "But, Christopher, if she tries to escape as soon as we leave, tie her down." She and the stylist exchanged double cheek kisses. "George, Woody and I will go to VitalSport for his fittings, and as you know they're providing lunch. Catch up with us if you can, and otherwise we'll meet at Holt Renfrew. They have a great selection for both sexes." She took Woody's arm and steered him toward the door.

He turned back, grinning. "See you later, Georgia. Have fun."

Once the pair had disappeared, Georgia studied Christopher's reflection in the mirror as he eased the clip from her hair and ran his fingers through the long strands. "I could use an inch off the ends," she suggested.

"You need a lot more than that, dear." He patted her shoulder. "You have lovely hair, but it's thick and heavy, and the weight pulls the natural wave out of it. I'll cut and layer it, give you something with body and personality." He studied her from all directions. "We'll definitely have to have feathery bangs."

"Bangs? I haven't had bangs since I was a kid."

"Hush, now, and leave it to me. I truly am a genius."

Georgia suppressed a whimper.

Sixteen

Woody walked to the Hotel Georgia, his muscles loose and pleasantly tired after a vigorous workout. He'd offered to pick Georgia up, but she said she preferred to take her own car to dinner. Since they'd cleared the air this morning, she'd been pleasant, even joked with him, but she'd kept things businesslike. Tonight, would she soften? He shouldn't want that. His focus needed to be on the playoffs. His mom's health and the VitalSport campaign were distraction enough.

The maître d' greeted him. "Welcome to Hawksworth, Mr. Hanrahan. Your guest has yet to arrive. We have you in the Pearl Room." He led the way, and Woody followed.

Weird how he could skate onto the ice with thousands of people in the stands and TV cameras aimed on him, and feel at ease, but walking into this classy place made him antsy. He sometimes went to upscale restaurants with the other players, but he preferred more casual places. Usually, he'd choose a sports bar, though he had to admit that restaurant Le Gavroche had been nice. Kind of cozy.

The Pearl Room was not cozy. Done mostly in shades of what he'd call cream but guessed must be pearl, with dark wood accents, it was elegant. A massive chandelier glittered with hundreds, if not thousands, of lights. The room was half-full, and the diners wore everything from evening wear to suits to jeans.

The maître d' seated him at a table for two, with a well-dressed couple on one side and an empty table on the other. He might not feel like he belonged here, but at least he looked the part, thanks to Christopher Slate and to Viv's selection of clothes from VitalSport. He had to admit, the guy who'd stared back at him from his bathroom mirror looked okay.

"Jeans and a jersey," Viv had said when she'd handed the clothes to him. "Can't complain about that, can you, Woody?" The jeans were black and slim-fitting, and the shirt was a brand-new design, whipped up when the company signed Woody. In the same caramel shade as the Beavers' emblem, it was styled along the lines of a hockey jersey but was tighter-fitting and made of a fabric that looked expensive. Surprisingly, it was as comfortable as a well-washed tee. Yeah, Viv had lived up to her promise that nice clothes didn't have to hurt you.

Now, sitting at a table decorated with a flickering candle in a glass holder and a small flower arrangement in—no surprise—shades of white and cream, he wondered what Georgia would wear. She'd participated in selecting his suits and tux at Holt Renfrew, but banished him when it was her turn to try on clothes. Fine with him. What guy would choose clothes shopping with a woman over a workout—or any other available option?

He expected her to wear another tailored suit. After all, she hadn't let Christopher Slate do much with her hair. When she'd joined him and Viv, it had been slicked back as usual. Christopher had given her bangs, which suited her face, and he must've cut her hair because a few curls escaped the usual knot, but the style wasn't much different.

Woody, keeping an eye on the entrance, gazed appreciatively at the lovely woman who was following the maître d' across the room. It took him almost until she'd arrived to realize it was Georgia.

She wore a dress. Not all bright and figure-hugging like the clothes Viv wore, but something silky and golden that skimmed her curves, revealed her collarbones, and ended just above her knees. Knees—and legs—that shimmered as if she'd been sprinkled with gold dust.

A fringed shawl, cream and black with gold threads running through it, draped her shoulders. And her hair was totally different: a mass of loose, silky curls. Curls that begged to be twined around fingers, to have hands plunge through them to grip her head. Curls that would tickle his belly, his cock, if she leaned over him and—

Remembering his manners, he jerked to his feet. "Wow, you look great."

Flushing, she sank into the chair across from him. "Thanks."

He seated himself too, his thickening erection reminding him that these pants were tighter than his usual jeans.

She fiddled with a curl of hair. "Viv said I should get comfortable with the clothes and hairstyle before I attend events with you."

"Huh." Last week, Georgia had told him about her mom dressing to attract men, and her own refusal to use feminine wiles at work. He was glad Viv had persuaded her that looking more feminine could be part of her job. "That's cool, and you even match the restaurant."

She glanced around as if she hadn't noticed her surroundings. "I guess I do. Except for my hair."

Her hair was the flame, the sexy highlight of the whole room. No, *she* was the highlight. But he didn't say stuff like that, much less even think it, normally.

"Fancy place," he commented.

"Viv's recommendation. I don't usually eat at formal restaurants."

"Me either." He gave a wry chuckle. "But you already knew that."

She smiled back, looking more relaxed. "We're quite the pair."

If only. With her looking like that, and his body throbbing with arousal, he wanted to forget all the reasons they shouldn't hook up. She'd admitted she was attracted. Could he persuade her to give in to it? He said, "You can say that again," giving it a hint of innuendo.

Unfortunately, she tensed again. "I didn't mean it that way. I meant, both of us trying out new clothes and hairstyles, coming to a place where we're fish out—"

She broke off when a waiter came over to ask, "Would you care for a cocktail? We have a number of specialty ones. Perhaps our signature Hotel Georgia cocktail?"

"Sounds like it's made for you, Georgia," Woody said.

The waiter, who had a subtle gay vibe, beamed. "Your name is Georgia? How perfect!"

"I don't usually drink cocktails," she said dubiously. "What's in it?"

"Plymouth gin, lemon juice—freshly squeezed, of course—and orange-blossom water, all frothed together with egg white. It's as smooth as silk. But please, study the cocktail menu. We have several excellent choices." He left them with the menus.

A minute or two later, Woody asked, "You having a cocktail?"

"I'm tempted."

"Go for it." If she gave in to one temptation, maybe he could tempt her further. Was he the only one at this table who was seriously turned on? "That Hotel Georgia thing?"

She nodded. "Usually I drink wine, but it sounds intriguing." She tapped the list. "So do a number of these." Her lips curved and she said, almost like she was talking to herself, "Marielle would love this menu."

"Marielle?"

"She's in my book club."

"You're in a book club? What kind of books do you read?"

For some reason, she flushed. "Mostly literary fiction."

He kept his mouth shut.

She grinned at him. "It's okay. You can say what you think."

He shrugged. "Sounds boring to me. But each to their own."

To his surprise, she said, "Sometimes they are a little boring. Sometimes they're great. I like that the club makes me read things I wouldn't otherwise pick up myself." Her lips twitched. "You can get some very interesting ideas from books."

He had some pretty interesting ideas right now, from being with her. "I guess. And surprises are good sometimes. Like that saying about not judging a book by its cover."

Her eyes flicked down, then up, and she gazed at him through dark brown lashes. "That's very true. And I'll admit, I judged you from the first video I saw. Maybe Billy Daniels gave me that one as a test."

A waiter came to take their orders: a Hotel Georgia for the lady with the same name, and a large glass of water for Woody.

When he'd gone, Georgia said, "You're not drinking?"

"Just a glass of wine with dinner. There's a game tomorrow night. What do you mean about a test?"

She gazed across the table into his eyes. "To see if I was daunted by a Neanderthal with blood running down his face and a gutter mouth."

He wasn't sure whether to wince or chuckle at that description of himself. He hadn't been at his best, but he'd been so damned pissed off, more about losing that last shot on goal than over the high stick that slashed his cheek. "You weren't daunted."

Humor lit her face. "Well, maybe a little."

God, she was gorgeous, and he liked it when they talked like this, easy and a little teasing.

"But," she went on, "if I'd turned down this account, I might not have been offered another."

"Backing down from a challenge isn't the way to get ahead."

"Exactly. And I want to build my career."

"What's your goal?" Not only was his body throbbing with sexual awareness of her, but he was interested in learning what made her tick. "To be your boss's boss?"

"Or to run my own marketing firm."

Ambitious. Maybe out of his league. But maybe not. Hell, he was ambitious too, if you counted wanting to play the game he loved for as long as his body held up, and then coach until he dropped in his skates. "You really like selling stuff?"

"It's a lot more than that. You're seeing that with the VitalSport campaign, Woody."

Their drinks arrived, she took a sip, and her face lit with pleasure. He wanted to caress her soft cheek, capture one of those long curls of fiery hair. Stroke the lobe of her ear and make her shiver. He figured she wasn't ready for that, though, so he took a long drink of ice water to cool down. "Guess so. But tell me what the job means to you."

"It's a challenge to put all the pieces together into an effective campaign, and fascinating to know we're influencing people's opinions. I get a kick out of turning the page in a magazine and seeing a dynamite ad that we worked hard on." She studied his face. "You find it hard to relate to."

"A little. I mean, I'm pretty basic. Ice, puck, goal."

"A man of pure action."

"Sort of. Though"—he thought for a moment—"there's strategy. Practice. Teamwork. A kind of second sense that tells you where everyone's at, out there on the ice. What they're doing, what they're planning to do."

She leaned forward, forearms on the table, the shawl slipping back so that he saw her arms were bare. Slim and cream-colored, matching the restaurant.

His fingers itched to stroke that bare skin.

"Terry says hockey takes intelligence," she said. "Smarts, skill, instinct, and discipline."

Woody nodded. "Good description. Different kind of smarts than book learning, though."

"Smarts that, Terry pointed out, make you more money in a year than we'll make in a lifetime," she said wryly.

Yeah, if he hadn't trusted Martin Simpson, he'd have a fortune by now. Trusting the man—trusting anyone—wasn't exactly "smart."

"Something wrong?" Georgia asked. "You're frowning."

Nah, he wouldn't let Martin ruin tonight, with him and Georgia getting along like this. Plus, he'd had good news today. His mom, who, together with her full-time nurse/caregiver, had arrived at the clinic in Switzerland last week, had told him on the phone that she was feeling better already. Experience had taught him not to trust her words, because she'd always hidden health problems— from broken bones to her cancer diagnosis—but he'd learned to read her voice. Today, it had held fresh energy.

Man, he wished he could be in Switzerland with her.

Of course, if he didn't pull up his socks and get back in the zone, the Beavers would lose the Western Conference and he'd have all the fucking time in the world. They'd won the first game against the Ducks, then lost the last three, and it was partly his fault.

"Woody? What is it?"

He realized he was scowling. "Sorry. Just got thinking about the last three games."

"They didn't go so well."

An understatement. A polite one. Normally, he didn't talk about stuff like this with anyone other than his teammates, but he found himself saying, "All that smarts and skill stuff, somehow it's not working for me right now. Gotta get it back."

She studied him with a concerned expression. "That must be disturbing. Do you have any idea what the problem is? It's not the VitalSport contract, is it, and the time we're asking you to put in?"

Sure it was. And worry over his mom, not to mention simmering anger over his agent's betrayal and his own stupidity in trusting the man. Having to wear a face shield didn't help his game, and nor did being distracted by Georgia.

But usually he had focus out on the ice. Nothing affected his concentration: not pain, not trash talk, not some dumb call from the ref, much less anything that was happening in his off-the-ice life. Oh sure, he slipped sometimes—he was human, not a machine—but mostly he got in the zone and stayed there. Why couldn't he do that now?

The concern in Georgia's eyes warmed him. "Nah, it's not the endorsement."

"Are you injured? Your shoulder—"

"What about my shoulder?" He cut her off, lowering his voice to a whisper. "Are people saying I'm injured?" They couldn't be; he'd have heard the rumors.

She shook her head. "I just noticed, when that player smashed into you in the last game, your shoulder took a beating and it took you a little while to get back up."

"Seconds. I was up in seconds," he defended hotly. He'd barely registered the pain, just leaped to his feet. Hell, if Georgia, who knew nothing about the game, thought he was slow, what were the Ducks seeing? Last thing he wanted was to look vulnerable. Besides, after a couple of days with no games scheduled, just light practice sessions, physio, and vigorous workouts, his shoulder was doing fine.

"You were. Sorry. I just"—she glanced away and picked up her cocktail glass—"I was worried about you. I don't understand how someone can get hit that hard and not feel it."

Somewhat reassured, he managed a grin. "Canadian tough guy, remember?" Was she worrying because she cared for him, at least a little? Or only because her marketing campaign depended on him?

"Right. I forgot for a moment," Georgia teased.

Wait. He didn't want her to care for him. All he wanted was sex.

Last thing he wanted was some woman looking for commitment, talking about the future.

"Well, I'm really glad you're not injured." Mischief sparked in her eyes. "And hey, things are bound to look up. You have that lucky haircut and beard trim. I have to agree with Viv. Christopher Slate really is a genius."

His teammates would give him shit tomorrow, but he liked the appreciation in Georgia's eyes. "Yeah, the man is. You look terrific." So touchable, so sexy, so irresistible. "When I saw you this afternoon, I didn't think he'd done much, but wow, your hair looks great tonight." Then, realizing he'd done one of those foot-in-mouth guy things, he quickly added, "Not that it doesn't look good usually. But I like it all loose and curly like that."

She tugged the shawl, which had slipped down, back up around her shoulders. "Why?"

Give a girl a compliment and she had to go all analytical. "Because, uh, it's pretty. Makes a guy want to run his fingers through it. Makes you look, you know, softer." Gave a guy ideas, and hopes. Gave him a throbbing ache and a driving need.

She frowned slightly. "Less professional. When a woman looks like this, a man doesn't take her as seriously. Not if he's thinking about running his fingers through her hair."

Did he agree? Working it through as he idly watched a sophisticated-looking Asian couple about his and Georgia's age take seats at the neighboring table, he said, "Viv dresses kind of that way for work. I take her seriously. She knows her job."

"What was your first thought when you met her?"

He thought back. "Pretty. I could live without the bright colors, but I guess that's her thing."

"What was your first thought when you met me?"

He remembered turning around and realizing George was a woman. One whose eyes were about ready to pop out of her head.

"That you were flustered. You were shocked at seeing a semi-naked guy in the conference room." He grinned. "Then you forgot about your broken heel and almost tumbled." He'd caught her arm, felt a zing of awareness rip through him. Now he didn't even have to touch her to feel that zing. Just sitting across from her was enough to make desire pulse through him, keeping him semierect.

"But not pretty?" she asked.

How had he gotten himself into this? "Not, uh, not pretty. But the way you were dressed and all, it took longer to sneak up on me. They called you George, you were all stiff and starchy and kind of pissed off, and—"

"You thought I was a lesbian."

Hard to believe, now that he knew her. "My brain thought that. My body had a different opinion." An opinion—a need—that intensified each time he was with her.

"Okay, but—"

She broke off as their waiter came over to ask, "Have you decided on dinner yet?"

Saved from getting himself into more trouble, Woody glanced at his companion. "Georgia?" Whatever she ordered, he'd do the same. Unless it was sweetbreads.

She smiled at the waiter. "Could you give us a couple more minutes?"

"Of course."

When he'd gone, Woody didn't want Georgia picking up where she'd left off, so he quickly asked, "What was your first thought when you met me?"

Her eyes widened, then sparkled as color hit her cheeks. But all she said was, "That you were a boor."

"And that's why you're blushing like that?"

Seventeen

Georgia couldn't get enough of looking at Woody tonight. He was easily the most handsome man in the restaurant. Probably in the entire city. Possibly the entire country. Viv had said he cleaned up well, but that was an understatement. And not only did he look amazing; his behavior was impeccable.

Maybe it was Woody, or the unaccustomed cocktail, or the fact that her new clothes and hair made her feel off balance—in mostly a good way—but a mischievous impulse hit her. "All right, if you insist on knowing my first impression." She glanced at the silver-haired couple seated on one side of them, then at the sleekly dressed Asian pair on the other side. Then, feeling deliciously daring, she leaned toward him and said in little more than a whisper, pronouncing each word slowly and carefully, "Tight, taut, amazing butt."

He blinked, then gave a surprised laugh, loud enough that both other couples shot them a questioning gaze.

Suffering from immediate second thoughts, she grabbed the menu and studied it again. "What looks good to you?"

"Oh, lots of things." His seductive tone made her lift her gaze again.

Bedroom eyes. Those were definitely bedroom eyes gazing at her, saying that his idea of a three-course meal was working his way down her body. She pulled the shawl more tightly around herself even as her skin flushed with arousal.

"How about you?" he asked. "What takes your fancy?"

Those eyes. The sharp planes of his face. The beautifully styled hair that looked so touchable, and the sexy scar that cut across his cheekbone. His broad shoulders and the strong muscles of his torso showcased by the jersey-style top. Not to mention the hard penis that would satisfy the needy throb in her sex.

No, this was a business dinner. She'd slipped and forgotten her own "strictly business" rule. "I'm sorry," she said stiffly. "That was completely inappropriate."

"Lighten up, Georgia. Just because we work together, that doesn't mean we can't have fun. Right?"

Define "fun." She swallowed, trying to ignore the man's blatant sex appeal. "I enjoy talking to you, and it is fun when we joke a little. But I crossed a line. It won't happen again." She hoisted the menu and hid behind it. "I think I'll have the apple and beetroot salad; then I think the slow-cooked halibut. How about you?"

"Uh, sure. I'll have the same."

She lowered the menu again. She'd chosen items that sounded light as well as tasty. Surely Woody needed more food than that. "You don't want something more substantial?"

He shrugged; then she realized he might have picked the same thing so he could imitate her. "Please, order what you want." She added, in a lower tone, "I'm sure you'll do fine." If not, she'd find a subtle way of giving him cues.

His jaw tightened and she worried that she'd embarrassed him, but he glanced at the menu again. "The scallop appetizer and the duck breast." He picked up the wine list and said tentatively, "A light red might work with both the halibut and the duck."

She raised her eyebrows. "I'm impressed."

He gave a relieved smile and handed her the list. "Good. Now I figure it's lady's choice to pick the wine."

"Since we're each only having a glass, we don't have to get the same one." She studied the wine list. "I think I'll go with a B.C. chardonnay." Then she handed the list back to him, curious what he'd do with it. "How about you?"

He opened the book-sized list and his eyes glazed over.

"You can never go wrong," she said softly, "by asking the waiter what the chef recommends to complement a particular dish."

Woody closed the menu, and when the waiter came back to take their orders, he repeated her words.

The man beamed. "I'm so glad you asked. I'll send a sommelier over immediately."

In a couple of minutes, a striking woman with a streak of white in her dark hair came over. With a hint of a French accent, she said, "Sir, I understand you're looking for a wine pairing for the duck breast?"

"Yes, please."

"We have an excellent shiraz, but I think perhaps, for you, a bigger wine. Yes?"

"Yes." He sounded confident, but Georgia guessed he had no idea what a big wine was.

"There is a very special Australian pinot noir I think you'll enjoy."

"I'll trust your judgment. Thanks."

The sommelier turned to Georgia. "You've chosen a wine to accompany your halibut?"

She had, but she was no wine expert. "I'd be interested in a recommendation too. Preferably a B.C. wine."

"There's a Blue Mountain sauvignon blanc that goes particularly well with that dish."

"Sold. Thank you."

"The sauvignon blanc will go well with the apple and beetroot salad, too," the sommelier said, then turned back to Woody. "But, sir, the pinot noir will be too hearty for your scallops. Perhaps a glass of something lighter with your appetizer?"

"Sorry; my limit's one glass tonight."

"Of course." To this point, she'd been professional and friendly. Now her lips tilted up at the corners. "And, Mr. Hanrahan, may I wish you luck tomorrow night? Bash 'em, Beavers!" The words, delivered in her cultured, French-accented voice, sounded totally out of place in this elegant restaurant.

Woody grinned. "Thanks."

A few minutes later, their waiter brought Georgia's white wine and a refill of water for Woody. She sipped her wine, smiled appreciatively, then slid the glass toward him. "Try it."

"A lesson in wine appreciation?"

Really, she'd just wanted to share something nice. But of course it should be a lesson. "Yes. Tell me what you think."

He lifted the glass, closed his eyes as he took a sip, then swirled the wine gently in his mouth, looking like an entirely different man from the one she'd lunched with. Those striking indigo eyes opened. "Grapefruit, new-mown spring grass, and the wind across a field of hay."

"Wow." Blown away, she took the glass back and sipped again. She'd have said "citrusy" and left it at that. But yes, she did taste everything he'd named. "How did you do that?"

"A friend told me to close my eyes and say whatever pops into my mind." He gave an engaging grin that was part boy and mostly sexy man. "The more outrageous, the better. He said wine snobs are into that stuff."

"I suppose they are. You certainly have a good palate."

"Thanks."

So many things about him intrigued her. She chose one. "Would your friend be Judge Westin?"

"Yeah. Viv told you we saw each other last night?"

She nodded. "How did you get to know him?"

"Met at a fund-raiser. He played hockey as a kid. He taught me to play squash and we have a game every week or so." He gave a wry grin. "Still beats me too, damn him."

"You're dinner friends as well as squash partners?" Last week, she'd have said they were an unlikely pair. Tonight, not so much.

Woody shrugged. "We're getting to know each other better." His eyes gleamed with humor. "He invited you over for dinner."

"What? Me?" Woody had mentioned her?

"He said his wife and son want to meet me. Then, when I said, uh, I'm working with you, he said I should bring you along."

How odd. But she could top him. She flipped a trailing end of her shawl over her shoulder. "My mother invited you for dinner. The moment she heard about the VitalSport campaign."

"How about that. She a Beavers fan?"

Her mouth tightened. "She's a fan of attractive men."

He gave a smug grin. "You think I'm attractive."

"*She* does." He was so irresistible, Georgia had to grin back. "All right, you know I do." She didn't believe in dishonesty. And tonight, what woman wouldn't find Woody attractive? As for a woman who'd seen that fantastic body naked, who'd felt his intimate touch, who'd climaxed so hard that it was a wonder her body hadn't come apart—

"Your salad." The waiter's voice interrupted her thoughts and a beautifully presented salad appeared in front of her, a ribbon of red-skinned apple making it look like a gift.

Trying to ignore the needy ache between her thighs, she picked up her fork and took a bite, then sighed her approval. Beets, apple, chèvre cheese, candied pecans, herbs, and a delicious dressing.

Woody tackled his own appetizer, using the correct fork and slicing a bite off a scallop rather than swallowing it whole. Then he put down his fork. "Mine's good. How's yours?"

"Very nice." Head tilted, she studied him. "Woody, you seem like a different man than the one I had lunch with. Were you having a joke at my expense?"

"A joke? No way." He ducked his head and toyed with his fork. "Guess I had a lot to learn. Having dinner with Tom really helped."

"You're a quick learner."

Still not looking at her, he said, "I wouldn't have even thought about how I eat if you hadn't said something."

"I'm sorry if I embarrassed you." Last week, she'd wondered about his upbringing. If he'd had a tough one, as his bio suggested, that could account for poor table manners. Rather than come right out and ask, she instead ventured, "Is it a guy-sports thing to rush through your meal?"

He glanced up. "I guess. We're usually either carb-loading before a game, or ravenous after one." He drew a breath. "But honestly, I've always eaten like that."

"Your parents . . ." She let the question go unfinished, hoping he'd pick up her hint.

He put down his fork again, and the muscles in his throat moved. Hard. "Guess we ate pretty quickly."

"Do you have brothers or sisters?" She'd heard that siblings often fought over food. Woody's bio didn't mention any, but then, it said remarkably little about his family.

"No. It was just my parents and me."

She waited, hoping he'd go on.

Finally, he said, "It wasn't pretty, the way I grew up. I don't talk about it. It's one of the reasons I've avoided interviews and endorsements."

His voice was steady, flat. That in itself spoke of the pain he carried inside, and her heart ached for him.

She touched his hand quickly, gently. "I'm sorry. It's lonely when you can't share with anyone."

He took another deep breath, then let it out audibly. "Yeah. When I was a kid, I didn't even tell my best friend. His dad guessed, and I guess his mom knew too. They helped where they could."

Guessed what? Abuse? Drugs? She waited, but he didn't go on. He hadn't told anyone, so she shouldn't be hurt that he wouldn't tell her. "Are your parents still alive?" she ventured.

He ran a hand roughly across his neatly trimmed beard. "My father died five or six years back."

"I'm sorry."

He shook his head. "Got in a fight he couldn't win. Took a knife in his guts and bled out."

Shocked, her breath caught in her throat. The grim satisfaction with which he said it confirmed her suspicion of abuse. Of him? Of his mom? "And your mother?"

"She's still alive." He cleared his throat. "They never traveled. She hated the long, cold winters and always wanted to go to Florida. After he died, I sent her on a long holiday there. She loved it. I'd have liked her to move to Vancouver, but she had some health problems. Cold and rain are hard on her."

Health problems resulting from being abused?

"I got her a place in Florida and visit whenever I can."

"She must be proud of you."

"That's what she says. Guess that's what all moms say, right?"

Ha. Her mom cared more about whether Georgia was dating than about her career successes. The two of them were just too different to ever be close, yet it still hurt that they weren't.

She was saved from answering when the waiter stopped by with a worried expression. "Is there a problem with the appetizers?"

She realized that, after those first tastes, neither she nor Woody had touched their food.

Woody smiled at the man. "No, they're great. We got talking." He picked up his fork.

How about that? Woody'd been so caught up in talking to her that he'd forgotten to eat. She reached for her own fork and her shawl slid off her shoulders.

Woody's gaze caressed her bare arms, heating them, and this time she didn't pull the shawl back up.

After a few mouthfuls, he said, "How about you? What's your family story?"

"I'm an only child too. My father—well, I never really knew him. He was around for the first couple of years of my life; then he and my mom split up and he didn't stay in touch. Since then, Bernadette's been married four more times. I learned not to get attached to any of my stepdads because they wouldn't be around long."

"That's rough. I'm surprised it didn't sour you on marriage." His tone made her guess that his parents were partly responsible for him being so anti-commitment.

She shook her head. "I'm the opposite of my mother."

"You must've been pretty young when you tied the knot."

"Twenty-one. And it would have lasted forever." She hadn't the slightest doubt.

He winced, and she figured that to him it must sound like a life sentence of hard time. But all he said was, "Your mom doesn't believe in that happily-ever-after stuff?"

"Kind of, but it never works. Bernadette is insecure, which you'd never believe if you met her. She comes off as vivacious, flirtatious, bodacious. Underneath, she needs men to give her validation. She meets a guy; he thinks she's wonderful; she's so happy and she thinks it'll last forever. But after a while, he's not paying her enough attention; he's looking at other women. There's always something. Either she leaves to look for another man, or the guy gets tired of her neediness and dumps her. It's a nasty cycle."

"Huh. Yeah, you're different than her."

"I believe that you should only marry if you find your soul mate.

I was lucky enough to find mine early on." And unlucky enough to lose him.

"I don't get it," Woody said slowly. "The soul mate stuff and all. But I see how much he meant to you, and I'm sorry you lost him."

Touched, she said, "So am I."

Across the table, his eyes were clear, the blue lit by sparkles from the chandelier above and the candle on the table. "I think it's great that you don't whine about how life dealt you a low blow. You picked yourself up and got on with things."

Pleased, she murmured, "Thank you. You're like that too, aren't you? You don't let things get you down. Not your rough childhood, not being smashed onto the ice, not even having me pick on your manners."

"Tough guy," he reminded her. The humor in his eyes, the softness of his mouth, made him look anything but, yet she knew there was a core of steel inside the man.

The combination was seductive.

Yes, to hundreds of women. And Woody liked it that way. Women, in the plural. He didn't even believe in serial monogamy. It was ridiculous to get moony over him. He wasn't her type. It was good, though, that she found admirable qualities in him. That would assist with the campaign, and it made working with him a lot more pleasant than she'd anticipated. She just had to make sure she didn't let it become so pleasant that she abandoned common sense.

Watching as he interacted with the waiter who'd come to clear their appetizer plates, bring Woody's red wine, and serve their entrées, she reminded herself she was with Woody only for business reasons.

Not temptation. Not orgasms.

She should have worn a business suit. The silky dress Viv had helped her pick out rode high on her thighs, thighs clad in panty hose that shimmered as if her skin had been dusted in gold. Her arms were bare, and she was aware that her V-neckline revealed a wedge of her upper chest, even a hint of cleavage. It was rare for her to bare so much skin, and that threw her off balance.

It was rare, too, to be in an elegant restaurant dining with a handsome man, feeling her body tingle and pulse with sexual awareness.

No, that last thing, the sexual awareness, wasn't just rare; it was unprecedented. Until she'd met Woody.

Once, he'd made her abandon not only her values but her common sense, and succumb to his wiles. Just like Lady Emma and the Comte. A second time, Georgia had been heading in that direction, but finally managed to pull back.

She wouldn't—couldn't—let it happen a third time. Though she hadn't had a chance to read more of the book, she was sure Emma would give in to the Frenchman's seduction. But Georgia wasn't Emma, and this wasn't fiction.

She had to make a success of the VitalSport campaign, and prove to her boss that he'd made the right choice when he picked her over her competition, Harry. Playing the role of puck bunny was *not* the way to do it, especially for a woman who believed that gender and sexuality didn't have a place on the job.

Not to mention that letting herself care for a man who didn't believe in marriage, much less even dating one woman at a time, would be purely stupid.

Eighteen

Woody finished dinner with a too-small yet delicious salad of exotic fruits and watched Georgia demolish something rich and chocolaty. The way she savored the chocolate and made soft moans of approval had him hard again.

Maybe there were good reasons for restricting their relationship to business, but hell, he was a guy. A horny guy, with a beautiful woman. "Feel like coming back to my place?" he suggested.

For a moment, he saw in her eyes the same naked hunger he felt; then she refocused on her dessert. "That's not a good idea."

God, she was frustrating. Tonight, she'd let herself look like the gorgeous, sexy woman she was. She'd shared with him, warmed to him, and he'd seen lust in her eyes. Yet she wouldn't let herself cross that damned line she'd mentioned. Didn't she know that the perfect dessert for tonight wasn't chocolate but sex?

He wished she'd had too much to drink, so he could have refused to let her drive home and taken her himself. He'd have turned off the engine, reached out for her in the darkness, and then he'd have been able to persuade her. She'd have invited him in, and once there, they'd have had slow, thorough, blistering sex. His hard cock throbbed as he indulged in that fantasy.

Then he came to his senses and realized she'd asked for and was paying the bill. Expensing it, he knew, because of course this was a business dinner. A dinner to train and test him.

That rankled, but he knew it was for his own good. Much as he hated revealing his inadequacies to Georgia, it'd be worse doing it in public, as the figurehead for VitalSport.

Georgia rose, draping that pretty fringed shawl around her even prettier shoulders.

He stood up too. The thought of his inadequacies had made his erection subside, so he didn't embarrass himself.

He rested his fingers on her lower back as they walked through the half-empty restaurant to the exit, and she let him. But once they were out on the sidewalk, she stepped away.

Turning to face him, she said in a rush, "That went very well. Congratulations, Woody. And good night." She looked up at him. "I really hope the next game goes well." A small laugh. "I suppose I should say, 'Bash 'em, Beavers.'"

"How about a good luck kiss?"

"I—" She was tempted. He saw it in her eyes, and in the way her body tilted toward his. Then she jerked back. "That wouldn't be wise."

Damn. "Are you parked in the hotel lot?"

"No." She waved a vague hand. "On the street."

Remembering her idea of directions, he hoped she'd be able to find her Toyota. And he hoped she'd fed the meter or there'd be another visit to the tow lot. "I'll walk you."

Her chin tilted up. "There's no need. I'm perfectly capable of getting to my car."

"Sure you are." He tried to sound like he really meant it. "But it's what a guy's supposed to do. It's proper *deportment*."

"I suppose it is. All right, if you insist." She headed down the street.

He sauntered beside her, not even commenting when she took a wrong turn and had to retrace her steps. Finally, she said with a note of triumph, "There it is. Thanks, Woody, and good night again."

"Night, Georgia."

She didn't offer him a ride. Because she assumed he'd driven, or she didn't trust him, or she didn't trust herself? Wondering about that, he turned and started to walk away.

An instinct made him look back, maybe to make sure she hadn't locked herself out of her car, or maybe just because he wanted one more look at her, all sexy and feminine. Somehow he knew that tomorrow she'd be back to a business suit and pulled-back hair.

What he saw brought adrenaline surging through his veins. He didn't stop to think. His body was in motion, pelting down the street toward her.

Frozen in a streetlamp's spotlight, Georgia cringed away from a man in dark clothing and a hoodie. The man's posture screamed aggression, and something in his hand glinted silver. As the sound of Woody's sprinting feet brought the mugger swinging around, Woody saw it was a knife.

Woody's entire being focused on that knife, only a couple feet away from Georgia, and he kicked out, hard and fast, aiming for the mugger's forearm. He heard the unmistakable crack of shattering bone. A howl split the night, almost drowning out the sound of the knife clattering to the pavement.

Woody needed that guy on the ground, out of commission, so he smashed his fist into his solar plexus, putting all his body weight behind the blow, and the man crumpled.

Woody drew a breath, the first he was aware of since he'd seen the mugger. He turned toward Georgia. "You okay?"

Out of nowhere, a body smashed into him, his bad shoulder taking the brunt of the attack. Caught off guard, his reaction was a moment slow, and in that moment a fist exploded into his face and he went down. Ignoring the pain in his shoulder, the gush of blood from his nose, he leaped to his feet, on the ready.

He didn't see a knife this time. But what if there was a third, even a fourth man? He had to deal with this asshole quickly.

When the second guy rushed him again, Woody dealt him one-two body blows, cracking ribs and punching him in the gut until he buckled to the ground.

Pumped, flying, Woody spun, doing a full circle, ready to take on any other attackers that materialized out of the night. But no one else came.

Relaxing a little, barely breaking a sweat, he took a quick inventory. Georgia was huddled against her car, her arms wrapped around herself, trembling and gasping, but he was sure neither man had hurt her. The muggers were out of the game, both curled up on the ground, moaning.

Yeah, he'd given them what they deserved. Woody smiled grimly.

He went over to Georgia. "You okay?" he asked again, his voice coming out nasal and choked.

She stared at him, wide-eyed. "Yes, they never touched me. Oh my God, you're bleeding."

Nasty throbbing behind his left eye and in his nose led him to probe gingerly. His nose, though gushing like a fountain, wasn't broken again, thank God. "I'm okay." He bent his head forward, pinching his nostrils, and heard the wail of sirens.

She fumbled a tissue out of her purse and began poking at his face. "Put your head back to stop the bleeding."

He batted her hand away. "I know how to look after a nosebleed."

Sirens whooped, stopped, and the police were there, rescuing him from her attentions.

When statements had been taken, the two attackers cuffed and dragged away, and the cops had wished him good luck in the game tomorrow night, Woody and Georgia stood alone by her car. His nose had stopped bleeding and he'd mopped most of the blood off his face with her tissues; then she'd fussed around, cleaning up the rest. His left eye was half swollen shut. Adrenaline was still a faint sizzle in his veins, taking the edge off the pain.

"We've got to get you to emergency, like the police said," Georgia said.

"Nah, nothing's broken. I'll be okay."

"But what if you have a concussion?"

He snorted. "I didn't hit my head."

"But that man hit you pretty hard. Maybe you've got whiplash or something."

Offended, he said, "He didn't hit me that hard. And he only got me at all because I didn't see him coming."

She nibbled her lip. "At least let me drive you home and make sure you're okay. There might be some kind of delayed reaction."

Her concern was sweet, but she was treating him like a wimp. "You don't know anything about injuries, do you?"

"Enough to know a person shouldn't be left alone if they haven't been checked out by a doctor." Her face was pale, her eyes huge and strained, yet he read determination in them. She might try to come across starchy and professional, but at heart she was a nurturer.

She was also sexy and beautiful. Even though the adrenaline was wearing off and Woody was feeling far less than 100 percent, he was still a guy. And it dawned on him that Georgia'd given him an opening. "Okay, Coach. I surrender. If taking on two muggers is what it takes to get you to go home with me, then it's a price I'll pay."

Her lips twitched. "I said I'd drive you. I didn't say I was coming in."

"What if I pass out in the elevator? Loss of blood makes a guy faint."

"I think you really must be concussed," she returned. "Or else you'd never admit you might faint."

He lifted a hand to his head. "Man, maybe you're right. I went down hard and all I was thinking was that I had to get back up and get that guy before he attacked you. Maybe I did hurt my head." It was all true except for that last bit, and yeah, he was being manipulative, but he didn't give a damn.

"Then you're going to the hospital," she said firmly.

He shook his head, and didn't have to fake a wince. "They'd just send me home and say I shouldn't be alone. I know about concussions. Someone needs to check on you every couple of hours, make sure you're not disoriented. Be there if you do pass out and don't wake up, so they can call an ambulance."

"I can do that," she said, eyes huge and serious.

Woody didn't feel the least bit guilty.

Nineteen

Georgia was so upset that she could barely force herself to get behind the wheel of her car and turn on the ignition. She glanced at Woody, who'd lowered himself slowly to the passenger seat, buckled up, then put his head back and closed his eyes. He must be in serious pain to admit that he needed help.

She gritted her teeth and pulled away from the curb. The man had saved her from two muggers. The least she could do was get him home safely. "Woody? Where's your place?"

"Yaletown." Not opening his eyes, he gave directions.

Though her hands—her entire body—wanted to tremble, she forced herself to focus entirely on driving and following his instructions. One thing at a time. Get to his building.

She pulled up at the security gate to an underground parking lot. "We're here. How do we get in?"

He opened his eyes, pulled a key ring out of his pocket, and pressed a button on a fob.

The gate lifted and she drove in and parked in a guest spot.

Inside the elevator, he hit the button for the thirtieth—and top—floor. "Thanks for doing this." He glanced at her, then away again, looking uncomfortable.

Her heart softened. Poor Mr. Tough Guy, hating to admit weakness. Little did he know, she was flattered that he would reveal his vulnerability to her and ask for her help. It made him even more appealing. And, though she was still traumatized by the attack, she would be there for him the way he'd been there for her.

He sure looked the worse for wear, his hair messed up, that lovely jersey stained with blood and dirt. His nose had begun to swell, his left eye was puffing, and a bruise was coming up. He looked like a total bad boy, which shouldn't appeal to a woman like her and yet it did. In a very sexual way.

How could she think about sex at a time like this, when she could have been seriously hurt and when Woody was injured and in pain—and all because she'd been silly enough to park her car on the street rather than in the hotel's nice, safe underground lot?

On the thirtieth floor, she realized there were only four apartments. Penthouse apartments, it dawned on her.

When he unlocked the door and she stepped inside, the windows drew her. Such an incredible view. She oriented herself, realizing his apartment was on the northeast corner. The living room windows showcased downtown Vancouver, Coal Harbour, and False Creek. Scattered across the dark nightscape was the yellow gleam of dozens of lit-up windows. But the darkness reminded her of the street, of the man who'd come out of the shadows, light glinting off the blade of his knife.

Shivering, she hugged her arms around her body and turned her back to the windows.

The room was filled with relatively masculine furniture, heavy on the leather, a large TV, a sound system, and a few large paintings of winter landscapes featuring frozen lakes.

Subconsciously, she'd expected a small, messy, bachelor pad. Woody didn't act like the typical rich person, and she'd almost forgotten about the money he earned. "What a lovely place."

"Thanks. I like lots of space." He caught the hem of his caramel-colored jersey in both hands and peeled the shirt upward.

Unable to look away, Georgia tracked its progress as it cleared his lean waist, rose up his six-pack, and revealed the lower curves of his pecs. The sight of blood matting the dark curls of chest hair brought her back to reality, and she hugged her body more tightly, wishing she was wearing a heavy sweater rather than a flimsy shawl.

When his face emerged from the crumpled fabric, lines of pain bracketed his mouth. "I need a shower. Get yourself a drink; put on some music."

"All right."

As he walked from the room, his movements were slower and less fluid than usual. Her fault. This was all her fault. Yes, she could use a drink. A double shot of something strong, something that might warm her frozen body.

A couple of minutes later, she heard the distant thrum of a shower. She imagined Woody, naked and sleek under the spray. His golden-brown skin wet, drops of water tracking down the center of his body.

She shouldn't be thinking of him this way. The man was hurt, and he'd quite possibly saved her life.

A long, cold shiver rippled through her body. Alone for the first time, she relived those moments by her car. She'd been utterly terrified, facing that mugger with the knife. She couldn't even draw a breath and call out for help.

But Woody'd known, somehow. He'd been there. If he hadn't—

No, she couldn't think about that.

She hurried to the kitchen, all silver and black, and checked the freezer to make sure he had an ice pack. In fact, there were assorted ice packs and a bunch of ice cubes. No chocolate ice cream, like in her freezer, just some frozen veggies, a steak, and a couple of packages of chicken breasts.

Clutching her shawl around her shoulders, she opened the fridge door, then didn't know why she'd done it. She stared at a carton of milk, juice, electrolyte drinks, eggs, multigrain bread, loads of fruit and vegetables, and a bottle of champagne. Champagne? Not, likely, for drinking on his own. That was probably his "date night" drink.

How many women had he brought to this penthouse, fed champagne, and taken to bed?

And why should that thought give her a pang of jealousy? If she wanted sex with Woody, she could have it. He'd made that pretty damned clear. And it would be utterly meaningless to him, not even a blip on his radar. It wouldn't be a distraction, and he wouldn't care if it was unprofessional.

No, she didn't want to be one in a long string of notches on his hockey stick. Maybe instead they could be friends.

She opened a couple of cupboards at random, finding a half dozen bottles of alcohol, and chose brandy. She didn't care for it, but it would warm her. She poured a couple of ounces into a glass and took a hefty slug, grimacing as the fiery taste nipped at her mouth and throat, then burned a path through her body.

Back in the living room, it was impossible not to glance out the windows. The landscape was glittery and golden, but there were dark spots too. Dark places where danger lurked. The kind of danger she'd faced less than an hour ago.

She wished Woody would hurry up. She didn't like being alone.

She took another drink and headed over to the sound system. Music, she needed music. Something with vocals, words that would fill up her mind so she couldn't think about what had happened. Couldn't remember how terrified and helpless she'd felt. If she let herself think about that, she might fall apart. She could feel it inside her despite the alcohol—a trembling tension that told her she was close to the breaking point.

Georgia drew a ragged breath and determinedly studied the array of black boxes and silver dials. Woody's system looked more complicated than the instrument panel for a jet, not that she'd ever seen one. "I can work this out," she muttered, and concentrated on the task.

"You figure out how to work that thing?" Woody's voice, coming from behind her, made her start. Her finger inadvertently jabbed a button, and the haunting notes of a saxophone poured into the room. He must've had a CD in the player.

"I guess so." She turned to face him.

Oh, my. He wore a terry-cloth bathrobe in a rich shade of royal blue a little darker than his eyes. The fabric was thick and bunchy, and even though it hid much of his body he still looked impossibly sexy. Maybe it was the damp, uncombed hair, or the vee of brown chest, or the well-shaped calves on display below the knee-length robe.

Was he naked under there?

That sax music was sexy and suggestive. It made her think of untying that loosely knotted belt, peeling back the sides of his robe, and all sorts of other things she had no business thinking. "What's that CD?" she blurted.

"Not sure. Haven't had music on for a while."

Dragging her gaze off him, she opened the cabinet and found an empty CD case on top of a stack. "*Sax for Lovers*. To go along with the champagne, and set the mood for seduction." She should replace the record with something less sultry, but she liked it.

"You got it." He walked to the kitchen, returned with a couple of ice packs, and sank into an armchair.

"How do you feel?"

"I've felt a hell of a lot worse." A flicker of pain creased his forehead. "Got a doozy of a headache coming on. Better take something before it gets worse."

He made as if to get up and Georgia said, "No, I'll get it. Tell me what, and where."

"Thanks."

On his instructions, she walked down the hall, past a room that, as she glanced through the door, seemed to be full of hockey trophies and pictures, and into a plainly furnished bedroom. Seeing the huge bed, she tried not to think about how many women he'd pleasured there.

The en suite bathroom was done in terra-cotta tile, and featured a huge whirlpool tub. The steam from his shower had dissipated but there was still a moist, warm quality to the air. Balmy, tropical. And a tangy herbal scent from his soap or shampoo.

His discarded clothes lay in a heap on the floor and a thick navy bath sheet hung crookedly on a towel rack. Georgia touched it, felt its dampness, thought of it rubbing Woody's body. All over. Reluctantly, she drew her fingers away.

He had told her to look in the cabinet by the sink. She saw all manner of liniments and bandages as well as the usual supplies: spare soap, toilet paper, toothpaste, toothbrushes. A large box of condoms.

Another reminder of the kind of man he was. A man who, even though he might be a surprisingly pleasant dinner companion, was the polar opposite of her beloved Anthony when it came to his views on sex and love.

She located the correct bottle, filled a glass with water, and returned to the living room.

Woody lifted an ice pack from his face. "Get lost in there?"

"I couldn't find the right pills."

"Sure." He took the medicine and handed the glass back to her. "It's okay; it's human nature."

"What?"

"Snooping."

"I wasn't."

"Yeah, you were." He shrugged, and winced. "If I ask you to do something, will you keep quiet about it?"

What now? "Uh, I guess that depends what it is."

He held out the second ice pack he'd brought from the kitchen. "Help me get into this thing."

When she took it, she realized it wasn't a pack, but a shoulder wrap.

"If you say anything to anyone about this, I'll have to kill you." The words were joking, but she heard the seriousness behind them.

"It's our secret," she said as she helped him strap it around his left shoulder. "How bad is it?"

"Nothing major. Dislocated it a while back and it keeps getting smashed again. Can't seem to get it healed. It was doing great until that mugger tackled me."

"I'm sorry. It was all my fault."

He eyed her. "You gotta be careful, Georgia."

"I know." She went over to the couch and perched on the edge, clasping her hands in her lap. When she stared down at them, she noticed flecks of dried blood on her fingers, from where she'd helped Woody clean up from his nosebleed.

No, she couldn't think about that, or she'd have a meltdown. She could feel it inside, hovering. She wouldn't break down in front of Woody. He'd been through enough tonight.

She shifted restlessly on the couch and something rustled under the couch cushion. She slid her hand down the crack, located the something, and pulled it out. A condom. "I should have known." Familiarity had brought a degree of composure, and this time she didn't drop the little package. "You really are prepared for female visitors, aren't you?" she teased, stuffing it back where she'd found it. Leaving it out might only give him—or her—ideas.

"Guy's got to be prepared for the best," he joked back.

She shook her head tolerantly. "You may have the morals of an alley cat, but at least you're smart enough to use protection."

He threw his chest out in that blustery way characteristic of the male of virtually any species. "I've never had unprotected sex in my life," he said proudly.

"You've never had sex without a condom?" she asked in disbelief.

"Never. I'm not going to take any unnecessary risks."

She stared wide-eyed. "You'll go up against two muggers in an alley, but you won't make love to a woman without a condom?"

He shifted in his chair. "Right."

"But . . ." No, she really shouldn't have this conversation with him.

"But what? I can't believe a smart woman like you believes in unprotected sex."

"No, not when it's, uh, casual sex." Which, of course, was all he ever had. "Yes, all right, I get it. You're right. It's just that when you love someone, when you're in a committed relationship, you don't want anything between you."

He cocked his head. "It'd take a lot to trust someone that much."

With Anthony, she'd never had a moment's doubt. "When you find someone special, your soul mate, it's different," she said softly. "There's love, trust, intimacy, and the lovemaking is amazing." That feeling of joining together, becoming one, had been . . . "Transcendent," she murmured.

Woody shifted position, and winced.

She came back to earth, and remembered something else. While the lovemaking had been transcendent, it hadn't been orgasmic. Only this man, this self-proclaimed tough guy, had brought her to climax. It made no sense at all.

"You should go home, Georgia," he said, his voice sounding tired and flat. "I'm fine, honest."

"You're concussed."

"No, I'm not."

Uh-oh. "You're acting disoriented," she pointed out. "Earlier, you said you might have a concussion, and now you say you don't. That's one of the symptoms, right? Disorientation?"

"I didn't hit my head when I fell. Just go."

Men didn't like having you around when they were sick. If Woody was feeling worse, that was all the more reason she shouldn't leave. "You said it all happened so quickly you didn't remember the details."

Nor did she. It had been like something out of an action movie, except it had been real. The knife; her panic. Woody suddenly being there, kicking and punching. The sickening sound of bone breaking. Nausea surged in her stomach and she fought it down.

"Did you have to hurt them so badly?" Her voice sounded accusatory, which was unfair, but it had all been so terrible, including the sight of those two men writhing on the ground.

Woody gazed at her from the eye that wasn't covered by the ice pack. "Guess I don't know my own strength."

"Oh, come on! After playing hockey all your life?"

"Georgia, I'm not a violent guy." He lowered the ice pack and frowned at her.

Not like his father, he meant. And yet, having seen him lay into those muggers, and seeing the way he threw his body at other players on the ice, she found herself wondering. She slugged down some more brandy, hoping the burn would quiet her nerves and settle her stomach.

Fiercely, he said, "I know how to gauge things. Hockey has rules, discipline."

"I guess so." She really wanted him to convince her.

"I don't react out of anger." He reapplied the ice pack to his face and sat back in the chair, crossing his legs, ankle over knee the way men do. The bathrobe split, revealing a portion of his thighs. "I don't use more force than necessary."

She was almost too focused on his words to ogle his thighs. Almost.

"I don't get off on beating up on someone," he said grimly. "Tonight . . ."

"That first guy had a knife and I had to disable him. When the second guy attacked, I didn't know how many more there were. I had to stop him, quickly, and be ready to take on someone else." He looked very male, an easy inhabitant of a physical world of strength and violence that was foreign to her.

Georgia's whole body trembled. She tried to control the quivering by sitting very straight, pressing her knees together, and clasping her hands tightly. "Were you afraid?"

"No. There wasn't time for that." He studied her. "Were *you* afraid?"

His words triggered the tension in her body. "Terrified!" She rose jerkily and moved away, trying not to glance out the floor-to-ceiling window that looked out over False Creek. "I've never had anyone threaten me. I've never been hit; my mom never even spanked me." A shrill edge of hysteria had crept into her voice and her muscles twitched as she relived her panic.

She turned to face Woody. The whole room was between them.

He took the ice pack from his face and put it down, then rose and came to stand in front of her. Gently he said, "It's okay, Georgia. Nothing happened."

"But it did." She raised a shaking hand to touch his swollen nose. The shawl slid off her shoulders to the floor, but she didn't pick it up.

"It did!" She said it again, her voice breaking. Her whole body shuddered violently as she reexperienced the terror.

Quickly, Woody put his arms around her and tugged her to him. Not tight, but warm, gentle, and comforting. That gentleness was her undoing, or maybe it was the ice wrap on his shoulder, a silent reminder of what they'd been through. Tears choked the back of her throat.

A sob burst out, and then she was crying in earnest.

He didn't say anything. He just held her, resting his chin on the top of her head and stroking soothing circles on her back.

Finally, the tears slowed. She sniffled. "If you hadn't been there . . ."

"I was." His lips were on her hair.

She didn't step out of the circle of his arms, but pulled back to lift her head and look up at his battered face. "I've never felt so helpless. I hate the idea of being dependent on a man."

"You're right. Women should be independent."

Why did that surprise her? She knew he wasn't really a Neanderthal. "Tell that to my mom," she said ruefully.

"Or mine." His voice was chilly.

An abusive father? A dependent mom who wouldn't leave him? Was that the truth of Woody's childhood? Did she dare ask?

"Here's what you need to do," Woody said firmly. "It'll give you power and confidence."

"That sounds good."

"Take self-defense lessons."

"I'm not the most athletic person in the world," she said doubtfully.

"You'll do fine." He sounded as if he believed it.

Maybe she could believe it too. "I'll look into it. If I research some places, could you help me pick the best one?"

"Glad to. I want you to be safe."

He could be so sweet. She couldn't stop herself from resting her head against his chest again. His bathrobe had shifted and now her cheek touched his bare skin, felt the tickle of crisp curls of hair. Was it horrible of her to enjoy this, to want more of it? To need this closeness and, yes, to feel aroused? It had been a unique night and her emotions were on overload.

He was injured, in pain, and yet he was being so nice to her. She smelled his warm maleness, and the scent was heady. Did he feel her breath against his body?

His chest rose and fell more rapidly.

She moved closer, snuggled tighter against him—and realized he was indeed naked under the bathrobe. Naked, and erect.

Twenty

Woody rested his chin on the top of Georgia's head. She fit perfectly in his arms. He liked it that this strong woman, so determined to be independent, felt safe with him. That he could protect her and she'd let him comfort her and offer advice.

He liked her curves too, which were much more accessible in that silky dress than in her normal suits. And the vanilla scent of her, both innocent and sexy. She smelled edible and he wanted to taste her.

Her breath, her tumbled hair, were soft caresses against his skin. Her shoulders and back felt delicate and feminine under his arms.

His body ached. His nose throbbed, his swollen eye burned, and his shoulder felt like someone had tried to wrench it off. But, overpowering those pains was the achy tightness in his groin, the driving need to have sex with her.

Sex. With a condom. Not lovemaking. Not that soul mate intimacy she'd spoken of, that made her face glow. That she found so damned *transcendent*.

He was—almost always—a good lover. Women moaned, cried out with pleasure, told him he'd made them see stars. They wanted to do it again.

But not Georgia. And now maybe he got it. It wasn't just that he'd been a jerk that first time, losing control and thinking only of himself. She'd climaxed, but he hadn't taken her to that special place she'd been with her husband. Hell, how could he? He'd never been there. Hadn't realized such a place existed.

Georgia'd had better sex than he'd ever had. Her husband, that skinny, intellectual-looking dude, had given her that.

She gave one of those little female shimmies that wriggled her whole body tighter up against his, and let out a sigh.

When Woody had played the "maybe I have a concussion" game, his goal had been to get her here and convince her to have sex. She had to feel his hard-on, and she hadn't stepped away. So maybe she'd be amenable.

He'd never be her soul mate, never give her fucking *transcendent* sex. But who cared? He didn't want all that stuff like commitment and marriage. Marriage could turn out bad. Real bad, like with his parents. Even a steady relationship was tough for a hockey player, with the guy on the road half the time and his girlfriend at home. Lots of couples broke up.

Some didn't, though. And yeah, maybe he felt a little envious of the guys who had wives and kids cheering for them at home games.

Oh hell. He wasn't concussed, but that blow to his head must have rattled his brain. He was standing here, naked and hard under his bathrobe, holding a gorgeous woman in his arms. His little head was screaming for sex and his big head had gone all girly and romantic?

"Maybe I am a little disoriented." He stroked down her back and rested a hand on the sweet curve of her ass. "But there's one thing I'm sure of."

She eased back so she could look up at him, the motion thrusting her hips more firmly against his hard-on. "What's that?" Golden flecks glittered in her hazel eyes, and her cheeks, which had been ghost-white since the mugging, were finally pink.

"This." He bent and captured her lips, grateful that the mugger hadn't punched him in the mouth.

Her response was immediate, telling him she felt the same need he did. Her lips were so soft, so full, and when his tongue licked inside her mouth she tasted faintly of chocolate. He'd never been a big dessert guy, but he could get addicted to vanilla and chocolate, served up Georgia style.

Heat surged through him and his body strained to get closer to hers. He wanted to rip off the stupid ice wrap, his robe, her pretty dress. To get flesh to flesh.

Seeing her in that alley, some hopped-up loser pointing a knife at her— Hell, it had been one of the worst moments of his life.

But she was here. Safe, warm, and responsive in his arms.

Or, no, maybe she wasn't. She broke the kiss, her hands coming between them to push against his chest.

Damn it, what now?

"Woody, we can't." Her breath came fast; her eyes were golden. "You're injured. You should go to bed."

That wasn't a "no." Not a real "no." He didn't let go of her. "Yeah, I should. And you should come with me. You can play nurse. Tend to my aches. All of them." He pumped his hips so his erection thrust against her belly.

"You need rest."

"What I need is you."

"But it would hurt too much." Her finger traced the edge of the shoulder wrap. "Wouldn't it?"

The wistful edge to her question made him grin. "I'm not gonna be feeling any pain when I'm inside you, Georgia." It was a lie, but he was used to pain—had been since he was a little kid—and the sex would be worth it.

"But if you have a concussion . . ."

"I don't. I lied. Sorry, but I wanted to be with you."

"You wanted to be with me?" She didn't sound mad, thank heavens.

"Yeah." And now, he realized, it had gone beyond *wanting* sex with her. He needed it. Maybe it was some primitive male instinct: he'd fought for her, and she was his prize. But it felt more like he needed to reassure himself that she was okay. Or to show her she wasn't a victim, but a lovely woman who should be treasured.

Treasured? Man, his brain really was rattled.

She was staring up at him, her thoughts clear on her face. She was tempted, but not sure it was a good idea.

"For once," he said, "don't take things so seriously. Don't worry about work; don't worry that I'm not your soul mate. Give us tonight, Georgia. We deserve it." Then, before she could answer, he kissed her, letting his lips and tongue persuade her.

After the briefest moment, she responded hungrily, giving him his answer and fueling his own need.

He wanted her in his bed. Now. He'd have hoisted her and carried her, but his shoulder had taken enough punishment. Instead, he caught her hand and tugged her along to the bedroom.

The room was big, like the rest of his apartment, and his bed was king-sized. It faced a huge window, but he didn't bother pulling the blinds because no one could see in. He clicked on a lamp on the dresser that shed a dim, golden light.

When he opened the fastener on the ice wrap, Georgia helped him peel it off, and he tossed it on the carpeted floor.

She stood there, looking nervous and very beautiful. "Are you sure you should be doing this?"

"Totally." He hated that he wasn't 100 percent, and that he must look like a freak with his swollen eye and nose. But he'd do everything he could to make this good for her.

He kissed her gently, then tossed back the duvet, revealing a white Egyptian cotton sheet. He might look a wreck, but his sheets were classy. "Let's lie down together." Again he took her hand, and tugged her toward the bed. Careful of his shoulder, he lay on one side of the bed, leaving room for her on his good side.

She studied him for a long moment, a smile curving her lips; then she kicked off her shoes. A hint of mischief in her eyes, she reached under her dress. "Let me guess. You want me to take off my panty hose."

He chuckled at the reminder of the joke he'd played on her. "Good idea."

She peeled off the gold-dusted fabric slowly, not revealing anything more than a few inches of thigh, but making it a sexy striptease all the same.

Then she came to lie beside him. In the soft golden light, her eyes were a little swollen, a little pink, and the small amount of eye makeup she'd worn was smeared around them. She looked tired, vulnerable, and he wanted to take care of her even if it meant restraining the need that raged inside him.

Lying on his side, he twined a curl of hair around his finger, then leaned over to bury his lips in the flaming mass. "Such pretty hair." He kissed her forehead, trailed a finger down the side of her face, followed it with his tongue and lips. "And such a pretty face."

She shivered, shifted position, her muscles loosening and eyes closing.

His tongue tracked the curve of her earlobe and toyed with a small gold earring; then he closed his teeth around her lobe and nipped gently.

She made a wordless sound of approval and curved her neck, offering it to him.

He kissed it leisurely, trying to ignore the pain from his injuries and the ache in his loins. Trying to focus entirely on her pale, silky skin, the hint of vanilla that rose from her, the warm pulse of her blood.

His tongue circled the hollow at the base of her throat and he pressed a kiss there.

She sighed. "Woody, that's so nice. This isn't what I expected."

He needed her to know that he could be gentle. That he could be patient and thorough; he could appreciate a woman the way she deserved to be appreciated.

He tugged at her zipper. "Don't want that nice dress to get wrinkled."

A grin curved her lips but she didn't open her eyes. "Oh no, we couldn't have that." She lifted herself as he peeled the dress down, revealing her lovely body clad in a semi-sheer flesh-toned bra and skimpy panties.

He rose, stifling a groan of pain, and hung her dress carefully over the back of a chair.

He turned and saw her watching. "Thank you," she said.

"No problem." Or, at least, her thanks made it worth the pain. For a moment, he just gazed at her, taking in the sight of her spread out on his white sheet. "You're beautiful, Georgia."

She shook her head, as if denying it. "Take off your robe."

He slipped out of it and stood, naked.

"You're beautiful," she said. Then, with a twitch of her lips: "At least from the neck down."

He laughed softly and walked back to the bed. Kneeling on the carpet, he leaned over to kiss her mouth. And then he worked his way down, set on kissing every inch of her, even those spots that tended to get ignored.

Yes, he wanted her breasts, her pussy, beneath his lips, but he also wanted the inside of her arm, her pointy elbow, the delicate bones of her wrist.

The ache in his groin was ever-present as he licked, kissed, and savored her, but, like the pain in his shoulder, he banished it to a far recess of his awareness. Worshiping Georgia's body was all that mattered.

Time stood still. The night stood still. Nothing existed except the scents of vanilla and arousal, Georgia's soft sighs and moans, the tiny movements as she shifted to give him better access to every secret place.

He could do this forever, and never grow tired of it.

Her bra came off, and her nipples were ripe berries under his tongue, firm and succulent. He teased and sucked them until she cried out and ripples of release shook her body.

Oh yeah, he understood why men wrote poetry.

His lips tracked the smooth skin over her ribs, the curve of her waist, the hollow of her navel, the flare of her hip. He hooked his fingers in the sides of her tiny panties and peeled them down slowly, his mouth following: across her flat belly, down through the neat vee of red curls, and between her firm thighs to her sex.

She was moist and hot, sweet and tangy, fragrant with the scent of desire. He ran his tongue across her swollen skin, between her folds, and around her clit. When he slipped a finger inside her, then another, her hips twisted and she whimpered, "Oh, yes."

He pumped gently, swirling his tongue around and around her clit, then sucking it gently until her body clenched, shuddered, and she cried out as orgasm swept her.

When the tremors finally settled, she said weakly, "What are you doing to me?"

"Does it feel good?"

"Oh, God."

He smiled against her damp skin, and began to kiss his way down her thighs. Her knees didn't escape his attention, nor her shins. He'd never thought much about women's shins before, but Georgia's legs were beautiful all the way from her soft inner thighs to her slim ankles. To finish off, he kissed every toe.

When he rose, Woody realized how much his aching body had stiffened. In that moment, he felt middle-aged. Then he gazed down at the woman who was staring up at him with a dazed smile, and felt like a god.

Her gaze sharpened and focused on his erection, and her smile turned into a sexy grin. "I think you've waited long enough." She rolled on her side and opened his bedside drawer. "I'm guessing . . . Yes, there we go." She pulled out a condom package and ripped it open. "Come here."

He stood beside her as she sheathed him, the touch of her fingers sheer torture on a cock that was ready to burst.

She lay back and opened her arms, and he lowered himself to lie atop her as her legs came up to hug his hips and her arms circled his back and pulled him close. Their lips met, and as he kissed her deeply, passionately, his cock finally found its way home, slipping into the welcoming dampness of her channel. He groaned with sheer pleasure.

Then, still kissing her, he rolled the two of them so she was on top. This was a good night to put her in control. Besides, this position was easier on his shoulder.

She sat up slowly, straddling him, and began to slide up and down his shaft, tentatively at first but soon finding her rhythm.

It felt fantastic, and he fought the urge to pump his hips and drive himself harder, faster, into her. He rested his hands on her thighs and felt the muscles shift, watched the soft bob and sway of her breasts, saw how the lamplight turned her hair to flame.

Her eyes were closed and she looked inwardly focused, but then they opened and she stared at him wonderingly. Breathing fast, speaking between little gasps for air, she said, "This feels so good. I can't believe how sexy you make me feel."

"Damn, Georgia, you *are* sexy. You're incredible." He thrust once, hard, then stopped himself.

Her body tightened around him and she moved faster, swirling her hips, letting him know she was getting close.

He found her clit with his thumb and rubbed it gently, making her gasp. And then, though his body urged him to roll her, pin her down, drive into her, and claim her, he let her set the pace as she took them both higher, higher, and over the peak.

His groan of satisfaction was soul-deep.

Her cry was music.

Their bodies shuddered together for ages, then slowly she collapsed down on him. Now he did roll them, settling her while he got up to deal with the condom and turn off the light.

When he came back, he pulled the sheet over them and lay back, contented, tucking her into the curve of his good shoulder, her cheek against his chest.

A chest that was growing damp. Damn it, she was crying. "Georgia, what's wrong?"

Twenty-one

The concern in Woody's voice made Georgia realize tears were sliding down her cheeks onto his chest. "Nothing," she reassured him, snuggling into the curve of his arm and blinking back the tears. "It was wonderful. It's just that I'm really emotional tonight."

His hand tightened on her shoulder. "I know that was tough on you, what happened with the muggers. I kind of hoped you'd feel better after, you know, we . . ."

Startled, she gave a chuckle. "You're not saying this was pity sex?" No, she was sure that wasn't true. Though she wasn't the most experienced woman in the world when it came to sex, she knew she wasn't the only one who'd had a good time.

"Hell, no. Or maybe it was you pitying the poor beat-up hockey player."

Her cheek rested on curly hair over solid muscle; her arm stretched across six-pack abs. Even injured, he was too strong—and not just physically—to ever elicit pity. Concern, though. "How *are* you feeling? I haven't been a conscientious nurse." The sex, even though it hadn't been strenuous, must have hurt him.

"I'm okay."

"You're in pain," she guessed.

He stroked down her bare arm. "Pain's a way of life for a hockey player. For most serious athletes."

Were they all insane?

When she didn't respond, he said, "You don't get it. Think we're all crazy?"

She nodded. "Pretty much. Why would someone opt into a career like that? The money?"

"I admit the money's nice." A pause, then, a little grimly: "More than nice sometimes. Yeah, no one's complaining about making that kind of money, and some people are into the fame. But for most of us, it's because we've found something we do well, and we want to be the best we can at it."

"That's why you do it?"

"Yeah. It's the one thing I'm really good at, but it's also the first thing in life I loved, pure and simple, no strings or complications." She couldn't see his face, but his voice had that same shadow she'd seen a time or two in his eyes. If he'd loved his parents, it hadn't been pure and simple. Poor Woody.

"Why did you love hockey so much?"

"It's fast, hard, clean in its own way. Blades cutting ice; there's nothing like it. And hockey's a world of its own. First it was a frozen lake, just me and my buddy Sam. Then indoor rinks, training, teams, games. But it's all focused, right? You know the goal." He gave a short laugh. "Hell, think about that word. Our goal's to score a goal. Being a team, playing fair, playing well, making it happen."

"You make it sound simple and straightforward, but I know it's not." That was a lesson she'd only recently learned.

"It is and it isn't."

"So, you felt all of that, from the time you were a kid?"

"Yeah. Plus it got me out of the house. Gave me something good."

"You said things were rough at home," she said tentatively, hoping he'd expand. Hoping he'd trust her that much, in the intimate darkness.

"I don't talk about those days."

She shouldn't feel hurt. Probably the only reason tears came to her eyes again was the emotionality of the night. She blinked them away before they could fall onto his chest.

Voice rasping, he said, "At home, I was powerless. On the ice, I could control the puck."

Those few words told her a lot. She wanted to probe deeper, but instead said, "You must have been a phenom. You were drafted into the NHL when you were seventeen."

He gave a soft laugh, his chest moving under her cheek. "Nah. I had natural skill, but it was pretty raw and undeveloped. I was drafted but I wasn't first pick like Crosby. I went to Atlanta, a team that was near the bottom of the league in standings. But I had better coaching than I'd had before, and playing at that level was incredible. I learned a lot. Then the Beavers traded for me. They weren't doing well either, but we turned things around. It's a great team, and I've been here ever since."

She couldn't get the thought of his childhood out of her mind. Pressing a kiss to his warm skin, she said, "If you ever want to talk about your childhood, I'd really like to hear."

He stiffened, the body she was curled up against turning wooden. "Why?"

A good question. Why was it so important for her to know? "Because you need to tell someone, and because I want to know you better. I . . . I like you."

He'd asked her to stop being serious and to give them tonight. She'd agreed. But if he revealed his deepest secrets, she'd like him more, care about him more. That was dangerous. She shouldn't be begging him to do it.

He didn't respond, and she'd begun to think he wasn't going to when he said, "You can't use any of it in the campaign."

That hadn't occurred to her, but now she reflected that her boss, Billy, would love an inside scoop to draw more attention to the campaign. "If there's anything that might be useful, I'd ask you first," she assured Woody.

"No," he said flatly. "Nothing. Period."

He was trying to tie her hands when it came to doing her job effectively. Yet it was his choice whether to reveal personal secrets, and he was doing it as a friend, not a business colleague. He was doing it naked in bed with her, after making slow, sweet love to her. "You're right. It's just between us."

He shifted position, moving away but only so he could turn on his side and study her face in the dim light from the big window. He frowned, not an angry frown but a puzzled one. "Why would I want to tell you this shit?"

She gave him a tentative smile. "Because we're becoming friends?"

"Yeah." He gripped her hand, where it lay on the sheet between their bodies.

Warmth coursed through her. She wove her fingers through his. "Tell me. Trust me."

"I'm not big on trust," he said gruffly. "Not after what my agent did, and Angela going to the tabloids with those lies."

She guessed his trust issues went back to his childhood, and squeezed his hand. "You can trust me. I promise."

He gazed at their clasped hands and, in a voice so low she could barely hear, said, "My father was an alcoholic with a violent temper. He took it out on my mom."

"And on you?" she asked quietly, aching for him.

He shrugged, which she knew was a "yes." "You never knew what to expect. Sometimes he didn't come home. Those were the good days. Once in a while he was nice, but he'd change in a second. We'd be eating dinner, everything calm, Mom and I quiet so we wouldn't say anything to set him off. Then next thing you know, he'd grab Mom's casserole dish off the center of the table and heave it against a wall. Then he'd yank her up, ready to pound on her, and she'd run out of the room."

Georgia shivered. "To get away from him."

He shook his head. "To get him out of the room. So he wouldn't hit me, and I wouldn't see him hit her."

She imagined a little boy eating dinner quickly, warily keeping an eye on his dad. And then the rest of it playing out until Woody was alone there, knowing—maybe even hearing—his father beating his mom. "You must have felt so powerless."

A shudder moved through him. "Even when I was tiny, I'd try to stop him. She wouldn't let me. Even slapped me once. It's the only time she ever hit me. She always said it was our fault. That I hadn't done my chores. That she'd burned the meat, not cooked the vegetables long enough. Worn a dress he didn't like, forgotten to buy ketchup."

"I know women often feel that way when they're in an abusive relationship." No one on the outside had the right to judge, and yet it was hard not to. His mom should have taken Woody away. Even if she was too weak to protect herself, she should have protected him.

"Yeah, I guess. And she said marriage was forever, so she'd never leave."

"Marriage should be forever, but not when it's like that," Georgia said vehemently.

He shrugged. "Alls I know is, I'd get out of the house whenever I could. On the ice, things were good."

He'd said "alls," slipping back into patterns of speech he'd learned as a child. She squeezed his hand again. "No wonder hockey means so much to you."

"It's my life."

He truly loved the sport, and it had meant survival as a child, his ticket out of a horrible situation, a career where he could use his skills and be respected.

And no wonder he didn't want to get serious about a woman. With his parents as role models, how could he believe that love and commitment could be the most powerful positive forces in a person's life, and that marriage could be heaven rather than hell?

He yawned, a movement that rippled through his torso and made him wince.

Feeling sorry for the boy he'd been and respecting the man he'd become, she murmured, "You need sleep."

"You're right. There's a game tomorrow night." He shifted to glance at the clock by the bed. "Tonight. It's past midnight."

"You're really going to play?" Then she amended, "Of course you are."

"Bet on it." He stretched out on his back again, and gathered her against him. "This is the critical game. We lose this one, we're out. I'm gonna be so in the zone, those Ducks won't know what hit them."

She hated to think of him playing injured, but from what he said, it wasn't unusual. So she tried to give him what he needed. "If I were a betting woman, I'd bet on you." She'd watch on TV, fingers crossed. She wanted that win, partly for the success of the marketing campaign, but mostly for Woody.

He yawned again, jaw-crackingly, and his arm grew heavy on her shoulders.

She should be tired too, but she wasn't in the least.

When his breathing became a slow, even beat, she thought how surprisingly comfortable this was, lying with Woody Hanrahan in his king-sized bed. They might never be soul mates, but they'd gone through a lot tonight. Yes, they'd ended the night as lovers, but more than that. They were friends.

It was a good feeling.

Knowing he needed his rest, and a clear, focused mind in the morning, she eased away from him and slipped out of bed. Quietly, she let the blinds down, marveling that she could stand naked in front of this big picture window with not a soul to see her. Then she took her clothing into the living room, dressed, wrote a quick note, and headed down to the parking garage, which fortunately was well lit and secure.

It was a short drive home, where Kit-Kat, no doubt unamused she'd stayed out so late, didn't greet her. But when Georgia found her cat curled up on a pillow, and stroked her, Kit sniffed her hand, then arched into it approvingly.

"Yes, I was with him," Georgia said. "And I let him tickle my tummy. Bet you're jealous."

In fact, the memory of Woody's touch on her skin was something she didn't want to wash away, so rather than shower she just pulled on a sleep camisole and drawstring-waist cotton pants, and got ready for bed.

Settled with two pillows behind her back and still not tired, she picked up her e-reader. Where had she been? Oh yes, Lady Emma had had sex with the Comte once, and had been pacing her bedchamber wondering whether those orgasms were the only ones she'd ever know.

"Let me guess," Georgia said. "You'll give in to temptation the way I did."

Maybe she should regret that decision. Perhaps tomorrow she would. But she doubted it. Tonight, being with Woody had felt right.

Doing it again, though . . . It wasn't professional. Dynamic Marketing didn't have a rule against it, but Georgia believed in separating her business and personal lives, and she didn't imagine her boss would be impressed by her behavior.

More than that, it surely wouldn't be wise. Nothing could ever come of it.

Except orgasms, of course.

Just how shallow was she? She, the woman who'd believed in celibacy until marriage.

Sighing, she escaped into Lady Emma's world.

The next morning, Emma took breakfast in her room, but knew she could not stay sequestered for the remainder of her visit. Venturing forth, she avoided the library, where the Comte might seek her out, and instead found herself in the music room.

Music had always given her solace, and especially when she put her fingers to the bow. She had not brought her violin with her, but Margaret played and had invited Emma to borrow her instrument.

Now, trying not to feel like an intruder, Emma riffled through Margaret's sheet music. Choosing a lively piece to lift her spirits, she drew her friend's violin from its case and stroked the burnished yellow-amber wood with reverence. It was a Guarneri, an instrument her friend assured her would one day be more famous than those created by Stradivarius. Whether or not Margaret's prediction would prove true, this was a far finer instrument than Emma had ever touched. She stroked it again. Odd, how she'd never before noticed what a feminine shape a violin had, with its lush curves and nipped-in waist.

When she tucked the base of the violin between her chin and shoulder, it felt surprisingly comfortable. Experimentally, she drew the bow across the strings, enjoying the resonance of the tone. As she warmed up, her soul was soothed. Almost, she could forget that the wanton interlude with the Comte had ever happened.

She launched into the spirited piece she had selected. At least to her own ears, she had never played so well.

When she came to the end of the number, a male voice called, "Brava!" and she heard clapping.

Startled, she turned to see le Comte de Vergennes, as darkly

*handsome and dashing as always, regarding her from the doorway.
He stepped inside, closing the door behind him.*

*Her entire body heated, from the tips of her toes to the roots of her
hair. Unbidden, her hand flew to her throat.*

"You permit me to join you, Lady Emma?"

*"I . . ." Shouldn't. Couldn't. She had let this man take the most
outrageous liberties with her body. Worse—or better?—she had enjoyed it.*

If she said no, would he truly leave her in peace?

Did she want to be left in peace?

*As he approached, her heart fluttered so wildly she could barely
think. His black hair gleamed. Had she really run her fingers
through it? His sensual lips widened in a smile. Had those lips really
touched— No, she could not even think it.*

*And yet . . . In scant months, she'd be forced to decide between
two forms of servitude: as wife to an older man chosen by her father,
or as caretaker to her brother's family. Was it utterly wrong to enjoy
a few moments of the Comte's attention?*

*She would draw a boundary today, though. If he even attempted
to touch her, much less kiss her, she would slap his face. Yes, she
would, and then she'd flee to safety.*

"A duet," he said.

"What?" No touch, not even an attempt to kiss her?

*"We will play a duet. Oui? I told you I play the piano, did
I not?"*

*Of course he had. He'd spoken of playing beautiful music to-
gether, and then he'd played her body like a maestro.*

*The seductive twinkle in his eye told her he knew exactly what
she was thinking, and was deliberately reminding her of it. Yet he
made not the slightest attempt to touch her.*

"I recall that," she said stiffly. Perhaps today he spoke only of

*music. After all, he'd taken what he wanted from her. Most proba-
bly, her naïveté had disappointed him, worldly man that he was.
And that was a good thing, of course. She would not have to fend off
unwanted advances—or debate with herself whether she wanted
those very advances.*

*"Let's see what we have." He helped himself to Margaret's music.
"How about this? It is a favorite of mine. I know it by heart."*

*She glanced at the music he held out. To her surprise, it was a
number she enjoyed herself. It reminded her of birds in flight. She
really should leave, and yet something held her there. The music.
Only the music. "One piece," she said, "and then I must go."*

*His lips curved and his dark, sparkling eyes held hers. "One
piece, in which to persuade you. You set a hard bargain, my lady."*

*To persuade her of what? But no, she would not ask. She would
not care. If it was something improper, she would indeed slap his face
and flee. In the meantime, she would focus entirely on the music.*

He seated himself at the piano with a showy flourish.

She put the violin in place, and lifted the bow.

*He held her gaze. "Here we go. One, two, three." His fingers de-
scended, as did her bow.*

*Rarely had she played duets, and it was invigorating, harmoniz-
ing with someone else, playing a note and hearing him answer, then
responding to him in turn.*

*The Comte's smile flashed bright and he threw his entire body
into his playing, as if the music filled him and swept him away.*

*In Emma's mind, birds swooped and soared, and she smiled and
let her body go with them.*

*This, right now, was quite perfect. If she could live in this mo-
ment forever, she would happily do so. But of course the music ended,
and with regret she lowered the bow and took the violin from its
spot under her chin.*

The Comte rested his hands on his knees. "What did you hear?"

"Birds," she confessed quietly. "Flying, swooping. Free and beautiful."

He nodded. "You were flying too. I saw it in the way your body moved. Beautiful, yes, and free."

She shook her head sadly. "Only for those short moments. I'm not the least bit free."

He rose and came toward her with that lithe grace of his.

Warily, she watched him approach, but all he did was reach out to take the violin and bow.

She placed them in his hands, careful not to actually touch him.

Rather than putting them down as she expected, he lifted them, one in each hand. "You can be free, Emma. You can choose to be free."

"You are not a woman—a widow—in this society," she said dryly, "or you would not say such a thing."

"You can have your moments, and not just when you lose yourself in the music."

He held up the violin. "She is lovely, yes? With her round curves, her glowing face. And here"—he raised the bow in his other hand—"when he touches her, he makes her sing. He makes her fly, takes her wherever she wants to go."

A bow was a rather male object, wasn't it? That thought had never before occurred to her. And it shouldn't now. It was a most improper thought, and it was improper of the Comte to talk this way.

She almost laughed. The Comte had, after all, done far more improper things.

Now he replaced the violin and bow in their case. "They will rest, and now it is your turn, dear Emma."

"My turn?" The words came out in a breathy whisper.

He knelt in front of her chair and finally—finally!—touched her.

Gently, he took her hand, raised it to his lips, and placed a kiss in the center of her palm. He didn't let go when he said, "You know what I mean. You know what I want. And you want it too."

"Wh-what?" she quavered. What she should want right now was to slap his face, but instead what she truly wanted was another kiss. This time on her lips.

"You are a bird who's been tethered in a cage. You want to sing, to fly, to be truly a woman. To experience all the things I can teach you."

Again, he lifted her hand to his lips and this time, shocking her, he licked her palm. The wet, deliberate stroke of his tongue sent tingling heat racing through her, setting a pulse throbbing in the womanly place between her legs.

God save her, she did want everything he offered. "It would be wrong."

He licked again, and she gasped. "Not wrong," he countered. "You are a widow and I am unmarried. We are betraying no one."

"Society would condemn us. That may be of little concern to you, but it is a serious matter to me."

"Ah, the lady has a sharp tongue. Yes, it is quite true that I don't give a fig what society says of me. However, I assure you I am a most discreet man."

"Ha! Everyone knows about that married woman in France."

"Because of her husband, not because of me. He was the one to issue the challenge and expose the affair."

There was truth in that. And considerable temptation in the tongue that now ran up the side of one of her fingers, into the dip between it and the next one, and then up the other. Shocking herself, she imagined that tongue on her most private flesh.

"No one will be hurt," the Comte said, dark eyes gleaming, "and you and I will experience more pleasure than you can even imagine."

"Why me?" she asked. "There are younger, prettier girls. They clustered around you the other night."

"Youth is no particular virtue, and you are beautiful rather than pretty."

He really saw her that way?

"But it's more than that," he went on. "You heard the music that night, inside your body and your heart. They barely listened. Their minds are a tangle of their own concerns. They do not know how to still their minds, how to experience something meaningful."

Still clasping her hand, he gazed at her. "You and I together, that would be meaningful. Making beautiful music together is meaningful, as it was with the violin and piano. With our bodies, Emma, it will be something incredible."

She couldn't look away. Couldn't halt the quivering that had taken over her body, radiating out from that warm, needy place between her legs. A life of dull servitude awaited her. An opportunity such as this man offered would never again come her way. For a brief time, in this lovely country manor, assured of the utmost discretion, she could experience something that she had no doubt would be incredible.

"Lady Emma Whitehead," he said formally, but with a gleam in his eye, "will you do me the very great pleasure of letting me undertake your sexual education?"

What could she say but yes?

Georgia put the reader down. She'd wanted to lose herself in Emma's world, but instead the heroine's situation only reminded her of Woody. Tonight, the hockey player had indeed played her body as skillfully as any musician. Yes, she could understand the temptation to enjoy a sexual education at the hands of a maestro. But wasn't that awfully shallow? And risky?

She was curious to hear what the other members of the book

club thought about Emma's decision. Too bad Monday night was so far away.

Last week, Marielle had e-mailed midweek, so why couldn't Georgia do the same?

She climbed out of bed, to return with her laptop. Ignoring a few e-mails in her in-box, she typed a message to the book club members.

> We agreed, more or less, that there's something to be said for giving in to temptation and having sex with a guy who's really talented. But one time is way different than an affair. Don't you think?
>
> The Comte isn't going to marry Emma, and she's not feeling an emotional attachment to him, so isn't it kind of slutty to opt into the whole "sexual education" thing?

Georgia had never, until Woody, felt the slightest inclination to have casual sex. God, her husband wouldn't even recognize her now. She'd always believed that physical intimacy was special, that it should be shared with someone you loved and were committed to. She'd belonged to a chastity club, been a virgin on her wedding night, and only a week ago reflected on how easy it was to remain celibate. She'd been career-focused, professional, and determined never to bring gender, much less sex, into her work life.

What had happened to her? And where would it lead?

Twenty-two

Woody woke from a sound sleep to the jangle of his alarm clock. Rolling over to turn it off, the ache in his left shoulder was familiar, but the unexpected pain in his nose and behind his eye made him wince. Shit, who'd high-sticked him this time?

Then he remembered. The muggers. Georgia.

Despite the minor aches and pains, he felt damned good. She was one sexy woman. And if he was quick, there'd be time to prove it once more before they both went to work.

He rolled the other way, and frowned. No Georgia. No sound from the bathroom, no sound from anywhere. Damn. Morning-after regrets?

"That woman blows so hot and so cold," he muttered as he dragged himself out of bed.

He retrieved his bathrobe from the floor, pulled it on, and went to the kitchen for ice. "Why do I bother? Every time she lets me get close, she runs away. If I had half a brain, I'd give up on her."

On the kitchen counter, he found a note.

Woody, I know you'll need to focus today, so figured I should leave you alone. But thanks for everything. Talk about an unforgettable night!

Best of luck with the game. I know you'll be wonderful. Bash 'em, Beavers!

Georgia

He grinned so hard it hurt his battered nose. "You bet we will. And then I'm calling you, woman."

Georgia was tired and confused the next morning. A large part of her wished she'd woken in Woody's bed and they'd had sex. The other part of her was annoyed at herself for wishing that.

When she checked her e-mail at the office, she found messages from Marielle and Kim.

Marielle said,

It's not slutty to have sex, for heaven's sake! It's natural. Poor Emma's been all stifled and constricted, and the girl's overdue for getting her rocks off. Nobody's hurting anyone, making any promises that'll get broken, or any of that shit. Rock on, Lady Emma!

Kim was next.

I see the temptation, but I'm more about relationships. In real life, I mean. I'm happy to read about Emma's raunchy adventures. LOL. But for me, I want the whole package: sex, caring, and commitment.

"And so do I," Georgia murmured. But wishing didn't make it so. She typed,

I agree, Kim. But what if you can't find that whole package? Emma is convinced she won't. So is she wrong to take the part she can get? The sex?

Viv tapped on Georgia's office door and called a bright, "Good morning."

Georgia clicked Send. "Hi. Come on in."

The blonde, today in an orange and pink dress with a pink jacket, seated herself in a chair across from the desk and crossed her legs. "How'd dinner go? Did Woody behave himself?"

"Amazingly well. But, Viv, I have to tell you what happened after."

Viv grinned. "There was an after? You and Woody? Wow, I didn't see that coming."

"No! I mean . . . That's not what I meant." She tried not to flush. "Woody walked me to my car, and ended up beating up a couple of muggers. He probably saved my life."

"Oh my God!" Viv's eyes widened with concern. "Are you all right?"

"Yes. They didn't get near me, thanks to him. But, Viv, we can't do any photos this week. He has a swollen nose and a black eye."

She winced. "Ouch. Poor guy. We should make him wear that hockey shield outside of the rink too."

"He'd love that."

They both chuckled.

"Let's hope he heals quickly," Viv said. "That was it, just the nose and eye?"

"That was it." She'd promised Woody that his shoulder injury was their secret. "He'll be on the ice tonight. I sure hope they win."

"And go on to win the Stanley Cup. It'll give our campaign serious buzz."

"I know." And it would make Woody so happy.

Terry came to join them, and the three of them discussed strategy for an hour; then they split up to each get on with their jobs.

At noon, Georgia popped out to grab something to eat. She was

thinking of indulging in a chocolate crepe, but remembered what
Woody had said about respecting your body and instead chose a
chicken salad. When she opened the take-out container at her desk,
she read an e-mail from Lily.

> They're different things, ladies. Yes, lots of women want a
> committed relationship, that whole package where love and sex
> are wrapped up together. But if you're not in one—or don't want
> to be, like Marielle—there's nothing wrong with a rewarding sex
> life. Great sex—safe sex between mutually respectful adults—is
> good for you.

Georgia typed,

> Lily, what do you mean about great sex being good for you?

She'd taken only a couple of bites of her salad when Lily's answer
arrived.

> To name a few effects: exercise, boosts your immune system,
> reduces depression, increases self-confidence, puts you in closer
> touch with your body.

Hmm. Those were all excellent points. It seemed the doctor pre-
scribed casual sex.

Was Georgia going to fill that prescription with Woody?

Georgia had never imagined that she'd cheer at a hockey game,
but there she was in her living room, jumping up and down in
front of the TV yelling for the Beavers. For Woody.

He was having a fantastic night.

When he'd stood for the national anthem, helmet off, she'd been glad to see that the swelling in his nose and eye had gone down, though he sure had a shiner. Along with a look of utter focus and determination.

When the game got under way, she studied his movements carefully and didn't see a hint of him favoring his left shoulder—but he'd be on guard against letting the Ducks know if he was hurting.

She stopped worrying about him soon, though, because he was on fire. When his stick connected with the puck, he couldn't miss. He made a goal in the second minute of the game, then got a shot to a perfectly positioned teammate who tipped it into the goal seconds before the buzzer ended the first period. The Ducks hadn't scored.

The Anaheim team managed one in the second period, but so did one of Woody's teammates; then he got another one himself.

In the Coach's Corner feature during the second intermission, the outspoken sports commentator Don Cherry, tonight in a flamingo-pink suit so bright even Viv wouldn't have worn it, said, "I've been saying the Beavers' captain should hang up his blades, but tonight Hanrahan's reminding us why he's been called 'the Next One.'"

In the third period, the Ducks did their best to stop Woody, but he scored again and the announcer yelled something about a hat trick.

The game finished with the Beavers winning five to one, and the Vancouver fans on their feet, trying to cheer the roof off the stadium.

When Woody came off the ice, pulling off his helmet and face shield, an interviewer stuck a mike in his face. "Terrific game, Woody."

Woody flashed a smile of pure pleasure. "It felt good out there. The guys did a great job and the fans were really behind us."

Georgia smiled at how happy he looked and how sincere he sounded, though in her opinion he was the player who'd won the game.

"Looks like you guys got the Beaver magic back. Good luck in Anaheim on Friday."

"Thanks."

When Woody's face disappeared from the screen, she clicked off the TV, grinning from ear to ear. A hockey star. She'd slept with a hockey star.

And she was tired of second-guessing herself. She knew what she wanted, and it was him.

Time to admit that she was no longer the goody-goody girl from the chastity club. With Woody, she had fun. He might not be her soul mate, but he was a fantastic sex mate.

She wasn't going to overcomplicate the issue. On the job, she'd remain entirely professional. As for her personal life, she was choosing Lady Emma's path: a sexual education at the hands of a master.

Woody glanced around the locker room. The vibe was testosterone and adrenaline. The guys were on a total high as they high-fived one another, joked with reporters, and stripped off their gear. The losing streak was finally broken—and in the nick of time.

Thank God.

His teammates had played well tonight, but the truth was, they'd been doing that all along. It was Woody who'd made the difference. For the last three games, he'd played like crap. Tonight, it had all come back: the joy of the game, his instincts, his skill. He'd been in the zone from before he even skated onto the ice, and he'd never stepped out of it.

Who cared that his eye was still swollen enough that his vision wasn't great? He was even getting used to the face shield, and was grateful for it when he took a high stick that might've split his cheek and taken him out of the game long enough to get stitched up.

Who cared that the Ducks were on top of their game too, and determined to stop him? As for his shoulder, he hadn't even felt it.

Some of the guys were jumping around in a masculine version of a happy dance, but he'd save that one for when they took home the Stanley Cup.

Finally, the reporters had gone and the players had showered and changed into their suits. Now his shoulder hurt, confined by that tight fabric. He hoped Viv was right, and his new suits wouldn't feel like straitjackets.

"Woody?" It was Mats "The Hammer" Hammarstrom, their star defensive player.

"Yeah?" Woody saw that the players were gathering, with the coaches and the GM in the background looking curious.

"We change our luck tonight," Hammarstrom said. "This is good thing, but why?"

"Why?" Woody asked, not sure what the Swedish player meant.

"What made the difference?" Dmitri Federov, their Russian goaltender, clarified.

"You did an amazing job of blocking shots, Dmitri," Woody said. "The defense shut the Ducks down at every opportunity; everyone was in the right place at the right time." He drew a breath, then admitted, "And I finally extracted my head from my ass and started playing real hockey, like you guys deserve from me."

There was a moment of silence, likely in acknowledgment of the truth of that last statement. Then Philippe Bouchard, from Quebec, who played left wing in the first line to Woody's right wing, said, "*Non*, it's your hair and beard."

"'Scuse me?"

"Yeah, dude," Stu Connolly, a rookie who was so good he'd moved into the first line in his first season with the Beavers, chimed in with his Texas drawl. "You got that lucky trim, right?"

When Woody had shown up today, the guys had been on his

case. They'd cursed about his "pretty boy" hair and beard trim, saying it could cost them the Conference. Knowing that a lack of confidence would hurt them on the ice, he'd said, "Nah, it's gonna change my luck."

Now Bouchard announced, "I'm gonna get my hair cut and my beard trimmed."

"Me too," Stu said. "Where'd you get it done?"

A little stunned, Woody said, "His name's Christopher Slate. But—"

"Got his number?" Stu asked. "We're flying out tomorrow afternoon. Gotta get in first thing in the morning."

Suddenly, BlackBerrys and iPhones were in everyone's hands.

Woody glanced at the coaches and the GM, and caught them exchanging quiet words and grins.

Yeah, athletes were superstitious. Woody didn't know whether the real power was in the lucky charms and rituals like putting on your left skate first that mattered, or whether it was the confidence they gave the players. But if his teammates believed they'd play better if Christopher Slate trimmed their hair and beards, then they probably would. Besides, it might psych out the Ducks.

He pulled Christopher's card from his wallet. The stylist had written his cell number on it. "In case of a hair emergency," he'd said in all seriousness.

At the time, the phrase "hair emergency" hadn't computed. But Woody knew one when he saw one. "Let me call and see if he can fix you up. How many guys want—"

A clamor of "Me"s and "Yah"s cut him off.

Christopher didn't even laugh when Woody told him what they needed, and he set up appointments for every single guy.

"Now we go get a steak," The Hammer said with satisfaction.

"Lobster for me," the Texan rookie said.

"Woody, you are coming?" Federov asked.

"Yeah, in a minute." He was starving too, and celebrating the victory with the team was an important part of being captain. "Just have to make a call."

As the guys trooped out, Woody heard Connolly joke, "Setting up a booty call."

Yeah, or so he hoped. The guys might have their theory about lucky haircuts, but Woody had his own. Georgia was his luck. When she was huffy, he was so distracted he played poorly. When she was nice—especially when they had sex—he felt so great that he fell into that natural zone that made the game such a joy.

Could he persuade her to keep being nice to him?

He dialed her cell.

She answered on the second ring.

"Hey, Georgia."

"Woody! Congratulations!"

"You watched?"

"I even left work early so I'd catch all of it. You and the team looked terrific out there. It was like you couldn't set a foot—skate—wrong."

He smiled at her praise, and the enthusiasm in her voice. "Thanks. Guess what the team's doing?"

"Uh, going out to celebrate?"

"Well, that too. But tomorrow they've all got appointments with Christopher Slate."

She laughed. "Seriously?"

"Hey, when the luck's running your way, you need to go with the flow." Speaking of which. "I really liked being with you last night."

"Me too," she said softly.

"Missed you when I woke up, but thanks for that note."

"I wanted you to know I wasn't upset."

"When I saw you'd gone, I wondered. You've said that stuff about how we should keep our relationship to business." Now he had to make his best argument. "But, Georgia, I don't see why. It's good, being together. That's not going to get in the way of work. It'll make us a better team, rather than being all tense and fighting and stuff."

"Hmm. That's an interesting perspective." Was that humor in her voice?

"I really gotta have dinner with the team, and I know it's a work night for you, but tomorrow afternoon we're flying to Anaheim, so—"

She cut him off. "You want to come over after dinner?"

He'd take that as an invitation, not a question. "Love to." Thank God for five o'clock games. It wasn't even nine yet. "I'd be there between ten thirty and eleven. That okay?"

"Sure. I'll just entertain myself with a book until you get here." Now there was definitely laughter in her voice.

One of those boring book club books of hers? Damned if he understood why that was so funny, but he didn't care. She wanted to see him. That was the only thing that mattered.

Georgia hung up the phone, grinning ear to ear. The star of tonight's game wanted to be with her. Not some over-endowed puck bunny, but *her*.

She checked her watch. She had an hour and a half to get ready. First, she'd make a trip to the drugstore and buy ice packs. And, for the first time in her life, condoms. Should she get groceries? Would he stay the night? Did she want him to?

Yes, she did.

That was . . . weird. A little scary.

There was no time to worry about it. She needed to go shopping, then have a bath, shave her legs, and change into . . .

Sadly, she didn't have anything worth changing into. The one time in her life that she wanted to look sexy, and no lingerie stores were open.

Twenty-three

The best Georgia had been able to come up with, after scrutiniz-ing every item of clothing she owned, was her usual sleepwear of a cami—worn without a bra—and loose, drawstring-waist pants made of light cotton.

At least she didn't look as if she was trying too hard.

She tossed her hair, enjoying the way the loose waves tumbled around her face.

Hmm. The Beavers thought Woody's haircut had brought him luck. Maybe hers had too, or at least the confidence to believe in her own sexuality.

"Of course," she murmured to Kit-Kat, "I'm really just tending to my health. Dr. Lily said so."

Ready with time to spare, she pulled out her e-reader. The Comte was making love to Emma in front of the fire in her room.

Erotica, Georgia knew by now, had the power to arouse the reader. Tonight, the sensual passages combined with her memories of last night, the experience of watching Woody on TV as he domi-nated the ice, and the knowledge that he wanted her. By the time his knock sounded at the door, her nipples were hard and the crotch of her pajama pants was damp.

She opened the door to him, all big and strong in one of his ill-fitting suits, the knot of his tie loosened and a couple of shirt buttons undone. His face was less swollen than last night, but his black eye was more pronounced.

His gaze swept her, and his smile flashed. "Jesus, look at you. You're so damned hot."

"Hi, W—"

Her greeting got lost in the kiss he planted on her lips, a kiss that carried her back against the wall of her entranceway. A hot, minty kiss that zinged all the way through her body to curl her toes. A kiss that had her thrusting her tongue into his mouth, driving her fingers through his hair, and twining her body around him like he was a maypole and she was one of the colored streamers.

No, the *only* colored streamer, because he'd chosen *her*.

Heart racing, panting for breath, she broke the kiss. "Woody, you won! You were terrific. How do you feel?"

"Fucking fantastic." Pinning her against the wall, he kissed her again, his lips and tongue hungry and demanding. His erection thrust insistently against her belly. This wasn't last night's tender, considerate lover, but his touch was just as arousing.

Finally, his whole body taut, he pulled his mouth away from hers. "Not here, not like this." He, too, was gasping for breath. "You deserve better."

But she wanted him now, here, with this urgency. It was like that first time, when he'd taken her on the conference table—but better, so much better. They knew each other, liked each other; they were lovers rather than strangers. And, God knew, she was ready—so ready—for him.

"No." She stared into his eyes, the blue of a deep, deep ocean. "I want you now. Here. Exactly like this."

She went for the knot of his tie, loosening it further until, standing on tiptoe, she could pull the strip of fabric over his head.

He looked a little stunned, then said, "Hell, yeah!"

She tackled the buttons of his shirt, but before she could undo more than a couple, he thrust her down so her heels hit the floor with a thump.

"No," she protested, then realized he was whipping off his suit jacket.

His hands went for the buckle of his belt, and she renewed her attack on his shirt. Between them, they had him stripped in seconds flat, and he'd found a condom in his pocket and put it on.

She'd barely had a chance to admire his sculpted nudity, his impressive erection, when she was blinded by him tugging her cami over her head. As soon as it was gone, he yanked her pants down her hips.

Before she could step out of them, Woody hoisted her free of them. She clung tight, arms and legs around him as he braced her shoulders against the wall and reached down, his fingers stroking between her legs.

She was wet, so hungry for him that dampness tracked down her inner thighs.

Woody's fingers parted her folds, the head of his thick cock nudged between them, and she gasped at how delicious it felt.

She wanted, wanted, wanted this, exactly this. More than this. Gasping, she tilted her hips, urging him to thrust into her, to go deeper, to stroke every part of her that was crying out for attention.

Already aroused beyond belief, pure erotic pleasure built with each stroke, climbed, came together. When finally, finally, he jerked his hips harder and thrust deep into her core, she exploded with a cry.

Gaze fixed on her face, he kept pumping, his cock stroking every sensitive cell, prolonging her climax as she shuddered helplessly around him until his wrenching groan signaled his own release.

Panting, drained, her body sagged, but somehow Woody still managed to hold her up, sandwiching her between his heaving chest and the unyielding wall.

Eventually she recovered enough presence of mind to think about his shoulder. "Let me down," she gasped.

He lowered her, holding her steady until her trembling legs managed to take her weight. "Man, Georgia, that's not what I expected."

She tilted her head and looked up at him. "What did you expect?"

His eyes twinkled. "I think there was a bed in it."

"That could be arranged." He might not be self-conscious about nudity, but she was, so she bent to slip on her pajama pants and cami. "Would you like something to drink? Ice for your shoulder? How's it doing?"

"It's"—he stepped into his boxer briefs and pants, picked up his shirt—"okay. Better than last night. Didn't get any hits on it tonight." He pulled on the shirt but didn't button it. "Wouldn't say no to some ice, though. And a big glass of water."

"Sit down in the living room and I'll bring them to you."

"You don't need to wait on me."

"You worked hard tonight. You deserve it."

"And you deserve more than a back-against-the-wall fuck in the hallway." His eyes peered down into her own.

"That was exactly what I wanted," she assured him. "Later, though, for round two . . ."

He chuckled. "Whatever you want, soon as I get my second wind."

Smiling, she went to the kitchen.

When she walked into the living room a few minutes later with ice packs, his water, and a glass of red wine for herself, Woody was sprawled on her couch, feet up on the coffee table. A second later, he dropped his feet to the floor. "Sorry. Forgot."

"It's okay. Assuming those are clean socks," she teased.

His feet went back up. He took the ice pack and applied it to his shoulder, then accepted the glass of water and drank thirstily. When he put the glass down, almost empty, he said, "Come here," and curved the arm on his good side invitingly.

She settled beside him.

"I'm glad you've stopped worrying about the work thing," he said.

"All the same, I doubt my boss would be impressed. So let's keep this private, okay?"

"Works for me. I'm a pretty private person anyhow." He took a deep breath. "There's something else. I don't want to, uh . . . Don't want you to think . . . I mean, you said you're pretty serious about relationships and—"

"It's okay," she stopped him. "I know we're not soul mates." After all, how many soul mates came along in a lifetime? "But I've decided there's nothing wrong with great sex."

He gave a relieved smile. "I like that attitude."

"I thought you might. Now, tell me about the game. How did it feel out there?"

"Felt the way it should," he said with satisfaction.

"You made that first goal so quickly. That must have been good for your team's confidence."

"And mine. Yeah, we needed that. We sure as hell needed to-night."

She nestled closer into the curve of his arm and sipped her wine. "It's great when you get the thing you need at just the right time." As had happened tonight, when Woody showed up at her door.

"Tell me about it."

"I want to understand the game better. Take me through it."

He complied, and as he talked and she asked questions, she thought how cozy this was. It reminded her of being with Anthony, of how they'd both relax in the living room in the evening, chatting about their days or relaxing with their books. Feeling at home together.

How strange. Her relationship with Woody was nothing like her marriage to Anthony. If she was thinking about the long term, about finding another soul mate, she'd choose a very different man. A man who was . . .

Smart and capable. A man who had principles and who looked after the people he cared about. A man who pursued a career because he loved it, not because of the status it might bring.

Fine. Woody had lots of good qualities. But the bottom line was that, in the long term, what she wanted from a man was marriage, and Woody wanted to be footloose and fancy-free.

She could opt into that for the short term, and reap the rewards. Yes, she would take a page from Lady Emma's book and enjoy being with a sexy, interesting guy who'd complete her sexual education.

Friday night, the Beavers did what they had to do. In a closely fought four–three away game, they tied up the Western Conference. When the team was showered and changed, free of the press, they climbed into limos to go enjoy a celebratory dinner.

"You guys played great tonight," Woody said to the players in his limo. And so had he. Maybe because of the kinky phone sex he'd had with Georgia last night. She'd seemed shy at first, and he'd enjoyed knowing she was blushing when he talked dirty to her and made her touch herself. As he pumped his cock, he'd closed his eyes and imagined her hands, her mouth.

He couldn't wait to get back to Vancouver.

"The Anaheim fans hate us tonight," Stu Connolly said with satisfaction. "You hear all the boos?"

"Wait for Sunday in Vancouver," Woody said. "Vancouver fans will lift the top off the arena." He paused for emphasis. "When we win."

"Damn right," The Hammer said.

"We're going all the way," Bouchard said. "I can taste that Cup now." He ran a hand through his neatly trimmed hair. "We'll take that fucker to Christopher's salon, let him touch it."

"Man's a fucking genius," Stu agreed.

"Who do you think we'll be up against in the playoffs?" Dmitri Federov asked.

It was the perennial question. Last night, the Pittsburgh Penguins had tied it up three-three with the Washington Capitals in the Eastern Conference. The winner would be determined Saturday night. "Wouldn't bet either way," Woody said.

They knew the strengths and weaknesses of each team and each player. Whether it was the Penguins or the Caps, they'd be in for a fight. But that was how it should be. The Stanley Cup had to mean something.

"We came so damned close last year," Dmitri said. "We're taking that Cup home this time."

"Damn right," The Hammer said again.

"What's it feel like?" Stu asked eagerly. "Skating around the rink hoisting that cup? Woody, Dmitri, you've done it."

"Best thing in the world," the Russian said, kissing his Stanley Cup ring.

"That's for sure," Woody confirmed, fingering his own. "All the hard work, all the dreams, they come together in that moment." He glanced at Dmitri. "Turns you into brothers, right? All those guys whose names go on the cup beside yours, it's a bond that'll always be with you."

"Hell, yeah."

He and the goaltender had both played for the Beavers when the team won four years ago. The experience had been incredible. Last year, his second as captain, they'd lost in overtime on the seventh game. This time, he wanted his team to have that experience of skating around the arena carrying thirty-four and a half pounds of hockey history, legend, and achievement.

In the back of the limo, there was a long, profound silence, and he knew each man was envisioning the same thing.

It was Stu who broke the moment. "What time's our flight in the morning? Once we eat, I'm getting together with that sexy Asian sports reporter."

"Flight's at nine," Woody said. "Don't be late."

He'd have told Stu that sleep was a better idea than sex, but hell, the kid was young and did fine with no sleep. The Texan liked to party a bit, but he didn't do drugs, never got drunk, and always showed up on time for practice and worked his butt off.

In fact, he wasn't all that different from Woody, though now Woody usually confined the late nights to regular season and kept his focus on hockey during the playoffs.

This thing he was into with Georgia was different. Now that they were finally in sync, she no longer distracted him on the ice. The thought of her gave him a charge of energy and happiness that made him feel even more in the zone when he was playing.

"You got a booty call tonight, Cap?" Stu asked slyly.

Call being the operative word. Oh, yeah, he'd be phoning Georgia. "That's for me to know." He fought back a smug grin.

Twenty-four

Late Sunday afternoon, Georgia joined the excited crowd streaming toward Rogers Arena. The only time she'd been here before was for the Stars on Ice figure-skating show, and then the crowd had been 90 percent female. Today, she saw men and women, young and old, and lots of families with excited children. Numerous people wore brown-and-caramel Beavers jerseys or tees.

The woman waiting by gate three, her red hair pulled up with artful casualness so that curly tendrils drifted free, wore a V-necked Beavers tee with her figure-hugging jeans. Was the neck of her T-shirt lower than everyone else's, or was it just that she was particularly well-endowed? Was it husband number three or number four who'd paid for those breasts?

"Hi, Bernadette."

Her mom hugged her. "Look at you! My little girl's finally turning into a woman."

Was that a compliment or a backhanded insult? Georgia wore a Beavers jersey along with beige pants. Neither garment was a size too small like her mom's, but the clothes accented her own curves. Her hair was loose and free, and she'd added dangly copper earrings.

"So," Bernadette said, eyes gleaming, "you're dating a hockey star."

"I keep telling you, he's a business colleague." No, she didn't want her mom knowing she was sleeping with Woody. Next thing, Bernadette would have them married off.

When Woody'd offered her two tickets, Georgia had thought twice, thrice, even four times before inviting her mom. When she'd mentioned the possibility to Woody, she'd said that, while she loved her mom, things were never easy between them. They always fell into the same old patterns.

He'd responded, "Then change it up. See what happens."

And so she had.

As the two women jostled their way through the gate among the boisterous crowd, Georgia tried to be nice. "I'm glad you came, but I'm surprised you were willing to leave your new guy."

"We're going to have a late dinner after the game. Fabio's golfing right now." She narrowed her eyes. "We're not bonded at the hip."

"Seems to me that when you get together with a new guy, it can be pretty, uh, intense." As in, bonded at the hip.

"That's what love's like, baby." She paused. "Well, maybe not for you and Anthony. You guys were so young when you became friends." For once, there wasn't an edge to her voice. Bernadette had approved of Anthony and his obvious love for Georgia.

"True." They'd been fourteen, and love had grown out of friendship, more mellow than intense.

With Woody, it could be pretty intense. But of course that was lust, not love. Which was likely what Bernadette was experiencing with Fabio. That, and her perpetual need to be half of a couple, to have some guy think she was wonderful.

Feeling a little sorry for Bernadette, Georgia looped her arm through hers. "A drink? I have a feeling beer's the popular choice."

"I feel more like wine."

Georgia couldn't help thinking that if her mom had been with Fabio and he'd wanted beer, that was what she'd have had too. "Sounds good. I'm buying."

In a concourse that smelled of pizza, burgers, and mini-doughnuts, they got plastic tumblers of wine, white for Georgia and red for Bernadette.

"Where are we sitting?" her mom asked.

"Woody offered me options, and I chose seats close to the ice."

"Cool. We'll get all that 'roar of the greasepaint and smell of the crowd' stuff up close and personal."

Trust Bernadette to find a way of mentioning a musical she'd once played in. A freelance graphic designer by profession, she was also an amateur actress. She was talented at both careers, but never achieved a lot of success because she didn't give them top priority. The men in her life always came first.

To Georgia's mind, a man who loved you should care about your career—and vice versa. That was how it had been with her and Anthony, who'd been working on his PhD in sociology when he died.

She and her mom found their seats, six rows up and roughly in the middle of the arena. They'd be able to see the action on both sides.

"This is exciting." Bernadette bumped her shoulder against Georgia's as people poured into the building to fill the seats.

"It is." The air almost crackled with it. A nervous shiver rippled through Georgia. The next three hours would determine whether Woody and the Beavers made it into the Stanley Cup playoffs.

If she was a praying woman, she'd have gone down on her knees. She knew how much the playoffs meant to Woody.

"You're looking great," Bernadette said. "Love the hair. The job's going well, and this new campaign you're in charge of?"

Surprised that her mom had remembered, much less commented, she said, "Yes, it's great. Thanks for asking."

"And you're feeling good? How about those headaches?"

"You know, I haven't had one in days." Hopefully, being with her mom wouldn't trigger one tonight.

Bernadette winked. "Great sex cures all ills."

"I'm not—"

The crowd's roar stopped her before she could finish the lie. The players were coming into the arena, and everyone leaped to their feet, chanting, "Bash 'em, Beavers!"

Georgia was with them, Bernadette right beside her. The din was so loud, Georgia could barely make out what her mom was yelling. "That's him, number seventy-seven, right?"

"That's him."

He skated toward her, and she pumped her fist in the signature salute. He pumped one back, and for a long moment their gazes connected. He was on fire with excitement and determination.

They were going to win. They had to.

To her surprise, her eyes were damp. Who'd ever have guessed she could feel so strongly about a hockey game?

Bernadette, on her feet beside Georgia, leaned close to yell in her ear, "Business colleagues? I call bullshit, baby."

Georgia pretended not to hear, and fought back a smile.

The national anthems played. Seeing the players shift restlessly, she couldn't even imagine their anxiety and eagerness. The sense of anticipation in the arena was so thick, it could be sliced with a hockey blade.

And it was, when the puck dropped and Woody slashed it away from the Ducks' player and swept it toward one of the Beavers, who was down the ice toward the Anaheim goal.

The action was fast, faster than in any of the other games Georgia had watched, or maybe that was because it was live. It was all so immediate. The huge men flying back and forth, the sound of blades slicing the ice, the whack of sticks hitting the puck, the players' grunts of effort. The thud of bodies hitting bodies, and the shudder of the Plexiglas when players slammed into it.

It was so physical and primal and utterly masculine.

Somehow, it was easy to forget that all this speed and skill and effort was directed to getting that little black disk into the opposite team's goal. She'd always thought it ridiculous how people got so worked up over players chasing balls—or in this case a disk—yet she was totally drawn in.

In the first period, both teams fought hard. One of the Beavers was sent to the penalty box, but even shorthanded, the remaining players—including Woody—stopped the Ducks from scoring on the power play. Every time Woody got the puck, one or more of the Ducks was on him, trying to block him, to hit him, to stop him from scoring. He battled back, came close with a couple of shots and assists, but at the end of the period, neither team had put a goal up on the scoreboard.

When Georgia and her mom got up and stretched, she realized her muscles were locked with tension. "This is stressful," she admitted.

"Course it is. That's your man out there."

"He isn't my man." At least not for the long term. Even so, there was something outrageously satisfying knowing that hundreds of women in the arena were staring at Woody with hungry eyes, and she was the one he'd saluted before the game started. She was the one he'd come home to tonight—to lick his wounds or to celebrate his victory.

She really hoped they'd be cracking open a bottle of champagne.

"I'll buy you another glass of wine," Bernadette said. "Maybe it'll settle your nerves."

"Thanks." They made their way to the line. "I wonder what Woody's saying to them in the locker room? He takes it so personally."

"How d'you mean?"

"He loves the sport, and he's committed to his team. He feels responsible when things don't go well, and he tries to keep them motivated and focused."

Bernadette handed her a second glass of white wine, smirking. "But he's not your man."

Rather than answer, Georgia said, "Let's get back to our seats."

There, she watched the second period with nail-chewing anxiety. Even to her inexperienced eye, something looked different out on the ice. The Beavers had been strong in the first period, but now their play was almost like a dance. An absurd analogy, considering they were giant men, padded and helmeted, yet the moves, the patterns, almost seemed choreographed. The team was in sync. Woody'd told her about spatial and situational intelligence, and she could see it at play.

As the Ducks tried to get the puck away from Bouchard, who was powering toward the goal, Georgia kept an eye on Woody, zipping across the ice. Bouchard deked suddenly and slapped the puck to Woody, who was now perfectly positioned on the other side of the goal.

The Ducks' goaltender flung himself across the crease, but not quickly enough. Woody flicked the puck over the man's shoulder and into the back of the net. The first goal of the game.

Georgia leaped to her feet along with the rest of the Vancouver fans, everyone screaming, whooping, whistling. She and her mom hugged each other, and on the ice, Beavers pounded Woody on the back and banged the top of his helmet with gloved fists. A jubilant grin split his face.

When he broke away, he gazed toward her, and she pumped her fist into the air, laughing with sheer joy.

As the crowd settled back into their seats, Bernadette said, "I never in this world thought you'd date a hockey player. I'm impressed."

"I'm not dating him." *Dating*, for her and her mom, meant a serious relationship. Woody'd made it clear that was the last thing he wanted. And yet . . . It felt like dating. They liked each other, talked about the things that mattered to them, and when they had sex it felt like more than just a physical act.

She was naïve. Woody didn't want love and commitment. She couldn't let herself care about him, not as anything more than a friend and casual lover.

Besides, when you dated, you told the world. You didn't hide it from your colleagues for fear your boss would think badly of you. Soon, Woody would be gone, but Georgia would still have her career. And, with any luck, more responsibility at Dynamic Marketing. But she had to be careful. Her competition, Harry, was keeping a close eye on the VitalSport campaign. He'd even read an early draft of their strategy, before she'd deleted mention of Ellen DeGeneres. Harry had snidely asked, "Any luck getting your guy on *The Ellen DeGeneres Show*?"

Oh yes, he had an eagle eye out for any weakness. She'd refused to let him get to her, merely smiling sweetly and saying, "You're out of date. We rethought that and decided it doesn't fit our overall game plan."

The puck dropped in the face-off, and Georgia's attention focused on the game. The play was fast and hard, both teams giving it their all. Once, Woody was slammed into the boards, smashing his bad shoulder. Georgia winced, but it barely slowed him for a second.

The period ended with the Beavers up one-zero, thanks to Woody's goal.

At the beginning of the third period, Woody smashed into a Ducks player who crashed onto the ice and just lay there. In an instant, players, refs, and coaches surrounded the man.

"Oh God," Georgia said, "I hope he's all right. It didn't look like that hard a hit. I mean, considering." All the hits were hard when the men were so big and traveling so fast across the ice, but Woody had explained to her that physicality was essential to the game, and there were rules about what was and wasn't okay.

The player finally rose. Shakily, with the help of a couple of others, he skated off the ice.

"He took a dive," Bernadette huffed.

"What do you mean?"

"He's exaggerating. Playing it up in hopes they'll call a penalty against Woody. That'll give the Ducks the power play, and the Beavers will be minus their most valuable player."

Georgia gazed at her. "You really know this game."

"What's not to like? Lots of hot guys. Speed, excitement."

A moment later, the announcement was made that a three-minute penalty was called. Woody, scowling, skated to the box as the crowd booed the referees.

Bernadette joined in loudly, and after a moment Georgia did too. She wasn't a demonstrative person, but the energy crackling in the air got to her. When the crowd began chanting, "Ducks suck, Ducks suck, Ducks suck," she screamed along with them.

The next three minutes crawled by as the Beavers, one man short, battled with everything they had to hold off the Ducks. They almost made it, but in the last few seconds the Anaheim team snuck the puck into the goal on a rebound, to a chorus of boos. The score was tied, one all.

Woody, after a three-minute rest, jumped over the boards and back onto the ice as if he'd been turbocharged. Dashing into the fray, he took the puck away from the opposing team, powered across the ice, and sent a slap shot whipping into the Ducks' goal.

Ten minutes later, the Ducks slipped a shot past the Beavers' goaltender, Federov, tying the game two all.

When only five minutes remained in the final period, the Ducks put together an incredible series of shots on goal, and Federov whipped up, down, side to side, blocking every shot until finally he dove on top of the puck, stopping it just outside the goal line.

Woody extended a hand, pulled the man to his feet, and caught him in a bear hug as other teammates slapped the goaltender on his back and the crowd roared.

When the puck was in play again, neither team let up for a minute—and neither scored. In the last minute, with the prospect of overtime looming, the Ducks again bombarded the goaltender, maybe figuring Federov's resources were drained. This time, Stu Connolly managed to hook the puck away.

He passed it to Woody, who took off. The Ducks, caught off guard, had only one defensive player in Woody's way.

The audience was on their feet, cheering him on, chanting, "Hat trick, hat trick, hat trick!"

The Anaheim goaltender looked huge, padded legs straddling the goal, shoulders wide, hockey stick at the ready. It was a battle of skill and of mind reading, Georgia realized, each man trying to psych out the other.

Woody deked left, right, and the goaltender shifted in anticipation. Then Woody shot, so fast Georgia's eyes couldn't follow the puck, but somehow it sliced past the goaltender's glove and slammed decisively into the net.

The arena exploded. There were twenty seconds left in the game, but it was over. The Beavers had won, and Woody'd made all three of their goals.

When the win was official, Georgia realized she'd screamed herself almost hoarse and happy tears dampened her cheeks. She and Bernadette hugged each other, bouncing up and down like kids.

The Beavers, sweaty and flushed, slapped and hugged and high-fived one another.

"It was Woody and Federov who did it," Bernadette said. "They won the game."

Georgia agreed, but said, "Woody says it's a team effort. The little things count as much as the big, showy ones."

On the ice, the Western Conference trophy was being presented, but Woody didn't pick it up; nor did any of his teammates. "I'd think they'd want to hoist that thing in triumph," she commented.

"There's a superstition about touching it," her mom said. "There's only one trophy worth touching, and that's the Stanley Cup. If they touch another along the way, it can jinx their chances."

Georgia shook her head. "Athletes and their superstitions. Did you know the Beavers all went to one hairstylist for playoff hair and beard trims, to bring them luck?"

They chuckled together, and Georgia realized something. "This has been fun. I'm glad you came." In fact, it was the most fun she could remember ever having with Bernadette.

"I'm glad you invited me." Eyes a shade darker than her own studied her. "You never ask me to do things with you, baby."

Georgia bit her lip. She'd told Woody that she and her mom got stuck in old patterns, ones she didn't like. He'd suggested changing things up, and it had worked. She could leave well enough alone, or be honest. "When we get together, you're always with the latest guy and it's all about him. It feels like . . ." She paused, chewed her lip again, then said it. "Like you care more about the guy, and the couple thing, than about—"

"About you?" Bernadette broke in. "Oh, baby, that's not true."

Georgia had felt that way, but that wasn't what she'd been going to say. She shook her head. "Than about you, Bernadette. It's like you, your identity, is all about pleasing this guy rather than being yourself." Or being a mom.

She expected denial, maybe anger, but instead her mom nodded slowly. "I hear you. Fabio told me the same thing."

"He did? Hmm. I might like this man."

"Then you have to come for dinner and—" Bernadette broke off. "Look, he's coming over."

Woody, helmet and face shield off, skated toward them. He gazed up at Georgia, an expression of pure happiness on his face.

She waved and then—oh, what the hell—blew him a kiss.

Laughing beside her, Bernadette did the same. Then, as Woody skated away, she said, "Bring him for dinner."

"It's not serious. There's no point."

Her mom linked arms with her as they climbed the stairs. "You don't *do* casual, Georgia. I know you."

The comment sent a pang through her heart. Was she wrong to think she could "do" casual?

Woody was such a different man from Anthony, and yet the pure pleasure she felt when she saw him, the way they were opening up to each other and sharing secrets, the intimacy of cuddling with him in bed were all things she'd experienced with her husband.

With Anthony, falling in love had been safe because they felt the same way about celibacy, commitment, and the sanctity—and desirability—of marriage.

With Woody, falling in love would be a recipe for heartbreak. That man wasn't about to shelve his condoms in just one woman's bedside table. She had to protect her heart. She'd enjoy the fun while it lasted, then move on.

"Bet you're going out partying with your guy tonight," her mom said as they jostled along with the jubilant crowd leaving the arena.

No, she and Woody weren't partying—he would celebrate the victory with his teammates—but she'd see him later at his place. "Nope. I'm going to curl up with a book." It wasn't a lie. Her e-reader was in her shoulder bag, along with a change of undies.

Woody had told her the guys wouldn't stay out late. The next game, the first of the Stanley Cup playoffs, was Tuesday. The Beavers would be facing the Washington Capitals, who'd won the Eastern

Conference last night. The other team had the advantage of an extra day to rest, heal, and work on strategy. The Beavers' advantage was that the first two games would be home games.

"A book?" Bernadette winked. "Well, I certainly hope he— pardon me, *it*—is a page-turner that keeps you on the edge of—"

"Stop!" Laughing, Georgia held up her hands in a T-shaped halt signal.

When Georgia had said to Woody that she guessed she wouldn't see much of him if the Beavers made it into the playoffs, he'd said, "Hey, you're my good luck charm. Course I want to see you." This, from the same guy who didn't usually date during the playoffs because it distracted him.

As for her, the woman who believed in independence, she'd agreed that they'd sleep at his penthouse apartment. He found his king-sized bed more comfortable than her queen.

She'd left plenty of food and water for Kit-Kat, and had Woody's spare key tucked deep in her pocket.

He'd given her his key. She had to be careful not to read more into that than he meant. Who knew; maybe this was really just about jock superstition. He'd decided Georgia was good luck, so he'd keep seeing her until the end of the playoffs.

Well, she felt lucky too. This whole experience was amazing— the sex and everything else—and she'd be fine when it ended. No heartbreak for her. She was far too practical.

She and her mom had finally made it outside the arena. The euphoric crowd was dispersing slowly, with laughter and triumphant whoops.

From here, Georgia would walk to Woody's place in Yaletown. "Thanks again for coming," she said.

"Thanks for inviting me. I had a great time. Anytime your guy"— Bernadette winked—"pardon me, your *book* gives you a spare ticket, I'd be happy to keep you company."

Twenty-five

Late Monday afternoon, Georgia, running a few minutes late, hurried into the Copper Chimney in Le Soleil hotel. The lovely art deco bar-restaurant was warm and welcoming, and three female faces gaped as she headed over to the book club's table.

"Wow, George." Marielle was the first to speak. "Love your new look." The others chimed in too, and Georgia thanked them.

She'd gotten in the habit of leaving her hair loose and casual, and, though she still wore tailored suits, she now teamed them with silky VitalSport blouses in pretty colors. She'd had a lot of compliments, and not a soul seemed to take her less seriously at work.

It wasn't just the hair and clothes, though, she thought as the group ordered drinks and snacks. She hadn't had a headache all week, her skin glowed, she was drinking less caffeine, and she had more energy. Dr. Lily—and Bernadette—seemed to be right about sex being good for you.

She studied Marielle, who wore jeans and a turquoise sweater that looked great with her coffee-colored skin and wavy dark brown hair. "You look great too. Is it casual day at the law firm?"

Marielle beamed. "The regular receptionist came back from sick leave. Now I'm a dog-walker and I love it. But hey, isn't it fantastic the Beavers are in the playoffs? How's your marketing campaign going? Can't wait to see photos of Woody Hanrahan."

Kim, in an eye-catching white tee with silk-screened pink

butterflies, said, "Oh, yeah! How's the hottie hockey star working out?"

Georgia tried to hold back a smug grin. "Very well." *In more ways than you'll ever know!* "We had the first photo shoot this afternoon, in Stanley Park, and he's as photogenic as we hoped he'd be." Today had been leisure wear. He'd posed in several different outfits, with props ranging from a golf club to sexy models. Georgia's favorite shots were the ones where he held a hockey stick and wore the same clothes as the night they'd dined at Hawksworth: black jeans and the classy takeoff on a hockey jersey, done in the Beavers' caramel.

She and Woody had kept their secret, but some steamy private looks, subtle touches, and double entendres—not to mention the sight of his fantastic body as he tossed leisure clothes on and off—had made her seriously hot and bothered. She couldn't wait to be alone with him later.

"Is he nice to work with, or an arrogant prick?" Marielle asked.

"He's nice." And even nicer in private. "He's not thrilled about being a model, but he tries to cooperate." Grinning, she said, "Poor guy had to wear makeup." Partly for the cameras, and partly to conceal the fading bruise around his eye. "Apparently that's not a tough-guy thing to do."

Kim and Marielle chuckled, and even Lily, who'd been frowning, gave a grudging smile.

Georgia noticed that the doctor's short, stylish blond hair looked tousled and there were tiny lines around the corners of her mouth that she hadn't noticed before. "Lily, are you feeling okay?"

Lily waved a hand dismissively. "I'm fine. It's been a long day and I missed lunch."

"Appies'll be here soon," Marielle said. Then: "I'm really looking forward to the playoffs. The Beavers are pretty evenly matched with the Capitals."

"If anyone wants to see Tuesday's game," Georgia offered,

"Woody says he'll give me four tickets. As, you know, a business thing," she added quickly.

Marielle whooped. "Yes, yes, yes!! I love your job perks."

"Me too," Kim said. "I'd love to come."

"Oh good God." Lily huffed. "Has everyone gone hockey crazy?" She picked up the martini their waiter had just placed in front of her and took a sip.

"Pretty much," Marielle said cheerfully, "and it's only going to get worse. I figure, enjoy the fun." She raised her cocktail, which she'd chosen for its name: a Passion Paradise Martini.

"You always figure that," Lily said a little snidely.

Marielle shot her a slitted-eye glance but said only, "The play-offs will be terrific. Our Woody against Alexander 'The Great' Ovechkin."

Kim ran a hand through her spiky hair, its streaks the same pink as the butterflies on her tee. "Too bad the Beavers aren't up against a weaker team."

"The tougher the fight, the more the win means," Georgia said. "And the Beavers *will* win."

"You bet," Kim said. "Here's to that win!" She raised her glass of designer beer.

Marielle clicked her cocktail glass against it, and Georgia followed suit with her wineglass.

Lily raised her martini glass, but only to take a drink. "Ladies, this isn't hockey club; it's book club. Much as I'm not enraptured with the book, could we at least discuss it?"

Georgia turned to her. "You're right. Sorry." Who'd have thought she'd rather talk about hockey than a good book?

The waiter delivered their snacks—Indian-style crab cakes, lamb kebabs, and samosas—and they all dove in. A few minutes later, Lily gave a sigh of relief. "Now I feel better. Low blood sugar. Sorry if I was bitchy."

Marielle flashed a smile. "No problem. And, Lily, I agree with what you said in your e-mail last week, about sex being healthy."

"It's like a vigorous walk," Lily said. "Burns calories, tones muscles, releases endorphins."

Marielle gave a wicked chuckle. "And it's a whole lot more fun than a walk in the park. As Lady Emma is finding out."

Kim, who'd been so quick to talk about hockey, said tentatively, "But sex is more than exercise. If it's just physical, then why not"— she glanced around and lowered her voice to a whisper—"use a vibrator?"

"Gotta love vibrators," Marielle said, "but let's face it, they're not all strong and muscular, you can't cuddle with them or go out for a drink with them, and they don't talk."

"Men don't necessarily talk either," Lily muttered, eliciting another round of chuckles.

No, Woody wasn't a chatterbox, but Georgia loved hearing the things he shared with her—about his team, his past, his love for the ice, his desire to be the best. It wasn't trivial chat about the weather; when he opened his mouth, she really wanted to listen.

"Besides," Marielle went on, "vibrators have a limited repertoire. They can't possibly measure up to a skilled, attentive, sensual lover like le Comte de Vergennes."

Georgia'd never had the slightest interest in trying a vibrator. "I'm with Marielle. There's a lot to be said for a real, live, talented lover."

"You're putting an awful lot of weight on sexual satisfaction," Kim said. "I mean, I have to admit it's really nice, and I guess it's healthy like Lily says, but it's not exactly essential to life."

"No," Georgia agreed, having survived quite nicely without it until she'd met Woody. "But it makes life more fun."

"Sure, but it's not the most important thing in a relationship," Kim said firmly. "You need other stuff like commitment and loyalty."

If Kim was having boyfriend troubles, as Georgia suspected, which things were missing in her relationship? One day, they'd know one another well enough to share more personal details rather than talk in the abstract.

"Yes, I agree," Georgia said. "You can have a wonderful relationship even if the sex isn't, you know, incredible."

"And you can have a rotten relationship even though the sex is good," Lily added.

"Gaah!" Marielle shook her head. "You're all making it way too complicated. Why does everything have to be about big-R *relationships*?"

"Because we're women," Kim said. She fanned out her fingers, pink-tipped like her hair, as if to illustrate her point. "It's men who enjoy meaningless sex, just to get their rocks off. Women aren't like that. For women, it's emotional. You can't have great sex unless it's emotional." She turned to Lily. "Right?"

"That depends on what you mean by great sex," Lily said thoughtfully. "Physically, you can have a satisfying, even wonderful experience, and you may not even like the man much. But if you're talking about lovemaking . . ." Her voice drifted off and her blue eyes looked sad for a moment. Then she straightened. "We've gone off track again. This isn't about the book."

"It is," Kim protested. "It's about understanding Emma's motivation. I mean, the book's hot and I love the sex scenes, but I can't relate to her. Unless she's falling in love with him."

"Which would be a totally stupid thing to do," Marielle said. "He's a rake, right? He's never going to settle down with one woman. Right, George?"

"No, he's not a one-woman man. And yes, Emma would be stupid to get emotionally involved with him, and she knows that. I think she knows what she's doing," she went on, speaking for herself as well as the fictional heroine. "She's been offered an opportunity she never thought she'd have. She's being appreciated as a woman, learning about her sexuality, and having a wonderful time."

"But what good does that do her?" Kim asked, frowning over the top of her beer glass. "He'll leave, and she'll be even less satisfied than she was before."

Taken aback, Georgia frowned.

Marielle shook her head. "No, she'll be hot, and she'll know it. It'll show. She'll have suitors. She won't be stuck marrying some old prick or playing slave to her brother's family. She can marry a rich, sexy guy, or be one's mistress if that suits her better. She'll be empowered." She glanced around the table. "That's what a good relationship—small R or large R—does. It empowers us. Don't you think?"

"I hope so," Georgia murmured. So far, with Woody, that was how it felt. When they broke up, it wouldn't shatter her because she knew it was inevitable. They were both in this for only the short term. So, she'd remain empowered.

Sad, though. She'd miss him. In such a short time, he'd become a big part of her life.

Oh God, surely she wasn't turning into a woman like her mom. One who based her life and identity on a man. No, she'd never let that happen.

"What if a relationship doesn't empower us?" Kim asked softly.

"Then it's bad," Marielle said decisively, "and we leave. We deserve better than that."

"Things are always so easy for you, Marielle," Lily said. "Wait until you're my age."

"Wait until you fall in love," Kim put in.

Marielle shook her head vigorously. "I refuse to even think about love and commitment until I'm, like, *seriously* over thirty. More likely thirty-five. Or forty!"

Georgia toyed with her wineglass, reflecting. Lily was married and Kim had been with her boyfriend for a while. Supposedly they loved their mates, yet neither sounded ecstatic about their relationships. Marielle was the happy one, and she was all about casual sex. And the same was true of Georgia, though she had to admit that, as fabulous as her fling with Woody was, in the long run she'd want more.

More, in fact, than she'd ever had before, she realized with a start. More than the other three women had. Some people must have relationships that paired incredible sex with loving commitment, mustn't they? If Georgia took what she'd had with Anthony, that sense of being soul mates and knowing they'd love each other forever, and added in the kind of amazing sex she had with Woody . . .

What would that perfect man look like?

Oddly, the image that sprang to mind was Woody's. Woody, in a dozen different varieties from naked in his whirlpool tub, to blazing down the ice, to wincing as she helped him wrap his injured shoulder with ice, to gazing intensely into her eyes during sex.

How disconcerting. And scary . . .

Since Lily had turned down a ticket for the Tuesday game, Georgia persuaded Viv to attend. The four of them—in Beavers jerseys except for Viv—met after work. The streets were full of fans and excited chatter about the game. The foursome grabbed a taxi to Rogers Arena, where they joined the boisterous crowd.

Kim, her hair streaks and fingernails caramel today in honor of the team, said to Georgia and Viv, "You two are so lucky, working with Woody Hanrahan. Guess you couldn't squeeze me in to see one of those photo shoots? Pretend I'm an assistant?"

"The guy'd see through it when you drooled all over him," Marielle teased.

In high spirits, the women got drinks and snacks, then found their seats. These weren't as close to the ice as on Sunday. It must have taken some doing for Woody to get four seats together in the first game of the playoffs.

When the players skated onto the ice, Woody gazed in their direction. Georgia knew that, in this sea of Beavers' jerseys, he'd never be able to pick her out. Just as well, since she didn't want Viv or her book club friends to find out about their secret fling.

Once the game began, all four of the women were on the edges of their seats, even Viv, who said, "I never realized it was so fast! So exciting!"

For Georgia, it still felt surreal to watch Woody power across the ice, slash at the puck, slam into another player—and to know he was her lover.

In the first period, he had an assist, and the Capitals also got a goal. In the second period, Woody scored and she cheered enthusiastically along with the rest of the crowd. She stopped worrying about giving away her secret, because Marielle and Kim were just as enthusiastic as she was, and Viv came a close second.

The period ended with the Beavers up by one.

In the intermission, the women went to get drinks. Four cute guys in Beavers jerseys, in line ahead of them, said, "Hey, let us buy the pretty ladies a drink."

"Thanks," Marielle said promptly. "That's nice of you."

Viv leaned close to Georgia and murmured, "Seriously?"

"What can I say? She's friendly."

The eight of them clustered together, chatting about the game and exchanging first names. Georgia was entertained by how each of the women behaved. Marielle was outgoing and genuine. Kim, who was in a serious relationship, was surprisingly friendly too, especially with a tall, sandy-haired guy who told her he loved the cara-

mel streaks in her hair. Viv, who was a few years older than the rest
of them, was friendly but in an impersonal way.

As for Georgia, she got into an involved conversation about
hockey with a blond guy named Glen, who had a great tan, sparkling
greenish-blue eyes, and a dimple. He was well-informed and she was
intrigued by his analysis of the game. When he praised Woody's
playing, she grinned and hugged her secret tight to her heart.

When it was time to head back inside the arena, the guys suggested they all get together for drinks afterward. Marielle and Kim
agreed, and Viv and Georgia both said they had other plans. Glen
looked mildly crushed and caught Georgia's arm, holding her back
as the other women headed for their seats. "Maybe I could get your
number? We could go to the next home game together."

"Thanks, but I'm not sure I'll be going." She didn't want to be
rude, but she also didn't want to miss a moment of seeing Woody on
the ice, so she hurried away.

When she joined up with her friends, Marielle said, "Man, he's
cute, George, and really into you. You going out with him?"

Startled, she said, "You mean, as in dating? No, but . . . Hmm. He
did invite me to the next home game, but I don't think it was a *date*."
She'd thought he suggested it because they were both fans.

"It was totally a date," Kim confirmed.

"Huh." She wasn't used to men finding her attractive. Was it her
new look, her increased confidence, or did she give off some kind of
sexual vibe she'd never had before?

"It was obvious," Viv confirmed. "Same thing with Marco Sanducci, right?"

"What?"

"Oh, come on. At the photo shoot yesterday, he was flirting with
you, but you didn't give him an inch."

Marco Sanducci was attracted to her?

Before she could ponder the thought further, the third period started, and she forgot all about Glen and Marco.

Both teams fought hard, and the score was two all when the period ended, with Woody having a goal and an assist. Four minutes into overtime, the Beavers' star rookie, first line center Stu Connolly, slipped the puck neatly off his blade and into the net and the crowd went wild.

"Three more games to go," Kim screamed, "and they bring home the Cup!"

After, when they were outside the stadium, Marielle said, "Don't you envy the girl who's hooking up with Woody Hanrahan tonight?"

Tongue in cheek, Georgia said, "He says he doesn't date during the playoffs because it's too distracting."

"What a waste!" Marielle said; then she raised her arm and waved wildly, and Georgia saw the four guys from intermission heading their way.

Marielle and Kim went off with them for a drink, Viv said she was meeting a friend for a late dinner, and Georgia headed home to feed Kit-Kat and give her some cuddles before packing a few things to take to Woody's.

The logistics of casual sex were complicated when your lover was in the Stanley Cup playoffs and insisted on sleeping in his own bed. She went along with it, knowing Woody was in constant pain. Anything that helped him get a good night's sleep—and helped the Beavers' odds—was fine with her.

It was only for, as Kim had said, three more winning games. After that . . .

Georgia didn't have a clue. Would they keep seeing each other? Or, if she was really only his lucky charm for the playoffs, would he be on to the next willing woman?

That would hurt, which was dumb. What she'd have to do was move on herself.

Before she'd met Woody, she was reconciled to being alone for the foreseeable future. Now she couldn't help but hope that somewhere there was another compatible, loving man like Anthony, one who wanted marriage and kids rather than random lovers. A man who thought that finding his soul mate was the best thing in the world.

In the meantime, for a few more nights anyhow, she had Woody. She'd make the most of them.

She drove to Yaletown, let herself in, and changed into the sexy purchase she'd picked up at Agent Provocateur at lunchtime: a black slip-style nightie made of silk and lace, over a matching thong. Then she curled up on his black leather couch and opened her e-reader.

Twenty-six

A little Lady Emma was the perfect way to relax and get in the mood for Woody. In the last scene Georgia had read, Emma had met the Comte for an afternoon tryst at a gazebo by the lake, out of sight of the Edgertons' manor home. The sex had been distinctly steamy.

Georgia turned to the next chapter.

Though she wore her drab widow's garb when she went down for dinner, Emma knew she looked her best, her blond hair gleaming and cheeks glowing. The tingly ache between her legs was a sensual reminder of the afternoon's erotic adventure.

As he handed her a glass of sherry, her host, Lord Edgerton, commented, "You look quite a different person from the woman who came to us from the city scant days ago. I do believe the country air suits you."

Le Comte de Vergennes joined them. A sly glint in his eye, he said, "I agree entirely. Lady Emma, you look splendid and I'm sure the country air is responsible. Indeed, I am having a most invigorating holiday myself."

It was a simple family evening, only Lord and Lady Edgerton, the Comte, and Emma. When they sat down to dinner, Emma was across the table from her paramour, and it was all she could do to remain decorous in word and deed.

The man used double entendres with sophisticated ease, and she wondered that their host and hostess remained oblivious. Yet, of course, the last thing they'd imagine was a tryst between the rake from France and the genteel widow.

Emma was torn between wishing the meal to end, and savoring every moment of watching the Comte's expressive face and graceful hands as he ate and drank. Remembering the caress of those hands on her naked flesh, shivers of pleasure rippled through her. Over the rim of his wine goblet, his eyes offered her a silent toast—and a seductive promise.

He would come to her chamber that night, when the household had retired. She could hardly wait.

At the close of the meal, she was not the least bit surprised when, upon Lord Edgerton proposing that the two men retire to his study for brandy and cigars, the Comte said, "I beg your indulgence, but I think not tonight."

Emma's heart raced. He wanted to be alone with her, and the sooner this evening was over, the sooner that would happen.

She was startled, then, when he went on to say, "I propose instead that we all retire to the music room. I had the good luck to discover that Lady Emma is an accomplished violinist, and I have a certain skill with the piano." His dark, bright eyes met hers. "What say the two guests pay for their supper by providing their gracious host and hostess with a little musical entertainment?"

Emma's cheeks heated. Playing with Alexandre was . . . Why, it was a kind of seduction. The man and the music together were far too heady. He wanted to do this in front of Margaret and her husband?

He intended to seduce her in public, with no one being any the wiser?

It was an outrageous idea. A shockingly scandalous one. A deliciously tempting one.

Demurely, she responded, "I fear I am not nearly as accomplished a musician as le Comte makes out. I still have"—she flicked her eyelashes in his direction—"much to learn. However, I do find the notion of playing a duet most stimulating." She put the slightest of inflections on the last word, knowing that her lover would appreciate the innuendo. "If I may be forgiven my inexperience."

Margaret rose, clapping her hands. "How delightful! We shall adjourn to the music room. Come, Edgerton." She stepped lightly to her husband's side as he rose, and slipped her hand through his arm.

The Comte held out his own arm, slightly crooked, toward Emma. "May I escort you, my lady?"

'Twas simple courtesy to accept. Yet there was nothing simple about the erotic heat that warmed her when she curled her hand around Alexandre's arm and he snugged that arm closer to his side. Her hand was quite trapped. Not that it had the least desire to escape.

Engrossed, Georgia read on as the Comte chose music that he knew spoke to Emma and aroused her passion. As he played, he caught her eye, smiled, and though the Edgertons wouldn't see anything amiss, Emma felt the heat in his gaze, the promise of delights to come when they were alone in the privacy of her chamber.

This was an exquisite form of torturous foreplay, with each stroke of the violin bow, each caress of the piano keys, a secret sexual message.

It was, Emma thought as she rested her bow after the last note of the third selection, a seduction that was as sophisticated as the man himself. And she could withstand it no longer.

When the audience of two applauded and begged for another piece, Emma said, "As enjoyable as this has been, I am afraid that I am out of practice." She darted a quick glance at Alexandre, seated

at the piano. "My apologies, but I confess that what I most wish at
this moment is to retire." There, she thought, I am not so hopelessly
unsophisticated myself.

His knowing smile was her reward. "By all means, Lady Emma.
I find myself quite ready for bed as well." He gave a small yawn.
"Perhaps it is the country air that has fatigued the two of us."

"It must be that."

Georgia smiled, reminded of the way she and Woody had behaved at the photo shoot. The hockey star was no suave French
count, and she wasn't as clever with double entendres as Lady Emma,
but she'd felt the same kind of sexual awareness and tension as they
pretended there was nothing between them but business. Emma
was right that it was a kind of foreplay. So, too, was watching Woody
on the ice and marveling at his power and focus, then reveling in his
victory.

The book she was reading was arousing too. She was glad the
club had chosen *The Sexual Education of Lady Emma Whitehead.* But
she had to wonder, if she'd been reading the book as a single woman
who wasn't dating, hadn't had sex in years, and had never climaxed,
would she be enjoying it half as much? As it was, the book was a
counterpoint to her own sexual education.

Georgia turned to the next chapter. It started an hour after the
group had left the music room. Emma lay in bed, a crackling fire and
two candles the only illumination in her chamber, when the Comte
crept silently in her door. And then, until long after the fire had died
to glowing embers, he made love to Emma.

Dazed with a passion she'd never believed possible, Emma trembled
and moaned as the Comte played her body from head to toe with an
even greater appreciation than he'd shown the music, his fingertips
stroking sensation throughout her body, to parts of her she'd barely

been aware existed before. He was patient, thorough, and always, always, he made her feel treasured as if she, like her friend Margaret's violin, was the finest and rarest of instruments.

This was the first time in her life she'd felt treasured. She must enjoy and remember every moment of this interlude, to brighten the days of her inevitable, and dismal, future.

"You are a most skilled teacher," she murmured, threading her fingers through the black silk of his hair.

"And you are a most adept student." He nipped her collarbone.

She let out a squeak of surprised pleasure. Who would have guessed that a collarbone could be so sweetly sensitive, yet the Comte had made a detailed study of her body, learning all her—

Woody's apartment door opened.

Georgia flicked off her e-reader and rose.

The Woody who stepped through the doorway looked very different from the man she'd first met. To start with, he was clothed in more than a thong—though she hoped to remedy that situation soon. His clothes were the opposite of the ragged jeans and jersey he'd first worn. Now his rangy frame was clad in one of his new suits—a charcoal one—and it fit to perfection, as did the tailored blue shirt. He'd loosened his tie, and the effect, with the lovely clothes, nicely styled hair, and trimmed beard, was rakish rather than sloppy. He looked unbearably handsome.

He strode toward her. "Now, that's what a guy likes to see when he gets home."

Though a foolish part of her longed to believe that he meant her, Georgia, waiting for him, she knew that really it was just a woman in scraps of black lace.

His kiss was warm, and she responded eagerly, then pulled back in the curve of his arms to say, "Wonderful game. You all must be so happy."

He gave a satisfied nod. "It's exactly the way we wanted to start the playoffs. Man, the Caps are tough, though."

"I'm sure you guys would rather play a wimpy team," she teased.

"What'd be the fun in that?" he joked back. The animation faded from his face and he looked tired. His arm around her shoulders, he guided her back to the couch and flopped down, kicking off his shoes and raising his feet to the coffee table. "Wouldn't mind winning it in four. The guys are pretty beat-up."

Including him. She went to the kitchen for an ice wrap for his shoulder and a heating pad for a nagging pain that was plaguing his lower back. When he'd shrugged out of his jacket and tie, she helped wrap his shoulder and settle the heating pad in the right place.

Ruefully, he gazed up at her. "Did you ever guess that dating a hockey player would be like looking after your granny?"

Georgia had never known her father's parents, and Bernadette's were dead. As for dating—his polite word for screwing—a hockey player, the idea had never entered her head. "It's an education." Thinking of Lady Emma, she smiled a private smile.

Going to the kitchen again, she brought him a bottle of water, then curled up beside him.

His blue eyes looked tired, but his gaze was steady. "Thanks, Georgia. I keep telling you, you don't have to wait on me."

In truth, she enjoyed looking after him, but that was too domestic—too intimate—a thing to admit. "It's my thanks for those four tickets."

"Your friends enjoy the game? How about Viv? Could she get past how unstylish the uniforms are?"

Georgia chuckled. "She managed, and everyone had a great time. They all sent their thanks."

"You didn't tell them about us?" He asked it as a question, but she knew he was pretty sure of the answer.

"No." Not only didn't she want her boss thinking she was

unprofessional, but if the book club women knew, they might pity her when she and Woody broke up.

"Your mom knows, though."

She grimaced. "She guessed. I didn't confirm it, but . . ."

His eyes crinkled at the corners. "Blowing me a kiss the other night might've been a giveaway."

"Mood of the moment." She grinned mischievously. "Hey, if Federov had skated by, I'd have blown him a kiss too."

"Sure you would. And so would your mom."

"That's definitely true."

He took a long drink of water, then sighed contentedly. "Man, this feels good."

"Did you take any bad hits tonight?"

"Nah, I'm okay. Just the usual wear and tear, and no time to heal."

"How are the other guys doing?"

"Connolly's got a cracked rib; Bouchard has a broken finger. The Hammer's got a bad knee; Smythe's got a groin injury." He waved a dismissive hand. "Every player's hurting in some way, but we're all in it to win."

She loved how he trusted her with the Beavers' secrets. Watching the games felt so much more personal when she knew what the men were suffering through. "The Capitals are in as bad shape, I guess."

He nodded. "Bet on it. Did'ya see the way The Hammer went after Norstrom? He hasn't been getting as much ice time and we figure it's his knees—he's had problems before—so we're going after them."

"That's cruel," she protested. "Would you want them going after your shoulder?"

"That's the sport," he said calmly. "It's all about strengths and weaknesses, both individual and team. When you find a weakness, you go after it. No matter whether it's a goaltender's blind spot or a forward's bad shoulder."

"Tough guys." Her lips twitched. "And on that note, shall I adjust your heating pad, Granny?"

"Cheap shot," he complained, "and you're gonna pay for it, woman. Just as soon as I rest a few more minutes."

"I'm only going after your weakness," she said demurely.

"Oh, well, if that's the game we're playing . . ." He put down the water bottle, now empty, and said, "Come sit on my lap."

He guided her as she swung across to straddle his thighs, facing him, and pulled her in for a long, sensuous kiss that sent ripples of arousal through her whole body. Because he was so big, she had to stretch her legs wide, which made her very aware of her sex, growing damp beneath her silk thong. If he got her any more turned on, he'd have to have those suit pants dry-cleaned, and she wouldn't feel the slightest bit guilty. Oh yes, kissing him was definitely her weakness.

Then, holding her shoulders, he eased her back and gazed at her appreciatively. "Did I tell you how pretty you look tonight?"

"Not in so many words."

"You're gorgeous. Fiery hair, creamy skin, black lace. You're like a fantasy, yet you're real. You're Georgia."

Did he think flattery about her looks was another vulnerable spot? She had to admit, she did love hearing it. "Thank you."

He leaned into her, heading not for her lips but her neck. He kissed his way down it with soft, damp presses of his lips, barely grazing the skin yet bringing her body to quivering life. Oh yes, he knew another weakness of hers. There was a spot . . .

Unerringly, his lips closed on it in a gentle nip.

She gasped with pleasure. As he strummed, licked, sucked that supersensitive spot, it was almost as if his mouth were on her clit, the sensation was so intense and blissful.

"You win," she said breathlessly. "I'll surrender—if you promise not to stop."

He raised his head. "What if I have to stop?"

Was he in pain? But no, he went on to say, "What if I have to kiss you?"

"I wish you had two mouths. No, three."

He laughed softly. "I wish I did too. Or why stop there? How about a dozen, and I could kiss you all over at the same time."

"I'd die of sheer bliss."

"Can't have that." Gently, he took her mouth, teasing and savoring it the same way as he had her neck.

She answered back, with tongue thrusts, licks, nibbles. Kissing Woody was like eating a wonderful chocolate. It was heaven, and you wanted it to go on forever, even as you anticipated the next candy in the box.

He shifted position to pull the heating pad from behind his back, and the hard press of his erection grazed her belly.

She wriggled closer. "For a granny, you're pretty hot."

"And getting hotter by the moment. Man, Georgia, you feel even better than you look, and that's saying a lot."

"You too." She leaned in for another kiss, and this time it went deeper, hotter, faster. She ground against him needily and moaned into his mouth. Damn it, she didn't want to eat the chocolates one by one; she wanted the whole box. Right now.

Gasping for breath, he tore his mouth away. "If you want slow and gentle, for Christ's sake, don't wear black lace."

She found enough breath to give a small laugh. "What should I wear?"

"Sweats. Two layers of sweats."

"I don't own sweats." And she didn't want slow and gentle. She tugged the fastener of the ice pack and together they peeled it off him.

"Then you're in deep trouble." He cupped her breasts and ran his thumbs over her budded nipples, the black lace a soft abrasion.

She shuddered with pleasure and attacked the buttons of his

shirt. "I like your kind of trouble." When she'd undone his shirt, she ran her hands over his chest, feeling the heat rising off his skin, the in-and-out movement of hard muscles as he drew air into his lungs. The crisp curls of hair tickling her fingers, the rapid thud of his heartbeat under her palm. "How fast does it beat when you're skating down the ice with the puck?"

"Not that fast."

"No, seriously." She scraped a fingernail across his nipple, then caught it between her thumb and index finger and rolled it.

He sucked in a breath. "Seriously." He leaned into her, forcing her to arch back. That wasn't a bad thing, because it brought her sex even more firmly against the erection that tested the strength of his fly. "On the ice, it's exciting, but I'm in control." He licked her nipple through the lace, around and around the areola; then he sucked the taut bud into his mouth.

Was he saying that, with her, he wasn't in control? What a flattering thought, almost as arousing as what his talented mouth was doing. She ground harder against him, and began to undo his belt.

His hands joined hers. When his zipper was unfastened, she lifted herself for a moment so he could shove his pants and boxer briefs past his knees.

His cock surged between them, unconfined and proud.

Georgia wrapped her hand around it, savoring the silky strength. The erotic musk of their combined arousal filled her nostrils. She wanted to lick him, to suck him, yet she was hungry to have him inside her where she needed him the most.

He touched her between her legs, stroking the damp crotch of her black silk thong. "I want you." His voice was husky, urgent. "Now. Here, like this." He shoved aside the strip of fabric.

So sexy, the idea of making out like this, both of them half-clothed, on the couch in a living room walled by windows. "Yes, like this," she breathed, pumping her hand up and down his shaft.

He took her by the waist, started to lift her, then groaned. "No condom."

No, she didn't want to stop. "Wait." She leaned over to thrust a hand between the seat cushions, found that crackly little package, and held it up triumphantly.

A quick grin flashed on his face; then he'd taken the package from her and was ripping it open, sheathing himself, lifting her again.

She held her breath in anticipation as the head of his cock probed between her folds and eased into her. Then she let out her breath in a gaspy sigh of pleasure. "Oh, yes! That's what I've been waiting for all day."

"You and me both." He tilted his hips, thrust deeper, found her core. His teeth flashed in a smile. "Oh yeah."

Gazing into Woody's deep blue eyes, she needed to move, to stroke the simmer of need, and so she did, lifting up and down on him.

"That's it," he said. "Ride me. Take me. Take what you need."

Her body demanded that she do exactly that. Moisture trickled down the insides of her thighs as she rose high on his shaft, then plunged down again. His cock stroked the sensitive walls of her vagina, nudged her aching clitoris.

Her body tightened with pleasure, with need. Chasing orgasm, she swiveled her hips as she raised and lowered herself. The musky aroma of sex was more pungent, and the only sound was the panting of their breath and the slippery suck-slap of wet flesh.

One of Woody's hands was under her butt, maybe to support her or more likely so he could explore the crease that ran between her cheeks and all the way down to where their bodies joined.

As she spiraled higher, closer, he lifted the bottom of her slip and gently rubbed her clit.

"Oh God," she cried. "Yes."

She rested the crown of her head on his chest and gazed down, seeing his big hand fanned out over her belly, his middle finger between her legs. Each time she rose, his shaft slid out of her; then as she sank down again it disappeared to fill her completely.

Anchored between his hands, front and back, impaled by his cock, all she could do was enjoy the sensations as he took her on a roller-coaster ride that went up, only up, until she crested the peak and cried out as her body came apart.

Clinging to him, she shuddered as waves of pleasure consumed her, then finally slowed until only an occasional tremor rippled through her.

Somehow, she managed to lift her head from his chest. He was hard as steel inside her, his cheeks were as ruddy as her own must be, and his blue gaze was fierce and primal.

"Your turn," she managed to say, wondering how she'd summon the strength in her legs to keep riding him.

But maybe she wouldn't need to. He surged to his feet and she barely managed to wrap her arms and legs around him so she could go along for the ride.

Expecting him to carry her to the bedroom, she was startled when, after kicking free of his pants and underwear, he merely walked around to the back of the couch. He eased her away from him so that his erection sprang free, and let her down to the floor. "Turn around."

Not sure what he had in mind, she slowly obeyed as he said, "Bend over, holding on to the top of the couch."

Hesitantly, she gripped the back of the couch with both hands and stretched out so her torso leaned toward the couch and her butt thrust toward Woody. She felt so vulnerable like this. She'd never had sex this way, and wasn't sure if she wanted to.

He raised her slip past her waist, but didn't pull her thong off. "You have the sexiest ass." He brought his body up behind hers, leaning over so his front met her back and one arm hugged around her. His cock nudged her tangled thong; then he tugged it aside again.

She was so slick with her own juices, he slid inside easily, fully, and she gasped with the delicious impact. Oh yes. She did want this. It felt amazing, being cradled against him as he pumped forward into her. Woody truly was giving her a sexual education.

He buried his face in the back of her neck, pressing kisses to her nape beneath the loose curls of hair. Her nape was sensitive—another erogenous zone he'd revealed to her. Shivers of arousal tingled from where his tongue teased her exposed skin, and deeper ones pulsed from her core, where he thrust harder now.

She gripped the couch, bracing herself to take his thrusts and push back against him.

"God, Georgia," he panted against her skin. "Can't get enough of you." He kissed his way around to that particularly sensitive spot on her neck, sucked, then nipped her.

"Oh!" A second orgasm built within her, more quickly than she'd have believed possible. Would Woody last long enough to carry her along with him when he came?

Bracing herself against the couch, she gazed down again, to see her breasts in black lace jiggling with each thrust, a strong arm holding her captive. Was this really her, this wanton, sexy creature arching to take the powerful thrusts of her lover?

"Damn, I need to come," he gasped. His thumb, rough with urgency, touched her clit. "Come with me."

She was so aroused, so sensitive, that one touch, one command, was all it took to topple her, and they climaxed together for what seemed like forever.

After, they remained like that, bent over, his body curved over hers. Finally, he groaned and straightened, and she gingerly did the same. "I should take yoga," she murmured, rubbing her lower back as she turned to face him. "I'm not as flexible as I should be."

"And I'm not as young as I once was." His eyes sparkled with humor. "What say we both go curl up in a nice, comfy, big bed?"

"That sounds very appealing." And not only because she could stretch out her aching back. She loved sharing the night with him, one of them spooning the other, or him on his back with her nestled in the curve of his arm.

Twenty-seven

How could a guy feel like an old man and a teenager, all at the same time? As Woody took his turn in the bathroom after Georgia, his body ached like he'd been run over by a Zamboni, yet he felt terrific. An endorphin high from the great sex, he figured. Not to mention the thrill of winning the first game in the playoffs, topped off by coming home to find Georgia looking über-hot in skimpy black lace.

A man couldn't ask for a better day.

He popped a muscle relaxant and a painkiller and, whistling, walked naked from the bathroom.

Draped over a chair by the bed was Georgia's black slip, and she was tucked between the covers, grinning at him. "Woody, you're a terrible whistler."

"Gotta have one thing I'm not perfect at," he joked back.

Was this woman really his lucky charm?

His life had sure improved since she came into it. Except for that VitalSport contract, but even the marketing campaign wasn't turning out so bad. People were giving him respect, not just because he looked good in the clothes, but because he was making a contribution to the campaign. Which reminded him . . .

"Hey, I forgot to tell you." He slipped between the sheets and gathered Georgia's warm body into his arms. "You know that *Ellen DeGeneres Show* thing?"

She gave a tolerant smile. "It's all right. I know it's not feasible."

He cocked his head. "Huh?"

"We didn't include it in our plans."

"You didn't think I'd come through," he realized, a little miffed. But then, how many guys could pick up a phone and secure a spot on the most popular TV talk show?

"Woody, it's all right. It would be really tough to—"

"How does Wednesday, two weeks from now, work?"

"Wh-what?" She gaped at him.

Smugly, he went on. "There's a spot if we want it. But I need to get back to Ellen tomorrow. What do you say?"

"Seriously? Oh, Woody," she squealed and hugged him tight. Tight enough to make him wince. "That's fantastic!"

"I'm glad you're happy."

She settled back, lying on her side so she could look at him. "While we're on the subject, there's something else I need to tell you about the campaign."

"Yeah?"

"You know we were planning a formal launch next week, just before the Boys and Girls Club fund-raiser on Saturday?"

He winced again, this time at the thought of his photos—in underwear—plastered everywhere. "Uh-huh."

"Well, Terry had a great idea. He suggested we use teasers instead, pretending they're insider leaks. Marco Sanducci's keen on it. Terry's setting up a Facebook page, supposedly written by an anonymous female fan, and it'll have sneak-peek stuff. Photos before they're retouched, which we'll label 'Woody: Raw.'"

He groaned.

"Man up, tough guy," she teased. "We'll have short clips on YouTube. Terry's been shooting video, right? 'Fangirl' will tweet everything. We're hoping it'll go viral. That's more contemporary and exciting than a traditional launch."

"I guess it makes sense," he said grudgingly. People loved the idea of getting insider scoops, and viral buzz was a big deal.

"We're starting tomorrow, so the confidentiality ban is lifted. Feel free to tell your teammates and friends—the more, the better."

"Oh, great." He'd be in for the razzing of his life when those underwear ads came out. Couple years ago, one of the guys had done a nude shoot for a women's mag and the rest of the team—Woody included—had made huge posters and stuck them up in the players' lounge.

"If you don't tell them, they'll find out on their own."

True, and maybe the timing wasn't so bad. He'd keep the guys so focused on the playoffs that the VitalSport thing would barely be a blip on their radar.

"On a happier subject," he said, tugging her back into the curve of his shoulder. "I talked to my mom."

"She's still feeling good?"

"Better every day. I think this is working." And how great it felt to share his happiness with Georgia.

Woody'd always kept pretty quiet about his personal life. With his teammates, he was a dedicated player and an easygoing guy to talk sports with in the bar. With women, he was an easygoing guy who liked females and sex. Somehow, with Georgia, he'd found himself revealing more and more about the shadows that haunted him. The only thing he hadn't told her about was his former agent's betrayal, because he'd promised to keep the fraud a secret as long as Martin stuck with Gamblers Anonymous. Though Woody'd told his judge friend in confidence, it didn't feel right to tell anyone else.

Georgia rested her head on his chest. "That's wonderful about your mom. You take good care of her."

"As much as she'll let me." Much as he loved his mom, it was hard to think of her without feeling guilty, and a little angry that she'd never looked after herself, or let him do it.

"Parents are supposed to love and protect us, and it's hard when the roles shift." She sighed, her breath warm against his skin. "It's also really hard on a kid when their parents don't protect them as well as they should."

He guessed his mom had done her best, but she'd stayed with that asshole when he hit both of them. She'd told Woody marriage was forever. To him, marriage had looked like hell.

He'd rather talk about Georgia's family. "You and your mom have some issues."

"We do."

"She's always loved you, though?"

"Yes." He heard an unspoken "but."

So, he said it. "But?"

"Her life centered on the men. Her husbands and boyfriends. She was all about being part of a couple, not about being an individual or a mom."

He knew that feeling, but this was her story so he kept quiet.

"It wasn't all bad, because it taught me to be independent and to think for myself. But . . . she didn't protect me as well as she could have."

Her body had tensed, and his did too. "Tell me," he urged.

She was quiet for a long moment. "She dressed me in clothes that were too sexy for my age." Another pause. "When I was thirteen, one of her boyfriends started coming on to me."

Anger made his hand tighten on her shoulder. "Shit, Georgia. He didn't—"

"No, nothing that extreme. But he brushed against me and . . . fondled me. I knew it was wrong, but I was scared to tell Bernadette because I figured she'd take his side."

Shit! Rage coursed through him. "I'd like to beat up the bastard." And castrate him.

"I was in bad shape. I gained weight, threw out all the clothes my mom had bought, and wore boy's clothes. Bernadette reamed me out for it."

"Oh man, you poor kid." Now he wanted to yell at her mom.

"Finally, in tears, I burst out with the story." Wonder in her voice, she went on. "I was sure she wouldn't believe me, but she did. She dumped the guy."

"Thank God." Too bad his mom hadn't had the guts to dump his dad.

"I started to feel better about myself and I lost the weight, but I never wanted to wear the kind of clothes she liked. I met Anthony the next year and—thank heavens—he didn't care how I dressed. He liked me for who I was. He respected me."

Woody thought about how she'd looked when he first met her. All tailored and stiff. She'd said she wanted to be professional, that gender didn't belong in the workplace, that she'd never use feminine wiles to get a promotion. All of that was true, he was sure, but there was more to it. A part of her was still scared that a man might try to take advantage of her.

No wonder she'd picked a sensitive, intellectual guy like Anthony. The surprising thing was that she'd given Woody a second look, much less let herself be seduced into having sex with him. He was an aberration—maybe a walk on the wild side.

She was an aberration for him too: as unlike his usual dates as a woman could get. And he, a man of action and not of sensitivity, was in way over his head.

"I'm really glad you met a guy who treated you right," he said gruffly. "And I wish your mom would, you know, *get* who you are and respect that." Anthony would've had something much wiser to say, but that was the best Woody could do.

"Actually, things are better between us, and it's thanks to you."

"Me?" Had he heard right?

"You were right about changing things up by inviting Bernadette to the game. We kind of bonded. And talked. It was good. But now she's nagging me about bringing you over for dinner."

He chuckled. "Her and Tom Westin. He's trying to fix a time for me to come for dinner after the playoffs, and he invited you."

"Woody." Her voice was tentative. "Does it bother you that they're treating us as if we're, um, a couple?"

He hadn't thought much about it, but now he did. Meeting her mom? Guys met the parents when a relationship was, well, a *relationship*. "Guess we'd better set them straight." And then a horrible thought dawned on him. They'd talked about this, but women's minds worked in mysterious ways. "You don't, I mean . . . You know that I, uh . . ." Crap, the last thing he wanted to do was hurt Georgia.

"You don't do relationships," she said flatly, lifting her head from his chest and staring at him. "That's what you're trying to say."

He shifted uncomfortably. "Well, yeah. I mean, not that you aren't terrific, but—"

"Stop." She shook her head. "Yes, I know this is just casual." She turned away to lie on her back and pulled the sheet snugly up under her armpits, securing it across her chest with folded arms. "Long term, I want something very different than you do. Commitment, marriage, fidelity. You've always made it clear you don't even believe in"—she swallowed—"serial monogamy, so I never—"

"Shit. You don't think I've been sleeping with someone else while we've been together?"

Her head turned and wide amber eyes studied him. "To be honest, I hoped not."

"I haven't." He hadn't felt the slightest urge to be with another woman.

A hint of a smile quivered on her lips, then faded. "Woody, I like you. I know you like me. We've shared something that's special to me. I'll always remember it."

"It's special for me too." He'd never spoken those words to a woman before, and they tasted odd on his tongue, yet strangely right. He would remember her too. He'd remember how she changed his luck, got him back in the zone out on the ice, set him on the path to the Stanley Cup. He'd remember coming home to her in black lace, having her take care of him, sharing secrets while they snuggled in bed.

And the sex, of course. He'd remember the mind-blowing sex.

Shit. He'd really miss her. Before, no woman had ever gotten close enough that he missed her. What the hell was going on here?

That little smile flickered again. "But don't worry. I never believed we had a future together."

Nor had he. So why did Georgia's words make him feel sad?

He was the guy whose parents had soured him on marriage. The guy who'd never even thought about a future with a woman. Not the guy who maybe, sometimes, secretly envied his teammates who had wives and kids cheering for them in the stands, and waiting at home when they came back from a road trip.

Nah, he wasn't that guy.

"Night, Woody," Georgia said, rolling onto her side with her back to him.

"Night, Georgia." He lay on his back for a couple of minutes, then couldn't resist moving over in the bed to spoon her warm, vanilla-scented body.

Wednesday morning, the team was scheduled for a light practice. When everyone was there, Woody called them together: players, coaches, athletic trainers, equipment manager, medical staff.

Before signing the endorsement contract, he'd cleared it with the NHL and with the Beavers' GM and coaches, but everyone else would be hearing about it for the first time.

"Just wanted you to know, I'm doing an endorsement for Vital-Sport, the American company that sells sports clothes and equipment. They're coming into Canada."

Though endorsements were normal for hockey players, everyone knew Woody had resisted, so he got some ribbing and questions.

"VitalSport makes good stuff," he said. "Their clothes are comfortable, look good; people can afford them. And we're not just promoting the product"—this was a point Georgia had impressed on him—"we're promoting recreation, fitness. If the ads get people to pick up a golf club or tennis racquet and get some exercise, that's a good thing, right?"

"And they're paying you the big bucks," Stu joked.

"That too," he admitted. Should he mention the underwear ads? Nah. He'd deal with the taunts when he had to.

Mike Duffy, the head coach, said, "I still can't believe you're doing this. You're the guy who hates promo. We're always dragging you to interviews. Though I gotta admit, you've been doing better lately."

"Yeah, well." Thanks to rehearsals with Terry Banerjee, Woody did feel more comfortable with the media. He'd always be most at home on the ice, but he was getting to where he could hold his own when a mike was thrust in front of his face.

"Okay, guys," Coach Duffy said, "let's talk hockey."

Grateful to no longer be the center of attention, Woody watched and listened as the coaches ran video of the game last night, freezing the action and using a Telestrator to highlight strengths and weaknesses. The players shared their perspectives, and they all talked strategy.

Before the team headed out on the ice to practice, Woody said, "You guys did great last night, but we can't rest on our laurels. You can bet, as much as we're strategizing, the Caps are doing more. They're the underdogs, and they'll fight back with a vengeance. We can't ease up for a moment. Imagine if it was us, one game down. Think how determined you'd be to turn things around."

Heads nodded as he went on. "We have to be that determined, and more. That focused, that skilled. I know you're all hurting. When you're off the ice, take care of yourselves. Massage, physio, lots of rest, eat properly, be careful with the booze. But once you set foot on the ice, there's no pain, no doubt, no hesitation. You're one hundred fifty percent. Body, mind, focus. You can't be anything less. None of us can."

He paused to glance at his team. He saw bruises and stitches but, as his eyes met those of each player in turn, he also saw total determination, a primal drive to win.

Though his shoulder was killing him, he held himself straight and tall, proud of the whole damned bunch of them. He kissed the Stanley Cup ring on his finger. "This is what we're doing it for. For the ring, the Cup. For going down in history. But more than that, for each other, and for the fans." He pumped his fist in the air and bellowed, "Bash 'em, Beavers!"

They all shouted back in unison.

He took a moment to savor their combined ferocity, then sent them onto the ice.

Before the game tomorrow, he'd give them a similar talk. But this morning had been crucial. He wanted them to feel pride in last night's victory, but not to get cocky.

One thing he knew for sure about hockey: you could never count on a win.

Twenty-eight

The practice went well, Woody got a massage that loosened up his bad shoulder, and he had lunch in the players' lounge with some of the other guys. He'd have been in a great mood except for one thing. The next item on his schedule was the underwear shoot.

There was only one way to deal with shit that was inevitable: suck it up and get on with it.

Shoulders squared, he entered the studio. Only to reel back in horror. He'd hoped for one photographer—male, of course—and one camera. Instead, the room was full of people and equipment. Terry Banerjee was there, and Marco Sanducci from VitalSport, but most everyone else was female.

Georgia, looking stunning in a dark gray skirt suit and a coral-colored blouse, came over to him. "Woody." She held out her hand as if to shake his.

He'd take any kind of contact he could get, so he put his hand into hers.

Rather than shake, she tugged him firmly into the room. "You look shell-shocked."

Viv came to join them and Georgia gave his hand a subtle squeeze, then released it.

The blonde winked. "This is the highlight of the campaign. I've really been looking forward to today."

A grin twitched the corners of Georgia's lips, but she held it back.

"As have I," she said evenly. "After all, it's the underwear line that's being launched first in Canada."

"What're all these people doing here?" he grumbled.

"The woman with Marco is the designer of the line—who's very disappointed we ruled out thong photos, by the way. Then there's the team of photographers, there's hair and makeup, and—"

"They're women," he protested.

Georgia's lips twitched again. "You're so perceptive."

Viv took over. "They'll do a great job at capturing the image we want to convey."

"I have to model underwear in front of all these people?"

"Got a problem with nudity?" Georgia asked, a wicked gleam in her eye. "You'd never survive in the locker room." Those were pretty much the exact same words he'd taunted her with, the day they met.

"Ha-ha," he said without humor.

"I'm sure we won't be the first women to see you in your undies," Viv joked.

"I'd bet on that," Georgia put in, and he could see she was fighting to hold back a laugh.

His mood lightened, but only a little.

"I'm still not sure we should have ruled out the thong," Viv said. "Maybe we should take some photos just in case."

"No fucking way," he said before he noticed the twinkle in her eyes.

Georgia touched his arm, bare below a VitalSport golf shirt that he wore with a pair of their casual pants. His skin heated with sexual awareness. If her plan was to distract him from his misery, it was working.

She gazed up at him, face serious now. "Woody, I'm sorry this is uncomfortable for you. But you've faced the media in a locker room in less than your underwear. You're a physical guy who's comfortable with his body. Right?"

"Usually."

She smiled and released his arm. "I think you have two options. One is to be the tough guy and grit your teeth and get through it."

That was what he'd figured on.

"But that's not the best approach," she went on. "You'll be miserable, and it'll show in the photos. Why not relax and have fun with it?"

"Fun? You gotta be kidding."

"You complained about going to Christopher Slate," Viv pointed out, "and look how well that turned out."

"It's a matter of attitude," Georgia said. "Like when the Beavers go on the ice, they could be intimidated by their opponents, worrying about how they'll measure up, feeling their injuries. But that's not what they do, is it?"

He shook his head. "We go in strong. Determined to play our best and to win."

"Attitude is a choice. You can make the choice to be positive about this."

Crap. She was right. He twisted his lips into a rueful smile. "You make a good argument, Coach Malone."

She beamed, eyes and smile lighting up her face.

Who could resist that smile? "Okay, I'll be positive." He winked and said, "Just for you, sunshine."

When he'd called her that at the first Dynamic Marketing meeting, she'd glared at him. Now she chuckled. "Thanks. Now, what do you hockey players say? Go suit up?"

"Yeah." Which meant putting on layers of protective gear, not stripping down to gonch. But hell, he was going to be positive.

Resignedly, he trudged over to the cluster of women and forced a smile. "Okay, ladies, I'm putting myself in your hands."

As they got under way, he felt self-conscious, but Georgia's warm smiles and nods of approval boosted his confidence, and all the women were professional and friendly. Georgia was right; being comfortable with his body helped. Being comfortable with women did as well.

It wasn't long before he was joking with the women who applied spray tan to body parts that never saw the sun, tousled his hair, and instructed him to stand this way, hold that prop, put his arm around the blond model, give a sexy smile.

What bugged him the most was that Sanducci was flirting with Georgia. The dude was handsome, successful, and he had the kind of poise and sophistication Woody would never master, no matter how many *deportment* lessons he endured. He couldn't hear what they were saying, but Georgia's body language told him she wasn't flirting back. Still, he wondered if, when the two of them split, she'd take up with Sanducci.

"Woody, what's wrong?" the photographer asked. "You're scowling. Frown lines are bad. Broody and mysterious is sexy. Frowning, definitely not."

He'd been scowling? Woody told himself there was no reason he should care whom Georgia dated down the road. Right now they were having a good time, and she knew she was his lucky charm. She'd never dump him during the playoffs.

And the Beavers would win the Cup. He focused on how it'd feel to skate around the ice with that massive trophy held high above his head, and it was easier to smile again.

When everyone finally proclaimed it a wrap, Woody sighed with relief and went to shower off the spray tan, body oil, and makeup. The pounding spray felt good on his aching shoulder. After this, he'd go for a run, soak in his whirlpool tub, then ice his shoulder. Georgia would come over for dinner and an early night. Good company, great sex, and a solid night's sleep. What better way to set himself up for tomorrow night's home game?

He hoped the other guys were behaving themselves. The married ones loved days like this, where they could pick their kids up from school. Some of them had wives who didn't have jobs or who worked from home, and they'd be getting in some couple time. It was the young guys like Stu Connolly he worried about. Vancouver loved the Beavers, and if a rookie hit a sports bar, it'd be less than a minute before someone wanted to buy him a drink. If he hit the Roxy, puck bunnies would swarm him.

At practice, the guys had been on their game and motivated. They wanted the Cup as badly as he did. He had to trust his men to stick to the program.

A couple hours later, Woody sprawled on the couch watching a soccer game on TV and anticipating the look on Georgia's face when she found out about the surprise he had for her. Oh yeah, they'd be having sex before dinner tonight.

His phone rang. When he answered, the sound that greeted his ears was hyena-like laughter.

"Who the hell is this?"

"Stu." One word came through amid the howls.

Shit. The rookie was drunk. God knew what trouble he'd gotten himself into. Woody straightened up and clicked off the game. "Where are you? What the fuck's going on?"

"You didn't say it was fucking gonch." The words came out in gasps strung out through more laughter.

Words that didn't make sense. "What're you talking about?"

"Oh man, it's going viral. I'm in this sports bar"—his voice sobered for an instant—"one beer, I swear, that's all I'm having. Anyhow, this girl's friend tweeted her, and she checked out YouTube on her iPhone, and now everyone's looking at it."

"At what?" Woody almost screamed.

"That video of the gonch shoot."

Woody clenched the phone in a death grip. "Video of a gonch shoot?" A sinking feeling crept through his body, chilling him.

"The girls are going crazy. They think you're the hottest thing they've ever seen."

Video of a gonch shoot? Phone to his ear, Woody hurried into his office, where he kept his trophies, photos, and business stuff. He turned on his computer.

"I'm texting the other guys," Stu said. "No one's gonna want to miss this."

"Stop texting; stop drinking," Woody ordered. "Go home and focus on hockey." With the phone hooked between his ear and shoulder, he typed YouTube's URL into his browser, then his name and, shuddering, "underwear."

"Hope they're paying you a lot of money for this," Stu said, then hung up.

Woody found the video: *Woody Hanrahan RAW—Canadian hockey star models VitalSport underwear,* posted by "Woody's insider fangirl." Two minutes long? He clicked on it, then sat, barely breathing.

Terry'd been unobtrusive today, moving around with his video camera so constantly that he was part of the background. And this was the result. Footage shot to look amateur, candid, furtive, of Woody in white boxer briefs joking with the blond model, Woody in skimpy chocolate-colored briefs as the makeup girl sprayed fake tan on the top curve of his ass. Woody's face in close-up, then a jerky pan down his body, lingering on his pecs, his abs, and, yeah—fuck it!—on his package barely confined in the pouch of black briefs.

He buried his face in his hands and groaned.

Then, remembering what Georgia'd said, he went to Facebook. Yup, there was a page—WoodyRAW—with several gushy updates posted over the course of the afternoon, accompanied by photos. Fuck. He studied them with morbid fascination, wondering which ones, blown up to poster size, would adorn the locker room tomorrow.

How the hell could Georgia do this to him?

Woody leaped to his feet and paced, and gradually sanity overcame anger.

He'd known, since the shock of that first morning, that he'd have to model gonch. Georgia had told him last night about the social media campaign. He sure wished she'd told him the details, though, so he didn't find out from a rookie who was laughing his head off over it.

He reminded himself of the bottom line. He had a damned good reason for doing all of this: saving his mom's life. He wished he could talk to her right now, but it was the middle of the night in Switzerland.

Still, he could call the clinic and leave a voice mail. "Hey, Mom. Hope you're getting a good night's sleep. Just wanted to tell you I'm thinking of you. I had kind of a rough day—nothing serious, okay?—and it made me want to talk to you. So, I'm just saying hi, and I hope you feel better every day." He paused. "Okay, good night, then. Or good morning, which is what it'll be when you get this message. Love you."

Feeling marginally better, he fought the urge to grab a beer. One drink was his limit tonight, and it'd be a glass of wine at dinner with Georgia. After he gave her flak for keeping him in the dark.

When she knocked on the door, then opened it, he went to meet her. She was wearing her work suit, and there was an anxious expression on her face.

"There's something I have to tell you," she said.

"You're an hour too late. I've seen the YouTube video and the Facebook page. Didn't check Twitter. Tell me there's nothing more."

She sighed. "No, that's it. I'm sorry. I'd hoped to get to you before anyone else did, and tell you in person. How upset are you?"

"Upset? I'm a guy. I don't get upset. I get pissed. Why didn't you tell me?"

She winced. "I told you that we'd be—"

"Yeah, yeah, but not that it'd start with a fucking video of me in fucking gonch."

"Terry was in charge of this part of the campaign. We held off on posting stuff from the Stanley Park shoot because, while it's strong, it doesn't have the same punch. Today, at the underwear shoot, he realized this material was seriously hot, so he started posting it."

"You should've told me before I left."

"I didn't know. Terry didn't tell me. He should have, but he was excited, and so sure it was right. He's young; he gets carried away. I've spoken to him about it."

Woody sighed. "It was gonna happen sooner or later."

Sympathetically, she said, "And this was the right timing. The video already has ten thousand hits." She touched his arm. "It's good. You look great." She moved closer. "Hot."

His annoyance faded. "You think?"

"Very hot."

Starting to feel a little cocky, he said, "Hot enough to turn you on?"

Her eyes glittered as she stared up at him. "Most definitely."

"How about if I tell you I'm wearing one of those damned thongs?"

Her eyes popped wide-open. "You are? I thought you hated them."

"Sure do. Can't wait to take the thing off. Or," he added suggestively, "have someone take it off for me."

Her hands were already at his belt, opening the buckle.

"It was so cool," she said, head bent as she worked the fastenings of his pants, "watching you at that shoot. All the women thought you looked fantastic, and I kept thinking, 'I'm the one he'll be with tonight.'"

Words like that really stroked a guy's ego. But even better were the hands fumbling inside his pants and caressing the front of his thong as his body stirred to life.

His pants slid down and he kicked them off. He pulled the golf shirt over his head and stood there naked but for a black thong.

A rapidly swelling black thong.

Georgia stepped back and twirled a finger. "Turn around."

He obeyed.

"You really do have a tight, taut, amazing butt," she said appreciatively.

"And it's touchable," he pointed out.

"I noticed that when the makeup girl was fake-tanning you," she teased. "She seemed to enjoy it."

The woman—Wendy—had slipped him her phone number. A number he wouldn't be using. Yeah, Wendy was striking, funny, and if Georgia wasn't in his life, he'd have held on to that number. But Georgia was in his life.

Wait. She was *temporarily* in his life. After the playoffs, she'd go looking for that soul mate guy—who *wasn't* Marco Sanducci—and Woody'd move on too. He always moved on.

Yet it was hard to imagine being with anyone other than Georgia.

Especially when her hands slid over the naked curves of his ass and massaged his glutes in a way that was totally different from how the male massage therapist did it.

She came around to stand in front of him, peeling off her suit jacket and tossing it on the couch. Then she stepped forward until the fronts of their bodies touched. "We never really said hello."

He put his arms around her as she did the same. "Hello, Georgia."

"Hello, Woody. Have you stopped being pissed?"

"You're distracting me nicely."

"I'm sorry the VitalSport campaign turned out differently than you expected."

"Not your fault." He grinned. "It has some unexpectedly good aspects."

"Would this be one of them?" She came up on her toes to kiss him, the front of her body pressing closer against his, and his cock grew harder.

She'd have felt better naked, but she still felt damned good as he held her and kissed her, letting her sweet mouth soothe away the days' problems. Oh yeah, sex before dinner was definitely going to happen.

Or maybe not. She pulled away.

But when she kicked off her shoes and sank to her knees on the Persian area rug, he liked where this was headed.

She leaned her head against his belly, her wavy hair tickling softly. "You're too big for that thong." Her tongue licked the crown of his cock, and he realized his erection had escaped the confines of the gonch.

"Only when you're around." Man, her tongue felt good, running in crazy circles around him, then flicking across the eye of his cock. "Feel free to take it off."

"Thanks. I think I will."

She eased the underwear down, bit by bit, following with her tongue, her lips. Lapping, sucking, teasing every inch of him until the blood surged hotly through his entire body.

When the brief garment hit the floor, he stepped out of it, wondering if she'd stop. Not sure if he hoped she did, so he could strip off her clothes and get inside her, or if she didn't, and kept torturing him this way.

Her hand grasped his shaft, her lips closed over the top, and she took him into the wet, silky warmth of her mouth.

"Oh, fuck," he murmured under his breath. "That's so damned good."

He tangled his fingers in her hair and held on as she began to suck rhythmically.

It was like she was milking an orgasm from him, pulling it from the base of his spine, to his tightening balls, to the root of his cock.

He groaned and clenched his muscles against the need to come.

Her tongue swirled around him as she sucked and her hair tickled him with fiery strands. She made wet, hungry sounds mixed in with "mmm" noises, and soft fingers toyed with his balls.

His climax gathered, urgent and demanding. "I can't hold on," he gasped. "Have to come."

Slowly, she freed her mouth. Tilted her head back. Looked up at him.

Georgia, on her knees, wearing her gray business skirt and coral-colored blouse. Her creamy cheeks were flushed, her red hair a wild tumble. She smiled. "Then do it."

She bent her head again, and sucked him in.

Every iota of self-control vanished. He let go. Let the orgasm surge through him in hot, pulsing waves that wrenched a cry from him, and crested in the heat of her mouth.

She hung on for the ride, swallowing, lapping, teasing every last ounce from him until he was empty. Drained, satiated. His whole body hummed with pleasure and exhaustion.

"Jesus, woman, you're really something."

Twenty-nine

Georgia gazed up at Woody. He was so masculine, so perfect, so sexy. She still had trouble believing she could use this spectacular body as her sensual playground.

Giving him a blow job, feeling and hearing his response—taking him, claiming him as hers—had been a total turn-on, and now her own body demanded reciprocity. One thing she'd learned: he wasn't a selfish lover. So she said, "Seems to me, it's my turn now."

She'd barely started to rise when he swept her up in his arms and carried her down the hall to the bedroom. On the way, she undid the buttons of her blouse, and when he let her down, she unfastened her skirt.

Together, hands getting in each other's way, they peeled her clothes off. She lay on the bed naked, basking in the approval she saw in his eyes.

"Fast or slow?" he asked.

Once, a question like that would have embarrassed her, but Woody had taught her to be proud of her sexuality. "Fast. I'm so horny for you I can't wait."

She guessed every straight woman who'd been at that underwear shoot, or seen the video, was horny for him. But it was her needy body—only hers—that would receive satisfaction.

He tossed her a pillow. "Put that under you."

She slid it under her butt, then planted her feet on the bed so her legs were apart, her knees up. Offering herself to him. Or, more accurately, demanding that he take her.

Take her to heaven. Now.

He stroked the length of her legs, then lowered himself between them. "So beautiful." Gently, he touched her inner thigh, running his fingers in circles, drawing her attention. The circles drifted higher, flicked the lips of her pussy, and she moaned. This was his idea of fast?

Couldn't he put her out of her misery now?

The circling, stroking fingers continued on their journey, brushing her clit as if by accident.

She whimpered. "Yes, more. Please."

He gave a chuckle, its soft, easy tone lulling her, fooling her.

So that the last thing she expected was two fingers spearing into her. Firm, deep, and delicious.

She cried out with pleasure as he pumped fast and hard, just the way she wanted. The way she needed. Oh God, that was good. Wonderful. Incredible.

That fast, she was close, so close, to coming.

He bent lower, sucked her clit, and that was all it took. She cried out again, loud and long, as spasms of sweet relief rocked her.

Finally. She'd been wanting, needing, this for hours, and he'd finally given it to her.

When the last tremor had quieted and she felt all soft and melty, Woody slid the pillow out from under her and kissed her. "Hungry?" he asked.

How romantic. And yet, she was. "Let's get dressed."

Moving slowly, they pulled on clothing. No thong for Woody this time; he went with the boxer briefs he preferred.

In the kitchen, they worked companionably. Together they

ripped romaine and radicchio and chopped up vegetables for a huge salad, talking about this and that. He threw chicken breasts on the grill while she prepared linguine Alfredo.

"Want to set the table?" Woody asked.

Georgia noted the way he favored his left shoulder, and the narrow lines that bracketed his mouth. "I bet you'd rather relax on the couch. Maybe watch a movie?"

"Man, that sounds good. You wouldn't mind?"

She shook her head. "Not if we can agree on a movie."

"Check the cabinet by the TV, or we could order Pay-Per-View."

Browsing, she found, unsurprisingly, a lot of action-adventure and sports movies. She pulled out one called *Slap Shot*. The cover image told her it was about hockey. It looked more humorous than macho, and it starred Paul Newman, back in the days when he was still pretty hot. She took the DVD into the kitchen, where Woody was pouring two glasses of chardonnay. "What about this one?"

He laughed. "Oh, man. You haven't seen that?"

She shook her head. "Is it good?"

"Matter of opinion. It's a cult movie. Every hockey player's watched it dozens of times. Yeah, you have to see it."

They took dinner and wine into the living room and settled in front of the TV.

The meal was pleasant, and the movie pretty bizarre. The most bizarre thing was that, according to Woody, much of the script was based on actual players and incidents in minor-league hockey.

When he paused the DVD and went to the kitchen to refill her wineglass and get a bottle of water and an ice wrap, Georgia asked, "How about the trash talk? Do players really do that, to try to get under another guy's skin?"

"Sure. It's part of the game."

"The underwear ads . . . They'll give the Capitals fuel, won't they? I'm sorry about that."

"Can't pay any attention to that shit. It's all about focus."

She helped him strap on the ice wrap, then curled into the shelter of his big arm as he restarted the movie.

When it came to the scene where the young, principled hockey player played by Michael Ontkean did a striptease on ice, all the way down to his jockstrap, they both howled with laughter.

"If—excuse me, when—you win the Stanley Cup," she teased, "will you do that?"

"Hell, what's the point?" he joked back. "The whole world's seen me in my gonch already."

This was fun, relaxing, domestic. As domestic as reading with Anthony, their feet touching companionably on the coffee table. A girl could get used to this.

No, she couldn't. Woody didn't want domestic. He'd made his views crystal clear.

This was one little interlude for him, during the playoffs, when he needed to rest and focus and he thought Georgia was his good luck charm.

She couldn't let herself want it to be more. She needed to be as sensible as Lady Emma, to enjoy the moment and not long for more.

Woody rose. "Time for bed."

She gazed up at him, and it hit her. She'd stopped being sensible. She cared for this man. Really cared. Was falling for him. Maybe had already fallen.

He was so different from Anthony, but he was so special. Could Woody Hanrahan be her soul mate? To her, the answer was clear. Yes.

But would he let himself be?

He held out his hand and she let him pull her to her feet. He had to see how good they were together. How couldn't he want the same things she did?

He'd proven he was a quick learner in a lot of areas, but maybe when it came to commitment, he was slow. His parents had made him cynical about marriage, but perhaps, over time, he'd realize that it was so much more rewarding to be with one special person than to have a bunch of meaningless flings.

Was she crazy to hope?

Wednesday started great, with Georgia in his bed, which Woody figured was a good omen. Yeah, he would suffer through a bunch of ribbing about the gonch photos, but the guys would get past it. Game days were laid out in a pattern, with routines that kept everyone focused on what counted.

Sure enough, when he entered the locker room, he saw that some jerk—probably Stu—had gotten posters made. Woody didn't let it rattle him. When he got the expected insults about the relative size of his package, he tossed them back. It was good practice for the trash talk he knew he'd face from the Caps on the ice.

He was about to change into his gear for the pregame practice when Coach Duffy stepped into the locker room. "Hanrahan, I need to talk to you."

Nothing unusual about the head coach wanting a private word with the captain, nor the fact that, when they sat down in the coach's office, Mike Duffy's expression was serious. It was a game day in the Stanley Cup playoffs. This was a time to be serious.

The coach's words weren't what he expected, though. "Woody, you've always kept quiet about your childhood and your parents. You didn't give us much for your official bio, and it's a taboo topic for interviews."

"Yeah?" he said warily. They'd been through this before.

"Has anything changed, like with this VitalSport endorsement?"

He shook his head. "Nah, I told them the same thing as you. That stuff's off-limits."

Coach Duffy ran a hand over his short, graying beard. "Then you don't know what's just hit the hockey gossip blogs?"

"You mean the gonch photos? Yeah, it sucks, and I didn't realize the contract included underwear, but I'm stuck with it."

The coach shook his head. "Not that. About your mom and dad."

"My . . . mom and dad?" Woody had the same sinking feeling as yesterday, but ten times worse. "What are they saying?"

Duffy's gray eyes, usually steely, held a touch of sympathy. "That your dad was an alcoholic who beat up on you and your mom, but she wouldn't leave him."

Woody sucked in a breath, feeling like he'd taken a hit to the solar plexus.

"That he was killed in a bar fight. That your mom's dying of cancer—"

"She's not dying!"

"Sorry. Just repeating what I read. The blogs say you sent her to Switzerland for some expensive alternative therapy."

"Shit!" Woody fisted his right hand, wishing he could slam it into the fucker who was responsible for this. "Shit, fuck! Where the hell did they get that?"

"I dunno." He scratched his balding head. "Is it true?"

Warily, Woody said, "Maybe."

"Who knows about your parents? Hell, I didn't know."

Woody shook his head. Only his old friend Sam, and Sam's dad, Martin, Woody's former agent. But they'd never said a word, not in all these years, and never would.

Georgia knew.

She wouldn't tell. She'd sworn to keep his secrets, and he trusted her.

But she was in marketing. She hadn't told him about the You-Tube video, not until he'd already seen it. If she thought it'd help the VitalSport campaign . . .

No, she wouldn't.

"Someone betrayed you," Coach Duffy said soberly. "You better figure out who that is. And what I want to know is, do they know about your shoulder? If the Caps find out about your shoulder—" He broke off.

Fuck! Not only did Georgia know about his shoulder, she knew about Bouchard's finger, Hammarstrom's knee, the whole fucking catalogue of injuries. If she spilled those secrets, the Beavers didn't stand a chance.

"I gotta go."

Duffy's eyes were steely now. "The captain missing pregame practice . . . That's not good. But this is more important. You gotta shut this down before it goes any further."

"No shit."

Betrayed. First by Martin, the man who'd been almost like a father—a *good* father—to him. And now by Georgia, the only woman he'd ever trusted. How the hell had he let her get that close to him?

"I'll talk to the team," Coach Duffy said. "They'll hear the gossip soon enough."

The captain was the leader, the one who was supposed to be the strongest, the one who guided the team and motivated them. Not the one who could cost them the Cup.

Furious, Woody stormed down the corridor and out of Rogers Arena. He'd walked here, since it was so close to his condo. Now he pumped it up to a run, heading toward the heart of downtown and the office tower that housed Dynamic Marketing. When that bitch Angela went to the tabloids last year, he'd been royally pissed, but this was way different. As fast as he ran, he couldn't outrun the hurt and anger at Georgia's betrayal.

What a fucking idiot he'd been.

Sandra was at reception, and greeted him with a bright smile—until she really took him in. Her eyes widened.

Sweat dripped into his eyes and he flicked it aside as he strode past her.

"Woody?" she called after him, but he didn't answer.

The door to Georgia's office was open and she sat behind her desk, phone headset resting amid her red curls. Her eyes widened too, and she jumped when he slammed the door behind him.

Two long strides took him to her desk. He planted his hands on the edge and leaned into her face. "How the fuck could you do it?"

Thirty

Georgia gaped at the sweaty, belligerent man looming toward her across the desk. The man who, only short hours ago, had kissed her good morning. The one she'd been falling in love with.

"I have to call you back," she muttered into the phone, then slowly pulled the headset off.

She'd seen Woody annoyed before, but this time a dark energy rolled off him that actually scared her. She scooted her swivel chair back a couple of feet and gazed at him warily. "Woody? What's wrong?"

"Like you don't know."

She frowned, shook her head. "Did the team give you a hard time over those photos?"

"Jesus! If that's all it was. Fuck, Georgia."

Clearly, he was furious about something, but that didn't give him the right to behave this way with her. The heat of anger brought her to her feet. "Don't swear at me. I don't have a clue what you're talking about."

"You betrayed me."

Her lips parted, but shock held her mute. She would never betray Woody. How could he think that?

"You leaked those stories about my parents."

"What stories?" Had he gone crazy?

Doubt flickered in his eyes; then he said, "If it wasn't you, it was one of your team. You told them, didn't you?"

"I—"

Before she could deny it, he went on. "Terry. Maybe he figured it'd help the campaign. Like how he posted the Facebook and You-Tube stuff before checking with you."

"I still don't know what stories you're talking about." She reached for her telephone headset. "Let me check."

She dialed Terry's local. "Do you know anything about some stories about Woody's parents?"

When he said no, and asked what she was talking about, she said to Woody, "Where did you see them?"

"Coach told me about them. They're on the hockey gossip blogs."

"Hockey gossip blogs," she repeated to Terry, sitting at her computer to do an Internet search. A moment later, she saw the headlines of the search results. It was all there: his father's alcoholism, the abuse, his mom's treatments in Switzerland. "Damn," she muttered. Poor Woody. He was such a private man, and now his carefully kept secrets were spilled all over the Internet.

Terry said, "Yeah, I see it. Where did this stuff come from?"

"It wasn't you?" she asked.

"I didn't know anything about his parents. He said his family was off-limits."

"I know."

"It's not bad, though," he said. "It humanizes him even more. Guy who rises above a rotten past. Takes care of his mom."

It might not be bad for the campaign, but it sure wasn't what Woody wanted. "Thanks, Terry." Slowly, she took off the headset again. "Woody, this is terrible. But it wasn't us."

He'd stopped leaning on her desk and was standing, hands fisted at his hips, still looking intimidating. "Viv, then, or Billy

Daniels." There was no uncertainty in his voice. "You told one of them."

Her mouth fell open. "I did not!" she snapped. How could he believe, for one moment, that she'd share his secrets? "You told me in confidence."

"And you broke that confidence."

"No." Shaking her head, feeling as if he'd stabbed her through the heart, she sank back in her chair. "I'd never do that." They were lovers. Yes, he'd said their relationship was casual, but she'd thought he trusted her, believed in her. Cared for her.

Yes, she knew what betrayal felt like. He'd just done it to her.

"Women gossip. You told someone. Maybe not Viv; maybe one of those book club girls. Or your mother. You can't tell me you didn't talk to them about me."

She forced herself to straighten her shoulders, though what she really wanted to do was curl up in a ball and cry. "Yes, but never about your personal life. I thought you knew me better than that."

"I don't know you at all," he spat out.

"And I don't know you either. I had no idea you were such a jerk!"

He leaned forward again, his face—her lover's face, now hard and cold as granite—mere inches from hers. "There's just one thing I want to know."

"What?"

"Did you tell anyone about the injuries? Are you going to? What'll it take to stop you?"

It took every ounce of willpower she possessed to not break down. To open her mouth and say, "Get out of my office."

"No." He glared at her, hands still fisted at his hips. "Not until you tell me. Damn it, I'm the captain and I screwed my team over by trusting you. I gotta make it right. Gotta stop you, whatever it takes."

She leaped to her feet, hands on her own hips. "Whatever it

takes?" She, who rarely raised her voice, was screeching now. "What are you going to do? Hit me? Pay me off?"

"George?" A male voice spoke from behind Woody's huge frame. "Woody? What's going on?"

Woody swung around, no longer blocking her view of the doorway. Billy Daniels had opened the door and stood staring at both of them.

"Tell her," Woody commanded. "Tell her she can't jeopardize the Beavers' chances at the Cup."

Slowly, feeling his way, Billy said, "George would never do that. Right, George?"

"Of course I wouldn't." She sank into her chair again. Could she go home, pull the covers over her head, and sob her heart out? No, she had to be professional. "Woody thinks someone at Dynamic has been leaking personal information to hockey gossip sites."

Billy shook his head. "Only photos. We don't have any information that could harm the Beavers. Right?" He looked at Georgia for confirmation.

She had that information. She knew the roster of injuries, information the Washington Capitals would love to get their hands on. But she'd acquired that privately, because she was—had been—sleeping with Woody. It wasn't Dynamic's information, and no matter how mad or hurt she was, she'd never use it against the team.

"No," she said firmly, "we don't. Tell Woody he has nothing to worry about."

Uneasily, Billy eyed the two of them. "Woody, you heard George. Now, let's all settle down, okay? There's a game tonight. Shouldn't you be at practice?"

With a final long, piercing glare at her, Woody stalked out of the office without speaking another word to either of them.

Billy stared after him, then turned to her. "Is there anything I need to know about?"

"No." He didn't need to know that she felt so miserable she wanted to die.

F ocus? What the hell was focus? How could a guy focus when his teammates were tiptoeing around him like they were fucking ballet dancers? When the woman he'd let into his life had betrayed him? When he didn't have an inkling whether the Capitals knew about the Beavers' injuries?

He'd told the coaches there was nothing to worry about, and could only hope he was right. When the puck dropped in Rogers Arena, he kept an eagle eye on the Caps. They were sure as hell trash-talking him, but they weren't going after his shoulder, The Hammer's knee, or any of the team's other physical vulnerabilities. Thank God.

Even so, the Beavers were having an off night.

Washington scored in the first period and again at the top of the second. The Beavers didn't get many shots on goal, much less actually get the puck into the net.

Midway through the second period, Woody took a penalty for boarding and, cursing under his breath, took his seat in the penalty box. It'd be just their luck if Washington scored on the power play.

The Caps tried their best, but Federov stopped every shot. Then Stu caught the puck on a rebound and, controlling it neatly, streaked toward the Washington goal. The Capitals' defense landed on him, sending him crashing to the ice and into the boards.

It was a hit, just like any other hit.

Except, it wasn't.

Woody knew he'd replay that moment in his mind, in his dreams, for months to come. The rookie star, the kid on the first line who'd scored the game-winning goal on Tuesday, just lay there. Knocked out.

Woody was leaping out of the box even before the whistle blew calling play. Everyone converged, the players and refs from on the ice and the coaches and medics from off the ice.

The medics forced everyone to stand back and Woody watched, heart in his throat as Stu finally stirred and groaned, his face twisted in pain. The damned kid, full of heart, raised his head, put his hands behind himself, and tried to push up onto his feet. But his legs didn't work.

Woody would never forget the gut-ripped expression on the kid's face when he realized his legs didn't work.

"Fuck," Woody cursed. How bad was it? He'd been around long enough to know that an injury like this could blow over in a day or two, or it could be serious. Really serious.

Would Stu ever play again? Hell, would he walk again? He was fucking twenty-one years old.

No, that was negative thinking. Woody had to believe it'd turn out to be something minor, and the kid would be playing beside him when they took home the Cup.

Stu was loaded onto a stretcher, and Woody skated alongside as he was taken off the ice. "Hang in there, kid. It's gonna be okay."

"Sure, Captain," Stu said, but his voice shook and his eyes were wide with fear.

Woody watched the stretcher go. Yeah, it had been a hit just like any other. Except . . . Had Stu been distracted by all the shit that had gone down today, and lost his concentration? That'd make it Woody's fault.

Play resumed, the Capitals taking a three-minute penalty, but the Beavers couldn't get it together to take advantage of the power play. They'd all taken that hit at some level.

At the end of the period, Washington scored again.

In the third period, the Beavers fought the good fight, but they were always a millisecond too late, too slow. At least they kept the Caps from scoring again and humiliating them even worse.

In the locker room, there was nothing to say. Not to one another, not to the reporters.

They all hurried to shower and change, then took off to Vancouver General Hospital.

The assistant coach was already there. He said Stu was in surgery, and he'd spoken to the parents back in Texas. They'd be flying out as soon as they could get on a plane.

Here in Vancouver, the team was the rookie's family. And so, they waited.

If Woody and Georgia were still together, he'd have called her. Hearing her voice would have helped him survive the wait.

But they weren't together. She'd betrayed him.

Besides, he didn't deserve to feel better. Guilt and worry churned in him.

Coach Duffy came over. "Stop beating yourself up. It wasn't your fault."

"I keep wondering if the shit that went down—my shit— distracted him. Hell, I've got a decade on him, and I lost my focus tonight."

"Stu didn't lose focus. He took a hit. You know this shit happens. It's the sport. The sport we all love."

He didn't love it so much tonight. Not with Stu in surgery, maybe never going to walk again.

Duffy settled back in a plastic chair and stretched until his spine cracked. "It's been one hell of a day."

"You can say that again."

Eventually, a doctor came out. The two coaches went to speak to him. Woody watched, not breathing, willing the news to be good.

The doctor disappeared again and the team rose to surround their coaches. "So far, so good," Coach Duffy said. "They operated; there'll be swelling in his spine. It's too soon to know for sure, but once the swelling goes down there's a really good chance he'll be on his feet again."

There was a long silence, then the coach answered the unvoiced question. "They don't know whether he'll make it back on the ice."

The players exchanged grim glances.

Coach Duffy ran a hand over his balding head, looking older than Woody'd ever seen him. "He won't wake up for a while, and you guys won't be able to see him. Go home. Home, not the bar. Get some sleep. We fly to Washington in the morning."

Reluctantly, the players wandered away. Woody stayed, and so did Mike Duffy.

"Can't use a cell here," the coach said. "I'm going outside to update Stu's parents."

He came back perhaps ten minutes later. "They couldn't get a flight until early morning."

After that, neither of them spoke; they just sat side by side in those hard plastic chairs. Woody's shoulder and back were killing him. He knew the coach's hip would be too. A former Stanley Cup champ himself, he had his share of aches and pains.

Woody's thoughts turned back to Georgia. When she'd seen those gossip blogs, her shock had seemed genuine. So maybe she hadn't leaked his personal business herself. But, no matter how much she protested, she had to have told someone. That person might not have even had it in for him, just been a chatterbox. A hockey fan who liked being in the know about one of the big-name players.

Women talked to one another. He should've known better than to trust one.

Except . . . Blabbing his personal business didn't seem like some-

thing Georgia would do. She'd sure been pissed off when he accused her.

But if not her, then who?

Sam wouldn't. He knew that. Absolutely knew it.

Nor would Martin. But then, Woody'd have said no way would
his friend and agent gamble away all Woody's savings. The man was
an addict, and addicts hurt people. Martin had called a while back
to say he'd joined Gamblers Anonymous and was sticking with the
program, but was that still true?

"I gotta get some air," Woody muttered. "I'll bring back some
drinks."

The coach nodded.

Woody headed out of the hospital. Outside, the street was quiet
and tree-lined. He pulled out his cell and called Martin. Who gave
a shit that it was the middle of the night in Manitoba?

The phone rang, kept ringing, went to voice mail. Woody hung
up and called again. This time, a grumpy male voice said, "Who the
hell is this?"

"Woody."

"Woody?" The grumpiness changed to concern. "What's wrong?
Is it Stu? I saw the game."

"Are you sticking with the program?"

"Program?"

"Gamblers Anonymous."

"Gotcha. Yeah, you bet. You gave me a second chance, and I'm
damned grateful."

It sure didn't sound as if Martin had betrayed him again. But
another possibility occurred to Woody. "You haven't been talking
to anyone about me, have you? Like, do you folks have those confes-
sional things, where you all say how you screwed up and who you
hurt?"

"Yeah, but I've never named you. Just said that a friend trusted me to manage his money, and I screwed him over. You said we should keep this between the two of us, and that's what I've done."

"How about other stuff, like my, uh, mom and dad? You talk about them to anyone?"

"No. God, no. Why'd I do that?"

"Someone did. The whole story's on the hockey gossip blogs today."

"Shit. I'm sorry, Woody. I know you didn't want people finding out about all of that." He paused. "You believe me, right? I know I'm a fuckup, but I'd never tell people about your parents."

He wanted to believe Martin. "But who would? No one else knows. Just you and Sam." And Martin's wife, but she'd been dead for two years. And Georgia.

"Sam would never—"

"I know," he interrupted.

"I swear I haven't told anyone. Maybe someone else from back home? No one knew the whole story, but it was obvious your dad was a drinker. Your mom's doctor must've guessed some stuff too."

His mom had avoided the doctor, even for broken bones.

"How is your mom, anyway?" Martin asked. "Last you told me, the chemo wasn't doing the trick. I've sure been praying for her."

A realization hit Woody. He'd found out about the alternative treatment in Switzerland just after Martin had confessed his betrayal. His former agent didn't know. The only person who could've told the blogs about that was Georgia.

That sense of betrayal sank into him again.

"Thanks for that, Martin," he said heavily. "Actually, she's in Switzerland, trying something new we heard about, and she's feeling better."

"That's damned good news."

"Yeah, it is." Woody squeezed his eyes shut, mad at himself. "Shit, man, I'm sorry. I just realized that some of the gossip on those blogs was stuff you didn't know. I was wrong to accuse you. It's been a rough day."

"Yeah, I bet. How's Stu doing?"

Woody filled him in, and they were both quiet for a long moment.

"Sure hope the kid comes out of it okay," Martin said. "He has so much potential."

"I know."

"He reminds me of you." A pause. "His parents flying in?"

"Yeah. They'll get here tomorrow. Coach Duffy and I are hanging around tonight so someone'll be here when Stu wakes up."

"Give him my best."

"I'll do that."

"Say, Woody," Martin said hesitantly, "there is one other person who knows all that family stuff. Your mom."

He snorted. "Yeah, like she'd talk about that shit."

"You're right. Course she wouldn't. Well, I hope you figure it out."

"Me too. And sorry again. For accusing you, and waking you."

"No problem." Martin cleared his throat. "It's good to hear your voice."

A part of Woody wanted to say, "You too," or apologize for not returning Martin's earlier call, but he wasn't ready to forgive and forget.

Not with Martin, and definitely not with Georgia.

Unless it hadn't been Georgia . . .

Thirty-one

Somehow, Georgia had managed to hold herself together at work on Thursday, but tears had glazed her eyes as she drove home. Once there, she'd rushed to the bedroom and collapsed on the bed in tears.

Kit-Kat licked her face a few times. Then, unable to keep up with the tears, she curled into a comforting ball at Georgia's side.

Now, hours later, Georgia was still berating herself for being such an idiot. She'd thought Woody knew her. Liked her. Trusted her. She'd thought he was a decent guy, not someone who'd fling unwarranted accusations.

Damn it, she'd let herself care. Let herself believe he might be her soul mate, let herself hope he might realize that commitment could be the most wonderful thing in the world.

She had no hope of sleeping and so, in an attempt to take her mind off her misery, she opened her e-reader. Lady Emma had such a sensible approach to her relationship with the Comte. Georgia had told herself she was following the heroine's example, but then somehow Woody had wormed his way into her heart. Would the same happen to Emma? Georgia almost hoped it would, so someone else—okay, a make-believe someone else—would be miserable too.

The screen flashed to life on the last page she'd been reading, at the end of a chapter where the lovers had just had sex in a pile of fresh hay in the stables. Georgia clicked to the next page.

"My dear Emma," the Comte said, "my sources inform me that the scandal in Paris has blown over, displaced by at least a dozen new ones. It is time for me to return to my home."

That was no big surprise. Their idyllic world of sensual trysts was never intended to last, the same as Georgia's fling with Woody. How would Emma take it?

He was leaving. She'd known this day would come.

Emma shifted position, and the hay beneath the rug he'd spread rustled, releasing a clean scent that was an intriguing contrast to the worldly cologne worn by her lover. Would he invite her to go with him?

If he did, she would not go. Her home was here, and this was where her heart belonged. It did not belong to this foreigner, no matter the erotic intimacies they had shared.

Drat that Emma. She'd managed to keep control of her heart. Georgia read on.

No, Emma realized, he would not ask. Nor did she want him to. He had given her exactly what she'd wanted and needed—she was a more fulfilled, confident woman—and now it was time to end it. Yes, she had dreams of the future, but they didn't include a rake. "I wish you well. When will you leave?"

"In the morning." He touched his lips to her temple, then trailed them down to her ear. "Which gives us one more night together." He nipped the lobe of her ear. "Will you miss me, my dear Emma?"

She smiled and arched her neck, so he could kiss his way down it. "Of course, Alexandre, but it is best that we part. I'm in danger of turning into a self-indulgent hedonist."

"You say it as if there's something wrong with that," he teased.

Or was he teasing? The man lived his own life in much that fashion. She, however, was a different person. As thrilling and enlightening as this sexual education had been, she wanted more out of life. Yes, she thought as her lover sucked her nipple into his mouth, she wanted a man who attracted and aroused her, a man who tantalized, sometimes shocked, and always satisfied her in a physical way. But she also wanted emotion.

"Damn right," Georgia muttered. "And respect. And trust. We both deserve that, Emma."

There was passion, but little emotion between her and Alexandre.

The man who teased her nipple with his lips and tongue, almost but not quite to the point of pain, had taught her to know and honor her body. Now she wanted a man who would also teach her to know and honor her heart.

She would find him. She had noticed that men's gazes turned to her now, as much or more than to the chattering, colorful young ladies. She might not have the virtues of youth and a dowry, but she had attributes that men wanted, needed, and prized even more highly.

"You are a delightful woman, Emma." He lifted his head. "You will not return to being a drab, unhappy widow."

She laughed. "Indeed I will not."

Her future did not lie with le Comte de Vergennes, but he had changed her future. No longer was she restricted to choosing between the bleak options offered by her father, of an arranged marriage like her first, and by her brother, of playing the glorified servant.

"Now," she chided her lover, "would you please stop talking? There are other, more intimate parts of my body that crave your attention. If we have only one night, pray, sir, make the best use of it."

Georgia flicked off the reader. No, the last thing she wanted to read was a sex scene.

And so much for Emma's story running parallel to Georgia's.

Yes, if her friends were to be believed, Georgia would have no trouble finding another man who found her attractive. But she didn't want another man. She wanted Woody.

She was such an *idiot*! The book club had talked about whether you could separate sex and emotion, and Georgia had believed—or wanted to believe—that you could. That *she* could. She'd been wrong, at least when that man was Woody.

She'd even fooled herself into thinking that he might come to feel the same way. But damn it, he should have.

Woody was such an *idiot*!

She was much, much better off without him. Maybe once she'd stopped sobbing her heart out, that truth would sink in.

Georgia thought about calling in sick on Friday. God knew, she felt sick. Sick at heart, and exhausted from a sleepless, tear-soaked night.

But she was a professional, and would not let her personal life interfere with her job. She dragged herself out of bed and into the shower. Lots of cold water reduced the puffiness in her face and the bloodshot appearance of her eyes. She'd plead a cold.

She dressed, then returned to the bathroom to take pills for her headache.

The image staring back from the mirror was the old Georgia. Without conscious thought, she'd harshly tamed the hair Christopher Slate had styled to be loose and curly, and reverted to her starchy clothing.

She studied herself. Professional, yes. No one would accuse her of using feminine wiles in her work.

But then, no one had accused her of that when she had curly, feminine hair and wore pretty blouses. She'd actually felt more confident—or had that been the knowledge that Woody found her desirable?

Damn it, she was the same woman. Woody might be a jerk, but that was his problem, not hers. Screw him. A woman should not let a man rule her life. If she let Woody have that kind of power over her, she was no better than her mom was—or, at least, used to be.

Georgia *was* attractive and she *was* professional, and there was no reason she couldn't be both at the same time. She liked her new look, and liked not having tightly pulled back hair tugging at her temples, and stiff collars rubbing her neck.

Georgia pulled the clip out of her hair and ran her fingers through the strands, releasing the natural waves to tumble where they would. Then she replaced her starchy clothes with a new suit she hadn't worn before, one in a soft shade of sage green, and a pale peach blouse from VitalSport.

She might be heartbroken, but it didn't show. She looked like an attractive, professional woman who had a cold.

Woody had taught her to know and honor her body, even if he hadn't been interested in her heart. Maybe there was a man out there who'd honor her heart as well. And if not, she was just fine on her own. She had a great career, good friends, and an improved relationship with her mother.

When she arrived at the office, Sandra, the receptionist, didn't comment on her new suit or her puffy, bloodshot eyes. Instead, she said, "Oh my God, did you see the game last night? Wasn't that terrible?"

"No, I didn't. Did the Beavers lose?" It served Woody right for being mean to his "good luck charm." She felt sorry for the rest of the team, though, and a win would certainly be better for the marketing campaign.

"Yeah, but that's not what I mean. When they brought that stretcher in—"

"Stretcher?" Georgia broke in, her voice a raw screech. "What happened?" Woody. Was Woody hurt?

"Stu Connolly took a hit and—"

"Stu? It was Stu who got hurt?" Her racing heart slowed a little.

"Yeah, and they carried him out on a stretcher. The news this morning is that he had surgery and he's out of danger, but it's a back injury. He may be crippled."

"That's terrible." The poor kid. And the team. The whole team must be hurting, and worrying. Woody, most of all, because he felt so responsible for his players.

Not that she cared about Woody's feelings.

Sick at heart, Georgia walked to her office. Stu Connolly was twenty-one. A real up-and-comer, according to Woody. A kid from Texas whose family was so proud of him. A young man who might never walk again. It put her own problems in perspective.

And now she felt twice as bad as she had before.

But, after a night of wallowing in misery, she was here to work, and that was what she'd do.

Not that she was terribly productive, she found as she tried to concentrate, and it didn't help that the biggest item on her plate was the VitalSport campaign. She couldn't escape Woody. She went from evaluating photos, to working out details with *The Ellen DeGeneres Show*, to meeting with Terry to brainstorm ideas for Woody's speech at the Boys & Girls Club fund-raiser. She even took work home with her.

When she picked up the phone that evening, she'd been so immersed in Woody this and Woody that, it almost wasn't a surprise to hear his voice.

She took a breath. She was a professional, and she had to work with this man. "I take it you're in Washington?"

"Just arrived at the hotel." He sounded subdued, and no wonder.

"What's the news on Stu Connolly?"

"There's inflammation in his spine, and until it goes down, they won't know the prognosis. It's hell for him." His voice grated. "For his parents. For all of us."

"I'm sure. Poor Stu. To have his life change in an instant like that . . . It makes me wonder if it's worth it, playing a sport like hockey."

"Yeah, but the letter carrier can get hit by a bus." He didn't sound argumentative, just sad. "The CEO'll die of a heart attack because he never gets off his butt. Every job has risks."

Even hers, though she'd never anticipated that a broken heart would be one of them.

She drew another long breath. "We've confirmed the details for *The Ellen DeGeneres Show*. You'll fly to—"

"That's not why I'm calling."

Damn. Was he going to sling more accusations at her? Coolly, she said, "Oh?"

He cleared his throat. "I want to apologize. I was a primo asshole."

Oh! Cautiously, she said, "Yes, you were." A trickle of warmth filtered into veins that had felt frozen for the last day. Had he realized she would never betray him? If he begged forgiveness, could she give it?

"I talked to my mom," he said.

What did that have to do with his apology? "Yes?"

"It was her."

"What was her?"

"Who leaked the details." There was no heat in his voice. He sounded more resigned than angry.

"Your mother? Why on earth . . . ?" Georgia realized, with a deep thud of sorrow, that no, Woody hadn't decided to trust her. Instead, he'd been told she was innocent of the horrible things he'd accused her of.

"I guess I was hot news after those gonch photos got out. Some woman from a sports gossip site decided to see if she could dig up some more stuff. She found out my mom lives in Florida, called the house and got the housekeeper, and spun some story so the housekeeper gave her my mom's number in Switzerland."

"But your mother has never talked about what happened."

"This woman told her there was some bad press about me. Like, that I was an overpaid, arrogant jock."

Georgia winced. It was exactly what she'd thought in the beginning.

"That I'd always led a privileged life," he went on. "The reporter said she wanted to show that it wasn't true."

"Your mother fell for that?"

He gave a long sigh. "The woman caught her when she was vulnerable and made it seem like I needed her help." Grimly, he went on. "Didn't help that I'd left a voice mail saying I'd had a rough day."

Did his mom have any idea how much the leak had upset him? "What did you tell her?"

"What could I? Told her thanks for trying to help me, but let's not share any more family stuff."

He hadn't let on that his mom had hurt him, and that didn't surprise Georgia.

"So, anyhow," he went on, "I was an asshole to you and I'm sorry. I was upset and I just reacted." He sounded exhausted, chastened, and genuine.

She appreciated the apology, but the fact that he hadn't trusted her rankled, and so did the way he'd flung accusations. "I remember something you told me about hockey. You said that being tough, checking opponents, hard body contact, they're all part of the game.

But you said a player shouldn't use them out of anger. That emotions need to be controlled."

He heaved another sigh. "I hear you. It took me a while to master that lesson on the ice. Guess I haven't mastered it off ice yet."

"That's for sure."

"What more can I say, Georgia? I was wrong and I'm sorry. I want us to get back together. Things aren't the same without you."

Another surge of warmth melted more ice in her veins. He missed her; he wanted her. Maybe he really did care. But did he trust her now?

His voice broke into her musings, tone lighter now, almost teasing. "'Sides, the Beavers want the Cup, and you're my lucky charm."

Now she got it. Heat flared through her at the thought that she'd even considered taking him back. No, she deserved better than Woody Hanrahan.

He wasn't good for her. He had been, for a little while, before she realized she was falling for him. She'd fooled herself into thinking he cared about her, but he didn't. He liked having sex with her and he had this crazy notion that she brought him luck. The superstition seemed ridiculous to her, but so did his entire team getting Christopher Slate to trim their hair and beads. Hockey players were weird.

Her tired body, her aching heart, felt every minute of lost sleep and every tear she'd shed. Heavily, she said, "I accept your apology. But our personal—whatever it was, because I know you don't *do* relationships—is over. We'll still work together. I wish you and the team the best of luck in the playoffs, and I hope Stu makes a full recovery. But that's it, Woody. I have no more to give you."

She took a breath and told him the rest of it. "In fact, I have *everything* to give to a man who deserves it, but that isn't you."

After a moment, he said, "Shit, Georgia. I've really blown it, haven't I?" He sounded so sad, so tired and worn down, she felt a touch of sympathy.

But she hardened her heart. He wasn't shedding tears over her. He just hated losing his good luck charm, and his ego, unused to rejection, had taken a beating. He'd pull out of it. Even though the Beavers were the visiting team in Washington, there'd be puck bunnies eager to cheer up the handsome captain of the Vancouver team. The guy who looked so damned hot in the photos strewn all over the Internet thanks to Georgia and her team.

She hoped he and the stupid puck bunny would be very happy together, for the whole two hours their steamy affair lasted.

Yeah, right.

Thirty-two

On Saturday, when Woody led the Beavers out on the ice at the Verizon Center in Washington, DC, he felt as if his skates were weighted down with lead. His energy and drive were in low gear, and he couldn't ramp them up. Maybe he was coming down with the flu.

He couldn't get Georgia out of his mind. He'd hurt her and she'd dumped him. And what if she really was his lucky charm, and without her he could no longer play?

Yesterday, when he'd called to apologize, he'd hoped that maybe bringing up that shared joke about her bringing him good luck would've softened her, but it hadn't.

He missed her. She'd become important to him, and not just on the ice. Every other woman he'd dated, he'd been able to put out of his mind. But not Georgia. She was like a freaking ghost, haunting his thoughts and dreams. Making him feel like crap.

On top of that, his shoulder and back were killing him. The other players' injuries were bugging them too. But their combined injuries were small potatoes compared to the fact that Stu's spine was still swollen. The kid was hurting, but less from the pain in his back than from the idea that his sports career might be over. Woody didn't think Stu'd even let himself think about the possibility of not walking again.

Woody eyed his teammates as they warmed up. Olssen, a second line player who'd been in the first line before Stu replaced him, was back on the first line, as center. The dynamic between him, Woody, and Bouchard was different, but he was a great player, a more seasoned one than the rookie.

This morning's practice had been okay, but not great. Tonight, they needed to function as a unit, to have power, speed, perception, and great instincts. Instead, they were dragging their fucking asses.

He could hardly yell at them because he was the worst of the bunch.

When "O Canada" began to play, he hoped the guys were all doing what he'd told them to. He did it himself. Focus, center, think about whom they were playing for: their country, their city, their club, their teammates, and their fans. Think about the reasons they were out here, the hard work they'd put in, the dreams that drove them. Find the quiet place, the place that was all determination and commitment, and shut out everything else.

When the national anthem ended, he felt better. Not great, but better.

He threw himself into the game. They all did. But it was an off night. There was no other word for it.

They ended up losing three-one. It was the third game in the playoffs and they were down one. The next game was two nights from now, Monday, here in DC. How the hell could he bring the team back to top form?

How could he motivate them when he felt like shit warmed over?

After the game, when the media'd been kicked out of the visitors' locker room, Coach Duffy gathered the players together. He didn't yell at them. Instead, he said quietly, "You played like a bunch of fuckwits out there. I know you've got stuff on your minds. You got injuries, personal troubles, shit going on. Stu's on everyone's mind."

Heads nodded tiredly, grimly. Seemed like the guys were so worn down they couldn't even straighten their spines and hold their heads up straight. Woody realized he was slumping on a bench, and forced himself to straighten even though it shot daggers of pain through him.

"I don't give a crap," Duffy said. "Not when you're on the ice. And you can't give a crap. None of that stuff exists. You hear me, men? It doesn't exist." He gazed at them, forcing each player to meet his eyes.

Then he went on. "You ask Stu, does he want you guys worrying about how he's doing? Hell, no. He wants you winning the Cup and giving him his chance to skate with it."

Now backs were straightening, heads nodding, and despite the players' exhaustion, a fresh sense of purpose and optimism filled the locker room.

Georgia didn't really want to go to book club on Monday, but then, she didn't really want to do anything except mope around feeling sorry for herself.

She'd done that after Anthony's death, until she decided she didn't want to be that kind of person. Nor did she now, especially when her loss was such a tiny thing in comparison. Her husband had been her soul mate. Woody'd been, at most, the fragile hope of a second chance at love.

She'd been silly to hope, and it was her own damned fault she felt so rotten.

Lily had picked the location for this afternoon's one-hour club meeting: the lounge at the Fairmont Hotel Vancouver.

When Georgia arrived, she gazed around the room. Its classic elegance—dark wood, upholstered chairs, and a man playing a grand piano—was marred slightly by the two huge TV screens on either side of the mid-room bar. One showed a boxing match and the other a football game. No hockey, thank heavens.

She spotted Lily, alone at a table where two club chairs upholstered in dull gold faced a small burgundy and gold sofa. The doctor sat in one of the club chairs, her usual martini in front of her, half-finished.

Georgia took the other club chair and forced her lips to smile. "Hi." She gestured to the martini glass. "You've been here awhile?"

The other woman had a Scandinavian look, with her very light hair and striking pale blue eyes. Right now those eyes looked a little dazed, as if she'd been deep in thought; then she focused on her martini glass. "Yes, I suppose I have."

"Everything okay?" she ventured.

A crease furrowed Lily's forehead. "I'm trying to figure out some work issues."

The waitress came to take Georgia's drink order. Normally, she'd have gone with wine, but now she said, "I'll have a martini too."

Then she turned to Lily and said hesitantly, because, after all, they weren't exactly friends yet, "Want to talk about it?"

"Thanks, but really, it's nothing. How about you?" Lily studied her with a doctor's critical eyes. "Have you been sleeping?"

"Not well."

"What are you going to do about that?"

The straightforward question brought a rueful smile to Georgia's lips. "Good question. I'd rather avoid drugs."

"Exercise," Lily said. "Exercise until you're exhausted. That might help."

Was that what she'd been doing herself? She looked lean and toned in a sleeveless white shirt, but more tired than full of energy.

As Georgia tasted the delicious and potent martini the waitress served her, she almost wished she and Lily could let down their hair and share their worries. That was the problem with a secret affair: when it went south, there was no shoulder to cry on. Instead, she said, "I've never been into strenuous exercise, but I am planning to take self-defense lessons."

"That's a great idea. I've taken them. I'll give you the name of the place."

Georgia had just finished noting it down when Kim hurried over, followed by a breathless Marielle. The pair studied the drinks menu and made their selections, Kim choosing an amber ale and Marielle ordering something called a Blanc de Fraises. Lily, whose martini glass was almost empty, ordered another.

Kim, still sporting caramel streaks and nails, turned to Georgia. "Bummer about the Beavers. Their luck's sure up and down."

"It is. But I'd rather talk about the book, okay?"

"I'd rather talk about those hot photos of Woody." Marielle winked. She was in jeans again, and her black tee sported a few dog hairs.

"Yes, they were hot," Georgia said resignedly, "and the campaign's going well, but it'd sure be better if the Beavers won the Stanley Cup. There, we've talked about it."

"Thank you," Lily said. "Finally, someone else understands the concept of a book club. Now, did everyone finish the book? What did you think?"

Kim leaned forward. "I really wanted Emma and the Comte to fall in love and end up together."

"I admit," Lily said, "I rather hoped the same. He educated her, and I hoped she'd educate him."

"Reform the rake?" Marielle asked, flicking her wavy dark hair back from her face.

Lily and Kim both nodded.

Marielle turned to Georgia. "How about you? Did you want the two of them to walk down the aisle?"

"Ha." Maybe at one point she'd secretly hoped for that, but she knew it wasn't realistic. "The Comte didn't have the slightest desire to change." Just like Woody. A future of puck bunnies and condoms stashed at the ready no doubt sounded like heaven to him. "And if he didn't change, then Emma would be crazy to fall in love with him because he couldn't possibly give her what she wanted. And deserved."

Lily cocked her head. "You sound a little, uh, bitter. Did the story strike a personal note for you?"

Embarrassed, Georgia muttered, "Maybe."

The waitress delivered Kim's and Marielle's drinks and Lily's second martini. Marielle promptly picked up the flute glass filled with a frothy pink concoction, sipped, and purred satisfaction. Lily lifted her glass too.

Kim didn't touch hers. She gazed steadily at Georgia, the serious expression in her near-black eyes a contrast to the playful caramel streaks in her spiky hair. "It brings up these issues, right? About sex and love, and what women want—and deserve, like you said—out of relationships." She squeezed her eyes shut for a moment. "It makes you think about the relationship you're in."

Was that why she'd agreed to have drinks with the guy she'd met at the game last week?

Georgia nodded agreement, and noticed Lily was doing the same.

"That's why it's better to do things my way," Marielle said. "Lots of guys, lots of fun, and no angst." Normally, she was breezy, joking, chiding them, bursting out with her own ideas, but now she seemed subdued. Almost as if she didn't really believe what she was saying.

Lily studied Marielle. "That's fine for a while. But people are meant to bond with others."

"I bond with lots." She sounded a little defensive. "And I'm happy on my own too."

"So am I," Georgia put in. "And it's better being on your own than with the wrong person."

She expected the others to jump in, either to agree or disagree, but all three of them picked up their drinks and took a sip. Georgia realized the pianist was playing the classic "When a Man Loves a Woman." How depressing.

Finally, Kim said, "Anyhow, once I got my head around the fact that the Comte wasn't going to turn into the man I wanted him to be, then, yeah, I liked the ending. The story's about Emma, isn't it? Not about him."

Happy to be back on the book, Georgia said, "Yes. It's called *The Sexual Education of Lady Emma Whitehead*, and she sure did get a sexual education, but she got more than that. She grew up. She figured out who she is as a woman, and how she wants to live her life."

"Knowing what you want is one thing," Lily said, "but the universe won't necessarily deliver it."

"Which is why," Marielle said, "you have to be happy with yourself, by yourself. And I think Emma's going to be. She'll take lovers, and have a wonderful time."

"No," Georgia said. "She'll find that one perfect man."

Lily studied her. "You're a romantic."

Was she? Maybe that was why she'd let herself care for Woody. Perhaps her heart had been looking for another soul mate, even though her rational brain knew Woody didn't want to fill that role.

"She'll have everything," Kim said. "She'll learn to be happy by herself, and she'll take lovers and enjoy them, and when the time's right, that one special man will come along and they'll fall in love with each other."

"And I thought George was a romantic," Lily said wryly, taking another sip of her martini. "By the way, is our book discussion going off course again? Usually we're more interested in the writing style, and so on."

"This is more interesting," Marielle said. "Look at how we all got caught up in the story. Who cares about the technical stuff? We care about Lady Emma, because each one of us identifies with her." She turned to Georgia. "Like, not to pry or raise a sore point or anything, but you had some guy you cared about, who you wanted to change, but he didn't. Right?"

Georgia nodded.

"And isn't that a futile quest." Lily said it as a statement, not a question.

"I don't think so," Georgia said slowly. "Some men are capable of change."

"You can never make anyone change unless they want to," Marielle put in. "Emma was ready, and she wanted to change. The Comte wasn't."

And didn't that exactly summarize Georgia's own relationship with Woody?

"I feel sorry for him," Kim said.

"He's perfectly happy," Marielle protested, flicking her hair back again.

"He's stuck," Kim said firmly. "Maybe he enjoys his life, but it'll always be the same thing, over and over. That's got to get boring after a while."

Would it, for Woody? And was Kim accusing Marielle of being stuck, or did she perhaps feel stuck herself?

Marielle slitted her wide, dark eyes, as if she was pondering a retort. Instead, she said, "Time's almost up. Next week we pick a new book, so bring your suggestions. More sex, anyone?"

"No," Georgia said. "I need a break from sex."

* * *

By Monday night, the Beavers had had some rest, massage, and physio. Best of all, Stu had called to say the swelling was almost gone and he could move both legs.

The players who took the ice in the Verizon Center were a stronger, healthier, happier group of guys.

Woody still missed Georgia, but he'd resolved to treat her the way he did his injured body. Yes, there was pain, but when he skated onto the ice, it wouldn't exist. It sure as hell wouldn't get in the way of playing the best damned game he could.

He played well, and so did the rest of the team. But the refs had it in for them. The Beavers spent more time in the penalty box than they had in any game this season, and the Caps exploited those power plays.

Federov, the Beavers' goaltender, almost worked magic, yet a couple of goals snuck in, and the Beavers managed only one of their own. They left the ice three games down.

If the Caps won one more—just one—they'd win the Stanley Cup.

Pissed off, the team gathered around Coach Duffy to hear what he had to say.

"You played well. Every single one of you. And Federov deserves a fucking medal. But, men, it's not good enough. Back in Vancouver, you're going to win. The Cup will be in the building, and no fucking way the Capitals are taking it home."

The players booed and cursed the idea of their opponents taking *their* cup back to California.

"You have to win," the coach said. "There's no option."

Every single head nodded vigorously.

Two days later, Wednesday, in Vancouver, they did win, four-two.

On Friday they were back in DC, with the Cup there in the Verizon Center. The energy in the building was kinetic with the Caps' fans hungry for the win, and a sizable group of Beavers fans yelling their lungs out. It was damned fine seeing those chocolate-and-caramel jerseys scattered among the sea of red-and-white Capitals ones.

Both teams were strong, and in the last two minutes of the third period, the score stood at two-two. Coach Duffy sent Woody's line onto the ice with one command: "Win this one for Stu."

They poured everything they had into an all-out assault on the Caps' goal; then Bouchard slipped the puck to Woody, who slammed it right past the goaltender's head.

The chorus of boos was music to Woody's ears. Back home, he knew Stu was watching the game from his hospital room and yelling his head off like the fans up there in the stands.

The series was tied, three games each.

Game seven, on Sunday, would decide the Cup. They'd be in Vancouver. Home ice advantage.

And tomorrow night, Saturday, he'd see Georgia. It was the Boys & Girls Club fund-raiser. He'd hoped to go as a Stanley Cup winner, but hell, he wasn't going as a loser.

And he'd see Georgia.

They'd spoken on the phone a few times and her voice had been cool and businesslike. He'd heard that voice murmur beside him in bed at night, moan as he tortured her with his tongue, cry out when he drove her to release. He hated how impersonal she sounded now, as if none of it had ever happened.

Georgia was driving him crazy and so, in a completely different way, were dozens, maybe hundreds, of other women. Those stupid gonch photos had made him a magnet for even more puck bunnies, and made him recognizable beyond the world of hockey too.

Didn't women have anything better to do than stare at semi-naked photos of guys and tweet their friends to take a look?

Wasn't it men who were supposed to get off on looking, and women were supposed to be more high-minded? Sure as hell couldn't prove it by him. If he had to autograph one more thong or scrawl his name across one more woman's cleavage, he'd look into becoming a monk.

Might as well. He didn't have the slightest interest in sex these days.

He told himself it was due to playoff focus, where nothing else counted.

Georgia had watched the last two games on TV.

After a series of losses and Stu Connolly's horrible injury, the Beavers had their fire back and were on a winning streak.

She was happy for them. Happy for the VitalSport campaign. Happy for Woody, even if she didn't want to care how he felt.

You didn't stop caring. That was a lesson she'd learned when she was young, with her mom. Even when Georgia had been mad at Bernadette, she hadn't stopped caring.

It would stop soon with Woody, though. Right now she missed him like crazy, and her heart ached whenever she spoke to him, watched him on ice, or even thought of him. But they'd been lovers for such a short time, it should be easy to relegate him to "just business" once the Stanley Cup playoffs and the Boys & Girls Club fundraiser were over.

The fund-raiser was tomorrow night. She had to be there, even though she'd far prefer to deal with Woody over the phone than in person.

But this event was big. The pseudo-leaks of photos and information from "Woody's insider fangirl"—aka Mr. Terry Banerjee—had brought lots of attention to Woody and the VitalSport campaign. Everyone would be watching him Saturday night. Smartphones and other devices would take photos and shoot video; people would tweet; images and posts would appear on the Internet as the event progressed.

Woody had been on the road a lot, and even when he was in Vancouver he'd been occupied with practices and game preparation, so Georgia's team hadn't had nearly enough time to work with him. Using e-mail and phone, Terry had developed a speech with him, and they'd gone over possible interview questions and answers. Viv had carefully selected his wardrobe. Georgia could only hope that the lessons in deportment she and his judge friend had given him were enough to get him through the banquet dinner.

And then there was the dancing. It was a black-tie ball, and when she'd asked Woody if he could dance, he'd said, "Yeah." She had a feeling that meant high school clutch-and-shuffle rather than fox-trot, waltz, and cha-cha, but there was simply no time for ballroom dancing lessons. So she'd said, "Try to stay off the dance floor. It's more important you mingle."

She'd have to keep an eye on him every moment.

That meant she had to keep a tight rein on her own emotions.

The night promised to be sheer torture.

Thirty-three

On Saturday night, fresh out of the shower, Woody dressed for the fund-raiser. Viv had chosen not only his tux and shirt but every other item in his wardrobe: the black VitalSport boxer briefs that he had to admit were more comfortable than the brand he used to wear; the blue-and-black patterned bow tie and vest that accented his custom-made tux and, according to Viv, made the blue of his eyes even more vivid; and the Italian cotton hankie she'd insisted the well-dressed man should never be without.

She'd wanted to come over to help him dress, and bring Christopher Slate to style his hair.

That was where he'd drawn the line. "I can dress myself," he'd protested irritably.

Now, as he did exactly that, he wished he was spending the evening in front of the TV, wrapped in ice packs.

He checked his watch. Ten to six, and the cab would arrive on the hour. The event didn't officially start until six thirty, but Viv had insisted on him arriving early. She'd also insisted on a taxi, even though the Four Seasons was only a five-minute walk. She'd said she didn't want him arriving windblown and sweaty. Like he'd sweat walking a half dozen blocks.

Viv was nice, smart, and she could be fun, but he was getting damned tired of being bossed around. The last order she'd given him was to meet up with Georgia the moment he arrived at the ballroom.

The Dynamic Marketing people didn't trust him not to stick his foot in his mouth.

Being with Georgia would be awkward at best. Yet, as he took the elevator down from his penthouse apartment, he knew he needed to see her.

The last two wins had shown that the sexy redhead wasn't his good luck charm. Now he hoped to prove to himself that his interest in her had passed; that she was just another woman, like those he'd dated before, and the ones who'd mobbed him at the airport when the Beavers flew home.

After tonight, he'd get over that weird feeling that something was missing. Even when the team won a game and the adrenaline surge of victory filled him, there was still a kind of hole. An aching hole. It had never been there before.

He kept having this desire to talk to Georgia, to see her, to hold her. It had been nice how the two of them discussed their days, whether it was in person or over the phone when he was out of town. He wanted to share his worry over Stu, and his happiness about how his mom's health was improving. Tell her how it had felt to score the winning goal in game six. Listen to her relate the ups and downs of her day. Have her tenderly wrap ice around his aching shoulder, then make him forget all about the aches when her lips touched his.

There was something wrong with him. More than his bad shoulder and back. How many women had he slept with over the years? He'd never obsessed over a single one.

The taxi arrived and he climbed in, saying, "Four Seasons Hotel, please," to the dark-skinned, turbaned driver.

The driver scrutinized him. "Aren't you Woody Hanrahan?"

"Yeah."

He pulled away. "Almost didn't recognize you, dressed up like that."

"Me either."

"You're going to win that Cup tomorrow night."

Woody liked the way he said it: a statement, not a question. He also liked that the man was talking about hockey, not gonch photos. "You bet we are."

"The Caps don't stand a chance."

They talked hockey for the rest of the short ride; then Woody gave the driver his autograph for his son, along with a big tip.

He climbed out of the cab, thinking that he'd sure been more at home talking with the cabbie than going into this black-tie *affair*, to use Georgia's term. He'd been to these things before and always felt awkward, at least until he met up with someone who was interested in sports.

Tonight, at least he wasn't in an ill-fitting penguin suit that pulled across the shoulders, with hair that needed a trim, and he could hold his own in the *deportment* area. He felt good about the speech in his pocket too. Terry Banerjee was great about suggesting topics and themes, then helping Woody find his own way of phrasing things so that the words and emotions were genuine.

Yeah, he was prepared. He was even prepared for seeing Georgia.

Or so he thought until he glanced through the doorway into the ballroom, elegant and glittering with the light of chandeliers and candles. There she was across the empty room, talking to a bartender.

She was stunning.

Women often wore black to these events. It was supposed to be sophisticated, but he thought it made them look like a flock of crows. Georgia would never be taken for one of a flock.

She looked so classy, he couldn't believe this was the same woman who'd moaned and writhed with pleasure as he plunged his tongue deep inside her. Her evening gown was the warm gold of a sandy beach, a color that made her skin look even creamier and her hair even fierier. He guessed Viv had persuaded her to accept

Christopher Slate's assistance, because her hair was fancied up, some pieces held away from her face with sparkly clips while other curls tumbled free to caress her neck and shoulders.

A neck and shoulders he'd explored in such detail that he knew exactly where to lick, exactly where to suck, to make her moan.

Deep in conversation with the bartender, she hadn't seen Woody yet, where he hovered outside the door. He didn't move, not wanting to draw her attention to him.

Right now, anything was possible. He could imagine that, when her gaze lit on him, she'd beam, hurry across the room to meet him, and throw herself into his arms.

And he wanted that. Damn it, he wanted that. The realization sank into him, deep and certain and terrifying.

He wanted it as much as—maybe even more than—he wanted the Stanley Cup.

His heart raced and his stomach did a somersault. Shit. So much for trying to convince himself Georgia was just another woman.

He'd fallen in love with her.

He'd never been in love before. No wonder it had taken him so long to understand the symptoms.

Hell, he didn't want to be in love. Love made people vulnerable. People did crazy things in the name of love. Like his mom staying with his dad all those years. If you loved someone, they had the power to shatter your heart.

That was why he'd felt like there was something missing. A hole, an ache. When Georgia had said she didn't want to get back together with him, she'd taken a chunk of his heart.

What had she said? That she had everything to give a man, but that man wasn't him.

Sorrow sliced through him, a blow to the gut, a whack that bowed his aching back.

But then he straightened. Damn it, why not? Why the hell

couldn't he be that man? Okay, he didn't have university degrees like her; he wasn't an intellectual like her deceased husband; he wasn't all suave like Marco Sanducci. But he was a decent guy. He might not know much about love, but he learned quickly. Georgia knew that. She could teach him.

He had to make her want to.

Determination strengthened and focused him. He had a goal now. The most important goal in his life. Taking long strides, he stepped through the doorway and crossed the room toward her.

Her gaze shifted away from the bartender and fixed on him. Her eyes widened. She didn't beam. She didn't immediately rush to him. But she did, after a long pause, walk slowly toward him.

When they met, she said, in that horrible polite, impersonal tone she'd been using with him, "You look very nice. Viv chose well."

"You look gorgeous, Georgia." Though, now that he was close to her, he saw that her face looked strained and the glow on her cheeks might be due to makeup. Gorgeous, yes, but not happy. Not the way she'd looked when they were together. That gave him hope. "How are you?"

"Fine," she said dismissively. Then, almost as if she couldn't stop herself: "Nervous. I'm not used to formal events like this."

"Same for me."

Her eyes narrowed. "But you're prepared? You have the speech?"

He touched his breast pocket. "Yeah."

"Good. Let's go over the agenda one more time."

"No. I know the agenda." He caught her hand and tried to tug her toward a corner of the room. "There's something I need to talk to you about."

She resisted. "About the event? You couldn't have thought of it earlier?"

"Not about the event. And I know this isn't the best time, but I have to tell you something." He tugged again, and this time she went, pulling back slightly against his hand to let him know she was dragging her heels.

He stood her in the corner, released her hand, and stepped in front of her so that his body blocked any view of her. Anyone looking across the room would see only the anonymous back of a big man in a tux. It was the most privacy he could give them.

"I'm a total idiot," he said.

A corner of her mouth flicked, but her eyes remained cool. "True."

"I acted like a shit and I hurt you, and I hate that I did that."

Her eyes lost their guardedness and he saw the real Georgia. "You didn't trust me, Woody. Yes, that hurt. A lot. I thought you knew me better than that."

"I did. I do." He shook his head. "It wasn't about you; it was about me. I don't trust easily."

"Go on." She wasn't making this easy, but she hadn't shut him down.

"It goes back a long way. Couldn't trust my dad. Couldn't trust my mom to look out for herself. Or for me."

"I know, but you can't let your childhood rule your life."

"No. And there's people I do trust, like the coaches and my teammates. But that's, you know, when it comes to the game. Not when it comes to"—he swallowed—"my emotions."

Something sparked in her eyes, a small glow of gold amid the amber. "Your emotions?"

"I had this bad experience recently. It's pretty much the only thing I didn't tell you about. But I couldn't because, well, it's someone else's secret too." Woody frowned. He'd promised Martin he'd keep the secret of his gambling and his fraud.

But this was important. And yes, he did trust Georgia. "I told you about when I was a kid, how my friend's father helped me out so I could play hockey."

* * *

Georgia hugged her arms around her body. Was there a problem with the climate control in this room? Since she'd seen Woody, she'd been alternating between chills and hot flashes.

Or maybe her body was echoing the roller-coaster ride of her emotions.

He looked so wonderful, despite the shadows around his eyes and lines of tiredness and stress on his face. The playoffs were taking their toll, and she hoped he wasn't in too much pain. She knew that, when he'd agreed to attend the Boys & Girls Club fund-raiser, he'd hoped the Beavers would've already taken home the Stanley Cup. Now, with the final game of a very tough playoffs tomorrow night, he should be home resting.

But here he was, honoring the commitments he'd made: to the Club and to VitalSport.

And here he was, apologizing again.

Last time, her wounds had been fresh and raw, and she'd heeded her brain and thrown up defensive barriers. Tonight, she found herself softening. He seemed truly upset and repentant, and the least she could do was hear him out.

People had their issues, their hot buttons. For Georgia, the biggie was to not be man-centered and needy like her mom. If trust was Woody's big issue, maybe she could understand that he'd overreacted and accused her, and now regretted it.

The fact that he had come to her and was revealing things that were painful for him confirmed that, whether or not he was ready to admit it to himself, he cared about her. Maybe she was foolish, but hope blossomed inside her.

"Yes," she said, "you told me how Martin took you to practices and games, and paid for equipment and coaching." Things his own father hadn't done. "He sounds like a wonderful man. You said you owe it to him that you got away from home and have your career."

"I do owe it to him. And more. He became my agent when I was fourteen. Coaches and players often suggested I sign with one of the big sports agents, but Martin did a good job for me. He *got* me, you know? He understood I hated doing media stuff and endorsements, and he didn't push, even though there'd have been more money in it for him." He grimaced, as if he was in pain.

Instinctively, she touched his arm. "Are you all right?"

He gazed down at her hand, then put his own over it, holding it there. "If you're touching me, I'm all right."

It was one of the sweetest things anyone had ever said to her, and it almost brought tears to her eyes. She realized that something more than hope was growing inside her: a deep sense of certainty that Woody truly cared.

His big body blocked her view of the room, but the increasing noise level told her the guests were beginning to arrive. They should be mingling, but this was more important. A few weeks ago, all she'd cared about was making a success of the VitalSport campaign, but her priorities had changed. "Go on," she urged.

"I trusted Martin. He was like a father and a business partner wrapped up in one. I trusted him to handle my career, and to handle my finances."

She nodded.

"Last month"—his voice grated—"he confessed he has a gambling problem. It got so bad that . . . that he used my money. My investments. He lost everything I'd made in my whole career. I'm even in debt on back taxes."

"Oh my God!" She gaped up at him. "That's awful."

"Yeah," he said grimly. "I was betrayed by the person I trusted the most."

Now she understood why Woody'd been so quick to leap to the conclusion that another person he'd trusted had betrayed him. "You said this is a secret? But surely you told the police." Why hadn't the papers and sports gossip sites jumped on it?

When Woody didn't reply, she studied his sad face. "No, you didn't. You couldn't. Despite the bad things he'd done to you, he'd done so many good ones too."

"Yeah." He squeezed her hand under his, and she felt the warm, reassuring solidity of his arm under his tux jacket and shirt. "And there's Sam to think of," he said. "His son. My best friend. It'd shatter him to know what his dad did."

She nodded thoughtfully, realizing something else. Woody, who hated doing endorsements, had signed with VitalSport so he could pay for his mom's treatments.

"Besides," Woody said, "gambling's an addiction."

"Yes, but . . ." Should she say this? "Your father was an alcoholic."

He sighed. "I know. I guess it's easier to . . . not forgive, but maybe understand Martin. He was good to me for a long time, before he got into gambling. And even then, it was just money he lost."

"Addiction isn't an excuse, though. Being an alcoholic didn't excuse your dad's abuse, and being addicted to gambling doesn't excuse your agent's fraud."

He shook his head. "Martin said it was a compulsion and he couldn't make himself stop. So I said he has to go to Gamblers Anonymous. If he sticks with the program and doesn't gamble, I won't turn him in."

"Oh, Woody." This time the tears didn't just threaten; they glazed her eyes. "You're a good man."

His brows lifted in apparent surprise. "Yeah?"

She gave a shaky laugh. "Yeah. The way you look after the people you care about."

His throat rippled as he swallowed. "I didn't look after you, Georgia. And I do care about you."

Her heart lifted. "You do?"

A slight smile touched his lips. "If feeling like there's a hole in my chest when you're not around is caring, then yeah, I do. A hell of a lot."

Her own heart filled with warmth. "You feel that way?" she asked tremulously.

"Yeah. For the first time in my life." He freed the hand he'd trapped, but only to catch both of her hands in his. "I think I'm in love with you."

Laughter and tears spilled in the same instant. All the defenses she'd erected crumbled and she knew the truth. She loved him too.

Doggedly, he went on. "So I need you to forgive me. To give me a second chance to prove that I—"

"Yes!" Rising on her toes, she cut him off with a quick, hard kiss. "Oh, yes. Because there's only one explanation for how rotten I've been feeling since we broke up. I'm in love with you too."

All the tiredness and stress left his face, to be replaced by pure joy. Then his arms circled her and his lips met hers in a kiss that, this time, was slow and tender. Loving.

Maybe she should have felt excited, but instead the sensation that flooded through her was peace. Like she'd come home, and all was right with the world.

Finally, she eased back in the circle of his arms.

He smiled at her, and to her astonishment pulled out a white hankie. "You have tear streaks in your makeup." Tenderly, he wiped her face, the fine cotton soft against her skin. "This'll get you through until you can make it to the ladies' room."

"I wish we could leave and be alone together."

"Oh, yeah," he said in a heartfelt tone. "But we've got a job to do here." Blue eyes gleaming, he added, "Besides, I want to dance with you."

"You really know how to dance?"

He winked. "Sure. You put your arms around each other tight and you shuffle and sway. Right?"

"Exactly right."

Thirty-four

After lots of schmoozing, a delicious but far too long dinner, and a speech by Woody that made her cry yet again, they finally got that shuffle-and-sway dance. It was pure heaven to be in his arms and know he loved her, but it was agony too. They were in public, no longer hidden in a corner with his back blocking everyone's view of them, so they couldn't kiss. She couldn't press against him, twine around him, untie his bow tie, and press her lips to his warm throat.

She wanted this—the slow, romantic dance—but she wanted it in private.

Easing back in the circle of his arms, she gazed into his gorgeous blue eyes. "You have a game tomorrow."

His lips twitched. "Yeah, I kind of remember that."

"Everyone will understand if you leave early. They want you rested and in top form."

The lip twitch turned into a wicked grin. "And what do you want?"

She met the grin with one of her own. "Oh, I want you in top form too. Come on, you've put in your time and done a wonderful job. Let's make our excuses and go."

As she'd predicted, the hosts of the event sent Woody on his way with best wishes and a hearty round of fist pumps.

It was a two-minute cab ride to his place, where the elevator took just as long, but that was okay because Georgia and Woody spent the ride plastered together, kissing.

When they were inside his apartment, he shrugged out of the tux jacket and was reaching up to undo his bow tie when she caught his hand, stopping him. "Oh no, you don't. Let's dance some more."

"You want to *dance*?"

Of course she wanted to make love, but he'd done such a good job of her sexual education that she had an idea or two of her own. "Mm-hmm." She put on the *Sax for Lovers* music, and held out her hand to him.

Head cocked, he studied her. "You have a plan, don't you?"

She studied him, elegant yet 100 percent male in the white shirt that set off his tanned skin and the buttoned vest that accentuated his broad shoulders and narrow waist. "Shut up and dance, my love." Oh my, it felt good to call him that.

Laughing, he pulled her tight, arms hugging her to him. "Can I say one thing first?"

"If it's nice." She wrapped her arms around him. Her man. So different from Anthony, and yet so wonderful.

"When I first saw you tonight, you looked beautiful, but the glow on your cheeks was makeup, not happiness."

She nodded, smiling up at him. "Perceptive guy. And now?" Her smile widened, showing him all the love in her heart. "Do I look happy?"

"Very happy." Slowly, he began to move. "Same as me."

If he never learned to dance any step other than the shuffle-and-sway, she wouldn't complain. Especially when they could do it alone, so she could cling as tightly as she wanted and feel the hard strength of his body underneath those classy clothes.

"Last week," he said, "when you were reaming me out, you said you had everything to give to a man, but that man wasn't me."

She nodded. "I knew what it was like to love and be loved, and I wouldn't settle for less."

"It's what you deserve. It's what I want to give you."

"Tell me again," she wheedled.

"I love you, Georgia Malone."

"I'll never get tired of hearing that."

"Me too. But you're going to have to teach me about love. You've been there before, but it's new to me."

It dawned on her that, while he'd taught her about her own femininity and sexuality, she'd taught him how to love. She'd taught this incredible man, this man so many women lusted after, to love. "We'll work it out together," she promised.

"If I start acting like a jerk again, just, oh—"

"Whack you with a hockey stick?" she teased.

"Yeah, that'd be good."

Both chuckling softly, they swayed together. It was romantic and sweet, but the hard press of his body was arousing, reminding her that she'd had a plan. An excellent plan. She tilted her hips, serving notice.

There was already a bulge behind his fly, and now it grew.

When they'd danced at the Four Seasons, it had been torture not being able to squeeze his taut butt or cup her hand over the erection pressing against the fly of those beautifully styled tux pants. Now, as they shuffled in place in his living room, the lights of sky and city through those huge windows the only illumination, she could do everything she wanted.

She started by reaching up and tugging on his bow tie. "Viv has great taste. She picks clothes that suit the person."

"I could lose the tie."

"You could." She worked the knot free, but rather than pull the strip of silk off, she left it hanging loose at his neck and admired her handiwork. "Rakish." She smiled a private smile because the word reminded her of Lady Emma's rake. Georgia had compared Woody to him, but Woody had so much more depth. The Comte had indeed been stuck, whereas Woody was willing to change, to mature. He would always be interesting, stimulating.

Stimulating, in every way. Right now, the slow stroke of his hand down her semi-bare back, while not blatantly erotic, was so sensual it made her quiver. His touch was like the physical embodiment of that sultry sax music.

She unbuttoned his vest, leaving it to hang loose. From there, she moved to the studs of his tuxedo shirt, starting at the collar and working down, letting her nails scrape gently. The hard, hot flesh of his chest burned her fingertips and sent arousal tingling through her. When she reached his waist, she tugged the shirttails free of his tuxedo pants and unbuttoned his shirt down to the bottom. Then she parted the sides of his shirt and vest, revealing a strip of brown skin.

She peeled the left side back and put her lips to his chest, feeling his heart thud beneath her kiss. He smelled of herbal soap and tasted slightly salty. She sucked his nipple until he groaned and thrust his hips against her.

Oh, that felt good, the hard thrust of his erection against her belly. She wanted him so badly, but tonight she wanted to go slow and savor every moment.

"Do I get to undo your clothes?" he asked.

"Not yet. I'm teaching you patience." And learning it herself.

He laughed. "Good luck with that. Didn't you learn that first day, I'm not so good with patience when it comes to you?"

"Yes, but I know you're trainable. Still, if you're really in a rush . . ." Her hands moved to the waist of his pants. She knew he expected her to undo the button and unzip the fly, and she was sorely tempted. Instead, she tracked her finger down the front of his fly, pressing against the insistent bulge beneath the fine fabric.

Her sex pulsed with need, and the ache between her thighs made it hard to keep shuffling in place.

She slid her hand into his pocket, intending to grasp him through the even thinner fabric. Her fingers encountered something else, though. Something she well recognized. A condom package. She drew it out and held it up. "You came prepared. You were so sure you'd win me over?" Should she be flattered or insulted?

He shook his head. "No, it's habit." A pause. "Look, I need to confess."

"Okay," she said warily.

"I hoped that when I saw you tonight, I'd realize I didn't have special feelings for you."

Her mouth opened. That definitely wasn't flattering.

"But when I saw you, it hit. Like lightning. Illumination and shock all at once."

Okay, that was better. "Sounds painful," she teased.

"Yeah, and especially when I thought you didn't feel the same way. But I decided I just had to win you."

"You do like to win, don't you? I'm afraid I made it too easy. What's the fun in that?"

"This. This is the fun." He dropped his hands to her butt, cupped it, and squeezed.

"Yes, it is." A thought struck her, and it halted her feet.

"What's wrong?" he asked.

She gazed into his eyes. "We're talking about exclusivity?"

His brows pulled together. "Damn right. We love each other."

Relieved, she said, "Good. But I had to ask. You're the guy with condoms tucked in every nook and cranny, just in case an opportunity presents itself."

"Love those opportunities." He winked. Then he touched her cheek. "But from now on, they'll all be with you."

Oh, yes. She slipped her hands around his neck and pulled his head down for a lingering kiss that curled her toes and dampened her sex. "Then let's scrap the condoms. I'm on the pill because I have problems with irregular periods."

Something intense and primitive darkened his eyes. "Hell, yeah. I've never done that before."

He'd given her her first orgasm, and she would give him his first truly naked sex. No, more than that—she'd give him his first true lovemaking.

Now. She'd had enough of dancing, at least standing up. She tossed the condom on the floor and reached up to grab both ends of Woody's unfastened bow tie. "I want you now. Naked in bed."

"Not complaining, but what happened to patience?"

"I've run out." She stepped away from him, keeping her hands on the ends of his tie and tugging him toward her as she backed across the room, heading for the bedroom. "Some other night, we'll be patient. Now I want you inside me."

"Man, I like it when you talk that way. Tell me what else you want."

Oh yes, a woman *could* have it all. Sex *and* love with an amazing man. She could be a dirty girl, a sexy woman, a loving partner.

In the bedroom, she said, "Shoes off, socks off."

As she spoke, he obeyed.

"I like this," she said. "My own personal sex slave." She deliberated. "Vest next, and shirt."

He was laughing as he followed instructions, but when she said, "Now your pants, but leave your underwear on," she saw how turned on he was.

As turned on as she was. It had been the most amazing evening of her life, and it kept getting better. The ache between her thighs demanded relief, and soon. "Much as I like you in a thong, I have to say the boxer briefs are classier."

"Thank God." His eyes twinkled with humor.

"Now peel them off."

When he did, and stood in front of her, so rugged and physical and beautiful, his cock jutting full and firm up his belly—hers, all hers, from now on—she beckoned with her index finger.

He took the two steps toward her. "What do you want, Georgia?"

She came closer, so the front of her body, clad in the lovely gown Viv had helped her pick out, grazed the front of his. "Unzip my dress."

"Thought you'd never ask."

The man was good with female clothing. She'd barely drawn a breath before the zipper was sliding down. She hooked a finger in each skimpy shoulder strap, pulled them down, then let the dress fall. She stepped out of it, then kicked off her high-heeled gold sandals.

"God, look at you," he said. "Now, that's nice underwear. You're the one who should be modeling."

She wore champagne-colored scraps of lace. "Strip me, Woody." The excitement of commanding him like this gave her voice a raw, husky edge.

"You women have been ordering me around for weeks." His fingers worked the clasp of her bra, then hooked into the sides of her thong. "This is the first time I've enjoyed it."

"It's about to get better," she promised as she let the skimpy garments drop to the floor.

He bent to kiss her but she put both hands on his chest, stopping him. "No. Not until we're in bed."

She pulled back the covers and stretched out on the bottom sheet, gazing up at him. Hers. So sexy, so perfect. So loving. Oh God, how she loved him. She couldn't wait to join with him, their bodies and hearts totally naked together. "No more foreplay," she said. "The whole evening's been foreplay. I love you, Woody, and I want you now. Inside me. Come here."

She bent her knees, spread her legs, offered her body in an invitation as blatant as her words.

Breath coming fast, he lay between her legs, the head of his naked cock nudging her moist sex.

He cradled her head between his hands; then his mouth crushed hers, taking it with a fierce hunger that resonated all through her. Whimpering with need, she reached down, grasped his beautiful cock, and eased it inside her.

He slid in slowly, relentlessly, until he'd filled her completely.

He stopped, and lifted his mouth from hers. "What do you want now, Georgia?"

"Make love to me."

"Oh, yeah." He caught her hands, raised them above her head as she arched her body into his, and twined their fingers together. He didn't kiss her again, but instead gazed deep into her eyes as he began to pump, their bodies creating a slow, sensual, consuming rhythm.

She felt him more intensely, more exquisitely, than ever before as he stroked deep, deep to her core, filling her, then retreating, then coming back even deeper.

Arousal, passion, love combined to make her body twist urgently against his, rising and falling, demanding and giving. Orgasm was building, the sensations now sweetly familiar yet always incredible.

Especially incredible now, when she knew this was more than simply a physical act.

"Tell me," she panted, struggling for breath, gazing deep into his eyes. "Say the words."

Woody's hands gripped hers tightly. "I love you, Georgia."

"I love you too. Now, here's what I want."

"Tell me."

"Make me come, Woody, and make me scream."

"Damn right, I will."

Thirty-five

Sunday night, Woody's body was battered and bruised, but he felt stronger, more confident, and happier than ever before. He'd never imagined that being in love could feel so incredible.

He'd achieved his most important dream: winning Georgia. Now it was time to make the second one come true, and he was going to do it in front of the woman he loved.

Minutes before the players would take the ice, he said, "Men, it's been one hell of a long season and here we are, one game from the end. *The* game. Tonight, the Cup will be in the building. *Our* building. We're gonna play our hearts out, and when the game's over we'll be skating that Cup around the ice. Each of us, one by one, holding it high."

Heads nodded firmly.

"Then you know what we're gonna do? We're gonna take it over to the hospital and drink champagne out of it with Stu."

"Damn right," Federov grunted.

And after that, Woody would go home to Georgia, for the sweetest celebration of all. Other players would celebrate with wives or girlfriends, children, maybe siblings and parents. He felt sorry for the single guys who had no one to hang out with but a flock of superficial puck bunnies.

"Sound like a plan?" Woody bellowed.

"Damn right!" they all shouted back.

"Then get out there, and bash 'em, Beavers!"

Woody had given her rink-side seats, and she'd invited her mother. They might have their differences, but there was no one Georgia would rather have beside her tonight. She and Bernadette were growing closer, and it felt wonderful.

When the two women met outside the arena, Georgia said, "Confession time. As of last night, Woody and I are a couple."

Her mother whooped, hugged her tight, then said smugly, "Tell me something I don't know. I'm so glad that *book* of yours makes you happy, baby. You deserve it."

"Thanks, Bernadette." She couldn't wait to tell the book club that she'd created her own version of Lady Emma's story, and she and Woody had given it a happy ending.

"So, when are the two of you coming over for dinner with Fabio and me?" her mom asked as they headed into the arena.

Georgia chuckled. "Soon. I promise." And she meant it. She was eager to show Woody off, and curious to meet the guy who encouraged her mom to be more independent.

"The folks at work know you're dating Woody?"

"I'll tell them tomorrow. I'm determined to convince my boss that I'll still do a professional job with the VitalSport campaign." He couldn't argue with her results to date.

"Of course you will. You're a very responsible person."

Wow, genuine praise from her mother. "You know," Georgia said, "I'm starting to think maybe I wasn't switched at birth, after all."

Bernadette's smile flashed brightly. "You and me both, baby. It took us a while, but I guess we both had some growing up to do."

Georgia sure did appreciate her mom's company during the first two periods as they cheered the Beavers, booed the Capitals, and Bernadette let her dig her fingernails into her arm.

In the intermission between second and third period, when neither team had scored, Georgia touched the red welts. "Sorry."

"Don't apologize. That's my future son-in-law out there."

"Bernadette, he hasn't proposed." In her heart, she knew he would. The two of them were so right together, it felt inevitable that they'd spend the rest of their lives loving each other.

She only wished the outcome of this game felt as inevitable. She wanted it so badly, for Woody and the whole team.

In the third period, the Capitals threw their best offensive line against the Beavers' goal. The Vancouver coach sent in the strongest defensive line, and together with the powerful goaltender Federov, they fought off the onslaught.

"Woody's going in." She grabbed her mom's arm again as Woody, Bouchard, and Olssen, the Beavers' top offensive players, took the ice.

She knew the three had played together last season, and earlier this season before Stu Connolly got moved up to replace Olssen. The three players had an ease together, and if Olssen didn't have quite the same speed and dazzle as Stu, Woody said he was more consistent.

The Capitals were all over Woody, knowing he was the highest scorer in the league. Every time he headed toward their goal, they got in his way.

He'd explained some of the strategies to Georgia and she watched in fascination as Olssen quietly insinuated himself in a position next to the Capitals' goal, while everyone, the goaltender included, struggled to fend off an apparently determined Woody.

Then Woody hooked the puck sideways, straight onto Olssen's

stick. Olssen, with all the poise in the world, sent it flipping into the corner of the goal.

She leaped to her feet, screaming, as everyone in the arena did the same. If anything could have taken the roof off, their cheers would have done it.

On the ice, the Beavers embraced and backslapped excitedly.

In the stands, she and her mom hugged each other, then were caught up in hugs by the people seated around them. Tonight, there were no strangers; the fans were one big family.

The game wasn't over, though. There was still almost ten minutes, and anything could happen. The players couldn't lose their focus.

Play resumed, and those ten minutes seemed more like hours as both teams threw every ounce of their energy and skill into the game. Woody almost scored, but the Capitals' goaltender threw his body on top of the puck and stopped it just short of the line. A clever Capitals' play almost snuck around Federov, but somehow he got his elbow pad in the way and flicked the puck away.

The last two minutes were intolerable. "Even if the Capitals score," Georgia yelled in Bernadette's ear, over the din of the crowd, "that'll only tie it. They'll go to overtime."

"They won't score. Our guys have a lock on it."

Georgia bit her nails.

In the last minute, the Capitals pulled their goaltender and stormed the goal with six men against five, giving it everything they had. Federov and the Beavers, with Woody in the middle of the fray, fought them off with just as much determination.

With less than ten seconds left, the Capitals' Ovechkin caught a rebound and slapped a shot toward the goal.

Federov dove on it.

For the first time that night, the arena went silent. Where was the puck? Had it crossed the line?

Carefully, very carefully, with the refs surrounding him, Federov separated himself from the ice. Georgia stared at the magnified image on the JumboTron.

The puck was two inches outside the goal line.

The crowd went crazy, the Beavers jumped on one another with crushing hugs, and Georgia and her mom, arms around each other, bounced up and down with joy.

The stands shook as fans jumped, screamed, and embraced, and the pandemonium kept up as the refs tried to restore order, and the last couple of seconds were played out on ice to make the win official.

Her mom handed her a tissue, and Georgia realized they were both crying and laughing at the same time.

Woody's team had won the Stanley Cup. Her man's name would be engraved a second time on that huge trophy.

On the ice, the Beavers were one big huddle of grinning, hugging bodies, more of them pouring onto the ice all the time. Helmets came off; then the giant huddle broke up as individual players embraced one another. Everyone wanted a piece of Woody, but he broke free, caught her eye, and pumped his fist in the air. Laughing, crying, she pumped hers back.

The teams formed two lines to do the traditional handshakes, and she felt sorry for the Capitals. Though they should be proud of what they'd achieved, they looked utterly drained.

She watched proudly and tearily as the Conn Smythe, which went to the player who was most valuable to his team during the playoffs, was presented to Woody. He hefted it, kissed it, and accepted his teammates' praise, but she knew he was waiting.

It wasn't that he didn't value the Conn Smythe, but he'd told her that, in the end, there was only one trophy that truly mattered.

And now she saw two smiling men carry that trophy into the arena along a red carpet, and place it on a table. How surreal to watch this and know that, at some point, that massive glittering cup would be sharing Woody's penthouse.

The speeches were brief, with congratulations to the general manager, coaches, players, and fans. And then Woody, as team captain, was presented with the holy grail of hockey.

He kissed this trophy too, the jubilation clear on his face. Holding it two-handed above his head, he pumped it up and down in victory as his teammates surrounded him.

She expected him to take it and skate around the ice in triumph, but instead he passed it to Federov. She nodded in acknowledgment. Without the big Russian, the Beavers never would have won.

After that, each team member took the cup, kissing it and skating around in jubilation. Tears ran down more than one of those rugged faces.

Finally, Woody reclaimed the trophy. He didn't look excited as much as gratified, a happiness that wasn't about just this moment but about the entire season and everything he and every other player had put into it.

He skated toward her and, smiling through her tears, she held his gaze.

He raised the Cup high above his head and shouted, "I love you, Georgia." By now, the noise had died down enough that she heard his words clearly.

"I love you, Woody!" she screamed back.

Bernadette grabbed her shoulder and pointed. "Look!"

Georgia followed her pointing finger to the JumboTron—and saw her own face, tear-streaked and joyful.

"You two just told the whole world!" her mom said.

Laughing, Georgia said, "Good!"

"Oh, baby, I'm so happy for you. I have to say, that's one fine *book* you've been reading."

Georgia stared at the man on the ice: cheeks rosy red, hair lank with sweat, wearing a jersey with the cartoon figure of a beaver. Tough, brave, caring, smart, sexy—and hers.

What had she learned in the past month? That in real life, just as in fiction, a happy ending can come in the most unexpected package.

She threw her arms around her mom. "He's the best damned book in the world!"

ABOUT THE AUTHOR

Savanna Fox is the new pen name for Susan Lyons, who also writes as Susan Fox. *Publishers Weekly* refers to her writing as "emotionally compelling, sexy contemporary romance."

Writing as Susan Lyons and Susan Fox, her books have won the Gayle Wilson Award of Excellence, the Book Buyer's Best, the Booksellers' Best, the Aspen Gold, the Golden Quill, the Write Touch, the More Than Magic, the Lories, the Beacon, and the Laurel Wreath, and she has been nominated for the RT Reviewers' Choice Award. Her book *Sex Drive* was a Cosmopolitan Red-Hot Read.

Savanna/Susan is a Pacific Northwester with homes in Vancouver and Victoria, British Columbia. She has degrees in law and psychology, and has had a variety of careers, including perennial student, computer consultant, and legal editor. Fiction writer is by far her favorite, giving her an outlet to demonstrate her belief in the power of love, friendship, and a sense of humor.

Visit her website at www.savannafox.com for excerpts, discussion guides, behind-the-scenes notes, recipes, giveaways, and more. She loves to hear from readers and can be contacted through her website.